"I like it here, Buck," Gina said. "I think God may have sent me and Bobby here for a reason. I'm thinking maybe I'd like to stay."

His ambivalence must have shown on his face, because she cocked her head to one side and spoke. "That bothers you, doesn't it? How come? Is it about my resemblance to your wife?"

"Somewhat." Actually, he was starting to wonder how he'd ever mistaken her for Ivana. She had a plucky strength and determination, a set to her chin and a way of holding herself that were all completely her own. Still, he had questions.

"Look," she said, "I'm sorry if I bring up memories for you. Maybe I'll get on my feet quickly and be able to get out of here. But meanwhile…"

"Meanwhile what?" He was holding her baby in the rainy twilight, looking at her and finding her beautiful, and feeling like he might be stepping into the biggest mess of his life.

THE GUARDIAN'S VOW

Lee Tobin McClain

AND

Brenda Minton

Previously published as *The Soldier and the Single Mom* and *Her Guardian Rancher*

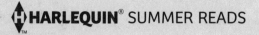 **HARLEQUIN**® SUMMER READS

Recycling programs
for this product may
not exist in your area.

ISBN-13: 978-1-335-00828-2

The Guardian's Vow
Copyright © 2019 by Harlequin Books S.A.

First published as The Soldier and the Single Mom by Harlequin Books in 2017 and Her Guardian Rancher by Harlequin Books in 2016.

The publisher acknowledges the copyright holders of the individual works as follows:

The Soldier and the Single Mom
Copyright © 2017 by Lee Tobin McClain

Her Guardian Rancher
Copyright © 2016 by Brenda Minton

Printed in U.S.A.

www.Harlequin.com

CONTENTS

Lee Tobin McClain read *Gone with the Wind* in the third grade and has been a hopeless romantic ever since. When she's not writing angst-filled love stories with happy endings, she's getting inspiration from her church singles group, her gymnastics-obsessed teenage daughter and her rescue dog and cat. In her day job, Lee gets to encourage aspiring romance writers in Seton Hill University's low-residency MFA program. Visit her at leetobinmcclain.com.

Books by Lee Tobin McClain

Love Inspired

Redemption Ranch
The Soldier's Redemption
The Twins' Family Christmas

Rescue River
Engaged to the Single Mom
His Secret Child
Small-Town Nanny
The Soldier and the Single Mom
The Soldier's Secret Child
A Family for Easter

Christmas Twins
Secret Christmas Twins

Lone Star Cowboy League: Boys Ranch
The Nanny's Texas Christmas

Visit the Author Profile page at
Harlequin.com for more titles.

THE SOLDIER AND THE SINGLE MOM

Lee Tobin McClain

To Porter, the real-world model for Spike.
Rescue pets rule!

Therefore if any man be in Christ, he is a new creature: old things are passed away; behold, all things are become new.

—*2 Corinthians 5:17*

Chapter One

It was 2:00 a.m. on a mild March night when Buck Armstrong saw his dead wife walking toward the town of Rescue River, Ohio, carrying their baby on one hip.

He swerved, hit the brakes and skidded onto the gravel berm. On the seat beside him, Crater—his chosen companion for the night—let out a yip.

Buck passed his hand over his eyes. It wasn't real— couldn't be. He'd made similar mistakes before, when he was tired, when the war memories came back too strong. Tonight, driving home from assisting in an emergency surgery out at the dog rescue, he wanted nothing more than to keep driving past the turnoff to the liquor store, lock himself in his room and shut it all off until morning.

He looked again, squinting through the moonlit fog.

They were still there. But they were running away from him, or rather, his wife was. Baby Mia was gone.

Where was the baby? He scrambled out of the truck, leaving the door ajar. "Stay!" he ordered the dog automatically as he took off toward his wife. "Ivana! Wait!"

She ran faster, but Buck had gotten back into military shape since he'd quit drinking, and he caught up easily. Was relieved to see that the baby was now in front of her, in some sort of sling.

His hand brushed against her soft hair.

She screamed, spun away from him, and he saw her face.

It wasn't his wife, but someone else. A complete stranger.

He stopped, his heart pounding triple time. Sweat formed on his forehead as he tried to catch his breath. "I'm sorry. I thought you were—"

"Leave us alone," she ordered, stepping away, one arm cradled protectively at the back of the baby's head, the other going to her oversize bag. "I have a gun."

"Whoa." He took a couple of steps back, hands lifting to shoulder height, palms out. A giant stone of disappointment pressed down on him. "I don't mean you any harm. I thought you were… Never mind."

A breeze rattled the leaves of a tall oak tree beside the road. He caught the rich scent of newly turned earth, plowed dirt, fields ready for planting. Up ahead, a spotlight illuminated the town's well-known sign, kept up and repainted yearly since Civil War days: Rescue River, Ohio. All Are Welcome, All Are Safe.

Ivana had been so proud of their hometown's history as a station on the Underground Railroad, its reputation for embracing outsiders of all types, races and creeds.

The good people of Rescue River had even put up with the damaged man he'd been when he'd returned from war, until he'd repeatedly broken their trust.

"Go back to your truck," the woman ordered, hand still in her bag. Now that he could see her better, he realized she was sturdier than Ivana had been, with square shoulders and a determined set to her chin. Same long tawny hair, but fuller lips and big gray-blue eyes that were now glaring at him. "Do it. Back in the truck, now."

He should do what she said, should turn around right now and get on home before the memories that were chasing him caught up.

Should, but when had he ever done what he should? "What are you doing out here in the middle of the night, ma'am? Can I give you a ride somewhere?"

She laughed without humor, shaking her head. "No way, buddy. Just drive away. We'll all be better off."

He had to admire her courage if not her common sense. There was no good reason for a woman with a baby to be wandering the countryside, but she was acting as if she owned the whole state.

"Sure you don't want me to call someone?" Truth was, he felt relieved. He could go home and crash and try to forget that, just for a minute, he'd gotten the crazy hope that Ivana and the baby were still alive, that he'd get a second chance to love them the way they deserved.

"We're fine." She ran a hand through her hair and patted the baby who, somehow, still slept against her chest. He caught sight of wispy hair, heard that sweet, nestling-in sigh of a contented little one.

Pain stabbed his heart.

She did seem fine, perfectly able to defend herself, he argued against the faint whisper of chivalry that said he shouldn't let a woman and child stay out here in the middle of the night. After all, he wasn't much of a protector. He'd lost as many people as he'd saved in Afghanistan. And as for Ivana and Mia...

The sound of a mournful howl silenced his thoughts. Crater. "It's okay, buddy," he called, and the scarred rottweiler bounded out of the truck's cab. As Crater jumped up on him, Buck rubbed the dog's sides and let him lick his face and, for the first time since seeing the woman, he felt his heart rate settle.

"Let's go home," he said to the dog. But Crater had different ideas, and he lunged playfully toward the woman and baby. Buck snapped his fingers and the dog sank into a sitting position, looking back toward him. The deep scar on the dog's back, for which they'd named him out at the rescue, shone pale in the moonlight.

"That's a well-trained dog." The woman cocked her head to one side.

"He's a sweetheart. Come on, boy."

The dog trotted to his side, and as they started back to his truck, Buck felt his heart rate calm a little more. Yeah, his shrink was right: he was a prime candidate for a service dog. Except he couldn't make the commitment. As soon as he'd paid off his debts and made amends where he could, he was out of here, and who knew whether he'd end up in a dog-friendly place?

"Hey, hold on a minute." The woman's voice was the slightest bit husky.

He turned but didn't walk back toward her. Didn't look at her. It hurt too much. She was still a reminder of Ivana and all he'd lost. "What?"

"Maybe you *could* give us a hand. Or a ride."

Buck drew in a deep breath and blew it out. "Okay, sure," he said, trying not to show his reluctance to be in her company a moment longer. After all, he'd made the offer, so courtesy dictated he should follow through. "Where are you headed?"

"That's a good question," she said, lifting the baby a little to take the weight off her chest.

He remembered Ivana doing that very same thing with Mia. He swallowed.

"What kind of a town is Rescue River?"

"It's a real nice town." It was, too. He'd consider staying on there himself if he hadn't burned so many bridges.

"Think I could find a cheap room? Like, really cheap?"

He cocked his head to one side. "The only motel had no vacancy, last I saw. My sister's renovating what's going to be a guesthouse, but it's not open for another few months…"

"Does she have a room that's done, or mostly done? We don't need much."

Buck wanted to lie, would have lied, except he seemed to hear Ivana's voice in his head. Quoting Scripture, trying to coax him along the path to believing. Something about helping widows and orphans in their distress.

This woman might or might not be a widow, but to be out walking the rural Ohio roads in the wee hours surely indicated some kind of distress.

"She's got a couple of rooms close to done," he admitted.

"Do you think she'd let me rent one?"

He frowned. "I don't know. Lacey's not the most trusting person in the world. A late-night guest she isn't expecting won't sit well with her."

The comment hung between them for an awkward

moment. It was the simple truth, though. Or maybe not so simple. The fact that the pretty stranger had a baby would disturb Lacey. A lot.

The woman gave him a skeptical look, then straightened and turned away. "Okay. Thanks."

Squeezing his eyes shut for just a second, he turned and tried to head back toward his truck. She wasn't his responsibility. He had enough on his plate just to keep himself together.

Nope. Like a fool, he turned around. "Hey, wait. Come on. We'll try to talk Lacey into letting you stay. At least for the night."

"That would be wonderful," she said, a relieved smile breaking out on her face.

Wonderful for her, maybe. Not for him. The last thing he needed was an Ivana look-alike, with a baby no less, staying one thin wall away from him.

"My name's Gina, by the way." She shifted the diaper bag and held out a hand.

"Buck Armstrong." He reached out, wrapped his oversize hand around her soft, delicate fingers and wished he'd driven home another way.

Gina Patterson climbed into the backseat of the handsome stranger's extended-cab pickup, her heart thudding. *Please, Lord, keep us safe. Watch over us. Don't let him be a serial killer.*

But a dog wouldn't be that friendly with a serial killer, and a serial killer wouldn't act that loving with a dog. Would they?

"Air bags," she explained when he looked over his shoulder, eyebrows raised. "Can't sit in front." Technically, she shouldn't even bring Bobby into the truck, not without a car seat, only she couldn't figure out what else to do. She couldn't give Buck the keys to get her car seat from her out-of-gas SUV, and she certainly couldn't leave Bobby with him while she walked the three miles back to her vehicle.

They were safer in the backseat, she figured, safe from him as well as from any kind of car accident. If he tried to kidnap them, she could at least hit him in the back of the head with her shoe.

She was ready to drop with fatigue after three long days of driving, and it was getting colder by the minute. Buck's arrival had to be the blessing she'd prayed for. Although he seemed pretty gruff for a rescuer.

"Right, I knew that. It's less than a mile," he said, and his dog panted back over the seat at her, smiling in the way happy dogs did. It made her miss her poodles, but she knew her best friend back home would take care of them.

She scratched the dog's ears for a minute and then let her head sag back against the seat, thanking God again for keeping her and Bobby safe during their journey.

Well, mostly safe. She'd been foolish to leave her bag on the sink while she'd changed Bobby's diaper. Who'd have thought there'd be a purse thief in a rest area in rural Indiana? Fortunately, she'd filled her tank just before the theft—with cash—so she'd kept going as far as she could, leaving the interstate so there'd be less of a trail.

The debit card she'd kept in her jacket pocket might help in the future, once things back home cooled down, but she didn't dare use it now.

After the theft, she'd gotten scared and timed things

all wrong. She'd thought she could make it to a hotel she'd seen advertised in a larger town up ahead, but the SUV was a gas hog and had sputtered to a stop a few miles back.

At which point she'd realized she didn't have enough cash for a hotel, anyway.

"All set?" Buck looked back at her and Bobby, brows raised over eyes the color of the ocean on a cloudy day.

Man, those were some haunted eyes. "We're set. Thank you for helping us."

She studied the back of him as he put the truck into gear and drove into the town. Broad shoulders, longish hair and stubble that made him look like a bad boy.

What had *he* been doing out at 2:00 a.m.? The question only now occurred to her, now that she and Bobby were safe, or seemed to be. "Excuse me," she said, leaning forward, "but you haven't been drinking or… partying, have you?"

His shoulders stiffened. "No. Why?"

Whew. She hadn't smelled alcohol on him, but alcohol wasn't the only thing that could mess you up. Her husband had been an old hand at covering his addiction to cocaine, right up until he'd lost control on a California mountain and skied headlong into a tree. The drugs had shown up in the autopsy blood work, but when he'd left the ski chalet an hour earlier, she hadn't even known he was impaired. Yet another mistake her in-laws had laid at her feet.

Her throat tightened and she crammed the memories back down. "Just wondering."

So maybe she'd done the right thing after all. When Bobby had started to cry, she'd decided it was better to risk walking than to stay with her vehicle. She'd scraped together change from the floor and found her emergency twenty in the bin between the driver's and passenger's seats. So at least she could get Bobby some food. At ten months, he needed way more than mother's milk.

Hopefully, she could find a church that would take her in, because calling in her lost wallet might put the police on her trail. She chewed on her lower lip.

How had she ever gotten into this situation? She tried to tell herself it wasn't her fault. While she'd committed to stay with her husband, she hadn't married her in-laws. Once he was gone, so was her obligation to them. When Bobby was old enough to know the whole story, he could choose to reconnect in a safe way if he wanted to.

"Guesthouse is right up there." Buck waved a hand, causing Gina to look around and realize that Rescue River was a cute little town, the kind with sidewalks and shops and glowing streetlamps, a moonlit church on one corner and a library on the other. The kind of safe haven where she might be able to breathe for a little while and figure out her options.

Except that, without ID and with just a twenty and change, her options seemed very limited. Worry cramped her belly.

The stranger pulled up in front of a rambling brick home. The outdoor light was on, revealing a porch swing and a front-door wreath made of flowers and pretty branches.

"I'll have to wake up my sister. You can wait here in the truck or out front." He gestured toward the house.

Well, okay, then. No excess of manners.

Except that, actually, she was the stranger and

he was doing her a service. "I'll wait on the porch. Thanks."

He seemed able to read her mind as he came around to open the truck door for her. "Sorry to leave you outside, but my sister is sort of touchy," he said as they walked up the narrow brick walkway. "I can't bring a stranger in to set up shop without asking permission. It's her place." He paused. "It's a very safe town, but I'll leave Crater out here if that will make you more comfortable."

"It will, thanks." It had been the dog, and the stranger's reaction to the dog, that had made her decide he was a reliable person to help her.

That, and the fact that she was desperate.

In her worst moments she wondered if she'd done the right thing, taking Bobby away from her in-laws' wealth and security. But no way. They'd become more and more possessive of him, trying to push her out of the picture and care for him themselves. And she kept coming back to what she'd seen: her mother-in-law holding Bobby out for her father-in-law to hit, hard, causing the baby to wail in pain. Her father-in-law *had* started to shake Bobby, she was sure of it, despite their vigorous denials and efforts to turn the criticism back on her.

Once she knew for sure, she couldn't in good conscience stay herself, or leave Bobby in his grandparents' care.

When she'd first driven away from the mansion that had felt increasingly like a prison, relief had made her giddy. She'd not known how oppressed she had felt, living there, until she'd started driving across the country with no forwarding address. Realizations about her dead husband's problems had stacked up, one on top of the other, until she was overwhelmed with gratitude to God for helping her escape the same awful consequences for herself and Bobby.

As she'd crossed state lines, though, doubts had set in, so that now her dominant, gnawing emotion was fear. How would she make a living? What job could she get without references and with few marketable skills? And while she worked, who would watch Bobby? She wouldn't leave her precious baby with just anyone. She had to be able to trust them. To know they'd love and care for him in her absence.

Inside the house, a door slammed. "I've about had it, Buck!"

She heard Buck's voice, lower, soothing, though she couldn't make out the words.

"You've got to be kidding. She has a baby with her?"

More quiet male talk.

The door to the guesthouse burst open, and a woman about her age, in a dark silk robe, stood, hands on hips. "Okay, spill it. What's your story?"

The woman's tone raised Gina's hackles, whooshing her back to her in-laws and their demanding glares. The instinct to walk away was strong, but she had Bobby to consider. She drew in a breath and let it out slowly, a calming technique from her yoga days. "Long version or short?"

"I work all day and then come home and try to renovate this place. I'm tired."

"Short, then. My purse was stolen, I'm out of gas and I need a place to stay."

The woman frowned. "For how long?"

"I…don't know. A couple of days."

"Why can't you call someone?"

That was the key question. How did she explain how she'd gotten so isolated from her childhood friends, how she'd needed to go to a part of the country where she didn't know anyone, both to make a fresh start and so that her in-laws didn't find her? "That's in the long version."

"So…" The woman cocked her head to one side, studying her with skepticism in every angle of her too-thin frame. "Are you part of some scam?"

"Lacey." Buck put a hand on the woman's shoulder. "If you're opening a guesthouse, you need to be able to welcome people."

"If you're serious about recovery from your drinking problem, you need to stop pulling stunts like this."

Buck winced.

Gina reached up to rub her aching shoulder. Great. Another addict.

The woman drew in a breath, visibly trying to remain calm. "I'm sorry. But you're blinded by how she looks like Ivana. Stuff like this happens all the time in big cities. We have to be careful."

Bobby stirred and let out a little cry, and as Gina swayed to calm him, something inside her hardened. She was tired of explaining herself to other people. If she weren't in such dire straits, she'd walk right down those pretty, welcoming porch steps and off into the night. "You can search me. All I've got is this diaper bag." She shifted and held it out to the woman. "It's hard to run a scam with an infant tagging along."

Buck raised his eyebrows but didn't comment, and scarily enough, she could read what he was thinking. *So you don't have a gun in there.*

Of course she didn't.

The woman, Lacey, took it, set it down on the table and pawed through.

Gina's stomach tightened.

Bobby started to cry in earnest. "Shh," she soothed. He needed a diaper change, a feeding and bed. She could only hope the trauma and changes of the past few days wouldn't damage him, that her own love and commitment and consistency would be enough.

"Look, you can stay tonight and we'll talk in the morning." With a noisy sigh, the woman turned away, but not before Gina saw a pained expression on her face. "*You* settle her in," she said to Buck. "Put her in the Escher." She stormed inside, letting the screen door bang behind her.

Buck felt tired, inescapably tired, but also keyed up to where he knew he wasn't going to sleep. "Come on," he said to the beautiful stranger.

But she didn't follow. "This isn't going to work out. I'll find something else."

"There's no place else." He picked up her bag and beckoned her inside, with Crater padding behind him. "Don't worry, Lacey will be more hospitable in the morning." Maybe. He knew what else had bothered Lacey, besides the fact that she'd rescued him one too many times from some late-night escapade: Gina's little boy. Just last year, Lacey had miscarried the baby who was all she had left of her soldier husband. Seeing someone who apparently wasn't taking good care of her own child had to infuriate her.

He wasn't sure his sister's judgment was fair; Gina might be doing the best she could for her baby, might be on the run from some danger worse than whatever she'd be likely to face on an Ohio country road.

He led her through the vinyl sheeting and raw boards that were the future breakfast room, up the stairs and into the hallway that housed the guest rooms. "Here's the only other finished one, besides mine," he said, stopping at the room called the Escher. He opened the door and let her enter before him, ordering Crater to lie down just inside the door.

Gina looked around, laughing with apparent delight. "This is amazing!"

The bed appeared to float and the walls held prints by a modern artist Buck had only recently learned about. The nightstand was made to look like it was on its side, and the rug created an optical illusion of a spiraling series of stair steps.

"Lacey was an art history major in college," he explained. "She's hoping to coordinate with the new art museum to attract guests."

"That's so cool!" Gina walked from picture to picture, joggling the baby so he wouldn't fuss. "I love Escher."

He felt a reluctant flash of liking for this woman who could spare the energy for art appreciation at a time like this. He also noticed that she knew who Escher was, which was more than he had, until Lacey had educated him.

His curiosity about Gina kicked up a notch. She appeared to be destitute and basically homeless, but she was obviously educated. He scanned her slim-fitting trousers and crisp shirt: definitely expensive. Those diamond studs in her ears looked real.

So why'd she been walking along a country road at night?

She put the baby down on the bed and pulled out a diaper pad. "Sorry, he needs a change."

"Sheets and towels here," he said, tapping a cabinet. "There might even be soap. Gina already let one couple stay here for a honeymoon visit."

She turned to him, one hand on the baby's chest. "I can't tell you how grateful I am."

"No problem." Though it was. "I'll be right next door if you need anything."

She swallowed visibly. "Okay."

Unwanted compassion hit him. She was alone and scared in a strange place. "Look, Lacey is a real light sleeper. She'll wake up if there's any disturbance. And... I can leave Crater here if you want a guard dog."

"Thank you. That would be wonderful." She put a hand on his arm. "You've been amazing."

He didn't need her touching him. He backed away so quickly he bumped against the open door. "Stay, boy," he ordered Crater and then let himself out.

And stood in the hallway, listening to her cooing to her baby while a battle waged inside him. He wanted a drink in the worst way.

He reached down, but of course, Crater wasn't there to calm him. He took one step toward the front door. Stopped. Tried to picture his recovery mentor.

Wondered whether the bar out by the highway was still open.

Ten minutes later, after a phone call to his mentor, he tossed restlessly in his bed. It was going to be a long night.

Chapter Two

A hoarse shout woke Gina out of a restless sleep.

Instinctively, she reached for Bobby. She found him in the nest she'd made with rolled blankets and towels. Thankfully, he slept on through more shouted words she couldn't distinguish in her sleepy state.

Sweat broke out on her body as she lay completely still, just as she'd done so many nights when her husband had come home drunk or high. Hoping, praying he'd sleep downstairs rather than coming up in the mood for some kind of interaction, whether affection or a fight. None of it ever ended well when he'd been using. Sometimes, his rage took physical form.

A knock on the door made her heart pound harder, but then she realized it came from the next room. She heard the clink of an old-fashioned key in a lock. A woman's murmuring voice: "It's okay, Buck. It's okay. You had another nightmare."

It all came clear to her: the guesthouse. The unfriendly landlady. Buck's haunted eyes.

Sounded like he'd had a nightmare and his sister had come to wake him out of it.

She drew in a breath and rubbed Bobby's back, comforted by the steady sound of his breathing. She'd landed in a safe place for the moment. The edges of the sky were just starting to brighten through the window, but she didn't have to deal with her day just yet. She could sleep again.

There were more murmurs next door. A hall door opened and closed. A toilet flushed. Then silence again.

Surprisingly enough, she did drop back to sleep.

"Good morning!" Gina walked into the kitchen the next morning with Bobby on her hip. He'd woken up hungry, and she'd nursed him and fed him her last jar of baby food. It was time to figure out her next step.

"Hey." Lacey's voice sounded unenthusiastic. She wore scrubs and sat with a cup of coffee in front of her. Her eyes were puffy and underlined by dark shadows.

No wonder, given last night's drama.

Lacey obviously wasn't going to make conversation, so Gina soldiered on. "Thank you so much for giving me and Bobby a place to sleep last night."

"Sure." Lacey glanced up from her newspaper and then went back to reading an article on the local news page.

"You headed to work?" Gina asked. "What do you do?"

The woman tried to smile, but it was obviously an effort. "I'm a CNA. Certified Nursing Assistant. And yeah, I leave in half an hour." A large orange cat wove its way between her legs and then jumped into her lap, and she ran her hands over it as if for comfort.

"You want me to fix you breakfast?"

That made Lacey look up. "What?"

"I'm a pretty good cook. If you're going to work, you need more than coffee."

Lacey let out a reluctant chuckle. "Is that so, Mom?"

Buck walked into the room, stretching and yawning hugely. He wore a plain, snug-fitting white T-shirt and faded jeans.

Gina swallowed hard. Okay. Yeah. He was handsome. At least, if you didn't look into the abyss that seemed to live permanently behind his eyes.

"How's everyone this morning?" he asked in a forced, cheerful tone.

Lacey pointed at Gina with her coffee cup. "She offered to cook breakfast."

"Sounds good to me," Buck said. "I've got comp time at the clinic from last night, so I'm gonna work on the house today. Could use some fuel, for sure."

Lacey waved a hand toward the refrigerator and stove. "Knock yourself out," she said to Gina.

Gina shifted Bobby and walked over to Lacey. "Any chance you could hold him? His name's Bobby, by the way."

Lacey scooted away so fast that the chair leg scraped along the freshly polished wood floor, leaving a raw scratch. "No, thanks. I... My hands are full with Mr. Whiskers."

Buck was there in a fraction of a second, concern all over his face. "I'll take him."

Gina cocked her head at the two of them, curious. She'd never met a woman who wasn't charmed by her son, especially when he was newly fed and changed, cooing and smiling.

Buck, on the other hand, held Bobby like a pro, bouncing him on his knee and tickling his tummy to make him laugh.

Gina rummaged in the refrigerator and found eggs, some Havarti cheese and green onions. It was enough to make a good-tasting scramble. Thick slices of bread went alongside, and she found some apples to cut up as a garnish.

When she placed the plates in front of the two of them a few minutes later, they both looked surprised, and when Lacey tasted the eggs, she actually smiled. "Not bad."

"I like to cook." Gina cleared her throat. "Is there any work you need done today? I have to find a way to get some gas out to my car, but other than that, I'd love to spend a few hours working around here in exchange for your letting me stay last night."

Lacey waved a hand. "Don't worry about it. This breakfast is payment enough."

"Truth is," Gina said, her face heating, "I might need to impose on you for another night. So we could consider it advance payment."

The other woman studied her thoughtfully. "Can you handle an honest answer?"

"Of course."

"I have a hard time trusting someone who can't afford a hotel but can afford shoes like that." She gestured at Gina's designer loafers.

Gina looked down at the soft leather and felt a moment's shallow regret. She wouldn't be wearing shoes like this anymore, that was for sure.

"She could work this morning while I'm here," Buck

interjected. "We need cleanup help, and anyone could do that. And this afternoon, she can work on getting her car and whatever else she needs to do."

Gina gripped the edge of her chair for courage. Asking for favors wasn't her favorite thing, not by a long shot, and she hated pushy people in general. But for Bobby, she'd do whatever was necessary. "What do you think about our staying tonight?"

Lacey's jaw hardened. "I'm not going to throw you out into the street right away," she said, "but you need to figure things out. Surely there's people you can call, things you can do. I don't want this to become permanent. The last thing either Buck or I needs is a stranger with a baby around here. You're poison to us right now."

Gina recoiled, shocked by the harsh words.

Buck held up a hand. "Lacey—"

"What? You know that's why you had a nightmare last night. Because she looks like Ivana and she's got a kid. It's too much for either of us."

"I'm sorry," Gina said, her heart going out to them. Underneath Lacey's brusque exterior was real pain that kept peeking through.

As for Buck, he'd looked down at his plate, but the set of his shoulders told her he wasn't happy. Something had happened to him, maybe to both of them, and Gina couldn't help wondering about it.

"I'll help this morning, if you'll allow it," she said, "and then work on doing what I can this afternoon with my car so I can move on. Maybe there's a police officer who can run me out to where it is. I'll need to take some gas."

And she'd need to rely on God, because twenty dollars wasn't going to buy much gas or baby food, and it was all she had.

Buck heaved a sigh as he put the last stroke of paint on the breakfast-room wall. Having Gina here was even more difficult than he'd expected.

She worked hard, that was for sure. She'd single-handedly cleaned one of the guest rooms that had been finished but a mess. Carried out vinyl sheeting and masking tape, swept up nails, scrubbed the floor on her hands and knees, polished the bathroom fixtures to a shine. Now she was removing the tape from the area he'd painted yesterday.

The only time she stopped working was when Bobby cried. Then she'd slip off, he assumed to nurse the baby or to change his diaper. She'd put together a makeshift playpen from a blanket and pillows, and he crawled around it and batted at a couple of toys she had in her diaper bag.

She was resourceful, able to compartmentalize in a way few women he'd known could do. Certainly, in a way Ivana hadn't been able to do.

Unfortunately, in other ways, it was way too much like having Ivana around. Some of their best times had been working around the house together with the baby nearby. They'd felt like a happy family then.

So having Gina and Bobby here now brought back good memories, but alongside them, a keen, aching awareness of all he'd lost. All he'd thrown away, really.

He shook himself out of that line of thought. He had a mission, and he needed to stick to it. *Find out what you can about her*, Lacey had told him.

He was curious enough that the job didn't rankle. Not only would they find out whether she could be trusted to stay in their house another night, but he could maybe get rid of the crazy impression that this woman was just like Ivana.

"Do you want me to help with the trim?" She came in now, a little out of breath, with Bobby on her hip. "Or I could work on the kitchen cabinets. I noticed they need cleaning out."

"I'd stay out of Lacey's stuff. You'd better work on the cabinets in here. Do you know how to use a screwdriver?"

"Sure."

She set Bobby up in the corner of this room and went to work washing the cabinet fronts, removing the handles, humming a wordless tune.

It was a little too domestic for him. "So, how are you gonna punt here?" he asked, his voice coming out rougher than he'd intended. "You got a plan?"

She looked up, and her eyes were dark with some emotion he couldn't name. "I thought I'd try the churches in town first," she said. "Where I lived before, some of the churches had programs for homeless families. Just until I can get on my feet and figure out what to do next." She paused. "I'd prefer finding work, but I don't know what's available."

So she thought of herself as homeless. That suggested she wasn't just traveling from point A to point B. Something else was wrong. And it was weird, because she did have that rich-girl look to her. Her clothes were stylish and new, her haircut and manicure expensive looking. But she also looked scared.

"Not sure if you'll find anything formal around here,

but the churches are big on outreach. I can take you to ours. And then…you mentioned talking to the police about your car?"

"They'll want to get it off the road as much as I do." She frowned. "I just hope they won't put my name in some kind of system."

"You hiding from someone?" he asked mildly.

Her eyebrows went together and her eyes hooded. "I… Yeah. You could say that."

"Boyfriend? Husband?"

She shook her head. "I'd rather not talk about it."

That figured. A woman as pretty as she was had to have a partner, and Bobby had a father. Had someone abused her? "I'm not asking you to tell me everything, but I can help you better if I know your situation."

Her cheeks flushed with what looked like embarrassment. "Thanks." She wasn't saying more, obviously.

"Where were you headed, originally?" he pushed on as he finished painting the crown molding.

She didn't answer, so he repeated the question.

"I don't know," she said finally. "Anywhere. It didn't matter. I just had to leave." She studied the cupboard she was sanding, one of the old-fashioned and charming parts of the breakfast room, according to Lacey. "I wouldn't mind finding a place to settle for a while. As long as it was safe."

Not here, not here. He didn't need any complications in Rescue River, and this woman seemed like a complication. "Safe from what?"

She shook her head. "Too long of a story." Her voice sounded tense.

"Okay, then, what would you like to work at? What are you shooting for, jobwise?"

"My line of work was being a housewife, but obviously I need to find something else."

Hmm. From the little she'd told him, he'd guess she'd been abused. And the last thing he and Lacey needed around here was an angry husband looking for his wife and child. She didn't show any bruises, but maybe they were hidden. "What are you good at?"

"Organizing things. Raising kids. Planning parties." She shrugged. "The type of thing housewives do."

He'd have said that housewives washed dishes and cooked meals. He had a feeling about what kind of housewife she'd been—not an ordinary one. With that breakfast she'd cooked, he could imagine her catering to some wealthy husband, giving brunches for country-club ladies.

So it was very interesting that she'd run away.

Gina was bone tired after her short, broken sleep and a morning of physical work, and stressed out about the eleven messages she'd found on her phone, her in-laws demanding that she return Bobby to them immediately. Of course she'd disabled the GPS on her smartphone, but she was still worried her in-laws could somehow find her.

But Buck had offered to drive her around and, tired or not, she needed to seize the opportunity. Once she had her vehicle nearby with some gas in it, she'd feel better. She'd have an escape route and she wouldn't be quite so dependent on the kindness of strangers.

When she went out to Buck's truck, he was leaning in through the rear door, adjusting something.

"Wow, where'd you get a car seat? That's wonderful!"

He cleared his throat. "It was sitting around here." He reached out and took Bobby from her arms without meeting her eyes, then settled him into the infant seat and expertly adjusted the straps.

Mr. Tough Guy continued to surprise her.

They stopped first at the grocery store, a small, homey market a quarter the size of the superstore she'd shopped at back home. The aroma of rotisserie chicken filled the air, and bushels of produce, labeled as locally grown, stood in rows just inside the front door. Gina held Bobby in his sling, facing out so he could see the people passing by, which he loved. Buck waved to a cashier and pounded a bagger on the back as they walked toward the baby aisle.

When they got there, she picked out six jars of the cheapest baby food available. She looked over at the diapers and bit her lip, hoping the single one remaining in the diaper bag would last until she got to the box in the SUV.

Buck held a plastic basket for their purchases and studied the shelves. "Look at this stuff. Turkey with pears. What self-respecting baby would eat that?"

"I know. We used to see the weirdest baby food at World Gourmet. Avocado risotto, vanilla bean with spinach…" But that was a lifetime ago, when she'd been able to shop at the most expensive healthy foods emporium in her California town.

"Buck Armstrong, is that you?" came a woman's husky voice.

They both turned. There in the food aisle of the Star Market was the most beautiful woman Gina had ever seen. Tall, super skinny, with high cheekbones and long shiny stick-straight black hair.

A little intimidated by the woman's breathtaking looks, Gina could only offer a smile.

"Amy Franklin?" Buck reached out and hugged the woman, then held her shoulders to look at her, a genuine smile on his face. "It's been a lot of years. Welcome home!"

"It's nice to be back. Kind of." The woman wrinkled her nose. "And this must be your wife and baby! I heard you'd married. He's adorable!" She reached out to tickle Bobby's chin.

"No, I'm not—"

"No, this isn't—"

They both broke off. Bobby reached out to grab for the woman's gold necklace.

"No, sweetie." Gina loosened his fingers from the shiny chain and took a step back. "I'm just a friend he's helping," she said to the woman.

"Oh! My bad." The woman looked apologetic. "I have a little one, too," she said, turning her attention to Gina. "I'm raising my nephew, Tyler, and he's about this one's age. Maybe we could get together for a play-date sometime."

"That would be great. I'm…" She paused, wondering how to describe her uncertain status. "I'm just in from California and I don't know anyone. Well, except Buck and his sister."

"I'm originally from California, too! We should definitely get together!"

Gina felt a surge of warmth. The idea of making mom friends on her own, rather than having acquaintances who were part of her wealthy in-laws' power network, was just what she hadn't known she was hungry for. "That would be great! Where's your nephew now?"

"Oh, I'm trying out a babysitter, so I came to the grocery to give her an hour alone with him. And it's killing me! I should go back, but give me your phone number and I'll be in touch."

They punched numbers into each other's cell phones, and then the woman gave Buck a quick wave and left.

"Wow, is this town always that friendly?" she asked Buck.

He nodded and tried to smile, but his eyes were hooded and lines bracketed his mouth.

"Buck?" She touched his shoulder.

He shook his head very quickly a couple of times. "We done here?"

"Um, sure. I think so."

"Let's go." He turned and walked toward the checkout, rapid but stiff.

She hurried after him. "What just happened?"

"Nothing. I think I'll go ahead on out, wait in the truck."

"But why?"

He stopped so quickly that she ran into him. "You look a lot like my wife. My dead wife. People who don't know me well and don't know what happened are going to think you're her."

"Ooh." Realization dawned. "And your baby? What happened to your baby?"

"Dead in the same car accident." His words were clipped, toneless. "Let's go."

It was what he didn't say that haunted her through the checkout and the ride to their next stop, the church.

She longed to ask him more about it but didn't dare push the issue.

Obviously, his pain was raw. And having her around was like salt in the wound.

Too bad, because she was really starting to like Rescue River.

Chapter Three

When they arrived at the church on the edge of town, Gina was captivated. Its white steeple shone bright against the blue sky, and the building was surrounded by a grassy lawn. A creek rambled alongside the church, and several long picnic tables stood under a shelter. It was easy to picture small-town church picnics on that lawn.

Gina hoisted Bobby to her hip and followed Buck toward the church. As they walked up the steps, the door opened and several men came out dressed in work clothes, followed by another in a police uniform. Everyone greeted Buck, and the police officer tickled Bobby under his chin, making him giggle. That close, Gina could see the name tag that indicated he was the chief. Her stomach tightened. For the first time in her life, she felt like law enforcement officers were her enemies, not her friends.

Buck introduced her and briefly explained her story, even though Gina was willing him to be quiet with all her silent might.

"Car broke down, eh?" Chief Dion said. "SUV? White?"

"That's the one," she said faintly.

"Saw it this morning. Ran the plates."

Gina's heart thudded like a doom-filled drumbeat. Had her in-laws reported her car missing?

"Our computers aren't communicating too well with those in California, so I couldn't get any information," he said. "Glad to know it's got an owner. Need any help getting back on the road?"

"It's just out of—"

"We might," Buck interjected. "We're headed out there in just a few minutes."

"Call me if there's any problem," Chief Dion offered. "In fact, I might be able to meet you out there or have one of our officers meet you. Make sure everything's okay."

"Sounds good."

As soon as Dion was gone, she turned to Buck. "Why'd you tell him we might need help? It's just out of gas. And I'd…rather not have police involvement."

"Oh? Why's that?"

"It's complicated." He'd been very helpful, and yet she couldn't fully trust him. She'd yet to meet the person who couldn't be swayed by her in-laws' money and power. The police detective she'd consulted privately about their unnecessary roughness had brushed aside her concerns and seemed more interested in how to get the wealthy couple to donate even more money to the local police department.

No, it was her and Bobby against the world. She headed on into the church, welcoming the dark, cool air.

"Come on—pastor's this way." As he took the lead, his shoulder brushed against her in the narrow hallway. An awareness clicked into her, something she hadn't felt since well before her husband had died. Whoa. What was *that*?

As they approached a doorway marked Pastor's Study, a middle-aged man stood up from behind the desk and came out to greet them, shaking Buck's hand heartily and then turning to her. "What a pleasure! Buck, we don't see you here often enough these days. You just missed the men's prayer group, fixing up one of the elementary classrooms. What brings you here?"

"This is Gina," Buck said. "She's looking for some help. Gina, meet Pastor Ricky."

Heat flushed Gina's face. She hated being in this position: helpless, homeless, asking for what amounted to a handout. *It's for Bobby*, she reminded herself.

The pastor invited them in, and Gina sat down, cuddled Bobby to her chest and explained their situation to a minimal degree. Homeless, purse stolen, looking for work and a place to stay.

The pastor nodded sympathetically. "The church isn't really set up for that," he said. "When we need places for people to stay, we usually ask families to put them up. In fact, Lacey, Buck's sister, has helped us out a few times."

"It would work better if she stayed somewhere else," Buck said.

Ouch! Gina had been an interloper back at her in-laws' place, where she'd been tolerated because she had given birth to the heir to the empire. But that feeling of always being on the outside, a burden, was a part of what she'd been fleeing.

The last thing she wanted was to feel that way at Lacey's place, but Buck was making it obvious that he didn't want her there.

"Let's see. There's Lou Ann Miller, but I think she's away visiting her sister. Maybe Susan Hayashi? Except her mom and brother are here visiting, and they're doing some renovations on Sam's house. Getting ready for the wedding, you know. Such a nice couple." He looked at Buck's impatient expression and waved a hand. "But you don't need to hear about all that. You're sure Lacey's place isn't an option?"

"Like I said, somewhere else would be better."

"Sure enough. I'll ask around. And I'll check the balance in the emergency fund." The pastor studied Buck with a level expression, obviously wondering what was going on. "I'd take you in myself, except we have a houseful of teenagers for the Artists for Christ Concert over in Mansfield. Not very quiet for your baby."

As if on cue, Bobby wiggled hard, trying to get down to the floor, and she gave the place a quick check for hazards and then set him down. "Do you know of any jobs?" she blurted out before she knew what she was saying. And wondered when Rescue River had become a viable place to live. "I don't want charity—I want to work, and I'm willing to do anything. I'm good at decorating, cooking and event planning, and I'm really organized. And I have most of a college degree." Her voice cracked a little on the last word. She'd been thinking about her job skills ever since she left her in-laws' place, and figuring out how to package her housewife background into something more impressive. Still, it was hard to brag about herself.

"Hmm. Again, we're a very small town, so I don't know of much. But what about Lacey? She's doing all that renovation. Surely she could use some help..."

"That's not going to work." Buck's words were flat, firm and final.

And that irked Gina. She scooped Bobby back up into her arms. "I'm sorry I remind you of your ex. I'll get out of your hair as soon as I can. But I have to do my best for my son. Why are you so against my working for Lacey, if I can talk her into it?"

He lifted an eyebrow, clearly trying to play it cool. "Because you're on the run and we know nothing about you." He rubbed the back of his neck with one hand. "And...look, Lacey's not as strong as she acts. Let's leave it at that."

What could she say? She nodded, feeling like there was more to the story.

The pastor put a hand on each of their arms. "Let's take it to the Lord," he suggested, and Gina felt ashamed she hadn't done more praying about her situation. She'd been too tired and too worried, but that was exactly when she needed to turn it over to God. Buck and Gina bowed their heads, and the pastor uttered a short prayer for Gina to find shelter and work and for everyone to get along. Something like that. Though she felt too upset and flustered to focus on the words, the pastor's heartfelt prayer offered a tiny sense of peace.

At the gas station, Buck pulled out a couple of five-gallon gas cans. "We'll fill both of these," he said to the attendant who came out to help, even though they were at a self-serve pump.

Gina touched Buck's arm, embarrassed. "Um, could we just fill one? About halfway? That should do me until..." She trailed off, her face heating. Never in her life had she been completely broke, not able to afford more than a couple of gallons of gas at a time.

He waved a hand. "Don't worry about it. We'll fill both."

"No, I'd rather just do what I can afford."

"I said don't worry about it."

"Trying to get me as far away as you can, are you?" She was half joking, and then she saw on his face that she'd guessed exactly right. "Fine, fill both." She slammed back into Buck's truck, feeling unaccountably hurt.

There was no particular reason why Buck should like her or want her to stay. Just because he'd rescued her last night, he didn't have responsibility for her future or Bobby's. That was solely on her shoulders.

The thing was, as she rode around Rescue River, even now as she watched the gas-station attendant clap Buck on the shoulder and help him lift the heavy gas cans into the back of his pickup, she *liked* this place. She could picture herself and Bobby playing in the park and attending the church and getting together with other friendly people. She could imagine herself a part of this community.

On the other hand, the idea of the man beside her resisting every moment of her presence was disconcerting. She hated not being wanted. She'd grown up feeling that way, and she'd married into a family where she felt like an outsider. Was she continuing her same sick pattern?

Rescue River was where the Lord had led her. It

seemed like the perfect place to stay, at least for a while.

She just had to convince Buck not to block the whole idea.

Buck helped Gina fill the gas tank on her loaded, late-model SUV, continuing to wonder what her story was, continuing to get distracted by the lemony scent of her hair. Dion was there, too, helping and subtly questioning, observing everything.

It was early evening, but Buck could still hear the steady *chink-chink-chink* of a rotary tiller off in the distance. Probably Rob Richardson, trying to get his field finished before the rain came on. Sun peeked through a bank of dark clouds, illuminating the freshly plowed acre beside them. Buck inhaled the sweet, pungent zing that indicated a storm was headed their way.

Gina thanked them both politely, strapped Bobby into the car seat and headed back to the guesthouse. Buck was about to climb into his truck when Dion gestured to him. "Stay back a minute, would you?"

Buck turned toward the police chief. "Sure. What's up?"

It wasn't like he was eager to get home. He was half hoping that Gina, now that she had a tank of gas and some baby food, would hightail it to the next town. Or the next state.

Then again, what would she do if she left Rescue River? Alone without money and with a baby to care for, what were the odds that she'd survive, let alone do well?

He didn't want to worry about her, because being around her disturbed him on so many levels. Her resemblance to Ivana evoked all kinds of feelings he'd had during his marriage. That initial attraction. Anger at how Ivana's love for him had cooled. Fear that he'd made a lifelong mistake in marrying her, and guilt that he'd let his feelings show.

Horrible guilt about how everything had ended. And with that, the way his drinking had spiraled out of control.

"We have a little bit of a problem," Dion said.

"With the car?"

"More so with the baby. Did you notice the bandage on his arm?"

Buck nodded. "She said it's a scratch."

"Mmm-hmm. Have you seen any other marks on the kid?"

Buck stared at Dion as the puzzle pieces started moving into place. "You're thinking…what? That somebody abused the baby?"

"Could be." Dion nodded, not looking at Buck, staring out over the fields. "Could be her."

"No." Buck reeled back against that accusation. "I've seen how protective she is. She wouldn't do anything to hurt him. I more got the impression that she's running away."

"That's my gut instinct, too, but she's a pretty woman and a mother, so guys like us can be a little distracted. Keep your eyes open for it, would you?"

"Did you find out something against her?"

Dion frowned. "Not officially. But I have a few friends in law enforcement on the West Coast. Apparently, someone tried to report the car stolen, only to find out that it's not even eligible for unlawful use for another four days."

"Unlawful use? So…"

"So she took a car that belongs to a family member or friend. Maybe she had permission to use it, but not to take off in it."

"What are you saying? What do you want to do?"

"I'm thinking she's either a woman in trouble, or she's trouble herself. Either way, that baby's the victim."

"So we should…"

"We should try to get her to stay in Rescue River, is what I'm thinking." Dion frowned, rubbed a hand over his chin. "No, it's not exactly our problem, and we can't make her stay, but it would be a good thing for her to stick around here until I can make some phone calls, find out what her story is. It's safe here, and I can monitor the situation, make sure she's not the abuser and maybe prevent those who are from finding her."

Something primal raised the hairs on the back of Buck's neck, and he gave Dion a narrow stare. "You like her, don't you?"

They weren't exactly friends. Dion had pulled Buck out of a couple of fights in his role as a cop, when Buck was drinking. Nowadays, Dion was more likely to evangelize him, which was almost worse. But at least it meant that Dion didn't think he was unredeemable, like so many in town did.

Maybe they had the beginnings of a friendship, but it wasn't enough to quell Buck's irrational twinge of jealousy at the thought of Dion liking Gina.

Dion's eyebrows came together. "What're you talking about, man? I don't even know her. I just see a Christian duty, and a judicial one, to watch out for her. And to watch her. Asking for your help as a citizen."

Buck chuckled, feeling relieved. "That's a first. You asking me to help you on the right side of the law."

"People change." Dion gave him a level stare. "Remember that, my man. People change."

Buck pondered that thought all the way home, and it gave him a spring to his step as he trotted up the guesthouse stairs, trying to stay ahead of the rain that was starting to fall. People changed. Maybe even him.

Just before he touched the door handle, he saw a movement on the far side of the porch.

Gina. Rocking gently on the porch swing, pulling a blanket over her shoulder, probably to shield Bobby from the sound of Buck's footsteps and the flash of lightning.

He walked quietly toward them, mindful of what Dion had said. He wanted to watch how she handled Bobby with Dion's questions in mind. If Gina was in trouble, he wanted to help her somehow. He couldn't push her away, no matter how disturbing it was to be around her. She could be in real danger.

"Hey," he said, keeping his concerns out of his tone. "You made it back okay? Vehicle's running well?"

She nodded. "Yes, and Lacey said we can stay one more night. Only one, though. Then we have to be on our way." She sounded sad.

"Do you...want to stay more?"

She adjusted Bobby with a tender care and private, loving smile. Then she looked out at the rainy twilight. "I like it here, and it feels safe. Like a good place to get my bearings."

"That's the town's history and reputation," he said.

"Rescue River's always opened its arms to those in need."

"It feels welcoming." She shot him a glance. "Well, mostly."

Buck decided to be honest. "I feel for your situation, but…" He trailed off as she adjusted Bobby again, and he realized exactly what she was doing.

She was nursing him.

He stood up quickly. "Whoa, I'm sorry to intrude. I didn't realize…"

"It's okay," she said, chuckling. "It's a natural thing and I know how to cover up. I've fed Bobby in all kinds of places."

"That's…pretty cool." He'd never been one of those guys who was turned off by nursing or pregnancy or childbirth. Just the opposite, in fact. He'd never loved Ivana more, never felt closer to her, than when she was in the height and glory of womanhood, pregnant with his child or feeding little Mia from her own body. The whole thing amazed him. God's creativity in action.

Rain was pounding hard now, bringing with it a fresh, clean-washed smell and cooler air.

He felt himself looking at Gina in a new light. His heart warmed toward her in a visceral way: that ancient male reaction to a mother and child in need. Yes, having her here was disturbing, but he thought he could handle it, at least for a short time.

And after all, he wouldn't be here for long himself. He was putting every penny he had into making restitution, repaying money he'd borrowed, getting back on his feet. Living here with Lacey rent-free in exchange for his renovation work. He didn't have the means to leave town, not yet, but he would soon.

"I like it here, Buck," Gina said. "I think God may have sent me and Bobby here for a reason. I'm thinking, maybe, I'd like to stay."

His ambivalence must have shown on his face, because she cocked her head to one side and spoke. "That bothers you, doesn't it? How come? Is it about my resemblance to your wife?"

"Somewhat." Actually, he was starting to wonder how he'd ever mistaken her for Ivana. She had a plucky strength and determination, a set to her chin, a way of holding herself that were completely her own. Still, he had questions.

She frowned and looked down at Bobby, who was starting to show signs of being done nursing. She turned a little away and wiped his mouth.

"Want me to burp him?" he asked before he could stop himself.

She quirked an eyebrow. "Can you?"

"Sure." He leaned down and picked up the baby boy and held him against his shoulder. He was sturdier than Mia had been. Gina had mentioned that Bobby was ten months. Mia had made it only eight.

But propping a baby with one hand, flipping the burp cloth over his shoulder, patting the baby's back, that all came right back to him. Like riding a bike. You didn't forget.

He pulled Bobby a little closer, breathing him in, cherishing the feel of the baby, pretending he was Mia. Pretending his little daughter was still alive and well and happy. That he hadn't driven Ivana from their home in a moment of anger and desperation.

If only none of it had happened.

"Look," she said, "I'm sorry if I bring up memories

for you. Maybe I'll get on my feet quickly and be able to get out of here. But meanwhile…"

"Meanwhile what?" He was holding her baby in the rainy twilight, looking at her and finding her beautiful, and feeling like he might be stepping into the biggest mess of his life.

And then, as he adjusted the sweet little bundle in his arms, Bobby's pajama leg came up and he saw it.

A bruise the size of a beer coaster. Or a man's fist.

"If it were just me, I'd leave for your sake," she said. "But this looks like the perfect safe place for Bobby, and I have to put him first."

He concealed his reaction to the bruise and stroked the baby's downy hair, his heart pounding. "Of course you do."

"But I don't know why I'm even talking to you about it. Your sister's the one who's determined to get rid of me." She was looking up at him with troubled eyes as the wind blew a strand of hair in front of her face. "I don't know what to do."

He could see that it cost her to admit that, to ask for advice. She'd do it, though, for her son. He could already tell she was that kind of woman.

He didn't think she could possibly have injured Bobby, which meant that someone else had done it. Someone she was running from?

And if so, what right did he have to push her away? Especially if it resulted in this little one being hurt again?

He patted Bobby's back until a loud burp made them both laugh. Then he sat down in the rocker across from the porch swing, still holding Bobby.

"Want to tell me about Bobby's father?"

She drew in a breath and let it out again, slowly, seeming to consider. Finally, she spoke. "Hank was... smart and handsome. And rich."

He smiled. "Bodes well for Bobby."

"Yes. I just hope he doesn't inherit a couple of the other genes."

"Like?"

"Like the addiction-prone one."

"Oh." Buck looked away, feeling ashamed. Addiction was considered genetic by some, but more of a character flaw by most. And it was a flaw he shared. "Did your husband ever do AA or anything like that?"

"He was more into cocaine," she said, "but sure, he did NA. Plenty of times."

"It never took?" That was discouraging. "You're talking about him in the past tense. Is he dead?"

"He died not long after Bobby was born. Ski accident."

"Drugs?"

She nodded. "Yes. He was high, skiing one of the most dangerous double black diamond slopes in California. He didn't have a chance."

"I'm sorry." Why did a guy do drugs when he had a wife and baby who needed him?

Then again, why did any addict do what he did?

"So that's not who you're running from."

She shook her head. "No. It's...my in-laws."

"Your husband's family? What's the problem there?"

She sighed. "Abuse, if you must know. I don't want to talk about it."

Buck's pulse rate shot up. There it was. He'd like to get his hands on those people. "If they abused you or Bobby, they should go to prison."

"They should, but they won't," she said with complete certainty.

"They're that powerful?"

"They're that powerful."

The sky was black velvet now, the air cooling more. She huddled under the blanket she'd been using as a nursing cover. She looked so pretty. So vulnerable. So in need of protection.

As was the little baby now sleeping in his arms.

He wasn't going to let anything happen between him and Gina, no way, but he had to let her stay. Dion had asked him to, and he had a lot to report to the police chief. And maybe, just maybe, it was a way for him to get over Ivana, move on. Maybe this was part of the restitution he was trying to practice in his recovery.

He was to make amends for wrongs he had done. Well, he was doing that with bar owners around town, with friends he'd borrowed from. With Lacey, who'd had to put up with a lot from him during his two-year drinking spree.

But the people he'd wronged the most were dead.

Could he make restitution through Gina and Bobby? Give something to them, and that way right the balance with his wife and child, who were beyond earthly help?

And once he'd made his restitution and saved up a little money, he'd leave. Leave, with a clean slate, and start over somewhere where nobody knew his past. It was what he wanted. All he wanted. All he was working for.

The wind blew the cool farm air toward the house, fragrant with fresh-plowed earth. Crickets sang out in a chorus. Streetlights flickered on down the block, where the shops were.

He slid one hand away from the baby and into his pocket where he carried his recovery coin. Six months sober. He could handle this new challenge.

"I'll talk to Lacey," he said gruffly. "Try to get her to let you stay awhile. And you can work on the renovation with me."

Chapter Four

Later that night, Gina had just closed her eyes when her phone buzzed. She grabbed it, not wanting to risk waking Bobby.

When she saw it was her friend Haley, back in California, she sat upright. "Hang on," she whispered and slipped a robe over her lightweight tank top and shorts.

Grabbing her phone, she hurried down to the small alcove on the landing of the stairs. It was one of the few public areas in the guesthouse that was finished, with lace curtains and a braided rug. She settled into the window seat, pulled her feet up underneath her and leaned back against comfortable cushions. She could see the half-open door of her room at the top of the stairs, so she'd notice if Bobby stirred.

"Okay, I can talk," she said quietly. "How are you? I miss you so much!" Ever since she and Haley had shared a room on the maternity floor, their babies born within hours of one another, they'd been close friends. Haley was the only person in whom Gina had confided about her plans to leave town.

"I miss you, too, but that's not why I called."

"Are the dogs okay?"

Haley laughed. "They're bad, and spoiled, but you know I love them. No, that's not the problem."

"Did you find anything out?" She was hoping, though not expecting, that Haley had figured out a way she could gain access to some of the money she should have inherited as Hank's widow.

"It's not good news." Haley cleared her throat and went into business mode, not a problem for her since she worked in a bank. "I've been nosing around, and it sounds like assets in probate can be tangled up for a year, eighteen months if the estate is complicated."

"Which it is." Hank's parents, seeing the mess Hank had made of his life after Bobby was born, had put most of his inheritance in trust. Gina even suspected that they'd gotten Hank to sign some CDs over to them when he was high.

"I talked to my manager—in confidence, didn't identify you—and she said that because there wasn't a will, there's no way around this long process. I'm so mad Hank didn't protect you and Bobby!"

"I know." Gina's chest ached, as it always did when she thought of Hank. He'd been so much fun when they'd first met; he'd swept her off her feet, had loved her madly. In the first two years of their marriage she'd realized his partying went further than it should— sometimes much further—but they'd still had a base of love and care for each other.

Bobby's arrival had changed everything. The responsibility of fatherhood had overwhelmed Hank, and Gina, sleep deprived and cranky, hadn't been as understanding as before. He'd gone off the deep end, dug into his bad habits and made the leap from recreational drug user to addict.

"He wasn't thinking straight," she said to Haley and left it at that.

"The good news is, within a few years, when it's all straightened out, you and Bobby should be okay." Haley's voice didn't sound all that reassuring, though.

"It sounds like there's a *but* in there somewhere."

"There is." Haley's voice sounded shaky. "Gina, there's a big problem."

"What? Tell me." Gina's heart felt like a stone. She wanted to start a new life, for herself but even more, for Bobby. But right now, it seemed like she'd never get free.

"It's your in-laws. When I saw Hank's cousin this morning, she told me they're going to report your car as stolen."

"What?" From the downstairs kitchen, Gina heard what sounded like an argument and lowered her voice. "That car's mine! Hank gave it to me!"

"But is the title in your name?"

Gina squeezed her eyes shut as if she could block out this unwelcome news. "No. It was in Hank's name."

"And since the estate's stuck in probate…"

Gina leaned her head back against the window, staring up at the ceiling. If they'd reported the car stolen, she was essentially a common criminal.

"Gina? Honey?"

Gina blew out a breath. "I'll be tracked down for sure, then, because the police department here has my vehicle information. What am I going to do?" Her voice broke on the last couple of words, and she swallowed hard, determined to maintain control.

"I've already thought about that. You've got to give it back, that's all."

"Give it back? When I'm here and they're in California?"

"Yep, and I've figured out how. You use one of those driving services. They load your vehicle on a truck and drive it across the country. It's done all the time."

Gina was still wrapping her mind around the facts: that her car wasn't her car, and that she was a wanted criminal. "It's got to be expensive," she said finally. "I'm almost out of money."

"Didn't you say you had a debit card?"

She did. "But it's not safe to use it." It wasn't as if there was a lot of money in the old joint account—Hank had drained most of it away in the months before his death—but there was something. Something for Bobby's future, if they could make it through the first couple of months.

Haley sighed audibly. "No. No, it's not safe, especially now that you're a wanted person. The police could track you to where you are."

Gina felt a sharp rush of shame that she had no savings of her own. If only she hadn't acquiesced to staying home with Bobby... She glanced up toward her room. No, she couldn't regret that decision. They'd both agreed that since they had the means, it would be best for her to spend Bobby's early years at home with him.

She shoved open the window, letting the rain-soaked breeze soothe her hot face.

"We've got to hire you a transportation service, have you send back the car. The way I see it, you don't have a choice." Haley cleared her throat. "I talked to Josh. We...we can pay for it."

"No." Gina couldn't let her friend do that. She and her husband had tons of student debt and no family money. Although they both worked, the high cost of living in their part of the state made it so that they barely scraped by every month.

And yet Haley was right. Staying out of trouble with the law was a bigger priority even than a financial safety net.

"Look, what if I mail you my ATM card? That way you can take the money out of my account, and if it's traced, it'll be local, not here." Gina couldn't believe how quickly she was able to flip into criminal mode when it was Bobby's safety in question. "If I do that, can you set it up for me? Do we just send the SUV to them? I'm afraid they'll find out where it came from and track us down."

"Nope. Overnight the card to me, and I'll get it all set up right away. As soon as the SUV arrives, I'll drive it over to your in-laws' place and leave it."

"How? In the middle of the night?"

"Maybe. Or maybe I'll figure out some explanation." She paused. "I really want this to work for you, Gina. I miss you, but you did the right thing. Bobby comes first."

"Thank you so much. You're an amazing friend." Her throat tight, she chatted for a couple more minutes and then ended the call.

How was she going to manage without a vehicle? And yet, what choice did she have?

She looked out the window at the streetlights of Rescue River. The main street glistened with today's rain. She could see the market, the diner, the library.

She could see them, which meant she could walk

to them. She looked up at the stars. "You knew what You were doing when You put me here, Father," she murmured in a low voice.

She let out a sigh and slid her feet down to the floor…only to shriek at the sight of a large figure standing a couple of steps down from the landing. When she recognized Buck, her heart rate settled a little.

He flicked on the hall light. "Sorry to startle you. I was talking to Lacey about your situation. Coming upstairs to my room." Unnecessarily, he gestured toward the upper floor. "I didn't mean to eavesdrop."

She remembered the raised voices she'd heard. "Let me guess," she said. "Your talk with Lacey didn't go well."

"I'm afraid not." He sat on the other end of the curved window seat, his face barely visible in the glow of a streetlight. "She's just not comfortable having you here. She said you could stay for a couple more days, through Monday, Tuesday if you really need to, but that's all."

The weight of her responsibilities pressed down on Gina. She couldn't stay, then, not unless she found another job. But she couldn't go, not with her transportation being taken out from under her.

"Hey, I'm sorry." He reached out a hand and patted her shoulder.

Surely he meant it as a friendly touch, but to Gina, the warmth of his large hand made her want to hurl herself into his arms. He seemed so strong and competent and kind.

And she couldn't give in to that desire to be rescued. "Thanks for trying. With God's help, I'll figure out something."

Rather than nodding and moving away, he gave her shoulder another pat and looked into her eyes. "When I met you, I thought you were one of those ladies who lunch, someone who never had a problem. But that's far from the truth, isn't it?"

"Miles away." She couldn't handle the compassion in his eyes, but she couldn't look away, either.

"If I wasn't knee-deep in problems of my own, problems of my own creation, I'd try to help you more." He squeezed her shoulder once and then pulled his hand away.

"Thanks." She actually believed him.

"One thing I *can* offer," he said, "is an invitation to church tomorrow. Nine o'clock. It's a great community church, the one we stopped by before, and who knows, maybe someone is hiring or can put you up." He sounded doubtful. And she couldn't tell whether he wanted her to stay or not. Probably not.

He was offering her solace, and shamefully, church didn't seem like a lot of help right now. But it was what she had, and she knew, intellectually at least, that God was big enough to handle any problem.

And she also knew that staying here in the dim moonlight, talking to a very handsome and compassionate man, wasn't the solution to anything. She stood and turned toward the stairs. "I'd love to go. Thanks for asking."

Minutes after Gina went into her room and closed the door, Buck trotted downstairs. He was putting on his coat when Lacey came out of the kitchen, holding her orange cat in her arms.

"Where are you going?" she asked. "It's late."

"Need some air." The conversation with Gina had thrown him off balance in more ways than one, and he knew he wouldn't sleep anytime soon.

Not to mention he was worried about the baby. Earlier tonight, when Gina had gone inside to fetch his binky, Buck had snapped a photo of Bobby's bruise to show Dion.

His sister cuddled the cat closer and studied him, her forehead wrinkled.

"It's just a walk, Lace."

"You're sure?"

"Yes!" Then, ashamed of his sharp tone, he put an arm around her shoulders and gave her a gentle squeeze. He shouldn't be mad at her when she'd bailed him out of so many problems. Between her own tragedies and his bad behavior, his waiflike younger sister had been forced to grow stronger than any woman should have to be. "I won't be out long and I won't do… what I used to do."

"I know." She leaned into his side. "I just got in the habit of worrying about you, know what I mean?"

"I know. But I'm fine."

At least, he *hoped* he was fine, he thought as he stepped out the door. In the past, he'd have for sure gone on a bender just because he felt mixed up about that encounter with Gina.

He was worried about what he'd overheard, but that wasn't all of it.

Turned out God had a sense of humor. He was *attracted* to the pretty, maternal stranger.

Buck blew out a sigh and strode through Rescue River's small business district. A farming community to the core, the town shut down early. The diner and the shops all had doors closed and lights off.

Clouds scuttled over the moon and a breeze rattled the tree limbs. Buck pulled his coat closer around him. Ohio weather. Yesterday had been springlike, but tonight it felt like a front was coming through.

There *was* one business still open, one place where light and happy noises indicated life: the Ace Tavern.

Buck straightened his back and told himself to keep walking. And he did. He walked past.

Behind him, the door of the tavern opened. Could he be blamed for turning back? Any combat vet worth his salt had it ingrained: know what's going on behind you.

A long-haired woman came out, alone. Wearing a jacket that didn't look too warm, skintight jeans and ridiculously high heels. There was a click, a flash, and she got her cigarette lit, then looked up and saw him. "Hey, handsome, come buy me a drink," she said. Then she squinted and leaned toward him, catching herself on the bar's wooden outside wall. "Well, if you ain't a sight for sore eyes. Buck Armstrong."

He stepped closer and recognition dawned. "Hey, Heather, how's it going?" He reached out to grasp her hand and ended up steadying her. "Been a while." Heather was at least fifteen years older than Buck, but they'd been good drinking buddies. Heather was one of the few people in town who'd been able to match Buck shot for shot.

The thought of that brought a tight feeling to his throat.

A glass of whiskey, he knew, would take that feeling away. Warm him right up, too.

"Gonna finish my smoke and then go back in.

C'mon, have a cold one and let me know what you been up to." She spoke slowly and carefully but still tripped over a few of the words. Did he used to sound like that?

"You planning on driving home tonight?" He knew Heather lived out in the country, had been to a couple of parties at her place.

"Sure, yeah. Why, want to come out my way?"

"No, not tonight, thanks."

"Your loss." She turned to go back into the bar and stumbled.

Catching her, Buck blew out a breath. He knew well enough what falling-down drunk looked like, and Heather was falling-down drunk. And he needed to make sure someone would take care of her. Holding her elbow, he steered her inside.

The bar wasn't crowded. A couple of guys playing pool, a man and woman talking intently in a booth, and three or four of his old acquaintances at the bar. Regulars, people who didn't have much family. Whether they hung out at the Ace because of that, or whether their drinking had pushed loved ones away, they didn't have another place to go, and the bar served as home to them.

"Hey, Armstrong!" Word circled around the place, and it was like he'd never left. Guys clapping him on the back, Heather clinging to his arm, proud to have brought in a popular old friend, the bartender turning over glasses, shot and a beer, his old favorite.

"Not tonight, Arnie," he told the bartender, leading Heather to a table and then extricating himself from her grasp.

Mild catcalls of disapproval greeted his refusal. Everyone here knew he was in AA and probably didn't want to tempt him too badly, but they'd welcome him back into the fold in a minute. His choice.

He stepped over to the bar and handed Arnie a couple of bills. "Get someone to take Heather home tonight, could you? She shouldn't be driving."

Arnie pocketed the money with a smile. "I'll take her myself."

"Thanks." *Get out of here, now.* He looked around at the beer signs, the glittering rows of bottles, ran a hand over the scarred wooden bar. This place had been here forever. A classic.

Get out now.

He turned toward the door.

"Sure I can't get you a drink? My treat." Arnie held up a glass.

Get out. Buck fingered his sobriety coin, squeezed it hard until the edges dug into his palm. Looked up at the ceiling, made a plea.

"No. No, thank you." Somehow, he got his mouth to form the words and got his feet to start marching. Like marching during wartime, when you'd been up twenty-four hours and more and didn't think your legs could carry you. One step at a time.

A moment later he was out of the bar and leaning against the wooden front of it, breathing hard. He pulled out his sobriety coin and, in the light from the bar's window, read the serenity prayer printed in tiny letters on the back. Or pretended to read it; actually, he knew it by heart. *God, grant me the serenity to accept the things I cannot change, the courage to...*

In front of him, a police cruiser stopped, and he was

still enough of a drunk that his heart raced before he remembered he hadn't done anything wrong.

Dion stepped out and walked over, stood a little closer than was polite. Undoubtedly trying to tell if Buck smelled of liquor. "In trouble, my friend?"

"Just got away from it." He held up his coin.

Dion narrowed his eyes, studying it, and then the light dawned. "Your recovery coin. Close call?"

Buck nodded, his heart rate settling back to normal. The fresh, cold air braced him. He could do this.

He hoped.

"Want to grab a cup of coffee? I'm done with my shift."

He *wanted* a drink. But no. He didn't intend to go back there, not ever. "Thanks—coffee sounds good," he said and got into the cruiser.

He'd definitely have something to share at tomorrow's AA meeting.

When they reached the truckers' restaurant out by the highway—the only nondrinking place open at this hour—the owner hurried toward them. He was a short man in a white shirt with pants pulled up high on his ample belly, and his hand was raised like a stop sign. "You're welcome, Chief, but him I won't serve."

Heat rose in Buck's face. He dimly remembered some late-night, postbar confrontation, some shouting, a few shoves.

The smells of coffee and fried food wafted through the air. A couple of uniformed waitresses stood near the cash register, watching. They probably remembered Buck, too, and not in a good way.

He turned to go.

"He's my guest," Dion said. His voice was quiet, but

he'd drawn himself up tall. He was a big man, and commanding, and the restaurant manager visibly cringed.

"Well, all right, if you'll take full responsibility. But if there's any trouble…"

"If there's trouble, I'll handle it, my friend."

The manager nodded and stepped aside, and Dion led the way to a booth in the restaurant's back corner.

Once they'd both ordered coffee, Buck let his head sink onto one fist and stared down at the none-too-clean table. "I'll never get out from under my reputation. I've got to leave Rescue River. Repay my debts and leave."

Dion shook his head, slowly. "You're a new creation. Did you think that was just words?"

"The outside looks the same, and no one around here believes in the change. It's dangerous," he added for clarification, remembering Arnie holding up the glass.

Instead of responding to that, Dion studied him. "What was it had you out walking so late?"

Buck looked at Dion's dark eyes, eyes that seemed to hold a depth of thought and wisdom beyond most of the people Buck knew. "Did you ever meet a woman you really liked, but you knew she was out of reach?"

Dion's mouth twisted a little and he looked out across the restaurant. "In a manner of speaking."

Daisy Hinton, the town's pretty blonde social worker, sprang into Buck's mind. He'd heard the rumors about her and Dion but didn't know whether there was any substance to them.

Dion rubbed the back of his neck. "What are we talking about here? You got a crush on someone unattainable?"

Buck sighed. "It's Gina. I like her."

"The new lady in town?" Dion lifted an eyebrow. "Back up, my man. What have you heard? How's the baby doing?"

"The good news is, Bobby is doing fine. Gina couldn't possibly be the one who was abusing him. He's thriving, and she's real gentle with him."

"Good." Dion sipped at his hot coffee. "What's the bad news?"

Buck hesitated. Should he tell Dion what he'd overheard, possibly getting Gina into trouble? But if he didn't tell Dion, and something happened to her that could have been prevented...

"I can tell you know something," Dion said, "so why don't you go on and tell me."

Buck shook his head. "Man, I feel sorry for your kids, if you ever have any. You're going to read them like a book."

A strange expression crossed Dion's face so quickly that Buck decided he must have imagined it. He stirred sugar into his coffee. "It was just a little something I overheard. One-sided phone conversation."

Dion lifted an eyebrow, waiting.

"She was talking about whether she and Bobby could be hunted down here. Something about mailing an ATM card to a friend so the withdrawal couldn't be traced." He paused, then added, "She also sounded worried about the fact that you have her vehicle information. And it sounds like she's going to ship her car back to California."

Dion's eyes narrowed. "So the vehicle *was* stolen."

"I thought so, too. But she seems to want to give it back."

Dion shook his head, a mirthless chuckle escaping. "That's what they all say."

"She wasn't saying it to make an impression. She was talking to a friend."

"And…there's nothing illegal about shipping a car. But if she doesn't have the registration or title or some identifying paperwork, no legitimate shipper will take it on."

"So we could just wait and see. If she's able to ship the car, that means she's got the rights to it."

"Or something." Dion frowned. "Tell you what. I'll do a little digging, but I'm not going to bring a lady in for wanting to ship a car. What I *am* going to do is to keep a pretty close eye on her."

Buck nodded. Dion had to do his job. And thinking of that reminded him of the photo he'd taken. "Look at this," he said as he pulled out his phone and brought up the image. "Zoom in on the baby's leg."

Dion's eyebrows rose. "Is that a bruise?"

Buck nodded and held up a hand. "After seeing her with the baby, there's no way she could be at fault. She's very protective of him. Protective like someone who's escaping an abuser, not someone who's an abuser herself."

Dion's brows drew together. "Maybe."

"Give her a chance," Buck said. "She could be a new creation, too."

"Touché, my man. But my job is to clean up the messes people make along the way." He leveled a pointed gaze at Buck. "And your job is to stay sober and help your sister. Not to get overinvolved with a pretty possible criminal passing through town."

"You warning me?"

"Let's just say we're not that far removed from the days I had to pull you out of that bar and toss you in jail to sober up. Worst thing a former drinker can do is to get involved with the wrong company."

Buck nodded, but he couldn't truly agree with Dion. He had the distinct feeling that he, with his miserable track record, was the wrong company for Gina. Not the other way around.

Chapter Five

Gina found the next day's church service renewing and refreshing, and afterward, friendly people talked her into attending the church luncheon and meeting to plan the Freedom Festival. After a quick check on Bobby, who was loving the church nursery, she found her way to the fellowship hall.

Amy, the tall, gorgeous woman she'd met in the grocery store with Buck, hurried over. "Hey, they're just finishing up the general meeting, and everyone's going to eat before breaking into committees. You should come sit next to me and we can talk about getting our babies together."

"That would be nice." Although she feared she wouldn't find a way to stay in Rescue River long enough to build real friendships, Gina was grateful to be able to sit with someone other than Buck and Lacey. She didn't want to impose on them.

After she'd gotten her plate of meat loaf, mashed potatoes and green beans, she headed over to where Amy was gesturing. And sighed. Amy was next to Buck and

Lacey at a table full of people. So Gina ended up sitting with them after all.

Conversation focused on the upcoming festival. Apparently, it had been going on for years, celebrating Rescue River's history with the Underground Railroad and the arrival of spring, which had meant easier travel for those seeking freedom.

Lacey was more animated today, talking about the guesthouse. "There's a room in the basement and another in the attic that were kept available for fugitive slaves. Apparently, at one time there were thirty people staying at the house."

"You should get a historic-landmark designation!" Gina said. "It's a lot of paperwork, but with a history like that, I'm sure you'd be approved."

Lacey didn't seem to hear her, speaking instead to Amy about how hard it was to get the renovation done while working full-time.

"I could help you with it," Gina offered when there was a break in the conversation. "At least to get it on the National Register of Historic Places, which is easier. I've helped a couple of organizations do it."

Lacey gave her a look, one Gina could read. It was the same look she'd gotten when she'd tried to connect with the popular girls back in high school. *You don't belong*, it said.

Gina bit her lip. "Look, I know I won't be here much longer, but I could print out the paperwork for you and give you some advice tonight. It's well worth doing. And it'll draw a lot of people to your guesthouse when it opens."

"I don't want to get the word out too soon. It's going

to take a long time to finish, with the hours Buck and I work."

"Hey, hey," said a man sitting across from Amy. "Don't blame me. Buck has worked so much overtime that he could do half days for the rest of the year and be okay." He looked at Gina. "I'm his so-called boss, Troy Hinton," he said, reaching out to shake her hand.

"Yeah, but I can't take time off, and the work we need to do now, like hanging wallpaper, requires two people," Lacey said. "I'm working extra hours myself, just to try to raise enough money so I can quit my day job and focus on the guesthouse when it opens. *If* it ever opens."

"I've hung tons of wallpaper." For Bobby's sake, Gina forced herself to persist. "I could just stay a little while and help—"

"No!" Lacey's voice cracked, causing conversation around the table to pause momentarily. "Not happening."

Gina felt her face heating with embarrassment.

Buck leaned toward his sister and spoke to her rapidly, and Lacey's eyes filled with tears.

One of the people who'd just come to the table, a pretty Asian American–looking woman who'd been introduced as Susan, shoved her plate away and came around the table to Lacey's side just as Lacey stood and murmured a broken apology to Gina.

"Come on," Susan said. "I'll take you home."

"Sorry about that," Buck said to Gina after Lacey and Susan were gone and conversation had resumed. "She has issues related to some stuff that's happened to her. She miscarried a baby, and quite honestly, I don't know if she'll ever recover. Lacey's strong in some ways, but she takes things hard."

"Oh, no! How awful!" Being a mother was the best thing that had ever happened to Gina, and she could only imagine how losing a baby would feel. "I'm so sorry I upset her."

"Not your fault."

It wasn't, but how sad. Gina sighed and distracted herself by looking around the room at the tables full of people eating and talking. Up by the stage, a group of kids tossed around a couple of sponge balls, their laughter and shouts contributing to the general noise. Near the pass-through to the kitchen, women were cutting and serving pie, and the scents of cinnamon and nutmeg made Gina's mouth water. It smelled like the home of the girl she'd most envied back in her grade-school days, a girl who'd come from a big, warm family.

Behind her, she heard the sound of a baby crying, and she stood and turned at the same moment as the man who'd spoken about Buck being able to take time off. In the doorway of the fellowship hall, one of the nursery workers scanned the room, holding a crying Bobby. When she saw Gina, she waved, indicating that she'd bring Bobby over.

"Oh, yours, not ours," Troy said, sitting back down.

"Woot!" The woman next to him gave him a gentle high five. "We actually get to finish our meals. I'm Angelica, by the way," she said to Gina.

"Yeah, until Xavier gets too wild and we have to rein him in." Troy put an arm around Angelica, looking at her with warm possessiveness. "I have to fight for adult time with my wife."

The loving look she gave him back made jealousy knife through Gina's heart. Would she ever have a relationship like that, or was she doomed to repeat past failures?

Shaking off the jealousy, Gina thanked the nursery worker and pulled Bobby into her lap, cuddling him close. He was what was important, not her own romantic longings.

"He's adorable!" Angelica said. "How old is he?"

"Ten months." Gina nuzzled Bobby's head and wiped his tears.

"He's a big boy!" Angelica leaned forward to tickle Bobby's arm, making him chortle. "My Emmie is nine months, but she's nowhere near this one's size."

"Mom!" A boy of seven or eight hurtled into Angelica's side and then looked curiously at Bobby. "Who's that baby?"

Another little girl, a year or two younger, hopped into Angelica's lap. "Xavier took my dancing bear, Aunt Angelica."

"I just hid it, Mindy. It's behind the curtain." Xavier gestured toward the stage and leaned forward to tickle Bobby's knee.

Mindy stuck out her tongue at him, slid off Angelica's lap and ran toward the stage. At which point Gina realized that the little girl was missing a hand.

"Be kind to your cousin," Angelica scolded her son gently. "Go play with her."

"But she wants to play dumb games."

"Listen to your mother," Troy said, his voice stern, and Xavier stuck out his lower lip, then nodded and ran toward Mindy.

As people watched and chuckled and asked to hold

Bobby, Gina felt a sense of homecoming unlike anything she'd ever experienced before. She loved it here. She wanted to raise Bobby here.

An elderly woman approached their table, pushing a rolling walker. "Are you going to finish putting my house back together before the festival?" she asked, pointing a bony finger at Buck.

"Um, I don't think so, Miss Minnie."

"Why not?"

"Too much to do and not enough time to do it, with Lacey and me both working."

Amy explained. "The guesthouse belonged to Miss Minnie until recently."

"Was it in your family a long time?" Gina pushed her mostly empty plate aside, too interested to finish her meal.

"Since before the Civil War," the woman said. "And to think that I would be the one to let it go out of the family…"

"Do you have any records, letters, stories?" Gina asked, fascinated as always by living local history.

"I certainly do, young lady. A whole trunk full of them. And you are…?"

"I'm sorry." Gina stood. "Would you like to sit down? I'm Gina Patterson. I'm…" She glanced around. "I'm just passing through, I guess. But I used to volunteer at the historical society where I lived in California. I hope those documents will be able to stay with the house."

"First time anyone's shown any interest," Miss Minnie grumbled.

"Sit down and join us, Miss Minnie," Buck said, standing too and holding a chair for the woman.

"No, sirree. I have more people to visit." And she was off, pushing her walker with surprising speed.

"Sure would be great if Lacey could open the house in time for the festival," someone said.

Let me help. Gina had to press her lips together to keep from saying the words out loud. "What kind of guests come to town during the festival?" she asked instead.

"Last year, we got over three thousand visitors." Troy had his arm around Angelica, unconsciously stroking her hair as he spoke. "City people, mostly, from Cleveland and Pittsburgh and Columbus. People who like the small-town scene."

"People with money?" Amy asked.

A pretty, plump blonde woman lifted an eyebrow at Amy. "You planning to pick pockets?"

"Daisy!" Angelica shook her head. "Be nice to Amy. She's newly back in town."

"And no," Amy said, laughing, "I'm not picking anyone's pocket. I'm hoping to take the visitors' money, but honestly. If I stay, I might open up a shop."

Gina opened her mouth and then shut it again.

"What?" Angelica asked, and Buck looked curious, too.

"It's just…you couldn't *pay* for the kind of advertising Lacey would get if she could have an open house during the festival. Even if it was just partially done, a few rooms. The people who come to town are already looking for the small-town experience. They're perfect customers."

"For sure," Buck said. "Just don't see how we could get it done in time."

Angelica looked at Gina. "Could you help them? Because this might be a God thing."

"I... Yeah, I could."

"How?" Buck asked sharply.

"It's not just the historical-society work and the fact that I've done a lot of decorating. I also majored in marketing in college."

"So you know how to showcase a place like the guesthouse to make it shine, right?" Angelica asked, smiling as if she already knew the answer.

"Yeah," Gina admitted, "I do. The place would be booked for months in advance even before it officially opens. Especially if there aren't a lot of competing guesthouses and B and Bs here."

"There's just the one other motel," Buck said, "and it's very basic." He looked thoughtful, as if he were really considering the possibility of having Gina stay and help.

"You and Lacey should totally hire her," Angelica said.

"Well, but it would mean having Bobby around a lot." Now that Buck seemed to be considering the idea, all the reasons against it flooded into Gina's head. "And we'd have to stay there. If we could stay, your sister could pay me pretty minimally."

"I can take Bobby some," Angelica said unexpectedly. "I'm at home with Emmie, and it would be fun for her to have a playmate."

"I couldn't pay much for child care," Gina warned, feeling uncomfortable with the need to economize. But she was determined to learn—or relearn—to live without the easy wealth she'd gotten accustomed to during her marriage.

Angelica waved a hand. "You wouldn't need to pay. It could be our contribution to the guesthouse. Rescue River needs it badly."

"No, I'd find a way to pay. But that would be great. There are fumes in some parts of a renovation, and that wouldn't be good for him. Would it, sweetie?" She reached out her arms for Bobby, who was snuggling now in Buck's arms.

"I'll hold him—it's fine," he said. "All of this is a good idea for Rescue River and for Lacey. But I have my doubts about whether..." He broke off, looked down at Bobby and then back at Gina, his face bleak. "Like I said, having a baby around would be hard on her."

And on you, Gina thought.

Around them, clattering dishes and bustling footsteps announced that the meal was coming to an end, but at their table, everyone was watching Buck.

Abruptly, he handed Bobby back to Gina and lifted his hands like stop signs. "All right, all right. I'll talk to her again. But I can't make any promises. I doubt she'll agree to anything of the kind."

As for Gina, she wondered whether Buck would present a fair case. He seemed almost as set against her staying as his sister was.

On Monday and Tuesday, Buck busied himself with work at the vet clinic. His boss, Troy Hinton, took in every animal who had a need, whether the owners could pay or not, so there was plenty of work.

Midafternoon on Tuesday, Buck was washing up after a procedure when there was a sharp click and then someone crowded behind him.

Adrenaline surged. Buck spun, wet hands up, and grabbed for his assailant's throat.

"Hey, hey!" His boss's surprised voice and familiar face made Buck drop his hands and step back, heart racing.

He looked away and drew in a couple of deep breaths, like they'd taught him at the VA.

"You okay?" Troy's voice was mild as he put away a pair of surgical forceps and started washing his hands at the other side of the sink.

"Yeah. Sorry, man."

"I should know better than to sneak up behind you." Troy dried off and then sat down at the computer.

It was a great thing about working for Troy Hinton: he was calm, an old friend, and he'd known about Buck's PTSD—and his other flaws—when he'd hired him.

His heart still racing, Buck stepped out the back door of the clinic for some air…and heard a whining, scratching sound at his feet.

There was a closed cardboard box, a couple of feet square, with holes punched in the sides and an envelope on the top. Uh-oh.

He picked up the box and carried it inside. "Drop-off," he said to Troy and set the box down on the floor. He handed the envelope to Troy, then grabbed a pair of forceps and used them to open the box gingerly. No telling what he might find. Could be something wild and scared, even rabid.

But when he got the box open, a dirty white mop flung itself out and planted front paws on Buck's leg. When he bent to pat what looked like its head, the little dog licked his hand, barking and whining.

He squatted down. "Okay, buddy. It's okay." He stroked the matted, dirty fur. "What's in the envelope?" he asked Troy.

Troy squinted at a sheet of notepaper and then read aloud. "'I'm sick, can't take care of Spike no more. My kids want to put him down. Please help.'"

"Spike?" Buck brushed back the excessive hair on the little dog's head and looked into anxious dark eyes. "You're a tough guy, huh?"

A couple of bills fluttered to the floor, and Troy picked them up, a five and a single. "Six dollars." He shook his head. "Guy probably went without something to leave that."

"Got room for him at the rescue?"

"I'll make room. Better check him out first." Troy got a small biscuit out of the jar they kept on the desk and whistled, and the mop waddled over to him. "Hey, big guy. How long were you out there?"

The little dog's whole body wagged.

"Sit," Troy said, and the mop sat down and held out a polite paw. When Troy offered the biscuit, the dog grabbed it and ran off to the corner of the room to eat. "He's hungry."

"Somebody trained him, though. Can't figure why anyone would want to put the little guy down." Buck stood. "Want me to do an exam?"

"No. I want you to take afternoons off like you're supposed to and go work on your sister's guesthouse. Why are you even here, come to think of it?"

Buck shrugged. "I meant to, but…"

"But what? What's going on?"

Buck blew out a sigh. He'd told himself he was needed here, but the truth was more complicated.

"Avoiding Gina and Bobby?" Troy sat down in the rolling chair and crossed his arms.

"Might be." Of course he was. He'd convinced his sister to give the new situation with Gina a try, and now he wasn't sure it had been the right thing.

"How come? You gotta deal with stuff, man, not let it slip under the rug."

And this was the bad thing about working for Troy: he was a little too insightful. "She's kicking up some memories, and not just for Lacey."

"Go home," Troy ordered.

"You're sure—"

"I'm sure."

So that was how, the next morning, Buck found himself just outside a smallish bedroom, listening to Bobby's baby chatter and Gina's murmurs.

He was almost wishing he hadn't talked Lacey into allowing Gina to stay and help. "Until the Freedom Festival and not a moment longer," Lacey had said.

Even that amount of time might be too long.

He, Lacey and Gina had talked last night, figuring out a plan. Lacey would open half of the house for the Freedom Festival, so people could see the progress and get excited about coming to stay, and then work on the rest of the house throughout the summer and possibly into the fall.

And right now, his role was to work afternoons— and possibly evenings—with Gina to finish the three rooms. Mornings, when he was working at the clinic, she'd be figuring out the historical-landmark paperwork and setting up a website to publicize the guesthouse.

Bobby was on hands and knees next to a table Gina had set up in the middle of the room. As Buck watched, the sturdy baby grabbed the leg of the table, hauled himself to his feet and then fell right back down on his diaper-clad behind. Undaunted, he reached for the table leg and began to repeat the process.

Gina bent over a book that lay open on the table. She tucked a lock of hair behind her ear and looked from the book to a can of something—paint, maybe—and then back at the book again.

Man, she's pretty. Buck's heart kicked up to a faster rate. Ignoring that, he tapped on the door frame.

"Hey." Gina smiled when she saw him, eyes sparkling, and his heart rate jumped up another notch. "I thought we'd start with the simplest project," she said. "Come see what I... I mean, we...have planned."

Calm down, buddy—she's not for you. He walked into the room, deliberately not focusing on Gina.

It was a corner bedroom with windows on two sides, and Gina had opened them. Birds chittered madly outside and a fresh breeze cooled his face.

"It's a little chilly in here, but I figure we'll get warm as we work. I like having the windows open, because we're going to be using primer today and I don't like him breathing it." She looked down at Bobby, her face curving into a smile, and Buck realized that the baby had pulled himself up again and stood, banging on the table leg, grinning.

"The fresh air is no problem. If you want to work on filling nail holes and doing repairs, I can do the priming in a different room from where you and Bobby are."

"I've already done that. And I cleaned the walls. So now, it's down to whether you prefer doing the edges with a brush or rolling." She held up a paintbrush and roller.

"Rolling is more fun for sure, but let's both work on the edges a little. That takes twice as long."

"Great."

While Buck opened two cans of primer and stirred them up, Gina brought out a pack-and-play. She put Bobby inside, along with a stack of plastic blocks and vinyl-covered books. "That'll keep him for a while, and when he gets bored, maybe he'll take a little nap." Gina bit her lip, her forehead wrinkling.

"You're short of toys for him."

She shrugged. "He's used to having a lot more stuff to entertain him, but it's okay. It'll develop his imagination."

"I know where you can get a bunch of baby stuff, free." He hadn't known he was going to offer until it happened, and the moment the words were out of his mouth, he regretted it.

Her forehead smoothed out. "I would love it, if you're serious. It's a challenge to entertain an active baby in the workplace."

"You've been doing fine." Maybe she'd decide she didn't want the loan.

"I'm fortunate that Susan Hayashi brought over the pack-and-play and a few toys. Apparently, they belonged to her fiancé and were just stored in his basement."

"I'm sure Sam Hinton had nothing but the best for Mindy. He's a pretty wealthy guy." But Buck didn't envy the CEO of Hinton Enterprises for his millions. The man had lost his wife and had struggled for a couple of years to deal with issues related to his daughter's disability and reaction to losing her mother. He'd only recently started looking happy and energetic again, since Susan Hayashi had come into his life last summer.

"So, where's this cache of baby toys?" she asked as she turned on the radio. "Is it your old stuff? GI Joes?"

"No…though I did have my share of those, and don't you dare call them dolls." He was hoping to distract her, and it worked.

"You grew up here in Rescue River, right? What did your parents do?"

Buck dipped his brush and started to paint a careful edge, finding the meticulous work soothing. "Yeah. Dad sold cars and Mom…" He paused, thinking how to explain it. "Mom taught piano when she could."

"Sounds like a story." Gina knelt to apply primer around a window frame.

"Yeah." Buck let out a mirthless chuckle. "It's a real old story. When Lacey and I were little, she just had a couple of cocktails before dinner. By the time we were teenagers, it was pills to get going in the morning and wine with lunch."

"Oh, I'm sorry." Gina glanced his way, compassion in her eyes, and shook her head. "That's so hard to deal with."

"Your husband had similar issues, right?"

She nodded, but didn't bite at the change of subject. "Is your mom still living?"

"No. Died when I was twenty-one." He was so used to saying it that he felt just a twinge of sadness, nothing more. Mom had been too talented for a small town, and too East Coast for Ohio, and actually, she'd been absent to him and Lacey for several years before her death.

The quick squeeze of his shoulder surprised him. "I'm sorry for your loss. And for having to grow up that way."

Quickly, Buck shook his head. "It wasn't like that. Lacey and I were blessed. Dad's a great guy. Everyone in town loved him. And his parents—my gram and gramps—they filled in the gaps when Mom wasn't doing well. It was hard on Lacey, not having a mom who could help her with the girl things. But for me, it was a real good childhood."

"So how come you started drinking?"

Just like that, Buck's easy mood shattered into pieces. Bobby was standing in the pack-and-play, waving his arms, and Buck put down his brush and went over to pick the boy up, craving the comfort. "Drank a little during the war. And a lot after. It would've taken a better man than I am to do two tours in Afghanistan without drinking."

She nodded, moving over to the next window frame and running the paintbrush along it with easy skill.

The fact that she wasn't looking at him, and the comfortable feel of Bobby in his arms, made him go on. "Got worse when I lost my wife and child. They say there's a genetic factor with alcoholism, and it looks like I inherited it." Gently, he set Bobby down in the playpen and, when the boy started to fuss, located his binky and popped it into his mouth. Then he pulled out the stepladder that had been lying along one wall and set it up. "What about you? Did you grow up in California?"

"Yes. Sacramento."

"What do your parents do?" He wondered why she

hadn't gone to them when she'd had the trouble with her in-laws.

"I never knew my mom," she said. "And Dad…well, he's got his own life. He's homesteading in Alaska with a group of friends. Kind of a back-to-nature thing."

She said it carelessly, similar to the way Buck talked about his own mother. "I didn't think homesteading even existed anymore."

"It doesn't, not the way it used to be, land for work. They're subsistence farming on public land. No electricity, no cell phones… It's pretty basic."

"Does he know you're in trouble? Can he help you?"

Gina just shook her head a little, a smile curving her lips. "Dad's not the type to rush in and save his daughter. He's a dreamer, always broke. I'm actually just glad he's got these friends to stay with. That way, I don't have to worry about him."

Interesting. Gina was in a tight spot herself, but she talked about her father like the man was another child, not someone she could turn to. "Have you been up there to visit?" He was wondering if it would be a viable place for Gina to go and stay with Bobby for a while. She seemed to want to hide.

The thought of her leaving Rescue River, though, put a very alarming pressure on his heart.

"I surprised him on his fiftieth birthday. Took a bunch of books and supplies. It was kind of fun."

"What was it like?" For whatever reason, he wanted to keep her talking. Her voice was low for a woman, a little husky, and the sound of it sent a pleasant sensation rippling down his spine.

"Well, fishing for our dinner was an adventure. And

hauling water really is good exercise." She flexed her arm, making a muscle, and tossed a saucy grin his way.

The air whooshed out of his lungs. She was, quite literally, breathtaking when she smiled that funny, relaxed smile.

"But there was a downside." She wrinkled her nose. "I really prefer indoor plumbing, especially when it's cold outside."

"I can imagine. And it doesn't sound like a good place for a baby."

"No. I never even considered it." Gina stretched her back and shoulders, flipped her ponytail and returned to work.

Which Buck needed to do, too. He didn't need to think about how lively and pretty Gina was, how her attitude toward what sounded like a pretty neglectful dad wasn't bitter. How she saw the humor in a situation that some would have resented.

Bobby had been pulling himself up at the edge of the pack-and-play, and now he started to climb. He fell back and immediately tried again.

"It's just a matter of time until he figures out how to escape," Gina said, watching him. "If you were serious about finding him some other toys, sooner might be better than later."

"Um, sure." *Be a man*, he told himself. But dread filled his heart.

Chapter Six

Buck really, really didn't want to do this.

And if he had to visit the place he'd avoided for a year and a half, he didn't want an audience. "Are you sure you want to come along? I can do it myself," he offered again as his stomach knotted tight.

"No, it's fine. I'd like to come. I know what kind of stuff Bobby likes, and if he has an outing now, he'll settle down better later on. We haven't gotten out much since I sent away my SUV." She was fastening Bobby into his car seat as she talked. Then she climbed into the passenger seat of the truck.

Which left Buck no choice but to get in and drive. He turned on the radio so he wouldn't have to talk.

All too soon, they approached the little cottage, set back from the road with a big grassy yard, a garden on one side. He looked away from the house and the memories.

Tightening his jaw, he drove down the rutted driveway to the garage, took his time about turning the truck around so it would be easy to load things into the back.

Then he couldn't postpone getting out any longer, so he cut the engine and opened the door.

The sound of the rushing creek and chirping birds filled his ears, and the smell of earth rose up to him. He couldn't help but glance at the garden, notice it was turned over. The tenant must be eager to get to gardening.

Like Ivana had always been.

"Who lives here?" Gina asked as she freed Bobby from his car seat and set him down, holding his hands so he could toddle. "See the bird?" she asked, kneeling and pointing to a robin that was hopping through the shining green grass.

"A single mom," he said noncommittally. "Couple of kids, I think."

"Don't you have to talk to her first?"

He paused, hand on the garage door handle. "It's my place. She rents the house, but not the garage."

He didn't look at her, but he heard her soft "oh."

The sooner he raised the garage door, the sooner he could get done and get out of here. "It's a mess," he warned and slid the door open.

He stared at the ground for a minute, not wanting to look. Not wanting to kick up the memories of the day when he'd cleaned out their house, alone, in a drunk frenzy of pain. He felt ashamed, now, of how he'd thrown everything in here. He'd probably broken some stuff that would have been perfectly useful to someone in need.

"It's actually kind of neat." Gina walked past him to stand in the doorway of the garage, squinting to see, and he looked up and realized she was right. Toys were stacked along one wall, alongside some labeled boxes. Furniture and more boxes lined the rest of the garage.

There was a sound behind them, and they both turned. A pretty redhead stood there with a couple of kids behind her, one probably first grade, the other littler, maybe three. "Hi, I'm Cassie. And you must be Buck Armstrong? I hope you don't mind. Your sister and I straightened everything out a couple of months after I moved in. We were afraid it was a fire hazard."

"It's fine." He introduced himself and Gina, welcoming the distraction. Then Gina introduced Bobby and showed him to the little kids, doing that instant bonding thing women—especially women with kids— were so good at doing.

Ivana hadn't been that good at it, and she'd complained about feeling left out at the playground and swimming pool. It was part of the reason they'd chosen to live out here: she'd been more of a loner.

"Would you like me to take Bobby into the backyard for a little bit, so you can focus?" Cassie asked. "It's fenced in and we have some fun climbing toys."

"Um…" Gina hesitated, obviously reluctant to leave Bobby with a stranger. "I wouldn't want to inconvenience you."

"Just bring him over if you'd like." Cassie started walking back toward the play area in the backyard, surrounded by a white picket fence.

He'd put in that fence himself, so Mia could play safely as she grew.

He clenched a fist and forced that thought away. "She's safe. A nice lady. Lacey checked her references."

"It would be so good for Bobby to be able to climb

and play with her kids. And I can watch him from here... Okay. I'll be right back."

Grimly, Buck strode into the garage and pulled out the two biggest boxes labeled Toys. He was going back in for more when Gina returned. "Go ahead and look through the boxes," he said as he pulled out a high chair. Mia's high chair. He put it down and turned to Gina. "Take whatever you think he'd like. We should do this quick."

She glanced up at him speculatively. "Look, I didn't realize... I totally understand if—"

"It's fine." It had been almost three years. He could deal with this. To prove it, he knelt beside the nearest box and started pulling stuff out randomly.

There were some toys he didn't even remember, a shape-sorter thing full of triangles and squares, a little phone, some dolls. Stuff that looked new. Gifts, probably, meant for when Mia got older.

Gina pulled an empty box out of the truck and sat down beside him on the grass. She started inspecting the toys he'd gotten out, murmuring almost to herself. "This one's got some little parts—better not take that. But he'd love that light-up ball. He doesn't play with dolls, not yet, but I think it's fine for boys to play with dolls. Maybe if there's a boy one..."

Her words soothed him. He was doing fine. He was handling this.

He pulled out a bucket and shovel, and an image of the week they'd spent at the beach came back to him. Sitting with Mia in the sand, showing her how to dig, watching her giggle as the water touched her toes. Ivana hurrying over with an umbrella, scolding him, but mildly. They'd gotten along great that week.

"Go ahead and take anything." He got up quickly and walked back into the dark garage.

He found the ExerSaucer he'd had in mind when he'd first proposed this harebrained idea. Beside it was a little seat on cables, and he remembered that it was a door jumper Mia had loved. He swallowed and grabbed that, too.

As he came out of the garage into the sunlight, Gina looked his way and her eyes lit up. "Oh, wow, that'd be so great if we could borrow the ExerSaucer!"

This was worth it, to see that happiness in her eyes, to find a way to lighten her burden.

And then he saw what she had in her hand.

Mia's pink elephant. Her lovey. The toy she'd slept with every night and nap time. She'd just started insisting that they take it everywhere, a new phase, when she and Ivana had disappeared that last, fateful time. When he'd seen it lying on the couch, he'd figured they'd be right back, had stopped worrying about them.

Mia hadn't even had her lovey in those scary, horrible final moments.

Without realizing he'd moved, he had the elephant in his hands. He turned it over to look at the toe she'd always sucked on. Held the slightly dirty-looking creature to his face.

When he smelled it—smelled *Mia*—everything he'd been trying to forget came rushing back.

He could feel her in his arms, could hear her cry. He remembered what it had been like to walk the floor with her, bouncing her gently, helping her calm down. Feeding her a bottle. Tickling her into a good mood.

Putting her down in her crib for a nap. And when she'd reach up her arms to him, wanting to be held when she really needed sleep, he'd put Pinky into her arms and she would sigh and cuddle her elephant.

Somehow, he found his way over to the side of the garage where he could be alone. He squatted down, his back against the wall, drawing his arms and legs in while physical pain racked his chest. His throat and eyes felt swollen and he could barely breathe.

He let his head drop to his chest, held the little pink elephant to his face and fell apart.

Gina steered the truck into its parking space at the guesthouse and looked over at Buck.

He was staring straight ahead, his whole body rigid.

Guilt washed over her at having been the catalyst for all this pain. She'd known plenty of grief herself, losing her husband, but the loss of a child was unimaginable. She opened the door and extracted Bobby from his car seat, held him close and looked at Buck.

Who could never hold his baby close again. She swallowed hard. "Do you want to…? Can I do anything for you? Call someone? Do you want to talk?" She was babbling, asking too many questions, but it seemed better than letting him deal with all of this alone.

She'd seen men cry before. Her dad had wiped tears when he'd learned that his sister had passed away. And her father-in-law had gotten a little choked up at Hank's funeral.

But to see this big, tough veteran truly break down… Whoa. That was a first. Even after she'd given him some privacy, had loaded the truck and gotten Bobby into his car seat, the sight of Buck hunched there, shoulders still shaking a little, had made her cry, too. She'd had to grab a handful of tissues and pull herself together before she could help him to his feet and drive him home. Because this wasn't about her; it was about him.

"No. I'm… Let's get this stuff unloaded. Got to do a couple errands." He opened the car door and got out, moving mechanically to the back of the truck.

"You don't have to…"

"I got this." He lifted the box and the couple of big toys out and carried them up to the house.

Unsure how to help, she followed him, carrying Bobby.

He had the things in her room before she'd gotten halfway up the stairs. "Can I have the keys?" he asked, his voice expressionless.

And then he took them from her and drove off for parts unknown.

A couple of hours later, when he came back, Gina deliberately gave him his space, staying in her room with a book she'd checked out from the Rescue River library. But when Bobby woke up hungry, and she heard voices downstairs, she decided she had to come out of her room.

Shifting Bobby on her hip—man, was he getting heavy!—Gina walked down the curving wooden staircase and into the large, old-fashioned kitchen.

Buck, pouring coffee at the counter, didn't turn around. But at the table, three curious faces turned her way, and two older gentlemen stood. "You sit down right here, sweetheart," said the one with an impeccable comb-over, a dress shirt and expensive-looking slacks and shoes.

"Don't be ridiculous, Hinton. My seat is closer." The other man, shorter and stocky, dressed in a flannel shirt and work pants, held the chair he'd been sitting in, at the end of the table.

Feeling like she was walking into something she didn't quite understand, Gina sat in the closest chair and set Bobby down beside her. "Thank you both. I'm Gina Patterson, and this is my son, Bobby."

"Pleased to meet you," said the slender, gray-haired woman at the table, holding out a hand to grasp Gina's. "I'm Lou Ann Miller, and this is Elias Hinton and Roscoe Camden. And you two men can sit down. Honestly! There are plenty of chairs."

Buck brought over cups of coffee, a sugar bowl and a creamer, waving off Lou Ann's offer of help. "You sit," he said. "The water's almost boiling for tea, if you'd rather have that."

Lou Ann held out for tea while Gina and the men accepted coffee.

"What brings you to Rescue River?" Mr. Camden asked bluntly. "We've been hearing different stories at the Senior Towers."

"Leave the woman alone," Mr. Hinton ordered. "You shouldn't listen to all of the tall tales over there."

"That place *is* a hotbed of gossip," Lou Ann said. "There's no need for you to fill us in on your personal business, dear."

"Thanks." Gina smiled apologetically at Mr. Camden. "It *is* somewhat personal, but I'm hoping to stay awhile. It's a lovely town."

"Quite a history, too," Mr. Hinton said. Bobby was holding on to the leg of his chair, looking up with curiosity, and Mr. Hinton reached down and picked him up, handing him a teaspoon to bang on the table.

"The house's history is just what I'm interested in."

Gina seized on the topic. "I'm helping Lacey apply to put this house on the National Register of Historic Places, and I'd like to learn more about the background of the house and the area. Do you all have any ideas where I could find out more?"

Buck chuckled as he sat down at the table, pushing a teacup toward Lou Ann and dunking his own tea bag. "You've just opened a big can of worms. These three know everything about the town. From three very distinct viewpoints."

Fifteen minutes and a rousing argument later, Gina had appointments to meet with all three of them, and the elders made their departure.

When Buck came back into the kitchen, Gina raised an eyebrow at him as she gathered up the coffee cups. "Why do I feel like I've been through a war?"

"Longest-lasting love triangle in Rescue River."

Buck looked at Bobby, who was chanting, "Up! Up!" He reached down and swept the baby into his arms.

A tingle of awareness passed through Gina's chest at the sight of her son against the rugged veteran's broad chest. A few teaspoons slipped out of her hands and clattered on the floor.

Instantly Buck was across the room, sliding Bobby to his hip and kneeling gracefully, helping her to pick them up.

The tingle intensified.

It wasn't just his physical grace or his good manners. It was what she'd learned about him this afternoon. Somehow, the fact that he had the capacity for that much emotion had made Buck twice as appealing to her.

Gina ducked her heated face away from him and

deposited the spoons in the sink. "Thanks. Clumsy of me."

He rose lightly, his white teeth flashing in a smile. "That's not the word I'd think of to describe you."

Their gazes held for a beat too long.

"Listen," Gina said, "I'm sorry to have opened up old wounds earlier today. Are you okay?"

He nodded. "Embarrassed. You think you're over something and then it hits you."

"That's grief," she agreed. "Don't be embarrassed. It's natural."

"I guess." He blew out a breath. "I don't mean to be rude, but could we drop the subject?"

"Oh, sure! I'm sorry."

He touched her chin. "Don't take it personally. At all. I needed to do that, I guess, but now... I feel like I've been hit by a truck. I can't handle getting run over again today."

"Makes sense." Gina tore her gaze away and rinsed dishes while Buck carried the rest of the dishes to the sink, still holding Bobby. "I guess I'll have to take a little time off from wallpapering to talk with the folks who were just here, but I hope that won't be a problem. I know you have to spend some time at the clinic, too. And we don't always have to be working together. There's some stuff I can do alone, or you can. A lot of stuff, actually." *Stop babbling, stop babbling.*

While she felt flustered, Buck seemed perfectly composed. "Time away from the house isn't a problem. We're not punching time cards here, just trying to get the work done."

"Hey, Gina." Lacey's voice, behind them, provided a welcome respite from her worries. "I came home for…" She saw Buck holding Bobby and swallowed visibly. "For an early dinner," she said, her voice quiet.

Gina's heart ached. She and Bobby didn't mean to, but they kept causing pain. "Sit down and I'll fix you something. Fix all of us something. We may as well eat before we go back to work," she added to Buck.

"No. Hey, I think I'll just head on back. I don't have much time." Now Lacey's voice sounded choked. Her cat, Mr. Whiskers, meowed loudly, and she picked him up and held him close to her chest. "Hey, buddy, where's your wife, huh? Where's Mrs. Whiskers?"

Gina shot Buck a glance, the same one he was sending to her. Again, that something arced between them. She took Bobby out of his arms, opened the fridge and grabbed a bowl of mashed potatoes and peas from last night's dinner. "On second thought, I think I'll feed Bobby first," she said as she headed for the porch.

She'd give Buck a chance to talk to his sister, give Lacey some space in her own house.

And meanwhile, she'd remind herself not to pay attention to the occasional sparks between herself and Buck. She needed to remember she had bad judgment with men. Just look at the mistake she'd made in her marriage.

Anyway, Buck had mentioned leaving Rescue River. He seemed to fit here, but he'd said he was moving on soon.

She looked down the street toward the library and restaurant that marked the beginning of the town's small business district. It was unusually warm for this time of year, and despite its being a weekday, lots of people were out. She saw two mothers walking along with babies in strollers. A small group of older people clustered on the benches in front of the Senior Towers. And a group of teenagers stood talking in front of the library, their excited voices floating to her on the warm breeze.

This was where she wanted to raise Bobby, God willing. She wanted to take him to the library and show him off to the seniors. To shop at the little market.

And this was where Buck *didn't* want to be. Another reason not to get involved.

Through the screen door, she heard Buck's rumbling voice and Lacey's quiet one. Good. That was what Lacey needed, to talk to her brother.

That, and not to have a baby in her face every moment.

Gina breathed in the smell of the earth, thawing in the weak sunshine of early March. A few daffodils were pushing up beside the porch steps, and she set Bobby's food down and carried him into the yard to let him crawl in the grass. She wished she'd thought to put a jacket on him, but she'd been rushing to escape.

She needed to do something different about Bobby if she was going to stay here and help with the renovations. His presence was causing Lacey pain, and while it was inevitable that he should be around Lacey sometimes, the woman ought to be able to come home for a peaceful dinner without getting her wounds, whatever they were, ripped open.

Bobby had crawled over to the fence, and as she watched, he pulled himself up to stare out between the slats. It wasn't good for him to be trapped in the house with paint and renovation tools and overbusy adults. The new toys were great, but he needed more stimulation, more attention.

She pulled her phone out of her back pocket and found Angelica's number. She was just finalizing the arrangements to have her care for Bobby three days per week when Buck came out onto the porch.

When she ended the call, Buck lifted an eyebrow. "You're taking Bobby somewhere?"

"To Angelica's," she tossed over her shoulder, jogging to get the baby before he figured out that the front gate was open. She swept him up and blew on his belly, causing him to chortle gleefully. Then she hugged him close and climbed back up the porch steps. "He's going to stay with her three days per week. That way, I can focus better on work."

"And Lacey won't see him as much." He gave her a half smile. "Thanks for that."

She nodded, holding Bobby, as the March sun tried to warm her back. His eyes warmed her more and she drew in a quick breath, unable to look away.

But all at once his face seemed to close and he turned. And that was good, she told herself firmly. She busied herself settling Bobby on her lap and spooning potatoes into his mouth, getting a little inside him before letting him try with the spoon, which would lead to a mess.

Best to remember that Buck had his secrets, his reasons to keep a distance. As did she. A little front-porch attraction didn't add up to anything in the lives of two people whose pasts were all too complicated.

Chapter Seven

Two days later, Buck held the door so that Gina could walk ahead of him into Love's Hardware. He tried not to notice the fruity smell of her shampoo.

They'd dropped Bobby off at Angelica's and now were picking up some supplies before another day of renovation.

He was spending too much time with her. The pink of her cheeks, the light smattering of freckles across her nose, the gentle sway of her walk—all of it held far too much of his attention.

"Wow." Gina stood staring at the crowded array of garbage cans, lamp oil, electrical cords, gutter spouts, hammers and pipes. "It's truly everything but the kitchen sink."

"We have those, too," said a voice above them. "Back left corner of the store."

At the sound, both Buck and Gina looked up.

As Buck had suspected, the voice came from Harold Love, the wiry, white-haired African American store owner, who stood at the top of a tall stepladder.

He was sliding a large box from the high shelf above the store's sales racks.

"Hey, Mr. Love, it's Buck Armstrong," he called, knowing the old man's vision wasn't the best.

"I was just praying for a little help here. Buck, son, if I drop this down, can you catch it for me?"

"But that's huge—" Gina's eyes widened.

"Right here." Buck stepped forward, feeling an absurd desire to impress her with his strength.

Mr. Love dropped the box, and Buck caught it easily. It was light, probably containing some type of paper product.

Gina touched his arm and nodded over at Mr. Love, who was now climbing down the ladder, slow but steady. "Is he okay?" she whispered.

Buck set the box down on the floor and nodded. "Don't worry about Mr. Love. He's been doing this for more than fifty years." All the same, he took a step closer, ready to help the man if needed.

"Grandpa!" A pretty, heavyset young woman came bustling from the back of the store. "Did you climb up there yourself after I told you not to?" She turned to Buck and Gina. "His vision is getting worse. He's not supposed to do things like that."

"Now you just let me be, Aliyah." Mr. Love reached the floor unassisted and smiled in their general direction. "Thank you for the help, young man." He headed back toward the counter, using his hands to unobtrusively guide himself, moving confidently. He seemed to have an inner picture of every item of stock and every inch of the store, so his visual impairment wasn't obvious to most people. He liked it that way, Buck knew.

Buck had renewed his old acquaintance with Mr.

Love when he'd started working on Lacey's house, and he valued their friendship. It was all about nuts and bolts, paints and primers, plumbing and wiring. Unlike most of the other people in Rescue River, Mr. Love knew nothing of Buck's alcoholic antics, or at least, he hadn't been affected by them. The eightysomething man was a nonjudgmental, easy part of Buck's past.

Aliyah scolded Mr. Love a little more before heading toward the back of the store, shaking her head.

Gina's phone pinged. She pulled it out, looked at it and frowned.

Curiosity tugged at him. Was she starting to make friends in town?

But whoever was texting her, it wasn't Buck's business. Deliberately, he focused on the familiar sights and sounds of the store. From hidden speakers, the sound of Smokey Robinson filled the air; it was all Motown, all the time here at Love's Hardware. A grinding sound in the back of the store told him a key was being made. The faint, acrid smell of lawn products permeated the very bones of the place.

Buck walked toward the counter, gesturing for Gina to follow along. "How's business today?" he asked the older man.

"Just fine, just fine, now that you've come in." Mr. Love patted his arm. "As soon as I heard it was you, I knew you wouldn't mind giving me a hand. Just like old times, eh, son?"

"That's right."

"Now, let me just carry this cleaning solution over to Miz Miriam's cart and I'll be right back to help you. Don't let anyone else take care of you. I want to help you myself. Aliyah and all the young folks want to put me out to pasture and I'm not having any of it." The old man hustled away, carrying the heavy jug of cleaning solution.

Buck saw Gina's raised eyebrows. "My first job when I was in high school. Mr. Love was a tough boss, but fair. He taught me a lot."

She smiled, and then her phone pinged again. Her face tightened, just briefly, but she didn't pull out her phone. Instead, she crossed her arms over her chest and looked around. "What an amazing place."

Mr. Love, returning to the cash-register area, heard her. "This hardware store has been in my family since 1901," he said proudly. "Now, what can I do for you people? Buck, son, you still working on Miss Minnie's old house?"

"That's right—trying to get some rooms open in time for the Freedom Festival."

"And we're looking to get it onto the National Register of Historic Places," Gina added. "If you've been in the area and familiar with the house for a long time, I might like to talk to you as I'm doing the paperwork."

"Have you talked to Miss Minnie yet?" Buck asked.

"We're supposed to meet soon. She's a busy lady."

"That she is." Mr. Love smiled. "I'd be honored to help. That house is a very important place to a lot of people in this town. *Very* important."

"How do you mean?" Gina asked. "If you have time to tell us about it."

Mr. Love perched on the high stool behind the counter. "Falcon Station was the stop before our place on the Underground Railroad."

"I knew the guesthouse was a stop," Gina said, "but

I didn't know there were others nearby. Is yours still standing?"

"Standing, but not much more than that. The house is gone, but the old barn where travelers hid is still around, about ten miles up the road. Has a rose painted on the side that you can barely make out. Served to let folks know it was a safe place."

"I've seen it." Buck remembered driving by during some high-school carousing. A couple of older boys had warned him that any spray painting, egg throwing or sign shooting should steer clear of the Old Rose Barn. In turn, he'd passed along the message to younger boys when he was a senior.

"Could it be made into a national landmark, too, I wonder?"

Mr. Love beamed at Gina's interest. "I don't know about that. It's just one of those weathered, falling-down barns, though I've taken the kids and grandkids up there and told the story."

"Maybe we could see it sometime, too."

"You surely could," the older man said, "but the Falcon home has plenty to keep you busy exploring. Have you looked for the secret treasure in the cellar?"

"Treasure?"

"Or something hidden, anyway. Never saw it for myself, but that's the story."

Gina's eyes lit up again, and she gripped Buck's arm. "Have you explored the basement?"

"No way. It has a dirt floor and nasty cobwebs."

"Wimp," she said, scoffing at him. Her hand was still on his arm, her eyes full of fun. "Tell you what, soldier hero. I'll protect you if you'll go down there and explore it with me."

He lifted an eyebrow. "Will you hold my hand?"

"If you're good." Her lips quirked up at the corners. *Wow.*

Her phone pinged again, and the smile faded from her face. She took it out, read the message, frowned and shoved it back in her purse, hard.

"Something wrong?" he asked as Mr. Love turned to assist another customer.

"Nothing. No big deal." She turned toward the rest of the store, straightening her shoulders, back to business. "Do you have a list?"

"It's all up here," he said, tapping the side of his head.

She rolled her eyes. "Great. Let's see how much you remember."

They headed to the drawer pulls and wall anchors they'd come for. Buck made his selections, and when he turned back toward Gina, she stood transfixed in front of a rack of gardening supplies, rakes and hoses and shovels. She was holding a packet of seeds in her hand.

He approached her. "You like gardening?" he asked.

"Just think what could be done with the little yard in front of the guesthouse."

He wasn't much for flowers, but he could imagine they'd look nice. The question was, if Gina planted flowers now, would she be around to see them blossom? Would he?

"I wonder why they called it Falcon Station?" she asked him.

"Miss Minnie's last name is Falcon." He lowered his voice. "Rumor has it that Mr. Love has been sweet on Miss Minnie for years."

She lifted an eyebrow. "The elders in this community are very…"

"Social? Romantic?" He grinned. "Something in the water, maybe."

Her phone pinged in her purse. And again. And again.

She squeezed her eyes shut for a moment, then pulled out her phone and looked at it. Her hand flew to her mouth.

"What's wrong?" Buck stepped closer, wanting to protect her from whatever was making her look so scared.

"They're cutting off my phone," she said faintly. "What am I going to do without a phone?"

"Who?"

"My in-laws. Bobby's grandparents." She shook her head back and forth, her expression despairing. "What am I going to do? They're going to…" She trailed off and squeezed her eyes shut.

Buck's eyes narrowed. "They have some kind of control of your account?"

She pressed her lips together and then nodded. "I didn't think about it, but yes. I'm on their plan."

"Does your phone have a GPS?" he asked immediately.

She shook her head quickly. "I disabled that right away, as soon as I left. And I blocked them from being able to see my call log and turned off location services. I just… I guess I wasn't thinking about how they could cut off my phone. And it's not like I'm a phone addict or anything, but I need Angelica to be able to contact me about Bobby. I need that phone for emergencies."

"Ma'am?" Mr. Love's voice came from behind

them. "We have some of those no-contract, prepaid cell phones."

She turned. "You do?"

"Right over here." He felt his way along the shelf to where a display stood. "Take your pick." He put a wrinkled hand on Gina's arm. "And if you're ever in trouble, you're more than welcome to seek refuge here at the store. We have a sitting room in the back with a refrigerator and coffeepot, and more than a few people have stayed a few days there over the years."

"Thank you so much!" Gina's eyes went shiny. "I appreciate your kindness." She fumbled at the phones in the display, picking up one, putting it back without looking at it and picking up another.

"This one's good. I've used these before." Buck identified a simple phone and pulled it off the rack.

"All right." Her voice was faint.

He was surprised that someone as competent and calm as Gina would get this upset over a piece of technology. "Look, it's just a phone," he said gently. "We can manage this."

"It's not just a phone!" She spun on him. "They're threatening… They want to…" She broke off, shook her head. "It's not just a phone," she repeated, her voice flat and dull.

"Here. We'll pay for it all together." But as Mr. Love rang up their purchases and Gina bit her lip, and her phone buzzed repeatedly, Buck was worried. So far, her former in-laws had taken away her transportation and her communication. What was next? Did they have no shame about mistreating the mother of their grandchild?

* * *

After a day of trying to drown her worries in work and avoid Buck's concerned glances, Gina hated to have to rely on him for a ride to pick up Bobby.

She'd realized a few days back that driving without a license could get her in trouble. Her license had been stolen along with her money, and she couldn't order a replacement without kicking all kinds of search engines into play. So when Buck and even Lacey offered her the use of their cars, she had to decline.

She disliked the lack of independence, would have tried hard to find a babysitter in town, except that Angelica's situation was so ideal: she was caring for her own baby and one other—gorgeous Amy Franklin's nephew—in a big, comfortable farmhouse. More important, Angelica was warm and loving and so, so good to Bobby.

Her own humiliation as she approached Buck, who was putting away plastering supplies, had to take a backseat to Bobby's well-being.

"Ready to go?" he asked, sparing her the need to ask. He was thoughtful that way. He seemed to anticipate what she might need and offer it, making it seem less of a burden and more of a friendly favor.

Still, the dependency rankled. "Yes, whenever you're ready, and thank you."

"No problem."

But when they arrived at the dog rescue farm, Buck stopped her from emerging from the vehicle with a hand on her arm. "I feel like you're uncomfortable with accepting help. But that's what we do around here— we help each other."

She twisted her hands on her lap. "Why are you doing so much for someone you barely know?"

He opened his mouth and closed it, his eyes snagging with hers.

"What?" Her heart was pounding.

"You're worth it. I don't know who made you think you're not, but you deserve to be helped and treated well."

Those words were like a balm to Gina's soul, but she didn't completely trust them. "I'll go in and get Bobby and be right back out," she said, her breath coming fast. "Unless you want to come in? It's up to you."

"I'll come in and say hello." He was out of the truck and around to her side to help her before she could climb down herself.

They walked into an idyllic scene. On the floor of the living room, all three babies sat, surrounded by toys. Amy's little one, Tyler, was shaking a rattle. Angelica's Emmie banged a truck on the floor, calling, "Ah-ah-ah." And Bobby sat up straight, staring at Emmie, the monkey in a circle toy in his hand forgotten.

On the comfortable couch, Amy and Angelica sat, keeping a relaxed eye on the babies.

Bobby saw Gina and waved his arms, a huge smile breaking out on his face. She picked him up and snuggled him to her. Even though this situation was obviously good for Bobby, it was hard to be away from him all day.

"Hey, Buck! Have we got a proposal for you!" Angelica glanced over at Amy and they both laughed.

"Why do I feel like I'm about to get talked into something?"

"We're having a girls' night," Amy said.

"And we want Gina and Bobby to stay."

"And we can drive them home after."

"So, thanks for bringing her out here, but—"

"We'd invite you to stay, but—"

Buck lifted his hands, palms out, and started backing away. "Hey, I get the message. I know when I'm not wanted."

At that moment, an ancient bulldog stood slowly from the dog bed where it had been resting and limped over to Buck. "See, Bull likes me even if nobody else does," he joked, squatting down to scratch behind the dog's ears.

Gina tried to feel upset that they hadn't even consulted her, just assumed she would stay, but truth to tell, she liked it. Liked feeling wanted, liked being around other women with babies. Liked having evening plans and something that felt like friendship.

Buck, though, noticed the omission and beckoned her over to where he was squatting beside Bull. "You want to stay or come on home? I'm fine either way."

"I'll stay." She felt absurdly conscious that she was planning her evening with him the way you would with a husband. "If that's okay with you, I mean, you drove me out here. But they said they'd bring me home…" She was babbling. She needed to stop babbling. She focused on Bobby, settling him back down on the floor beside the other babies.

"All right. See everyone later." With a final pat to Bull, Buck was gone.

Turning to face two women she didn't know well, Gina felt a moment of shyness, thrown back into a high-school world where, because of her dad's eccentric lifestyle and lack of money for stylish clothes, she hadn't fit in well with other girls. But Angelica stood and took her by the hand, tugging her toward the couch. "Here, hon, sit down. I'm just going to check on the salmon, and then we can pick up where we left off. You know Amy, right?"

"We're already friends," Amy said, and Gina's heart warmed. "Bobby's so adorable." She tickled his chin. "Wow, how many teeth does he have?"

"Five, and I think he might be cutting another. He was super fussy last night."

"I hear you. That was us a week ago."

"You guys are having salmon? If I'd watched three babies all day, I'd barely be able to order pizza." Gina sat down on the couch next to Amy.

"She claims it's easy. And low calorie. And if we're good at dinner, we can eat the chocolate mud cake I picked up at the Chatterbox before I came out here."

Gina's mouth watered. "I am so there. I love chocolate. But what's the occasion?"

"Actually, we're second choice. Angelica was cooking for Troy and Xavier, but he'd forgotten to let her know they'd rescheduled a game for tonight. Basketball," she clarified. "Troy coaches. So she called me and asked if I'd bring dessert. I stopped by the café for three pieces of cake, and presto…it's a party. I think she tried to call you, too, but couldn't get through."

That comment punctured Gina's pleasure. She pulled out her phone, looked at it. "I sent texts earlier today. In fact, I sent you a text, to see if we could get together this weekend."

"Didn't get it," Amy said. "Did you forget to pay your bill? Because when that happened to me once, I could text, or it seemed like it, but nothing sent and I couldn't receive messages or calls."

She'd sent the texts after the exchange with her in-laws, when they'd threatened to cut off her phone. So they had actually done it. That fast, she was severed from her old life. Suddenly, the salmon didn't smell so good. Her stomach churned.

The old bulldog came over and nuzzled at her hand, and she scratched his ears distractedly, trying to look on the bright side. She was actually slightly relieved that she wouldn't be getting texts or calls from her in-laws anymore. And she could give Angelica the number from her new, no-contract phone.

She could do this.

The only thing that worried her was, if they'd cut off her communication so quickly, would they come for Bobby next, as they'd threatened to do?

Amy was still looking at her quizzically, but Gina turned away, unsure of whether she could reveal any of her problems to these women she didn't know well. Fortunately, Angelica called them into the kitchen and they picked up the babies and went in.

"You have three high chairs?" Gina asked, surveying the neatly set table with chairs alternating with high chairs.

"I'm married to a Hinton," Angelica said wryly. "They have everything."

The farmhouse kitchen was warm and comfortable, even sporting a couch in the corner. They served themselves and chopped bits for the babies, and soon they were all digging in, talking like old friends. The kids babbled and guitar music played quietly in the background, and Gina felt her worries slide away.

"So," Amy said, turning to her purposefully, "I have an idea."

"What's that?"

"I want to rent a little space in downtown Rescue River, maybe start a craft and yarn shop."

"Wait a minute," Angelica said. "You're staying in Rescue River for sure?"

"It's a good place to raise Tyler, and I can't go back to New York." Amy didn't explain why. "With this craft shop, I'd like to link it in with the town's history. You're helping to restore Lacey's house and you know all about the historical-landmark stuff. Wonder if we could reclaim one of the old buildings in downtown and get grants to renovate it?"

Gina's eyebrows lifted. "That's an interesting idea," she said. "I've always dreamed of opening a shop for interior decorating, but I have no money to start something like that."

"That's why we need grants," Amy said. "I don't have a lot to invest, either, but I would guess a couple of the buildings on the edge of downtown are dirt cheap. Some of them may have historical significance. Isn't it worth checking them out?"

"Probably." Gina started to say more and then broke off. Could she be honest about her fears and limitations with these women?

She wanted so much to belong. To have true friends, not just acquaintances impressed with her fancy home and car.

But the more people who knew of her situation, the more likely someone would let slip some information that would lead her in-laws to Bobby.

She couldn't take that chance.

"I… Everything about my life is up in the air right now. I don't know how much help I can be." To avoid the pain of the cold shoulder that would inevitably follow, she turned to Bobby and helped him spoon up some food.

To her surprise, she felt a hand press her arm. "I understand problems," Angelica said. "When I came back to Rescue River, my life was pretty messed up."

From her other side, Amy sighed. "We all have issues. I don't know if I'll ever be able to be open about what happened to me in New York."

"Even if your problems are too big for you, they're not too big for God," Angelica said gently. "That's what I had to figure out before I could really be happy. Really open my eyes to what was around me, all the good stuff."

"Good stuff like Troy?" Amy teased gently.

"Exactly."

Gina felt some of the tension leave her shoulders. These weren't judgmental high-school girls; they were real Christian women, who weren't going to let the fact that someone didn't have a perfect life push them away.

Yet another reason she was glad she'd landed in Rescue River.

"Speaking of men," Angelica said, "what's going on between you and Buck?"

"You saw that, too?" Amy said to Angelica.

Her cheeks warming, Gina grabbed a wet cloth and focused on wiping off Bobby's hands and face. "Saw what?"

"It's not so much what I saw as what I felt," Angelica said.

"Vibes," Amy agreed. "Major emotional vibes between the two of you. And I was glad to see it. Buck's a nice guy."

"How long have you known him?" Angelica asked, and there was something in her voice, some guardedness that made Gina curious.

"We were in school together," Amy explained. "All through, from kids' birthday parties to high-school track to his goodbye party when he went in the service. Knew his family, knew Lacey. Loved his dad."

Angelica nodded. "From what I heard, everyone loved his dad."

"Didn't you know Buck, too?" Gina glanced up from putting Bobby's sock back on. "You went to school here, right?"

"I was a year younger and on the outside of the main group in high school, but he was always nice to me."

"He's a good guy." Amy lifted her baby out of the high chair and took him over to the sink to wipe him down. "His mom had a pretty bad drinking problem, but Buck's dad and Buck and Lacey were so well liked, someone usually stamped down the gossip before it got too bad."

"It had its impact on Buck, though," Angelica said quietly. "Well, that and the war."

"So I hear." Amy came back to the table and sat down, holding Tyler on her lap. "I haven't been around for a few years, but wowie! The stories of his drinking reached me all the way in New York City."

"It was pretty bad." Angelica leaned back in her chair and looked at Gina, the skin between her eyebrows pleated. "One time before Troy and I got together…"

Gina lifted an eyebrow, waiting, her heart sinking.

"It's just… Buck and I were going to go out. He came out here—I was staying at the bunkhouse with Xavier. Anyway, he came to pick me up and he was really drunk. Too drunk to drive, so Troy and I called Lacey to come get him. He got pretty belligerent."

"I heard there were a lot of incidents like that," Amy said. "After he came back from Afghanistan, right? Substance abuse is a huge problem for vets. A way for them to cope with the things they saw and had to do."

Amy's choice of words—substance abuse—reminded Gina of how careful she needed to be. No judgment. She had absolutely no judgment where men were concerned.

She'd fallen for an addict before, and she was doing it again.

Angelica reached out and put a hand on Gina's arm. "I don't want to gossip, and I really like Buck. I'd just… I saw how you two were looking at each other, and I worried… Just be careful, okay?"

"Well, but he's in recovery, right?" Amy rocked Tyler gently. "That can really work. I saw it dozens of times out in California. And shouldn't we try to help him, not judge him?"

"Of course, and I feel for Buck—I really do. He's had so much to deal with." Angelica frowned. "It's just…sometimes recovery programs don't work. And families are devastated."

Gina knew about that firsthand. She nodded, her thoughts chaotic.

"I would never tell you what to do," Angelica said. "I'd just suggest you be careful. With Bobby and all."

Gina nodded. "I will." Restless, she stood and paced, Bobby on her hip.

On a built-in shelf beside the sink was a photograph in a wedding frame. Troy, Angelica and Xavier, all dressed up in wedding clothes, with the ripe harvest fields behind them.

Her throat closed. She remembered her own wedding day, the hopes, the promises. She'd thought that the biggest decision of her life was over and done. And done well.

There was so much she hadn't known on that day. So much suffering in the future.

But for someone like Angelica, who'd chosen the right man, the future *was* bright.

Amy and Angelica were still talking about Buck. "I just don't think he can handle a lot of stress. It's likely to push him back into drinking."

"That's so sad, but you're probably right."

"Troy says he plans to leave Rescue River as soon as he's repaid the debts he incurred during his drunk phase."

Gina gripped the edge of the sink as she listened and stared at the picture. No matter her romantic dreams, she and Buck weren't going to get together. There wasn't a potential relationship. She wasn't going to be saved by him.

She had to save herself…and leave Buck alone.

Chapter Eight

"So, why have you been avoiding me?"

The moment Buck asked the question, he wished he hadn't. He and Gina had to work together this whole evening—they'd set it aside to wallpaper after Bobby was in bed. She'd just come downstairs and into the front guest room. Lacey was away, working her third double shift this week.

"I haven't been avoiding you. We've been working together every day!" She stood by the table they had set up for spreading paste, her hand on her hip.

"Working together, yeah, but no talking. Did I do something wrong?"

He figured he knew the answer. It had started after her evening with Angelica and Amy. No doubt she'd been told some of the details about him and his past escapades.

She opened her mouth like she wanted to say something and then shut it again.

"Are you going to tell me or not?" He didn't know why he was pushing; it was like he'd lost control. Like when he'd been drinking, only he wasn't drinking. And he probably shouldn't make a big deal of it, but it was bugging him. The way she acted toward him mattered.

He definitely needed to discuss this with his sponsor.

She looked down, then lifted her eyes to his again. "It's just… I don't want you to get the wrong idea. We can't…you know."

He nodded, defeat blasting his heart. "You heard the truth about me." And he knew it, knew he had to get out of Rescue River for just that reason, but never had it discouraged him so much.

"It's not exactly that." She wasn't entirely denying it, he noticed, because she was honest to the core. "It's just…there *is* a spark." She lifted her eyes to his, looking troubled.

Heat rose in him at her words. "On your side or mine?"

She looked down, color staining her cheeks.

Was that because she felt the spark herself or because she didn't?

When she didn't answer, that told him everything. She'd noticed that he was attracted but she didn't feel the same herself.

In awkward silence they worked together to paste, lift and spread the wallpaper. The moments in between, while they were waiting for the paste to permeate the paper, felt uncomfortable. And when they got to the big break, when they had to let the whole room dry before putting the moldings back up, the silence was excruciating. He was just about to get up and go to his room when she spoke up suddenly. "Let's go explore the basement."

"What?"

"There's supposed to be a secret room or hiding place. Let's go try to find it."

Great. It was the last thing he wanted to do, the only way of breaking the silence he'd much rather have said no to.

But she was already out the door, and a gentleman couldn't let a lady go into the dark alone.

They made their way down the house's wooden cellar stairs. There was no railing, and a single bulb hung down to illuminate the old stone walls.

Something brushed his leg and he kicked out, barely restraining a yell, heart pounding.

An indignant yowl sounded, and the reclusive Mrs. Whiskers ran past him up the stairs.

Gina had grabbed a flashlight and she shone it around, but the darkness was so heavy that the light barely penetrated.

A sick feeling rose in him as they reached the low-ceilinged, dark main room, but Gina wasn't affected the same way; she was giggling, grabbing his arm at the scuttling sound of some little creature, shuddering openly. To her, it was obviously a trip through the fun house.

Sweat trickled down his back. He tried to focus on her and not on the memories.

"I wonder what's here. Have you even been down here before?"

"No." He could hear the hoarseness in his voice and wondered if she could, too.

"We'll go over the walls, see what we can find." She shone the light around, scanning the stone walls, exploring.

He took deep breaths of cold, dank air and told himself he was fine. He was in a basement in Ohio, not a cave in Afghanistan.

Still, when a rock she was fiddling with came out of the wall and fell to the floor with a thump, he grabbed her shoulders, heart racing, and pulled her back. "Come on. Let's get out of here."

She tried to move out of his grip, but he held on. "Come on!"

"Buck. Hey, Buck!" She twisted away but kept hold of his hand, shining the light in his direction. "Hey, what's wrong? You look awful."

He blew out a breath and drew in another lungful of musty cellar air. "Bad memories."

"Memories of what?" She tugged him over to where they could sit on the stairs.

Light came in from the open door above, illuminating an escape route. His breathing calmed a little. "Afghanistan. There were…lots of caves."

"And you had a bad experience in one." It wasn't phrased as a question.

"Yeah." He took another minute to breathe, feeling his body steady, his heart rate settle. He was cold from the sweat, but he no longer felt sick. And since he'd already wimped out on her, and since she didn't have any romantic interest in him anyway, he might as well tell her. "A buddy and I got ambushed in a cave. Separated from our unit, and we didn't know the country near as well as our enemies did. It got ugly." He ran a hand over his face.

"But you got out okay, in the end?"

"I did." A bleak sense of failure overwhelmed him.

"And your friend?"

He shook his head. "He didn't make it." And that

was the shame of it. He should have been able to save John, but he hadn't. They'd made a plan to run for it, knowing they couldn't cover each other, but he should never have agreed to it, because John had gone down. And he'd never forget the misery of walking down off that mountain without his buddy.

"That must be hard to deal with." She'd never let go of his hand and now she gripped it tighter. "I can't imagine. Wow."

And then she just sat with him, quiet.

Her simple acceptance of how bad it had been, her comforting silence, surprised him. He hadn't told anyone—outside of his shrink—about that particular failure. He'd worried that he'd be condemned. Thing was, no one could condemn him more harshly than he condemned himself.

She was kicking at the bottom of the stairs and a loose board fell down. She picked it up and studied it.

"Look at that," she said.

"Is that a keyhole?" he asked at the same moment.

She squatted down and shone the flashlight under the stairs, and he had to marvel that she seemed to have no fear of mice or spiders or whatever other nasty thing could be down there.

Instead, she pulled out a wooden box, deteriorated, rotten on one side.

Her eyebrows lifted. She looked at him and then held it out.

He met her eyes and then, slowly, lifted the lid.

Inside was a tarnished silver cross necklace.

She studied it. "Wonder who this belonged to?"

"I don't know. Maybe there's some information in Miss Minnie's paperwork."

"Or maybe Mr. Love would know something."

He put the necklace back into the box and closed the lid. "We didn't find a secret room," he said, "but we found something interesting."

"There could be an amazing story behind this. We can display it in the guesthouse!" She sounded excited.

"You did the right thing, dragging me down here."

She looked at him and their eyes held. Hers sparkled with the excitement of their find and then darkened. Her tongue flicked across her lip.

It took everything in him not to kiss her.

"Buck?" she said faintly.

"Yeah?"

"It wasn't one-sided."

He lifted an eyebrow, wondering if she meant what he thought she meant.

"That…spark. I… I felt it. *Feel* it."

What was a man supposed to do when he'd faced his fears and found a treasure? How was he supposed to remember to do the wise thing?

He put a hand on either side of her face, reading her expression, trying to figure out whether she'd mind. Her eyes were wide, but not afraid.

He pulled her closer and lowered his lips to hers.

Being in Buck's arms, immersed in his sweet but intense kiss, Gina felt like she was floating. Never in her life had she experienced anything like this.

His lips were firm. He definitely knew what he was doing, kissing her. She sighed and settled into the strong, warm circle of his arms.

He lifted his head to look into her eyes, and she couldn't hide her dreamy satisfaction. He nodded and dipped down for another kiss, his hands stroking and touching her back, but not straying anywhere that made her uncomfortable.

He was careful, protective. He was looking out for her rather than going for anything he could get. That alone set him apart from most men she'd known.

And the closeness she felt wasn't just physical. He wanted to know about her, to help her; he cared. More than that, tonight he'd let her know him more. What he'd revealed, his vulnerable side, made something burst free in her heart, a seed that could grow.

And then, through the baby monitor she'd left in the kitchen, she heard mild fussing.

"Bobby's crying," she told Buck.

He dropped his arms immediately. "Better check on him," he said, and she stood, steadied herself and then turned and hurried up the stairs, the little wooden chest still in her hand.

As she trotted up two flights, the euphoria of kissing Buck faded and doubts rushed in.

He's an alcoholic!

He's too vulnerable to take on the mess of your life!

He's leaving Rescue River!

She reached her room and found Bobby tossing, face red, half-asleep. He'd gotten himself into the corner of his crib and was too sleepy to find a more comfortable position.

She moved him and patted his back until he settled down.

Touching her baby brought her back into line with her goals. She needed to remember them.

She was here to take care of herself and Bobby, to

protect her son from harm, and find a safe place to raise him.

She wasn't here to get involved with another risky, dangerous person.

The door creaked. "Is he okay?" Buck asked, coming up behind her, putting a hand on her shoulder.

A hand that felt possessive. And although everything inside her wanted to curl toward him, to feel his arms around her again, her responsibility for Bobby overcame it.

She braced herself. "That can't happen again," she said and looked up at him.

Hurt flashed across his handsome face, making her remember that he wasn't a carefree, blustering addict like Hank had been. He was a man who'd fought for his country and bore the emotional scars from it. A man who'd lost a wife and child.

She closed her eyes for just a minute, confused.

When she looked at him again, his mouth and eyes had gone flat. "All right. If you're both okay, I'm going to turn in."

His words were flat, too. When he walked away, his shoulders looked stiff.

Her mouth opened to call him back, and she pressed both hands over it to stop herself. It hurt to nip this thing between them, but it was best to do it now rather than ripping apart a full-grown love affair.

And it had to be stopped. It was best for Bobby. Ultimately, it was best for Buck, too.

But what about me? What about what I want? She wrapped her arms around her middle. She felt like she was breaking apart.

When you were a parent, you made the decisions that were best for the child. That, she knew.

Doing the right thing was hard, but in the end, it would lead to less pain.

She walked over to her bed and sank down on it, arms still wrapped around her middle. She tried to pray, to cry out to God, but rather than finding comfort, she saw Buck's hurt face before her eyes.

Why did she have to hurt someone else to do the right thing by Bobby?

Why did she have to hurt herself?

No answers came. So, slowly, she closed the door to her room and got ready for bed. Went to check one last time on Bobby and saw the wooden box she'd been clutching in her hand when she'd run upstairs.

There was the cross. But now, studying the box in brighter light, she saw that it should be deeper than it was, suggesting that it had a false bottom. She tried to pry it up, and when her fingers wouldn't do the job, she found a metal nail file and slid it between the bottom of the box and the side, prying upward until the old piece of wood gave way.

Inside was a slim leather book filled with careful, old-fashioned handwriting.

Immediately, she thought of telling Buck. She wanted to share this with him. And she would, but not tonight—they were both too vulnerable, too hurt.

She flattened the pages out and began to read.

Buck paced the guesthouse, feeling like a caged dog. He picked up a magazine and then threw it down again. Started to straighten up the wallpapering supplies and then realized they'd just need to get them out again tomorrow. There was nothing to do now, and no way he was going to sleep.

He'd opened himself up to Gina, had experienced her sweetness and the hope of some more substantial connection with her.

But she'd shut him out.

He slammed a hand into the wall of the downstairs hallway and relished the pain of it. She'd responded to him; he was experienced enough to know that. Her breathing, her quickened pulse, her dark, lidded eyes told him that she'd enjoyed the kiss. And he hadn't pushed it too far; he'd been careful to respect her boundaries. He knew what kind of woman he was dealing with. Gina was a lady, through and through.

No, it was worse than that. When she'd gotten away from him and had had a moment to think, she'd realized she didn't want anything to do with him. What had she said? *No more of that.*

Maybe she'd had time to think about the drawbacks of a man who was afraid of small dark places. Or a man with a bad history everyone in town knew about. Or a man from a modest background, rather than the wealth she was accustomed to.

Or maybe it was just something about him.

For the second time this week, he thought back to his marriage. Not the loss of Ivana and Mia, but the months leading up to it, when he'd heard repeatedly about his failures and inadequacies as a husband.

He hadn't had it all together when he'd come back from Afghanistan. He'd needed counseling, time to figure out the right professional direction. The fact that he hadn't been sure of himself, combined with Ivana's weariness as a new mother, had made for stressful times.

It wasn't that he hadn't tried. He'd practiced listening skills he'd learned in counseling, brought flowers and gotten sitters so they could go out on dates. But none of it had worked.

You're not the man I thought you were. Those words, the ones he'd stuffed down and tried to forget, came ringing into his brain now.

He'd like to rip that brain right out of his skull. He could feel himself going down.

What did it matter if he had a drink, or ten? His life was never going to get any better. Work, sleep, try not to drink. Always alone.

At least at the bar, he'd have companionship. Not the kind he wanted, but something was better than nothing.

He paced some more. Looked up at the ceiling, where he could hear Gina moving around.

Was she upset, too? Uncomfortable hearing him roam around the house? Ambivalent about pushing him away?

Maybe she was, but she'd sounded sure of what she was saying. She'd made a decision.

Just for a moment, he'd thought he might get the girl. He'd thought that life could open up for him again, that he could have the companionship he craved. Not just someone to hold in his arms—although Gina fit beautifully there—but someone to talk to, someone who understood.

He had to get out of here.

Grabbing his jacket from the hook beside the door, he ran to his car and drove.

Twenty minutes later he was parking beside the big,

dark barn out at the dog rescue farm. When he opened the door of his truck and slammed it shut, all the dogs started barking. Only then did he realize he needed to text Troy and Angelica, who lived with their kids in the adjacent house, to let them know he wasn't an intruder.

It's just me, out at the barn.

You okay? came the text back from Troy.

Yeah. Just forgot something.

He went inside, breathing in the familiar smells of hay and sawdust, feed and dogs. Rather than put on the main light, he just turned on the lamp on the desk near the door, found a flashlight and headed back.

The dogs continued barking, of course, and he got drawn into petting some of the needier ones. When he saw Spike, the Maltese mix from the alley the other day, he opened his crate, picked him up and carried him around. He'd turned out to be healthy enough, just your average senior, overweight dog with bad teeth. But with most of his matted hair shaved off, he was a little guy. He didn't fit in with the bully breeds that made up most of the population at the rescue.

"But somebody loved you, huh?" He rubbed behind the dog's ears, thinking of the note and the money.

The dog licked his face gratefully.

"Your breath smells worse than a garbage dump," he chided the old dog.

Yeah, he was talking to a dog. Which might mean he was crazy, or might mean he was sane.

Finally he got to the kennel he'd been seeking. There

was Crater, in the back of it, licking his paws. When the dog saw Buck, he came bounding forward.

Buck opened the kennel awkwardly, still holding the Maltese. "Hey, buddy," he said. "Want to come home with me tonight?"

He only did that on the bad days. Lacey hadn't bargained for a big, clumsy dog in her house. But she knew he needed the company sometimes.

Crater trotted confidently beside him, mouth open, tongue hanging out. He seemed to laugh at the other dogs, still in their kennels.

When they got back to Spike's small crate, Buck bent down to put the little guy in.

Spike struggled, looking up at him with big, dark eyes, letting out pitiful cries.

"I don't even like small dogs." Firmly, he shut the crate and headed for the door.

Above the noise of the other dogs, he could hear Spike's high-pitched howl.

All the dogs were barking. All of them needed a home. He was giving one of the unadoptables an outing, that was all. He reached down to rub Crater's head and the dog stared up at him adoringly.

That high-pitched howl again.

Buck groaned. Stopped. Started walking again.

Crater looked at him quizzically.

His steps slowed. He turned around. Then he jogged back to Spike's cage, opened it and swept the fat Maltese into the curve of his arm. "One night on a real bed. Just one, you hear?"

Twenty minutes later, as he let himself into the

guesthouse and went upstairs—Crater beside him and Spike in his arms—he realized he hadn't even considered taking the turnoff for the bar.

Chapter Nine

A scratching sound tugged at Gina's consciousness. Was Bobby scratching, or was it Buck? Someone was in a box and she needed to help him get out of it, she knew that, but she couldn't make herself move.

More scratching, and then vigorous, high-pitched barking.

Barking?

And then an indignant yowl, some growling and more barking.

Gina sat up in bed, her eyes barely able to open. When she saw the bright daylight outside her window, she jumped up. How late had she slept?

Automatically she checked on Bobby, but he was sleeping through the sounds of an animal fight right outside their door. She shrugged into her robe and went out to see what was going on.

Buck was coming up the stairs at the same time, already dressed and covered with a fine white powder, like he'd been plastering.

"Hey." He snapped his fingers and the big dog, Crater, bounded over. Buck pointed at the floor, and Crater sat.

The orange cat, Mr. Whiskers, and his reclusive lady friend perched on a high, built-in ledge. They both glared disdainfully at a small, fat white dog who continued to bark furiously at them.

Gina bent down and picked up the little dog. It quieted down and licked her face before twisting toward the cats.

She wrinkled her nose. "Dog breath, wow!"

"His teeth aren't the best. That's Spike."

"Spike?"

"Uh-huh."

"Okay." She studied the ten-pound dog doubtfully. "These guys weren't here when I went to bed."

"I needed company," he said gruffly. "Sorry they woke you."

His words brought back the night before, and she immediately thought of their kiss. Her face heated and she started to touch her lips, then cuddled the little dog closer instead.

He'd needed company. Why had he needed company? Because she'd hurt him?

She remembered the old journal she'd found and opened her mouth to tell Buck about it when Bobby called. He was always hungry in the morning.

She pressed the little dog into Buck's arms and went to her son.

As she changed him and prepared him for the day, she heard Buck whistle to Crater and go back downstairs. Good. And she'd keep Bobby with her today, maybe do some paperwork instead of working beside Buck. They were making good progress on the renovation, and it looked like there would be several rooms ready to display for the festival if they all stayed on task. It was time to figure out a publicity plan.

And it was time for her to spend a day apart from Buck. Exactly what she *didn't* want to do, because the thought of working with him, beside him, filled her with longing. Made her want to share another sweet kiss.

But she couldn't reopen that wound. It was kinder to be cruel.

After feeding Bobby some breakfast, she went out onto the front porch. She sat on the steps and put a blanket and toys in the yard for Bobby. As he banged plastic together and plucked at grass, she updated the marketing plan.

At one point, Buck opened the door to let the little dog out and saw her there. "Will it bother you if Spike hangs outside with you? He's getting into everything." Buck's voice was toneless, exquisitely polite.

"No problem. I like him. C'mere, Spike."

Normally they'd have laughed together about the ill-fitting name. He'd have told her the dog's story. But today, he just nodded.

He was turning away when Bobby started shouting. "Buh! Buh!" He waved his arms at Buck and started to crawl toward him.

Buck looked back, and a muscle twitched in his jaw. He stepped inside and closed the door.

Pain twisted in Gina's chest. She didn't like being estranged from him. Didn't want this coldness. Didn't want Bobby to get sad from rejection, although truthfully, her son had spotted a robin and turned toward it, easily distracted.

If only she could be distracted that easily.

It's better this way. She tugged the little dog closer to her side and determinedly went on writing out her plan.

An hour later, she heard the sound of a camera clicking and looked up to see Amy, phone in hand, snapping photographs. "You just look so cute, with Bobby and that little dog," Amy said. "I'll send these to you. You working hard?"

"Yeah. Getting some paperwork done."

"For the national-landmark thing?"

She nodded as Amy opened the picket fence and let herself in. "Some of that, and I'm working on marketing. We need to send out some blasts on social media, get the word out about the guesthouse and how it'll be open for the festival."

"I can help with that," Amy offered. "You think you're going to make it, then?"

"It's looking good." Then it came together for her. "Hey, we need to take a bunch of pictures of the renovation. We can post them, and the fixer-upper crowd will think it's awesome."

"That's for sure. Want me to take a few more of the outside?"

"The inside, too, if you're willing. I'm a terrible photographer. But where's Tyler?"

"Out at Angelica's. Why isn't Bobby there today?"

"He's only there three days per week." Gina didn't add that she needed the comfort of keeping her son close today.

They went inside and Amy walked around snapping photos. In the kitchen Gina put Bobby in his high chair, placating him with dry cereal while she fixed a tray of fruit, cheese and crackers for an early lunch. She made a separate plate for Buck to find when he was ready. She and Amy could sit outside to eat, away from him.

She could hear Buck and Amy talking, but she stifled her desire to listen. It didn't matter. Wasn't her business.

The voices came closer, and then they both walked into the kitchen. When Buck saw her, he stopped in the middle of a sentence. He stammered something, turned abruptly and left.

Amy frowned after him and then looked at Gina. "Why's the tension so thick in here?"

Gina so wanted to tell her. She was suffering from a serious shortage of girlfriend consultation.

But what could she say? *He kissed me and I liked it and then I cut him off? It'll never work for me because of who he is and who I am? I'm crazy about him?*

She blew out a sigh. "Grab those glasses, will you? I'll carry the pitcher and we can have some lunch outside."

Once they were settled on the porch, Gina rocked Bobby and held him against her, and just as she'd hoped, he relaxed into sleep. After he drifted off, she ate some snacks with one hand and held him, and then Amy made a nest for him and they laid him down.

"You're still not off the hook. What's going on between you and Buck?"

Unable to think of a real excuse, Gina settled for half the truth. "We went forward a little bit in our…friendship. And then we… I…decided not to go further."

"Why?" Amy poured another glass of lemon-infused water for both of them.

"Because Bobby comes first," Gina said firmly.

"And? Is Buck somehow anti-Bobby?"

"No, he's great with him. It's just…men mostly aren't reliable, and Buck…well, you heard what Angelica said that one night. He's got a drinking problem, and I—"

"He's in AA, right?" Amy interrupted. "Have you ever seen him drink?"

"No, I've never seen him drink. But still…"

"Why did you say men mostly aren't reliable?"

Man, Amy was like a bloodhound on the scent. But Gina didn't know whether to get into talking about her dad. "Just…past history."

"But Bobby's a boy. It would be nice if he had some male role models in his life."

"That's true, and yet…" She sighed. "I don't know." She leaned over to check on Bobby, hoping Amy would take the hint and get off this line of questioning.

But no chance of that. "What was your childhood like?" Amy pressed. "Was your dad in the picture?"

"Yes." Gina thought of her dad, and as always, the shaggy, smiling image of him brought a fond feeling. "He was my only parent. My mom passed on right after I was born."

"Good relationship with him, I assume? Because you're smiling."

"I'm smiling because I love him to pieces," Gina said. She was about to stop there, to brush it all off as she usually did with inquiries about her childhood, but Amy's understanding face, her receptive silence, made Gina feel like she could share a few details. "But my childhood was a little different."

"Different?"

Wondering how to explain, Gina thought back, and

a memory flashed into her head. "Once when I was about seven," she said, "I invited a couple of girls to come over after school. We all got notes from our parents and they rode home on the bus with me." She put her elbows on her knees and leaned forward, remembering. "When we got off the bus, we were running up toward the house, but one of the girls stopped. She wanted to know why my house was so little, and why the porch roof was sagging, and why the driveway was made of dirt, not asphalt."

"You grew up poor," Amy guessed.

"Yeah. I explained it away, and we went inside. And there was nobody home."

"Your dad was gone?"

She nodded. "I was used to being alone, but they both got scared and started to cry. They wanted their moms."

"What did you do?" Amy asked.

"I fixed us all a snack. Showed them how to put butter and sugar on white bread, and they loved it. And then I told them stories until their moms came to get them."

Amy nodded, looking sympathetic and nonjudgmental. "Sounds like you were pretty mature. Did the moms find out?"

"My dad rolled in just as they did, and somehow, he smoothed it over. He really was handsome back then, and super articulate. There wasn't a woman within miles who couldn't be charmed by him." She sighed. "But of course, the girls weren't allowed to come over again, and they spread the word. Pretty much nobody trusted my dad to do what he said he'd do."

Amy nodded. "And so you don't trust men," she said. "Makes sense, with that background."

Gina hadn't really put it together like that before, and she wasn't sure she bought it. "I got married, though. I was happily married." For a while.

"And what was he like? Your husband."

Gina thought. "He was the playmate I never had," she said, her eyes filling with tears. "When we were first dating, and when we first got married, we had so much fun together. He really *was* like a little boy, and I got to be a kid again with him, too."

"That sounds good," Amy said, "but it also sounds like you married your father. Someone else irresponsible, you know? How did he do when Bobby came along?"

Gina frowned. "Not well. I couldn't party anymore, and he couldn't cope with responsibility, and…" She blew out a sigh. How to explain the disaster their marriage had become? How to explain the issues with his parents, who'd morphed from kindly caregivers to monsters with the arrival of Bobby?

She pushed her plate away. "I should probably get back to work. I'm sorry to do all that talking."

"It's okay," Amy said. "I was the one asking all the nosy questions."

"I'm glad you came over." And she was. Gina hadn't had much girl talk since she'd been here, aside from a couple of phone calls with Haley back in California.

They hugged, and then Amy held her shoulders. "Remember," she said, "the past doesn't have to determine the future. Buck isn't your dad. And he's not Bobby's father. Give him a chance, okay?"

Except he was all too much like them, Gina thought

as she settled back down to work. And though she'd put her trust in two men who hadn't repaid it, she wasn't going to make the same mistake a third time.

She watched her baby's chest rise and fall with his sleep breathing. No mistakes. Not this time. The stakes were too high.

After lunch, Buck changed into scrubs and headed out the front door, Crater trotting behind him.

Gina still sat there, working on Lacey's laptop. Bobby slept beside her and the little Maltese pressed against her side. In the spring sunlight, she looked so pretty that his throat hurt.

He swallowed. "C'mon, Spike. Time to go back to jail."

"Do you have to take him?" She put a protective hand on the dog.

"We're not set up for a dog here." He looked around, anywhere but at her. "No little-dog food, no dog bed…"

"I know, but he looks so sad!"

As if to prove her point, the dog peered up at him from beneath shaggy fur, his dark eyes pleading.

"I know—that's why I brought him home. But Lacey…" His sister hadn't okayed it. She also was never home these days; she was working double shifts at the hospital, ostensibly to earn extra cash, but really, probably, to stay away from the painful memories Bobby evoked.

"Oh, of course. I wasn't thinking." She sat up straighter, scooped the dog off the wicker couch beside her and deposited him into Buck's arms.

The dog whined and struggled to get back to Gina.

"Hey, come on, buddy." He scratched behind the

dog's ears until it settled into his arms as if confident he'd do the right thing.

Gina was watching him expectantly, too.

"Okay, look, I'll work on it. But no promises."

"Of course!" She was beaming. "Thank you!"

Buck would do just about anything to make her smile like that again. Which was really bad.

It was almost like he was falling in love with her.

Stuffing down that very disturbing thought, he spun away and hurried down to his truck.

Out at the rescue, after Buck had put Crater and Spike back into their kennels, he and Troy did a couple of procedures, working together like a well-oiled machine. Buck prepped and assisted, grateful for the distraction from his troubled thoughts.

One of the local farmers brought in a goat that had gotten tangled in some barbed wire, and Buck cleaned and bandaged its leg. In town, Troy's practice was mainly small animals, but out here, they did what was needed.

Spike barked and whined every time he walked by, so when they hit a lull and were doing paperwork in the office, he brought the Maltese out and let it run around. After a cursory sniff of the room, the dog settled beside Buck's office chair.

"What's up with that?" Troy asked, nodding toward Spike. "Thought you went for bigger dogs, like Crater."

"Yeah. He's just so…" Buck trailed off and reached down to scratch the shaggy little guy's ears.

"Needy?"

"Yeah."

Troy nodded and changed the subject abruptly. "How are Gina and Bobby doing?"

"Great, I guess." Buck focused on the intake form in front of him, filling in the details.

Troy leaned back in his office chair and put his hands behind his head. "You guess? Thought you'd know."

Buck shook his head and kept on writing.

"I thought something was heating up between you."

"No." Buck looked up to meet Troy's assessing gaze. "Can't."

"How come?"

Impatiently, Buck gestured toward himself. "Look at me, man. I'm a mess. Not a good choice for anyone."

"I don't know about that. Your life is more stable than hers."

Stable wasn't a word Buck had applied to himself, ever. But if he thought about how he lived now, he realized, it was accurate. He stayed with his sister, went to work at one or the other of his jobs, came home, went to bed. Got up and did it all again. Even went to church on a regular basis, and got something out of it.

But he'd seen the expression in Gina's eyes after that night she'd gotten together with Angelica and Amy, and then again after they'd kissed. She'd heard things. She had doubts about him, and understandably so. "I have a history, and it keeps wanting to chase me."

"People see you changing," Troy said mildly. "You're not chained to your past."

Buck stood, restless. It was what Dion had said, too, but he and Troy were both looking at life with rose-colored glasses. The past *did* come back to bite you. "I gotta get back, do a little more work tonight." He paused then, fingered his sobriety coin and made an abrupt decision. "Hey, listen. You know I'm working the steps in AA."

Troy nodded.

This was never easy. "One of the steps is making amends, and I need to do that with you."

Troy tipped back in his chair. "You're doing great now. That's all that matters."

"No." Buck forced himself to stand there and go through with it. "I was a jerk in a number of ways, but a day I remember in particular, I came in to assist with surgery when I'd been drinking. Started to botch things up, and you had to kick me out and finish it all yourself."

"I remember. I think I had a few choice words for you."

"I deserved them. I put the dog you were working on at risk, and I'm sorry." As soon as he said that, a weight he hadn't known he'd been carrying lifted off his heart. "I'd like to find a way to make that up to you."

Troy let his chair fall forward with a gentle bang. "You don't owe me anything. But—" he waved an arm toward the dog area "—you might owe something to those guys. Or, at least, to one of them." He looked down at the Maltese that stood patiently at Buck's feet. "Think about it."

"I will." He shrugged into his jacket and headed for the door. Spike trotted confidently after him. When he started to go outside, the dog ran out and jumped at Buck's truck.

Afternoon sun heated Buck's back, and a cardinal sang its "Birdie? Birdie? Birdie?" from the top of a bare-limbed tree. Buck took a minute to breathe in the spring air.

Troy stood in the barn's doorway, watching as Buck walked to the truck, opened the door and lifted the little dog in.

"Hey," Troy called. "The half-drunk guy who used to stumble in here wouldn't have given that dog a second glance," he said. "You're changing, whether you know it or not."

"He's crazy, right?" Buck said to the little dog as he put the truck in gear.

The dog propped its front legs on the door to look out, making nose smears all over the side window. Buck sighed, lowered the window a little so the dog could at least catch a whiff of springtime and drove back to the guesthouse at a sedate pace that wouldn't knock the Maltese down.

Troy was right. On days like this, Buck barely recognized himself.

Chapter Ten

Two days later, Gina was drinking a glass of lemonade on the porch, trying to muster the energy to either cook dinner or take Bobby to the park, when a shuffling sound drew her attention to the street.

Miss Minnie Falcon was approaching the house, pushing her walker. She stopped in front of the gate and shaded her eyes with her hand, looking up toward the house.

"I'll get it, Miss Minnie," Gina called. She hoisted Bobby to her hip and hurried down to open the gate. "Would you like to come up and sit for a while?"

"I would, thank you. I'll just leave my trusty steed here." She parked her walker beside the porch steps.

Gina laughed, helped her up the steps and into an upright rocking chair and then brought her a glass of lemonade.

Bobby crawled over and pulled up on Gina's leg, looking curiously at Miss Minnie.

"Why, look at him stand right up!" the older woman said. "Is he walking yet?"

"So far, he likes crawling better. It gets him around

faster." Gina replaced the baby gate at the top of the porch steps and handed Bobby the colorful roll-and-crawl ball they'd gotten from Buck's stash. Bobby batted it, chortling when a tune started to play and then crawling after it. "I feel like he's ready to walk. He cruises all around holding on to things, but he just hasn't done it by himself yet."

"Everything in its own time. Once he starts to walk, you won't be able to hold him back." Miss Minnie leaned forward and took a sip of lemonade. "My, this is delicious. Thank you, dear. I won't bother you for long."

"It's no bother. Truthfully, I'm glad for the company." Gina meant it, too. Not only because she'd been feeling a little lonely, but because it was mostly the older generation who shared her fascination with history. "In fact, I'd love it if you'd tell me something about this house. Were you born here?"

Miss Minnie nodded and relaxed back into the chair. "Oh, yes. I was born here and lived my whole life here. My parents wanted to fill it with children, you see, but there was only me. I did have a lovely childhood, though. Right here in the middle of town, everyone stopped by."

"It's a perfect location," Gina agreed.

"Everyone from all the farms would come to do their Saturday shopping in town, and of course, they came Sunday for church, so we always had something going on." Miss Minnie looked off into the distance as if she were able to see the past. "Father passed when I was in my twenties. But Mother lived to be quite old. Almost as old as I am now." Miss Minnie looked down at herself and chuckled, then shook her head. "I'd bring her out onto the porch every day and we would have a little tea before dinner. She loved to watch the people go by."

Gina smiled and nodded, hoping the older woman would continue. "Has Rescue River changed much?"

Miss Minnie gestured toward town. "The Chatterbox Café has been here for as long as I can remember. Lyman's Tailors and Sadie's Stout Shop are gone. But Love's Hardware, that's still there."

"I met Mr. Love last week."

"Oh, that man." Miss Minnie shook her head with a little smile.

Gina suddenly remembered Buck's comment that Mr. Love was sweet on Miss Minnie. "He seemed charming," she said, lifting an eyebrow.

"Indeed he is." Two high spots of color appeared in Miss Minnie's cheeks. "Now, that's enough about me. Tell me, child, are you planning to stay here in town?"

Gina looked around at the sunny street and sighed. "I love it here. But I only have my job of helping with the renovation a couple more weeks, until the Freedom Festival." Something about Miss Minnie's inquisitive, sparkling eyes made Gina want to confide. "It's hard for Lacey, having Bobby here. He reminds her of all she lost." Although to be fair, Lacey had been trying to get comfortable with Bobby, asking Gina questions about him and even, a time or two, offering to hold him.

"Of course." Miss Minnie shook her head. "That poor child, she's had so much heartache. As has her brother."

"But…it's strange. Buck seems to like babies, even though he lost his daughter."

"Men and women are different." Miss Minnie set

down her lemonade and rocked gently. "Although I never had children myself, I know how women hold on to things. And then Lacey's husband…" She rocked faster for a moment, shaking her head. "Well. I'm not about to spread gossip." She looked at Gina with curiosity. "Some folks seem to think you and Buck Armstrong make a good couple."

Heat rose to Gina's face, revealing too much, and she laughed weakly. "Oh, well…"

Miss Minnie's face crinkled into a smile and she patted Gina's arm. "Let an old woman give you some advice. Life is short, and the things you think will always be there one day are gone." She looked around at the porch and the house, her chin trembling a little. "One day, everything's gone."

Gina's throat tightened. Not sure of what to say, she reached out to squeeze Miss Minnie's hand. "I'm so glad you came over. I'd like to hear more about the house and its history."

Buck's truck pulled into the driveway, and a minute later, he trotted up the stairs, holding the little white Maltese that had made its way into Lacey's heart by now, as well as Buck's and Gina's. "Hey, Miss Minnie, how's it going?" he asked cheerfully.

"Well, I declare, this house is Grand Central station." The elderly woman's voice was cheerful again. "And my mother would turn in her grave to know there were dogs living here."

"He's just a visitor," Buck said, "but if I remember right, you and your mother were all about cats." He opened the door and whistled, and the orange tabby walked out, tail high.

"Now, is that Mister or Missus?" Miss Minnie asked.

"It's Mister. Can't you tell he's a tough guy?" Buck picked up the cat in his free hand, chuckling, and deposited him in Miss Minnie's lap.

After they'd visited a few minutes more, Miss Minnie petting the purring Mr. Whiskers, the older woman headed back to the Senior Towers.

Gina fixed a quick dinner and they made short work of the dishes. Gina settled Bobby in his crib and then, feeling more comfortable with Buck for the first time since their kiss, came back downstairs. "Do you have time to look at something?" she asked Buck.

"Sure." He looked surprised but not unhappy that she'd reached out to him.

She showed the box and the journal to Buck. "This journal was in the box we found."

He studied the first pages. "Who wrote this? One of Miss Minnie's relatives?"

"I read the whole thing," Gina said, "and I think it was written by a young fugitive woman who stopped here on the way north."

"Really?" Buck examined the pages with more interest. "That's some history."

"Read it!"

She watched as Buck turned slowly through the old pages, deciphering the spidery handwriting, getting as caught up as she had herself at the tale of Minerva, a young fugitive who'd fallen in love with Abraham Falcon, the eighteen-year-old son of the Falcon family.

He looked up at one point, shaking his head. "He proposed? And gave her a fancy ring? That must have raised some eyebrows pre–Civil War."

"Apparently so. Especially since she was expecting a baby. But the people who were most upset were those she'd escaped with. They didn't think Abraham—or any white man—could be trusted."

"Understandable." He read a little more. "So they tried to talk her out of it and she wouldn't listen."

"Right, and wouldn't come along as they were getting ready to go to the next station."

"Which was the Old Rose Barn, I guess? Mr. Love's family place?"

"It must have been. It's not very far away, but I was reading that stations were pretty close together in this area." Gina was glad Buck was as interested in the story as she was. "Apparently, she didn't trust Abraham completely, because she concealed the fact that she could read and write. When he found out, he was angry she'd concealed it, and she was angry that he couldn't understand why."

Buck whistled. "*I* can understand it. Teaching a slave to read and write was a crime in the old South. She'd probably had to conceal her ability for years."

"Anyway," she said, too impatient to wait for him to read the whole journal, "they had a big fight. Minerva got mad and gave the ring to her sister as she was leaving. She told her sister to use it to get to freedom. But her sister said no, she'd hide it in the roses for Minerva to find when she got over being angry."

"If she was that mad at Abraham, why didn't she go along with the others?"

"She said she knew it would slow everyone down. She was near her time of giving birth."

"So did they make up, Minerva and Abraham?"

Buck had given up all pretense of reading the diary for himself.

"They did. The last entry is about how happy she is that they've come to understand and trust each other even better than ever before."

"The last entry? So we don't know what happened?" His forehead wrinkled as he turned to the last page. "It just stops. There was no ring with the journal, no description of a wedding?"

She shook her head. "She must have started another journal, or else been busy with the baby. At least, I hope that's what happened. I hope she didn't have to give up on marrying him."

Buck nodded. "Totally understandable that her friends didn't want her to trust Abraham."

"But she believed in him."

A curious expression crossed Buck's face and then was gone. "I wonder what roses she's talking about. Where her sister hid the ring, and whether Minerva and Abraham ever found it."

"She said she'd hide it in the roses. I wonder if that was around here? The roses couldn't still have survived, I don't think."

"I don't know," he said. "There's a rose garden right by the sign coming into town…"

"Oh, there are a million possibilities, and this journal is really old. We probably wouldn't find anything now." Gina felt disappointed. "At any rate, mementos like the journal should be preserved."

"Since Abraham is one of her ancestors, Miss Minnie may know what happened to them, whether they got married," Buck said. "Or maybe Mr. Love will. He's also familiar with the town's history." He studied the ragged, leather-bound book again. "This reminds me of hunting for treasure when I was a kid."

"Hey, I have an idea," Gina said without thinking it through. "We should go digging."

"Are you asking me out?" he shot back. And then he blew out a breath. "Sorry. I know you're not."

She looked into his eyes and read the confusion there. She was confused, too. She'd made the decision that he should not be in her life, and she hadn't had a moment's happiness since. "You don't need to be sorry."

"No. I *am* sorry. We can't go there. I'm leaving, and you're focused on Bobby. It's fine."

The thought of him leaving crushed her happy feelings. She was lonely, plain and simple. Bobby was wonderful, but he was a baby. She was starting to make some friends, but that didn't fill the gap in her.

"Tell you what," he said. "After Bobby goes to sleep, and Lacey's home in case of any problem, let's go out searching."

"You mean it?" If they were going to be apart, a little time together wouldn't be bad. Would it? Especially if there was a mystery involved?

And the idea of a mystery sparked another thought. "I wonder if we could also look at Miss Minnie's old materials about the house," she said. "We might find answers there. And we might find some stuff that would make awesome decorations for the guesthouse. We can have cases and shadow boxes. Guests will love knowing more about the history of the place."

He was looking at her, smiling. "You don't do things halfway, do you?"

She flushed. "Just stop me. I'm getting carried away again."

"No need to stop. I like it."

High-pitched barking from the ground broke their gaze. Spike, wanting attention.

"Hey, buster, don't be jealous," Buck said to the concerned little dog. And then to Gina: "Meet me here after Bobby's asleep?" He touched her hair, pulled his hand back with a wry grin and then disappeared up the stairs, Spike trotting behind him.

When the doorbell rang around eight o'clock that night, Buck was knee-deep in plaster supplies, but he wiped his hands off and tried to get downstairs before whoever it was rang again. This was about the time Gina put Bobby down, and Buck didn't want to wake him up.

Didn't want anything to interfere with their plans for later. Idiot that he was.

But when he got there, Gina was already at the door.

She listened, opened the door to take a business card and then opened the door wider to let the person in.

Danny Walker.

Local banker and resident womanizer.

"Come on in the kitchen," she said. "We can talk in here." She led him toward the kitchen, only belatedly noticing Buck standing there in the hallway, clothes a mess compared to Danny's nice suit.

"Hey!" Danny held out a hand and pumped Buck's. "I heard you were living here, working on the place. That's just great, what you and Lacey are doing here."

"Thanks. What's up?" In his not-that-friendly voice was the question *Why are you here?*

"Got some business to talk over with Gina here," he said easily.

Buck cocked his head.

Gina lifted an eyebrow at him. Her message was plain: *not your affair.*

And she was right. It wasn't. He stomped back upstairs and applied plaster with extra energy, then did some repairs downstairs until, finally, he heard Danny leave.

It took him about thirty seconds to think of an excuse to go into the kitchen. And then he wished he hadn't, because Gina was smiling.

"What did he want?" he asked.

"He wants my business," she explained happily. "He'd heard about my interest in possibly starting an interior-decorating place, and he wanted to talk about loans and options."

Buck frowned skeptically. "Do you really think it was your *business* he was after at eight at night?"

"What else?" She looked puzzled.

"Maybe…to hit on you? You're a beautiful woman."

Gina didn't seem to love the compliment. "So the only thing I have going for me is my looks? Nobody would want my ideas or my creativity or the work I can do?"

"I didn't mean that. It's just… I know Walker. He has a track record."

"Thanks a lot for undermining my confidence." Gina shoved back her chair and started noisily putting dishes away. "He was totally respectful and businesslike. I'm meeting him for coffee next week to talk more about it."

"There you go. He was after a date and he got it."

"It is *not* a date! Every outing isn't a date!" She came closer and stuck her finger in his chest. "And what's more, I don't appreciate your stomping around upstairs, or pounding nails in the next room, when I'm trying to have a business meeting!"

It had been obvious, then. And even though he knew that Danny wouldn't have called on a homely woman with such alacrity, he still felt bad. "I'm sorry. I guess I'm jealous."

She'd turned away with a flounce, but at his words, she spun back. "Jealous? Of what?"

Now he was truly and deeply in it. He studied the toe of his work boot, scraped it across the floor. "Of a guy who might be hitting on you. Wanting to date you."

"We've already discussed how nothing can happen between us, Buck!" She crossed her arms over her chest, looking exasperated. "So even if I *did* want to go out with this Danny guy—which I don't—I don't see where you'd have a leg to stand on, being jealous."

"I know," he said miserably. "It's true. I'm sorry."

She had opened her mouth to say something, but now she shut it. "You're sorry?"

"I was wrong," he added. "I shouldn't have come in here or asked you anything about it. Or banged around while you were talking to him."

She laughed and rolled her eyes. "When you apologize so well, how can I stay mad at you?"

It was like the sun came out again. "So, you still up for hunting treasure?"

"As soon as Lacey gets home, as long as she agrees to keep an ear open for Bobby. He shouldn't wake up— he was exhausted, but there's always a first time. She can call me and we won't be far away."

Lacey came in the door just then, wearing scrubs, looking tired. "Hey," she said, waving to them. "You two look like you're up to something."

Gina explained about the journal and showed it to Lacey, quickly explaining their quest. Watching them together, Buck was guardedly optimistic. Lacey seemed to have come around to where she liked Gina, and she was doing better with Bobby, paying him a little bit of attention, giving in to his cute ways.

And now Lacey said she was willing to listen for Bobby, even asking Gina to put her baby monitor in her room. "Because I'm just grabbing a sandwich and going to bed. I want to make sure I hear him."

So the women organized that while Buck got cleaned up. He and Gina both emerged from their rooms at the same time, and Buck was absurdly pleased that she'd put on a pretty skirt and sweater. He'd worn khakis himself, something different from his usual scrubs and jeans.

All of a sudden, holding the door for her and walking down the porch steps beside her, Buck felt like he *was* on a date. Even after all their discussions to the contrary.

They strolled through the darkened downtown, gently lit by old-fashioned streetlights. There was a March chill in the air, belying the day's earlier springlike weather. A family headed into the Chatterbox Café. Someone emerged from Love's Hardware, and then the illuminated sign clicked off.

Gina shivered and pulled her jacket tighter, and Buck wanted to put an arm around her and pull her close. Wanted it so much that he pressed his arm tight against his side to make sure he didn't slip up and do it.

When they passed the Ace Tavern, it served to remind him of why he shouldn't make any move toward a relationship with Gina.

As they got to the edge of the town, traffic thinned out, pedestrian and vehicular. Finally they reached the Rescue River sign, on a little garden spot with a bench and some bushes, and Buck pulled out the canvas bag of gardening tools he'd brought.

"I remember when I first saw this sign," Gina said. "It seemed like a fantasy, that I'd ever be welcome and safe. But I do feel that way now."

"I'm glad," he said and risked taking her hand to tug her over to the bench. "We'd better wait until full dark. I doubt digging up the ground around the town's welcome sign is smiled upon."

She hesitated and then sat down beside him, and this time, he couldn't resist putting an arm along the back of the park bench. It was there, for her to lean into or not.

She did, and nothing felt so natural as to tighten his arm around her.

They sat and talked as the stars peeked out and the moon rose, its silvery light casting shadows. When she shivered, he pulled her tighter against him, but the way her closeness tugged at his heart, the confusing little sigh she let out, made that seem like a bad idea. "We should dig," he said, forcing briskness into his tone. "We don't have all night. You'll get frostbite."

She laughed but stood and walked around, looking at the little plot of land. "If I were hiding a romantic memento, I'd hide it…here."

"Under the sign?"

"Yep. According to Miss Minnie, there was always a little garden here, welcoming people to town."

"But the sign wasn't here back in the day," he argued, just for the sake of talking to her, hearing her voice. He knelt down where she'd indicated, though, pulled out a shovel and started to dig.

"It should be under the rosebush, if that's a rosebush," she said. "Are you finding anything?"

"I don't... Wait. I'm hitting something, but it's probably just a rock."

He dug a little more and was about to pull a giant stone out when headlights illuminated them.

Gina clutched his shoulder and he stood quickly, stepping in front of her. Adrenaline surged in him, but not the crazy kind. This was Rescue River, not Afghanistan.

"Not the criminals I expected." It was Dion's deep voice. Behind him was his black-and-white police car.

"Hey, man." Buck reached out to grasp the chief's hand. "Thanks for not using the siren on us."

"What are you two doing?"

"We're trying to solve a mystery," Buck explained. "Show him the diary, Gina."

She fumbled in her purse and brought it out, encased in a large plastic bag, and they took turns telling the big police chief an abbreviated version of the story it contained.

Dion shone his light down on the book, looking thoughtful. Then he turned the flashlight on the hole Buck was digging. "You find anything?"

"We thought we might find the ring her sister hid. It was supposed to be among the roses." He shook his head. "Hit something down there, but I'm pretty sure it's a rock."

"Are we in trouble?" Gina asked at the same moment.

Dion chuckled. "As crimes go, this isn't the worst. I might let you off with a warning if you fill up the hole all nice."

"You never heard about anything hidden here?"

Dion frowned. "I've been in Rescue River a long time. I've heard a few things, but not about here."

"Where, then?"

He studied them thoughtfully as if trying to decide whether to tell them. Finally, he nodded. "You ever been to the old cemetery?"

"The one by the church? That's the only one I know about," Buck said.

"No. There's another one. I'll show you."

After they'd filled in the hole and replaced the sod, Dion drove them out one of the country roads to a tumbledown church. Behind it was an overgrown yard with multiple depressions and a few stones. "This is a cemetery?" Gina asked, stepping closer to Buck.

"It's the AME cemetery," he said. "Not used anymore, but some folks still have kin buried here. And look." He led them across the rutted ground and to a stone bench that backed up against the woods. "Know what that is?" he asked, touching a tangle of vines that grew as tall as he was.

Buck shook his head.

"Is it…a rosebush?" Gina guessed.

"That's exactly what it is. I wonder if what's referred to in your journal is buried here."

Buck studied the bench and the bush. "Could be."

"Have a look around, but don't dig. We don't want to disturb anyone's remains."

Gina knelt in front of the little bench, looking at the rosebush, its buds just starting to come out. "What a lot of history is here," she whispered, touching the carving there.

Dion shone his powerful flashlight on a couple of stones next to the bench.

"'A friend loves at all times,'" Buck read from one of them. "Proverbs 17:17."

"Look at this," Gina said, kneeling to trace the inscription on a nearby headstone. "Minerva Cobbs. She didn't write her last name in the diary, but could this be her grave? How many Minervas could there be in a town the size of Rescue River?"

"Are there dates?"

"No. And if this is her grave, she didn't change her name to Abraham's." Gina bit her lip. "I did an online search for Minerva Falcon and nothing came up. I really wonder what happened."

They looked around a little while longer but didn't find a ring or anything else that would help fill in the blanks of the story, a story Buck was getting curious about himself. Or maybe he just wanted to keep that interested sparkle in Gina's eyes. "How are we going to find out the rest of it?" he asked her.

"Talk to the old folks," Gina said promptly. "They're more likely than anyone to know. Are you in?"

Dion raised an eyebrow, his mouth quirking a little at one corner.

"I'm all in," Buck said. Right or wrong, he wanted to spend every moment he could with this woman. Every moment he had before leaving town.

Chapter Eleven

The next week went by in a flurry of renovations. They worked hard to get the first floor ready for the Freedom Festival, and when the Monday before the festival arrived, Gina could look around the guesthouse and feel assured that what she'd promised Lacey would come to pass. They'd be ready.

She and Buck had postponed their meeting with Mr. Love and Miss Minnie, but this morning, as they returned from dropping Bobby at Angelica's place, they settled on the next day.

"Should we take them out to lunch?" Gina asked. "I know Miss Minnie likes to go to the café."

Buck turned down the road into town. "If we want to look at Miss Minnie's materials, maybe we should meet at the Senior Towers."

"Great. If you can pick up Mr. Love, we'll meet there right after lunch." They were driving through downtown. "Speaking of the Chatterbox, can you drop me off there?"

"Sure." He pulled up beside the place, and Gina told herself she didn't need to provide Buck with an accounting of her day, where she was going or whom she was with.

At the same time, they'd gotten in a rhythm of working together. "This shouldn't take long," she said, "and I'll be back at the house to work on that crown molding."

"Take your time," he said, his voice expressionless. "There's your breakfast date, right there."

"It's not a date!" She gathered her purse and briefcase and slid out of the truck without waiting for Buck to get the door for her. Nonetheless, he got out and stood beside the truck, for all the world like a protective father. She rolled her eyes.

"Gina!" Danny greeted her happily. "Come on—I've got us a table." He nodded at Buck and escorted Gina inside, a hand on the small of her back.

When Buck did that, she liked it. But when Danny did it, it felt…creepy. She walked faster to get some distance from his touch.

As they sat down to discuss more details about a possible loan, Gina felt uneasy. Why *did* Danny need to meet with her again? And why were they doing it at a restaurant instead of at the bank?

She didn't have much experience with men; she'd been awkward in school, and then soon afterward she'd gotten attached to Hank. She wasn't the flirtatious, frequent-dating type. So she couldn't tell what vibe Danny was putting out. Did he want to date her? Couldn't he read her lack of interest in him?

As she got out her notes and ordered coffee, she cast a glance in the direction where Buck had roared off and frowned. Why had he put this insecurity into her head? Why couldn't he accept that women could be businesspeople, meeting with other businesspeople? That it wasn't always about dating?

"We're really looking forward to working with you," Danny said after their coffee had arrived. "Have you thought any more about what your business might entail? Had the chance to look at any storefronts?"

"Not really, Danny. I've been totally occupied with getting Lacey's house ready for the festival."

"How's that going?" he asked, and she told him about what they were doing. "That's great, great," he said. "But let's focus on your business as soon as that's over."

She frowned. "Can I ask why you're so interested in working with me? I'm not a high-capital investor, believe me."

"Oh, we like to help small-business people in Rescue River. It's a community outreach kind of thing. Keeping the downtown strong."

She nodded, studying him without making it obvious. He just didn't seem sincere. "I have to give all of it some thought."

She wished Buck were here so she could ask him his opinion, learn more about Danny's background. If only he weren't so touchy about her having coffee with another man! With concern, she realized that Buck was the person she most trusted right now, most wanted to share the details of her life with, big and small.

When did *that* happen?

"You're staying in town, though, right? You'll be here through the festival and beyond?" He looked so eager that, against her better judgment, she was flattered. Even though she wasn't going to pursue a relationship with him, it was nice to have a man show interest.

"I'm planning to stay, at least for a while," she said. "Rescue River is a wonderful place. So warm and safe and welcoming."

An odd expression flashed across his face and then was gone. "Right," he said smoothly. "Rescue River *is* a safe place."

And as they parted ways, she wondered again why Danny was so interested in her business, even though she'd been open about the fact that she didn't know how long she'd be able to stay.

That afternoon, Buck drove Gina out to pick up Bobby in a thoughtful mood. As he waited for them in the truck and then headed back to Rescue River, he considered his own progress.

In the past, he would have been royally mad that Gina had had coffee with Danny against his advice, to the point where he couldn't have had a reasonable discussion. He remembered, with some embarrassment, a couple of occasions when he'd gotten jealous about Ivana. Both had led to huge fights. But today, he'd managed his feelings with just a little mild argument.

And out by the Rescue River sign last week, when Dion had flashed his lights, he hadn't freaked out. Yeah, he'd been startled, but he hadn't grabbed Gina and taken her to the ground or some crazy move like that.

Counseling and AA and prayer must be starting to have an impact, even on a hardheaded creature like him.

Gina cleared her throat like she'd been trying to

get his attention for a while. "Hey," she said. "If this is too much trouble, I can start asking Angelica to bring me home."

"What?" He glanced over at her and was surprised to see her lower lip out and her eyes blazing. "It's no trouble. What are you talking about?"

"You've been completely silent during this whole drive. You didn't even say hi to Bobby!"

"Well, excuse *me*." Was he supposed to put on some kind of show for her? He paused, took a breath. *She's a woman. She has different needs.* "I'm sorry. I didn't know I was acting weird."

"You're not sulking about my having coffee with Danny Walker?"

He frowned, thinking. "I'm not thrilled about it. I don't trust the guy."

"So you *are* mad." There was the satisfaction of being right in her voice.

"No." He shook his head. "You're an adult. And… although I feel a lot for you, we're not a couple. I don't have the right."

They were driving through Rescue River now, getting close to the guesthouse, and he didn't want to leave things like this. On an impulse, he pulled over beside the town park. "Look, since I neglected Bobby before, how about we take him to the playground for a little bit?"

He turned off the truck and looked at her. There were two vertical wrinkles between her eyebrows, and her lips pressed together.

"We don't have to," he said. He put his hand back on the keys, waiting for the put-down that might be coming. You never knew with women.

But then she smiled, her cheeks going a little pink. "Okay. Sure. That would be great."

Happiness flooded him. He'd been able to get her from upset to happy. He *was* learning, maybe at a slow pace, but still. He came around to her side of the truck, opened the door for her and helped her out.

Her hand was soft, delicate. He pulled in a breath.

She shot a glance at him and then got very busy unhooking Bobby from his car seat in the back.

He shouldered the diaper bag while she carried Bobby, wiggling with excitement, on her hip.

"I have to say," she said as they headed toward the play area, "I *was* uncomfortable with Danny this morning."

"What did he do? Did he make a move on you? Do you want me to talk to him?"

"No, no!" She laughed a little. "I just… Well, I question his motives."

"I can tell you his motives," Buck groused.

Her laugh rang out like a bell. "I love this park," she said, waving her hand around. "We didn't have this kind of friendly-feeling place in my neighborhood in California."

"I used to play sports here as a kid," he said, accepting the change of subject. "And do less wholesome things when I was in high school."

"You're such a bad boy." She rolled her eyes and then looked wistful. "This must have been a great town to grow up in."

"It was." And for a second, Buck got a hard, hot yearning to stay, to raise a family here like had been the plan with Ivana and Mia.

They reached the playground, and Buck set the diaper bag down on a bench. A couple of moms on the other side of the colorful play structures stood talking while their kids climbed the taller one, yelling out their after-school joy. Off in the distance, someone was stringing lights and people were unloading something from a truck, probably getting ready for the festival at the end of the week.

Gina carried Bobby over to a bucket-style swing and eased him into it, and then stood in front while Buck pushed it gently from behind, making Bobby giggle each time he swung toward his mom. A light breeze rattled the still-bare tree limbs and the sun warmed the back of Buck's shoulders.

When Bobby tired of the swing, Buck lifted him out and helped him toddle over to a play structure. Bobby pulled himself up and climbed through an opening, landed on his hands and then pulled himself through. Immediately, he turned around and did the same thing again.

"He is *so* close to walking." Gina squatted down and reached into her pocket, then looked at the basic flip phone with disappointment. "Oh, man, I wish I'd brought my other phone to take a picture!"

So Buck pulled out his phone and snapped a bunch of photos and a video—of Bobby, mostly, but also of his pretty mom. She'd be happy to have memories of herself and Bobby together as he grew.

He sure was a cute kid. As cute as Mia had been, though in a different way. Sadness and nostalgia washed over him, but gently, a spring shower rather than a storm.

He could think about Mia now. And yeah, it hurt, a

lot. That was only natural. Losing her and Ivana would always be the biggest sadness of his life.

He glanced up at the sky, pale blue with fluffy white clouds scudding by. Mia and Ivana were with Jesus now. And he didn't know what heaven was like, but he was sure that mother and daughter were together and happy. Maybe there was a big swing set somewhere up there.

His throat tightened. He swallowed, then focused on Bobby. "Come on, little man. Ever gone down a slide before?"

Gina watched as Buck lifted Bobby halfway up the plastic slide, then whooshed him down. As Bobby laughed, Gina's heart melted a little.

Buck was so kind. Even when they were arguing, even when she'd been a teeny bit unreasonable, he didn't blow up or sulk. Instead, he tried to make things right.

She was starting to trust that Buck had her best interests at heart, that he wasn't trying to manipulate her the way Hank—and, yes, her father as well—used to do.

Moving to the bottom of the slide, she knelt down so Bobby could glide into her arms, safely guided by Buck. A couple more trips, and he wanted to wander over to a low play table. She helped him, and he stood banging the table like a drum.

"Sit down over there," Buck said, pointing to a smooth stretch of rubberized play surface. Then he lifted Bobby and set him down a few yards away, holding him by his shoulders. "Walk to Mommy," he said.

Gina's mouth dropped open. "Do you think he can?"

"Call him," Buck said. "I won't let him fall."

So she held out her arms to her son. "Come on, sweetie."

Bobby chortled and lifted one awkward leg after the other, staggering unsteadily toward her. Buck was supporting him—and then he wasn't.

Never taking his laughing eyes off her, Bobby toddled into her arms.

"Oh my word! His first step!" She was laughing and crying at once as she pulled Bobby to her and hugged him tightly. Such joy. And such sharp pain that Hank wasn't here to see it.

A movie of memories flashed through her mind, the good ones this time: Hank in the delivery room, flourishing the scissors as he fearlessly cut the cord. The way he'd insisted on taking Bobby to visit every friend he had, the moment the pediatrician had okayed it, just to show off his brand-new son. How he'd swept her into a huge hug when they'd seen Bobby's first smile.

Hank hadn't been perfect, not by a long shot, but he had loved his son. And he would have loved to see this milestone.

Buck knelt beside her and wrapped both her and Bobby in his arms.

Tears flowed down Gina's face even as she laughed and kissed Bobby. "I'm happy and sad at the same time," she said to Buck.

"Me, too." His voice was a little choked.

She looked into his eyes and realized it was true. He'd lost as much as she had. More.

She tightened her arms around both of them—Buck, who'd seen so much, and Bobby, who was only beginning to explore the world. Closed her eyes and lifted a wordless prayer.

Bobby struggled free, used Buck's arm to pull up to a standing position and then looked from her to Buck expectantly. "Go!" he demanded.

"Has he said words before?" Buck asked, laughing as he scooted a few yards away and held out his arms for Bobby.

"Not that clearly." Gina wiped her eyes and steadied her baby and let him go, lurching from leg to leg with undeniable independence.

The next day after his lunchtime AA meeting, Buck stopped by the hardware store as planned. He picked up a few needed supplies while he waited for Mr. Love to finish giving detailed instructions to his granddaughter, who'd run the store alone in his absence.

"I got this, Granddad," she said good-naturedly. "You can take an hour off to do some visiting!"

Reluctantly, Mr. Love headed out the door. Buck crooked his arm for the older man and alerted him to curbs during the three-block walk to the Senior Towers.

"Now, see," Mr. Love said, lifting his face to the spring sunshine, "isn't this nicer than riding in a car? Not that I didn't appreciate the offer. But any chance to be active and outside, I take it."

"A good philosophy." Buck listened to the birds singing in the trees, just beginning to offer a few buds, and smelled the earthy scent of spring. He'd like to share in that feeling of new life, but truthfully, his insides were in turmoil.

He'd spent more time with Gina and Bobby during the past week than during any of the previous weeks since she'd arrived in town. They'd worked long hours, and tag teamed on child care and cooking and dog walking, since Crater and Spike were now established residents of the guesthouse. They'd shared conversations about their pasts, argued amiably over final paint colors and finish details, and generally made a great team.

They'd shared Bobby's first step.

Passing the Chatterbox Café made him think of Gina meeting Danny. He shouldn't begrudge her starting to establish other friendships, and he didn't—as long as the friendships were female. But Danny Walker's obvious interest in Gina bothered him.

Danny was too slick for Gina, and he didn't think them a good match, but then again, he had no right to comment on or criticize her choices. What say did he have?

"What's got you bent out of shape?" Mr. Love asked.

"Who says I'm bent out of shape?"

"It's more than obvious. You're wound up tighter than a drum. And I'm a fast walker, but you're rushing me here. Cut me a break. I'm eighty-seven!"

"Oh, man, sorry!" He slowed down. "And…you're right—I'm a little uptight."

"Woman problems?" Mr. Love asked.

"Now, why would you jump to that conclusion?"

Mr. Love chuckled. "I couldn't help noticing the attention you paid to that young lady in the hardware store. Gina? Is she going to be there today?"

"She'll be there." Buck debated denying everything, but Mr. Love had known him a long time. "And yeah," he said. "I like her. But she's got issues, especially with addicts and drunks. And I'm leaving town. *And* someone else is after her."

"You've got problems." Mr. Love nodded. "Serious problems, but there's one thing—you're not defined by being a drunk. Kid I knew, who worked so hard in the store, he wasn't a drunk."

"I've changed."

"Yes, you have. More than once. A man can be forgiven for going a little crazy after the losses you had, but that doesn't mean you'll be crazy forever. You seem kinda sane to me right now."

"Maybe."

"And why are you leaving town? Rescue River is your home!"

Buck shook his head. "Burned too many bridges. Bad reputation. I need to start fresh."

"Like my mama used to say, no matter where you go, there you are. You think your problems won't follow you into another town?"

Buck guided the man around a broken section of sidewalk. "That's exactly what I think. In another town, they won't look at me like the criminal who busted up a restaurant or got his license taken away."

"You're going to give up your woman just so you don't have to have hurt feelings?"

The question echoed in the air, and Buck wondered: Was that what he was doing? "Sounds kind of cowardly," he admitted.

"Yes, it does. And you've never struck me as a coward."

Buck blew out a breath. "Speaking of women…anything you want me to do to promote your case with Miss Minnie Falcon?"

"Hey, hey now." Mr. Love held up a hand. "Show respect for your elders."

Buck chuckled. "You can dish it out…"

Mr. Love bumped a fist into Buck's upper arm. "We almost there? I'm getting tired of talking with you."

"As a matter of fact, we are. But I've got my eye on you." Buck was grinning, satisfied with having turned the tables on the old man.

When they walked into the homey, plant-filled lobby of the Senior Towers, Gina and Miss Minnie Falcon—and a whole cadre of Miss Minnie's friends—were waiting for them.

"Trust a man to be late," Miss Minnie said, leaning forward to check the grandfather clock. "No sense of time."

Buck took a breath, but Mr. Love squeezed his arm, communicating nonverbally not to respond.

"They're right on time," Gina soothed, "or maybe a few minutes late is all. Should we head up to your apartment, Miss Minnie?"

"We should. I've got everything all ready."

After a few words with the other women in the lobby, the four of them went upstairs and were soon looking through the trunk of materials Miss Minnie had saved or inherited over the years.

"We're looking for something from 1850 or thereabouts," Gina said, her face flushed with excitement. "How much do you know about what's in here, Miss Minnie?"

"I surely do wish I could see better," Mr. Love said wistfully.

"There are letters from some of my ancestors," Miss

Minnie said. "And drawings, jewelry, even some early photographs. A good deal of family history."

"We'll respect your privacy," Gina said. "Are you sure it's okay with you if we go through it?"

Buck loved that about her, that she was sensitive to the older woman's concerns. Gina hadn't had an easy life, and maybe that was how God was using her trials: to make her kinder than the norm.

"It's perfectly fine. I'm so old now, I don't care who knows my business."

"I know exactly what you mean, Minnie," Mr. Love said.

Miss Minnie blushed. "Look for a pair of daguerreotypes in a brown leather case. From what you've told me, they'll be very interesting to you."

Buck and Gina knelt in front of the trunk and opened the lid. Inside was a jumble of letters, a blue military uniform, jewelry in worn velvet cases and pewter candleholders.

Gina sat back on her heels, very close to Buck. "Wow, Miss Minnie, this is awesome! It belongs in the historical society for sure!"

"If we had one, I'd gladly donate it to them."

Buck carefully picked up a brown leather case. "Is this the one?"

"I believe," Miss Minnie said, "that those photographs are images of the couple in your old diary, Abraham and Minerva."

Gina's eyes sparkled as she studied the images: on one side, a beautiful African American woman in an elegant wedding dress; on the other side, a handsome white man in a formal suit, including a vest and short tie. "So they did get married!" She practically glowed with excitement.

Miss Minnie shook her head. "No, dear. Those photographs were taken weeks before the wedding was to happen. You'll notice the style of dress conceals her pregnancy."

"I imagine any pictures had to be taken in secret, given the times and her status as a runaway," Mr. Love said.

"Wait—I'm confused." Buck was studying the photograph. "Did she have Abraham's child?"

Miss Minnie shook her head. "It wasn't Abraham's child, you see. She arrived pregnant. She'd been assaulted by a plantation owner down South."

"How awful," Gina breathed, glancing over at Buck.

"I respect the fact that he was willing to marry her in that circumstance," Mr. Love said. "It must have been quite unusual back then."

Miss Minnie nodded. "What happened to her was awful, and yet if she hadn't found a safe place to bear her baby, I wouldn't be here."

"You're a descendant?" Buck looked up from the trunk. He'd known Miss Minnie for years, ever since she'd been his Sunday-school teacher, but he hadn't known that she had a slave ancestor.

"That's right. Miss Minerva Cobbs was my great-grandmother."

"Wow. You were named after her," Gina said.

"Yes, young lady, and proud to be. Since that day, there has always been a Minerva in the Falcon family."

Buck was impatient to hear the end of the story. "You said they didn't marry. Did she decide to move on with the others headed north?" Buck was remembering his Ohio history. "Because the Fugitive Slave Act would've put them at risk, right?"

"The rest of the group wanted her to come with them. They were worried Abraham would take advantage of her, that he wasn't serious about marriage, but they were wrong."

Gina moved a little closer, her shoulder brushing Buck's, and he felt his blood pressure rise. Did she know what she was doing to him? He leaned back against the couch and put up a pillow for her back, and she scooted back and sat right next to him, the side of her leg burning into his.

He shot up a prayer for calmness.

"Tell us what became of them," Gina asked, seemingly unaffected by their closeness.

Miss Minnie shook her head, looking sad. "Like many women of those times, she died in childbirth. But Abraham and his parents raised her son, Ishmael, as their own and gave him their last name."

Mr. Love whistled. "Even despite his mixed race."

"They were staunch abolitionists and strong Christians. They believed all people were equal."

"Wow." Buck tore his attention from the woman beside him to focus on the story. "There are people nowadays who could learn a lesson from your ancestors."

"They very nearly made a full-time job of assisting fugitives to freedom. It's said that eight hundred people came through the Falcon home." Miss Minnie smiled proudly.

"That's amazing!" Gina was practically rubbing her hands together. "We have *got* to tell this story."

"Miss Minnie should be the judge of that," said Mr.

Love. "She may not want it known that she has some mixed blood."

She inclined her head at him. "My father was one of Ishmael's five sons, the youngest, and he inherited the house. And while he didn't advertise his ancestry, he didn't hide it within the family, nor in Rescue River. He always encouraged me to be proud of my great-grandmother, and I am."

"And you should be." Gina gripped the older woman's hands. "But what do you think about making it public? There's no pressure to do that."

"It's not widely known," Miss Minnie admitted. "In fact…" She trailed off and looked at the floor as if lost in thought.

"Are you okay, Miss Minnie?"

"I've never married," the older woman said. "But I was engaged. When my fiancé discovered my background, he broke off the engagement."

"For racial reasons?" Gina asked. "That's awful."

She nodded. "I'd left this area, gone away to school. People in other places weren't as open as those in Rescue River."

Mr. Love shook his head. "My, my. I always wondered why a fine-looking woman like you didn't have a husband. You had plenty of suitors as a schoolgirl."

Miss Minnie chuckled. "I did make a few conquests, didn't I?"

"Hearts were broken, right and left."

Buck didn't ask, but he wondered whether Mr. Love's heart had been one of those broken, or at least bruised, by a younger Miss Minnie.

"And so you stayed single," Gina said.

"Don't feel sorry for me, young lady. I've had a wonderful life in this town. And it may be that I don't have the temperament for marriage. I always did have strong opinions of my own, and when I was young, not many men could tolerate having a wife on an equal plane."

"Not many men in your circle had any sense," Mr. Love said. "Why, I would have…" He shook his head. "But times were different then."

"Yes, they were."

As the two elders began sharing stories of people they'd both known in years past, Buck glanced at Gina to find her watching them, her face a study in care and concern. As if in common accord, they moved to the trunk and started sorting through the items now brought to life by the story they told.

Ribbons and photographs and letters. "Where do we begin to sort these out?" he asked quietly.

"We start small," she said. "I think we should find just enough to make a display for the Freedom Festival. And if Miss Minnie is feeling up to it, maybe we could ask her to come talk to visitors."

"Mr. Love as well," Buck suggested. "He's done presentations for the festival before." He looked up to ask Mr. Love about it, but he was talking intently to Miss Minnie, their heads close together.

He turned back to Gina and found her lifting an eyebrow at him. "Senior romance?" she whispered.

"Love is beautiful at any age," he said, and Mr. Love's example gave him courage to reach out and touch Gina's shoulder, gaze into her eyes. "We may have barriers, Gina, but it's nothing like people faced in times past."

She looked from the old diary in her hand to him and then back again, color rising to her face.

He touched her chin. "No pressure," he said, "but maybe, when things settle down, you'll give this a little thought."

She looked at him, her eyes darkening. "Give *what* a little thought?" she almost whispered.

He let his hand caress her soft cheek and tangle in her hair. "Us," he said. "Give *us* some thought."

That night, Buck was going into the Star Market just as Dion was coming out.

"Any news about the mysterious buried treasure?" Dion asked, grinning.

Buck filled him in on the conversation they'd had with Mr. Love and Miss Minnie.

Dion whistled. "I had no idea. Definitely need to record them telling their stories, and sooner rather than later. Did she know anything about the ring you were hunting for?"

"You know, in the midst of all the storytelling, we completely forgot to ask."

"Makes sense."

Buck was about to turn away when he thought to ask Dion about Gina's California in-laws. "Hey, any news about Gina's situation?" He knew Dion had been monitoring the police airwaves and had also contacted colleagues in California to keep updated.

Dion lifted his hands, palms up. "It's strange," he said. "According to my friend in California, there was a ton of inquiry and investigation for the past couple of weeks. But yesterday, it stopped."

"Stopped?" Buck tilted his head to one side. "What do you make of that?"

Dion shrugged. "Maybe they've given up."

"Maybe," Buck said.

"Or maybe… I don't know. Let's keep our eyes open."

"Will do," Buck said, an uneasy prickle crawling up his neck.

Two days later, Gina finished the dishes, strolled toward the sitting room and looked in. Buck was there, leaning back in a big chair with Bobby on his lap, turning the pages of a board book. In front of the fireplace, Crater and Spike nestled on a folded blanket, and Mr. and Mrs. Whiskers curled up together on the back of the couch. Pretty lamps stood on end tables, and paintings of local landscapes graced the walls. They'd all worked late last night, dragging furniture out of storage, to get several of the rooms finished.

She stopped in the doorway to survey the scene, her heart swelling with happiness.

Her son was thriving here, that was the main thing. He got all the attention he needed, and even though he had a case of the sniffles, Buck was cuddling him close. He treated the boy like kin.

She took pride in the beautiful room. The walls were a light chocolate shade, set off by white moldings, and this afternoon they'd put up the ornate chandelier she'd found in a local antiques shop. Heavy gold draperies added weight and warmth, and the chesterfield sofa and wing-back chairs gave the room the look of an old library.

At that moment, Buck looked up and saw her, and the light in his eyes sent warmth all the way to her toes. Maybe they had a chance after all.

"Ready?" he asked. They were planning to do the

finish work on the final room tonight, in preparation for the start of the festival tomorrow.

"I'm ready. But you two look comfortable."

"We are. He's a little stuffy." Buck studied Bobby and brushed his wispy hair off his forehead. "Almost asleep. Can he stay down here with us?"

Touched by the big veteran's care for her son, she scanned the room. "We'll be right next door. He can rest in here." She folded a couple of blankets, put them on the floor and set up the baby monitor.

They worked in the connected room as the sun slanted low and golden, making hazy squares on the polished wooden floor. Gina painted baseboards with glossy white enamel while Buck put a door back on its hinges.

Buck set his phone to play quiet contemporary music. They chatted a little as they worked.

Gina's heart was full to breaking. After tomorrow, this interlude of renovation would be done. Lacey could find someone else to do the work, or she and Buck could do it themselves at a more leisurely pace.

And whether Gina stayed in Rescue River or moved on, her time of working closely with Buck would likely come to an end.

She didn't want it to; she wanted to go on working with this man. Her attachment to him was growing daily, and her fears about his past were lessening. She was starting to think that maybe, just maybe, she'd fallen for a winner this time.

But he wouldn't be around. He had a plan and knew what he needed. And that was, apparently, to leave Rescue River.

She finished her painting and tapped the lid back on the can, then stood to survey the room.

"Penny for your thoughts," he said, coming up behind her.

She looked over her shoulder at him. "This has been fun, renovating the place," she said, surveying the room. "I'll miss it."

"You're talking like it's over."

"You know what Lacey said. Only until the festival—no more."

"Okay," he said, "but you'll stay in Rescue River. Right?"

"I don't know. I'd like to stay, hire out as a historical renovation consultant or open a shop for interior decorating, but I'm not sure it would be wise to take that on." She sighed. "It's a lot of responsibility, being a single parent, you know?"

She felt him nod behind her. And then he put his arms around her and pulled her back against him. "Whatever happens," he said, "I hope you know you've got a friend."

But, oh, she wanted more. "Is that what we are? Friends?"

"What do you think?" he asked, his breath warm against her ear.

The feel of his arms enfolding her, warming her, circling her, set her heart pounding. She felt him nuzzle her hair. The music swelled and the light was dying and the poignant contentment made her close her eyes. "I think I could stay like this forever," she whispered.

His arms tightened, and for a moment, they just breathed together, their whole bodies in sync.

Suddenly, the dogs went crazy, Spike's hysterical yip combining with Crater's deep growl.

And then, before she could step away from Buck to investigate, she heard a sound and saw a sight she'd hoped never to experience again: her former mother-in-law, holding Bobby, standing in the connecting doorway. "How nice," Lorna said. "You're cozying up to a derelict while our grandson rolls around on the floor with the dogs."

Chapter Twelve

Buck took in the situation instantly.

"Art! Lorna!" Gina's voice was a breathy gasp. Based on her stricken expression and the well-coiffed older couple's words, these had to be Gina's husband's parents.

The sight of that fist-size bruise that had marred Bobby's leg when he first arrived came back to Buck. Bobby's grandparents. His *abusive* grandparents.

Two long steps put him directly in front of them. "Bobby needs to go to his mother. Now."

He reached for the baby.

The older woman turned away. "Step back, young man," she said, her voice scornful, but also a little scared. "Don't you dare touch me or this baby."

"I don't want to touch you," he said, "but if you don't give Bobby back to his mother right now, I will."

He'd commanded men to do things they'd never have risked on their own. He'd frightened macho Afghan militants into backing down. Dead drunk, he'd glared down punks with guns in the seediest parts of Cleveland.

Never had his powers of intimidation felt so important.

Gina seemed to draw from his strength; she came and stood beside him and held out her arms.

The older woman looked sulky, but then some kind of nonverbal signal passed between her and her husband.

She handed the baby to Gina.

Gina seized Bobby, pulled him close against her shoulder and stepped back. Her face was white. "How did you find us? What are you doing here?" She ran her hands over Bobby's arms and legs as if she was worried that they'd already hurt him.

The man, Art, stepped between Buck and his wife and turned his back, effectively excluding Buck from the conversation. He was probably six feet tall, his sports jacket stretched across his shoulders, his khaki-clad legs planted wide. He crossed meaty arms over his chest and glared at Gina. "Did you think we couldn't find you, with our connections?"

She swallowed visibly and clutched Bobby closer. "You don't have connections in Ohio," she said in a hoarse voice.

The woman cackled. "We know people everywhere. We aren't like you, a nobody from nowhere."

Buck mentally scanned through everyone he knew in Rescue River, wondering who would run in these folks' elevated social circles. Sam Hinton, maybe? But Sam would swallow glass before he'd betray a woman and child in need.

"Our friends Bernice and Jerry Walker just happened to see their son's post about a new guesthouse on social media," the woman said. "They thought the woman and baby looked familiar. They got in touch with us, and we spoke with their son."

Gina gasped. "Danny Walker. And those publicity pictures Amy was taking that one day. I never even thought—"

"After he met with Gina and assessed the situation for us, he was concerned," Art interrupted. "He saw you getting involved with someone you shouldn't. Said that you and Bobby were practically homeless."

Betrayal was written all over Gina's face.

"And I must say," Lorna added, looking around the room, "he was right to be concerned. You're working as a common laborer."

"Place is dirty." Art brushed imaginary dust off his sleeve.

"And our grandson, lying on the floor unsupervised, with a couple of dirty, dangerous dogs. He could have been bitten."

"Or hurt on these nails and wood." The burly man nudged at a small pile of scraps with his toe.

"Art. Lorna. Come on. There's a baby monitor, and the dogs are perfectly safe," Gina said. But her voice sounded insecure.

Buck felt a quake of doubt, too. *He* was the one who'd suggested that Bobby stay downstairs with them.

But he'd trust Crater with any child, and Spike wouldn't hurt a flea.

Whereas these folks had already hurt Bobby. "You're trespassing in my sister's house," he said. "Get out."

"Door was unlocked," the man, Art, said. "Anyone could have walked in. You might want to think about that."

"It's a safe town," Gina said. "Or was, until the two of you came in."

Dion. Buck needed to call Dion.

He got out his phone and scrolled through his contacts, tapped Dion's name. "You need to get over to the guesthouse," he said the moment Dion answered, not trying to hide his words from either Gina or Bobby's grandparents. "The people who abused him before are here. Gina needs help."

"Be right there," Dion said.

Lorna's penciled-on eyebrows lifted almost to her hairline. "*We're* the danger? Us?"

The man pointed at Buck, thumb and forefinger out like a gun. "We know all about you, son. If anyone's a danger to Bobby, it's you."

"We talked to the nice people next door, in the Senior Towers," Lorna said, hands on hips. "They told us about *your* reputation. Drunk all over town, breaking places up, getting yourself arrested. Why, the very idea of our grandson anywhere near you has us terrified."

"And not that she's treated us well," Art said, "but we'd hate to see Gina take up with the likes of you."

"Do you even have a job, aside from day work?"

"We heard you're in AA but that you were also seen at a bar recently."

"Once an alcoholic, always an alcoholic."

Gina was looking at him, her eyes stricken. "You were at a bar recently?"

"Not to drink," he tried to explain. "Not to drink."

But the words, true as they were, sounded false in his own ears. Like the excuses he used to make to Lacey. Like the lies every alcoholic knew exactly how to tell.

"You're a danger to both Gina and Bobby," Lorna declared. "We'll certainly take steps to keep you away from our grandson. And, Gina, what on earth were you thinking, leaving safety and comfort in California for this?" She swung a scornful arm around. "For *him*?"

The words went on, spoken by all three, an argument the older couple was clearly winning. It all started to blur together in Buck's head as he backed slowly out of the room and toward the guesthouse's front door.

What *had* he been thinking, getting so close to a nice woman and her innocent baby? Thinking he could have a normal relationship with them, be good for them, even?

He'd been the downfall of Ivana and Mia, and he was headed toward being the downfall of Gina and Bobby.

He opened the door and stepped onto the front porch. He had to get out of here. Had to make Gina and Bobby safe by leaving. But he couldn't go until she had another protector.

"If you think you'll be able to keep custody after this, you're wrong," he heard Art say through the screen door.

"When we go back to California, we're taking Bobby with us," Lorna added.

A police car squealed to a halt in front of the house, and Dion was out of it and up the porch stairs in seconds. When he saw Buck, he stopped. "Fill me in."

"The grandparents from California. Making threats, scaring Gina and Bobby." As if to back up his words, a loud wail came from inside the house.

Dion nodded and hurried inside, leaving the door open like he expected Buck to follow. When Buck didn't, he looked back, eyebrows lifted. "Come on, man."

But Buck knew what was best for everyone, and he wasn't it. He grabbed his wallet and keys. "You handle it," he said and headed out, bent on getting far, far away from here.

Gina survived the next hour of shouting and accusations by clinging to Bobby, soothing him, reminding herself to stay strong for him. She reeled from the force of Art and Lorna's hatred, her stomach churning with fear. Could they take Bobby from her?

Could she prevent them, with her complete lack of money and power?

Her mind darted in all directions, but it kept coming back to one question. Where was Buck? Why wasn't he here, standing by her?

Of course, it wasn't his problem or his obligation. She shouldn't feel betrayed. Still, she'd trusted him and felt he was a friend, if not more.

If not a whole lot more, if their sweet embrace was any indication.

But now, in her hour of need, he seemed to be gone. True, he'd gotten Dion here, for which Gina was incredibly thankful, but still. She'd expected something different from him.

Then again, if he'd been frequenting bars…

As Art and Lorna talked heatedly to Dion, heaping on accusations and innuendos, Gina shot up prayers for help and safety with every breath, her body cringing from the onslaught of lies and bitterness that seemed almost physical in its intensity. She didn't see how God could deliver her, but she tried desperately to remember all the biblical promises she'd ever memorized.

Dion was a force of calm and reason. Obviously sensing that she was near her breaking point, he pulled Art and Lorna aside for quiet moments of conversation while she took Bobby upstairs to calm down. As she let him nurse, she prayed hard, and bits of verses came back to her.

The Lord is my strength and my shield.

We are more than conquerors.

Thou preparest a table before me in the presence of my enemies...of my enemies...of my enemies.

She wanted to stay in her room, to shut out the hateful forces downstairs. But she needed to pay attention. She couldn't shrink away as she used to do.

She put Bobby down in his crib, but he fussed and lifted his arms, so she picked him back up and carried him downstairs, stopping in the doorway of the living room to listen to what was going on.

"You wouldn't understand," Lorna was saying in a patronizing voice. "You people are used to all that drinking and rough behavior."

Gina blinked. Had Lorna really said that? To *Dion*?

"Did you want to elaborate on just what kind of *people* you mean?"

Lorna hemmed and hawed.

"I didn't think so." His answer was quiet, with steel underneath. "Now, I suggest you go back to where you came from and leave the decent folks of Rescue River alone."

Art and Lorna both started talking at once, even as they backed toward the door. Phrases like *back tomor-*

row and *with a warrant* and *custody hearing* and *abducted out of state* flew from their mouths.

Gina stepped out of the kitchen in time to see Dion take a couple of steps toward the couple.

They turned and left, slamming the door.

Gina sank down onto a bench in the entryway. "I'm so sorry about them," she said to Dion. "They're awful."

"I can see that." He leaned against the wall, looking through the window beside the door as a car engine started up outside. "But it's not your fault."

The sound of spitting gravel as the car sped away took some of the weight off Gina's heart. "I caused them to come here and disturb your town."

He shook his head. "That was their decision. We just have to make sure they don't get access to Bobby."

"You knew about his bruises?"

He nodded. "Your in-laws aren't the only ones who have connections. Did you ever get a restraining order against them?"

"I tried. The officer I talked to advised against it." She paused. "They donate a lot to the local police fundraisers."

Dion just shook his head.

Car headlights flashed through the window, and fear clawed at Gina's stomach. Had Art and Lorna come back?

Or had Buck? Now, after the trouble was temporarily over? She braced herself to yell at him, but truthfully, all she wanted was the protection and comfort of his arms.

But it wasn't Buck who came through the door. It was Lacey.

"Hey, guys, are we all set for tomorrow? I heard we're supposed to have record turnout at the festival…" She broke off, seeing Dion. "What's wrong? Where's my brother? What's he done now?"

Gina flinched. Lacey, who knew him so well, had made the automatic assumption that Buck had gotten into trouble.

The truth clicked into place, like pieces from a puzzle. His sister assumed he'd fallen off the wagon. He'd been seen at the bars.

She blew out a breath as her hopes and dreams about him shattered around her. She'd thought he was a great guy, wonderful. She'd even begun to dream of a future together.

But he is *a great guy!*

Yes, he was. Her husband had been, too, when he wasn't high.

But she knew where this road led. Despite the twists and turns, despite the promises and the calm periods, and, yes, the happiness, in the end, what you got was a couple of cops on your doorstep.

Ma'am, are you Gina Patterson? We have some bad news…

Her eyes filled with tears as disappointment congealed into a huge lump in her stomach. When would she ever learn? Why had she let it happen again? She had to understand that love wasn't meant for someone like her, too needy, too hopeful, too ready to look past fatal flaws when they came in the guise of a charming guy, someone like her dad.

She couldn't subject Bobby to that. But look at her—earlier tonight, she'd been ready to jump into Buck's arms, to make a commitment that she and Bobby would be his family.

She was a fool.

Dion and Lacey were talking quietly, glancing over at her. She heard Buck's name. And then they both took their phones out, punching in numbers. Waiting.

No answers.

Gina felt the same discouraged hurt that was written on Lacey's face, the same tight-lipped anger that flattened Dion's mouth.

Buck hadn't cared enough about her and Bobby to stay. The siren call of the bottle had been louder to him than Bobby's cries.

She knew it was an illness, that he couldn't help himself.

But he was helping himself! He was in recovery! You never saw him drunk, not even once!

But if he was well and whole, he'd be here now.

They all waited for another hour, drinking coffee, checking phones, talking a little. Gina took Bobby upstairs and put him to bed, then came back down. Too restless to sit, she cleaned up the little bit of remaining mess in the room she and Buck had been working on.

Before everything had gone straight downhill.

When she came out, Dion was shrugging into his jacket. "I've got to get back on patrol, but I'll make sure you're all locked down," he said. "We'll have frequent surveillance. And, Lacey, you stay here with Gina and Bobby, okay?"

Gina opened her mouth to protest, then closed it again. She didn't want to be an obligation. But Bobby's safety took precedence over her own embarrassment.

"Of course." Lacey moved to stand by Gina. "We'll be fine."

After Dion checked the locks and all the downstairs windows, he drove off with another promise of frequent patrols.

Gina turned to face Lacey. "I'm sorry to have involved you in all this. I know you didn't want us here, and that you've been working extra to avoid being around us, getting all your memories kicked up. As soon as I can find a way to keep Bobby safe, I'll be out of here and you can go back to life as normal."

Lacey took her hand and tugged her into the kitchen. She filled the kettle with water and put it on the stove. And then she came to sit across the table from Gina. "It may not seem like it," she said, "but you and Bobby have been a help for me. Forced me to face some things about myself. To get my thoughts and plans together." Lacey closed her eyes for a minute and then opened them again. "It's been painful. But I understand some things better now. I'm not going to *get* better, not completely."

"Oh, Lacey, with God's help—"

"I know." Lacey held up a hand. "I'm praying all the time, looking for guidance, asking for forgiveness. And I realize I'm never…" She swallowed hard.

The teakettle whistled, and she stood and poured hot water over tea bags, brought two cups over to the table.

"We don't have to talk about this now," Gina said. "It's late. I'm sure you want to go to bed."

"Do *you* want to? This has to have been an awful, scary day. I don't know the whole story, but you must be exhausted."

"I'll never get to sleep. If you can distract me by

talking about something other than my horrible in-laws, go for it. Please."

Lacey dunked her tea bag repeatedly, not looking at Gina. After a moment, she spoke in a low voice. "I realize I'll never be able to love a man and child again. Not like I loved Gerry, problems and all. And maybe that's why…" She broke off, opened her eyes wide as if that would make the tears stay inside. "That's why God made me infertile. Why I can't have another baby."

"Oh, Lacey." Compassion for the other woman flooded Gina's heart, making her own worries recede. "Are you sure?"

"Pretty sure. I just got results from a few more tests."

"And here I've been preoccupied with work and all my problems and never even thought of what you might be going through. I'm sorry. That must be so hard to deal with."

Lacey grabbed a napkin and started shredding it. "It's like I'm frozen inside. Maybe I'm going to stay that way. But when I get over this initial…hurt, I'll figure out what to do with my life as a single person. There's nothing wrong with being single."

Gina nodded. She needed to start remembering those ideas herself. "That's what the Bible says."

"Exactly. And maybe that's His mercy to me, stopping me from even trying to connect with a man and have a family. Because I can't." Her voice was quiet and bleak.

"Oh, Lacey, don't give up if that's your dream. There's all kind of medical advances, there's adoption, there's—"

"I know," Lacey interrupted. "I know, and I know

it's not going to happen for me. But let's get off my issues. I feel like a rat, talking about this when your baby's at risk."

"I *want* to talk—"

"No." Lacey raised her hand like a stop sign. "Please. I can't… Look. I've got a burglar alarm, and Dion made me turn it on. The locks are great—Buck made sure of that. We'll be safe through the night. And things will look better in the morning." She blew out a breath and banged the table with a fist. "I just can't believe that brother of mine. I thought he was making such good progress."

"Me, too." Gina's voice broke a little and she pressed her lips together.

They finished their tea in silence and then hugged good-night and went upstairs.

"Tomorrow is another day," Lacey said.

Gina nodded. *Another day when Bobby's at risk of being taken from me.*

Chapter Thirteen

Buck didn't know how long he drove. It could have been minutes, or it could have been hours. Finally, when he couldn't outrun his pain, he pulled off the highway into a little rural strip mall's parking lot.

It looked familiar, and he figured he'd been here before. In his drinking days, he'd spent a fair amount of time traveling, doing odd jobs, letting whatever town he was staying in cool off.

There was a Chinese restaurant at one end of the strip mall, still open, and he thought about going in to get tea and something to eat. But since the place looked familiar, had he been here before? In what condition? He couldn't face another manager barring the door, another rejection.

The words of Gina's former in-laws rang in his ears.

Drunk all over town.

Once an alcoholic, always an alcoholic.

A danger to Bobby and Gina.

It was that last one that hurt his heart and scared the daylights out of him. Bobby and Gina meant the world to him. He loved them both—he knew that now. He wanted them to be his family.

Only, if he was a danger to them, then no dice. He couldn't put them at risk. If he were the cause of some-one else dying, another woman and child…well, that would be unforgivable. Better to keep running and never come back than to harm them in any way.

He remembered his wife's words in their final bad days. *Terrible husband…don't know why I married you…disaster as a father.* He'd had enough counsel-ing to know that words spoken in anger couldn't fully define who he was. At the same time, if the sources all agreed, then you'd come upon truth.

Even the people at the Senior Towers had con-demned him. His old friends, the people who'd known him since childhood.

And Dion…his disappointed expression when he'd looked back and seen that Buck wasn't coming along. It was a killer.

The truck cab was getting stuffy, and he needed to move. He got out and leaned back against the side of the truck, looking around the small plaza. Yes, he'd been here before, had seen that dollar store, that gas station.

He knew without looking behind him that there was a bar across the street. His back actually tingled, as if the place were pulling him magnetically toward it.

He was far enough from Rescue River that no one was likely to know him there. He had money. He could easily go in and get a drink or a couple. No one from home would find out.

And even if they did, who cared? His reputation was already in the sewer.

Some part of his mind recognized the dangerous direction of these thoughts, and he fumbled in his pocket for his sobriety coin. But he was still wearing work clothes, and he hadn't put the coin in his pocket this morning. Had missed doing it a lot of days lately, in fact. He hadn't been thinking about alcohol.

He'd been thinking about Gina.

He blew out a breath and tried to latch on to what he'd learned in AA. He should call his sponsor. He reached back into the car, and only then did he realize he didn't have his phone on him. He'd left in such a hurry that all he'd grabbed was his wallet. His phone was on his dresser at home, turned off so it wouldn't wake the baby.

Bobby.

He looked heavenward. "I've tried, Lord. I've really tried here."

Of course, there was no answer. God wasn't on speaking terms with a loser like him. God was in agreement with all the good people of Rescue River.

He banged a fist against the top of the car, stupidly. It hurt, and he winced as he climbed back in and started the engine.

Washing his mind clean of any thought, he drove over to the little bar's parking lot, pulled up close, got out.

As he approached the door of the roadhouse, a light flashed next door. Curious, he looked over.

It looked like another bar beside the first one, only where the first bar flashed beer signs, this one had the message—Jesus Saves—along with a blinking cross.

He hadn't seen it the last time he was here. Lacey would have called it tacky.

Was it some kind of joke? But no, above the door

was a small sign: New Country Church. Along the storefront windows were painted slogans and verses: "Sinners Saved by Grace" and "All Welcome" and "Because He Loves You."

Buck shook his head. Some crazy Christian, or a bunch of them, making a church along the highway. Trying to, anyway. He had to admire the effort, however futile. How would a church compete with a roadhouse full of light and color, with pulsing music, laughing people?

Whereas the little church...

Ridiculing himself for being a fool, he walked over to the door. A Thursday night, late—no way would it be open.

He tried the door.

It opened.

"Really, God?" he said out loud. Took one last glance back at the roadhouse. Then walked into the storefront church.

The next morning, Gina was already up and dressed after a restless night, feeding Bobby, when there was a pounding at the door.

Lacey didn't come down, and Gina wasn't sure whether or not she'd left for work. So she answered the door herself, Bobby on her hip.

Standing on the porch was Dion in full uniform, and Daisy, a woman Gina had met briefly at the church lunch.

But Daisy acted official rather than friendly as she shook Gina's hand. "Daisy Hinton. I'm a social worker, here to look into a couple of things for Children and Youth. Is this your son?"

Gina's heart pounded so fast she thought she might pass out. "Yes, this is Bobby," she said and clutched him tighter.

"May I come in?"

"Okay." Gina stepped aside.

"I'll leave you to it, then," Dion said to Daisy. "Call me if you need anything. I won't be far away."

In the hall, Daisy took off her coat. "We had a report of child neglect. I'm just here to ask a few questions."

Gina's knees went limp and she sank down on the hallway bench, clutching Bobby so tightly that he fussed a little. They'd done it. They'd reported her. She was going to lose her son.

He leaned his head against her and clutched her hair in stubby fingers, and she straightened her spine. No way would she let them win.

"You can't take him." Gina stood and gauged the distance to her car, wondering whether she could outrun this woman. No doubt Dion's presence and assurance that he was near was meant to forestall just that.

"No, that's not what this is about. Not at this point. Can we sit down and talk?"

Manners. Show her you're a good mom. Gina gestured the other woman into the kitchen. "I'm sorry— I'm a little upset. Would you like some coffee?" She looked at the high chair where Bobby had eaten his breakfast. Cereal was scattered over the tray and on the floor, and there was a smear of banana on the chair itself. Too late, she noticed that some of it was in his hair as well.

Why, oh, why hadn't she cleaned things up before answering the door?

"No coffee, thanks. Can you tell me a little about

your routines with Bobby, where he stays while you're working, that sort of thing?" As she spoke, Daisy watched Bobby, not staring, just observant.

Gina blew out a breath and tried to speak, but no words came. She reached for her own coffee and lifted it, thinking it would calm her, but her hand shook so badly that she sloshed some out onto the table and banged it back down too hard.

"Hey," Daisy said gently, "it's okay. Take a minute."

The kind tone brought tears to Gina's eyes. Still, she knew she shouldn't trust it. Daisy was just trying to get her to open up.

Never had she felt so alone. Sure, she liked it here in Rescue River; she'd made a start at some friendships. But the reality was that she was new in town, not really a part of things. She was an outsider, and it was her word against two other outsiders, Bobby's grandparents, so much more wealthy and powerful than she was.

The one real friend she'd thought she had was notably missing: Buck. He hadn't come in last night, as far as she knew; he must be out carousing or else sleeping it off. She'd chosen the wrong person to attach herself to, as usual.

The loss of him, of who she'd thought he was, opened up a hole in her chest, so painful she almost gasped with it.

Bobby struggled to get down and she set him on the floor, then immediately wondered if that was the right thing to do. Lacey kept the kitchen clean, but the mat below the high chair held the remains of breakfast.

Daisy watched as Bobby pulled up on the chair and moved toward his race-car push toy. A couple of steps, and he fell forward onto his hands, then moved into his preferred crawling mode. Gina went over to make sure he didn't run into anything, and Daisy stood, too.

"Seems like his development is normal," she said. "What's he doing lately?"

That, she could talk about. "He's pulling up a lot and taking a few steps, like you just saw. He's not steady yet." Remembering how he'd taken his first step when Buck was watching, her throat tightened. She'd felt so close to Buck then. She'd trusted him.

Bobby pushed his car into the hallway and down, banging it into the doorway of the front room. He looked back at Gina. "Da? Da?"

"He wants the dogs," she explained, and then her hand flew to her mouth. "Is that bad, that I let him be around the dogs? They're gentle as lambs, but my former in-laws were upset…" She trailed off, not wanting to incriminate herself.

"Being around animals is actually good for babies. Helps them not get allergies."

"That's what I've read." Relieved, Gina opened the door and Spike and Crater cried to get out of the crates they stayed in at night.

She opened the crates, picked up Bobby and let the dogs go outside. "Sorry," she said over her shoulder. "Mornings, they need to get out and get fed."

"I understand. I'm Troy Hinton's sister, after all. I know rescue dogs, and I know Crater." She gave the large dog a head scratch as he bounded back inside. His tail wagging, Crater soaked up the attention and then ambled toward the kitchen, pausing to lick Bobby a couple of times. Bobby giggled and sat down hard on his diaper-clad behind.

Gina's adrenaline spiked again. Was that bad, letting a dog lick a baby? But it was too late to change it.

Spike tore in, barking, and ran in front of Crater to get to the kitchen. "He thinks he's the alpha," Gina explained. "And Crater lets him think so. Do you mind if I get them their breakfast? They'll settle down after that."

"I have all morning," Daisy said, "and this is actually great, to see your household, and your care of Bobby, in action."

Way to make me self-conscious, Gina thought as she scooped dog food into bowls. But the daily routine relaxed her a little, as did Daisy's apparent friendliness.

Don't get too trusting, she reminded herself.

"So," Daisy asked, "while you're working on the house, where does Bobby stay?"

Gina tensed. "Sometimes we—I mean, I—I gate him in an adjoining room. Sometimes he's in his jumper, although he doesn't like it as much as he liked his jumper in California. He doesn't like to be confined." She looked down at Bobby, only to realize he was crawling rapidly out of the room. "Bobby!" She put down the dog food and hurried over to close the kitchen door. "Exhibit A," she said and pulled out a couple of pots and pans for him to bang.

"Do you have alternative care if you're doing something he shouldn't be around?" Daisy asked, so Gina explained about Angelica.

They walked around the house slowly, with Gina showing Daisy the places Bobby played, his toys, his crib. As they talked about his routines, Gina started to relax. Daisy just didn't seem like an enemy; she seemed fair.

After they'd gotten back to the kitchen, Daisy sat down at the table and pulled out her tablet computer. "I'm going to make a few notes here, if you don't mind," she said. "No guarantees, but I don't see anything that would warrant removing Bobby from the home."

Relief washed over Gina, and she offered a quick prayer of thanks.

Daisy typed rapidly on her tablet, and Gina started wiping down the high chair while Bobby pulled more pans out of the cupboards.

The kitchen door opened. "Hey," Lacey said. "I slept in a little, since I'm off today. Daisy, what's up?"

"Just looking into a few things." Daisy tapped away on her tablet.

"Like, professionally?"

Daisy nodded, still typing.

"The in-laws," Gina explained. "They filed a report against me and she's investigating."

"What?" Lacey stared. "You're the best mother I've ever seen!"

Gina's jaw just about dropped. "I… I have to say I'm surprised, but thanks."

Bobby had picked up a plastic bowl, and now he put it on his head, making them all laugh. Gina hurried to get it off so he wouldn't be scared, but they were still laughing when Art and Lorna flung open the kitchen door. Spike barked fiercely from behind Gina's legs while Crater walked out to stand, alert, in front of the intruders.

"Where's our grandson?" Art demanded.

"I don't recall inviting you into my home," Lacey said.

"We were given to understand a social worker would investigate. Can't you quiet down that dog?"

"I'm a social worker, and I'm investigating," Daisy said calmly, snapping shut the case of her tablet. "Come here, Spike. Good boy." She swept the little dog up onto her lap.

"But...but it looks like you all know each other," Lorna argued. "That's hardly a fair investigation."

"In this town, we all know each other," Lacey said.

"And we like it that way," Daisy added.

Gina swung Bobby to her hip and stepped forward, empowered by the other two women's presence. "And that's why I want to raise Bobby here," she said. "It's a warm, safe environment. A real community. He'll grow up happy here."

Lorna's hands went to her hips. "Once we get a *real* investigator in here, I'm confident that our home will be determined to be a better environment for him."

Gina's stomach dropped. Could they do that? She wouldn't have thought so, but she'd been surprised before at what their money could buy.

She opened her mouth to protest, but Lacey stepped forward and put an arm around Gina. "Since you're uninvited guests and this is my home, I'd like to ask you to leave."

Crater stepped forward with them, emitting a low, almost inaudible growl.

Lorna took a step back, but Art huffed and didn't move.

"I have the police on speed dial," Daisy said pleasantly. "Shall I call them?"

"Come on, Lorna. Once I make a few phone calls, they'll be singing a different tune." The older couple turned and walked out onto the front porch, and Gina followed to make sure they really left.

And there was Buck, trotting up the steps, looking much the worse for wear.

"You again!" Lorna sputtered. "So it's true you live here. We ought to have you arrested. A common drunk in the same house as our grandson!"

Dion's police car cruised slowly by, and Art hurried toward the street to flag him down.

"He's not…" Gina broke off. She didn't know *what* Buck was or wasn't. She couldn't deny the burst of happiness in her chest when she saw him, but she couldn't trust it, either.

"What are *you* still doing here?" He asked the question of Lorna, politely, but with steel in his voice.

"Getting ready to take custody of our grandson, if it's any of your business."

"No, you're not." Gina lifted her chin and glared her in-laws down. "I'm through putting up with your manipulation and…and abuse. Bobby's staying here with me, and that's that."

"Abuse? You've been watching too many trashy TV shows."

"I saw Art hit him." She narrowed her eyes at Lorna. "And you were holding Bobby still so he could do it. Don't even try to deny it."

"I do deny it," her mother-in-law said, her lip curling. "And no one's going to believe you over me."

"I think they will. Wait here. Everyone, please." Buck pushed past Lorna and into the house, giving Bobby a brief chin tickle that made him chortle, looking into Gina's eyes with something inexplicable in his own. Then he disappeared up the stairs.

Hearing some noise on the street, Gina stepped out onto the porch. Dion was walking toward the house with Art, but something off to the side made him stop and stare.

Gina looked, and then she stared, too.

From the direction of the Senior Towers came a parade of white-haired people, some striding, some using walkers and some being pushed in wheelchairs.

They appeared to be headed…here.

When they reached the gate in the front of the guesthouse, the clatter of canes and the scrape of wheels on concrete trailed off. The crowd parted to allow Miss Minnie Falcon to march to the front, her eyes blazing.

Instinctively, Gina went down to meet the older woman, holding Bobby on her hip. "What's going on, Miss Minnie?"

"I'll tell you what's going on." She stopped her walker and drew herself up, pointing a long, bony finger at Art, then at Lorna. "We were having breakfast this morning when word came around that you two are attempting to take little Bobby away from his mother."

"And that they're using things we said as evidence, which is just plain ridiculous," Gramps Camden contributed from the front of the crowd.

Behind Gina, the door of the guesthouse opened. She looked back as Buck hurried out, still in his bedraggled clothes, and then stopped. Crater stood at his side.

"For one thing, that young man," Miss Minnie said, gesturing at Buck, "is a fine, upright person, and any child would be safe with him."

Gina blinked at the vote of confidence.

Ninetysomething Bob Eakin, the Towers librarian,

came forward, adjusting his Proud WWII Veteran baseball cap. "He may have had some troubles in the past, but who here hasn't?" he asked, his voice ringing out loudly. "Who will cast the first stone?"

Realization swept over Gina. She *had* been casting stones, had been believing the worst of Buck even against the evidence of her own senses. "Buck Armstrong is totally safe," she said. "I'd trust him with Bobby's life."

Buck descended the steps slowly, his forehead wrinkled. He opened his mouth as if to speak and then closed it again.

"And what's more," said Lou Ann Miller, who was pushing a wheelchair, "Gina Patterson is a wonderful mother. I've visited her and seen her with Bobby. There's no reason on earth to take that baby away."

Seeing the white heads nodding, Gina's throat tightened. When in her life had people ever stood up for her this way, taken her side?

Art made an abrupt, waving gesture, seeming to discount their words. "The truth will come out, and then we'll get custody."

Buck took an intimidating step forward, and despite his ragged clothes, his straight posture and steely gaze made everyone quiet down.

"The truth *will* come out. I had occasion to take a picture of Bobby right after he and his mother arrived in Rescue River," he said, holding up his smartphone. "And if you'll look where I'm zooming it in, you'll see the fist-size bruise on Bobby's leg." He looked at Gina. "I'm sorry to make your story public, but these people have to be stopped. The reason she left California," he said as he turned to the crowd, "is that these two were beginning to abuse their grandson. This bruise is just the outward mark of some pretty awful behavior."

Art and Lorna sputtered and looked at each other. Before they could formulate a response, Dion's voice boomed out. "Is that true, Gina?"

She cleared her throat so she could say it loud and clear. "They hit him and shook him. I was afraid for his safety."

A murmur came from the Senior Towers crowd, rising in volume. Indignant voices stood out.

"That's an outrage."

"They should be prosecuted."

"We don't tolerate that kind of thing around here."

Lorna's face was red and her eyes shiny with tears. Art looked apoplectic. "You haven't heard the end of this," he snarled at Gina. "It's not against the law to discipline a child."

Dion stepped toward the couple. "I'll be following up with my colleagues in California. Now, I'd suggest you get out of our town and don't come back."

Assenting voices came from the white-haired crowd.

Art and Lorna looked at each other, then turned and hurried down to their car, hunching away from the disapproving stares and comments of those watching. A moment later, their car pulled away.

Gina stood, dazed, as voices and activity swirled around her. Finally, a gentle hand patted her back. "I brought down a chair," Lacey said. "Come on—sit."

So she sank into an Adirondack chair, Bobby in her arms, and Lacey sat down beside her. Spike jumped up, licked her leg and Bobby's, and then squeezed in beside her, panting. And as people came up to express their indignation or sympathy, offering help and comfort, something long empty inside her started to fill. She was cared for. She was protected. She was home.

Chapter Fourteen

It was now or never.

Buck hitched his duffel to his shoulder and walked out into the moonlight. He'd thought about it all day today, had prayed, had found moments between the busy festival activities to discuss things with Lacey.

He'd gotten his life and his sobriety back in Rescue River, had learned he could love again. He'd even, at the storefront church, come to see that he wasn't to blame for Ivana's driving off the road with Mia. But he was still some distance from being fully recovered, and he didn't know if he'd ever get there. The wise pastor he'd talked to last night had reminded him of what the Bible said about being single: it could be a blessed state, allowing a person to devote himself to God's work.

But Buck knew he couldn't get to that point while being in Gina's presence. He'd come to care too much. At the same time, he'd seen how she didn't trust him, might never trust him, because of her own past. The minute Art and Lorna had started lobbing accusations, she'd believed them.

He didn't blame her for that; he did have a past,

and so did she. But he owed it to himself and to God to go somewhere he could make a difference and rebuild a life.

He'd debated over and over whether to talk to her before he left, but in the end, he'd decided that a quick departure would be less painful for both of them. He'd left a letter for her with Lacey, explaining why he was leaving.

He strode out the front door, intent on reaching his truck before he changed his mind.

"Where are you headed?"

The soft voice nearly shattered him. Slowly, he turned toward the source of it: Gina, on the front porch, bathed in moonlight and holding Bobby.

Nod and run! His brain made that very practical suggestion. But his heart and soul tugged him toward the pair, so he dropped his duffel by the rocking chair and walked over.

Gina smiled at him, looking relaxed. She'd always been gorgeous, but from the time she'd arrived in town, tension had tightened her face and haunted her eyes. Now that was gone, and the effect of her genuine, full smile was stunning.

"Wh-what are you doing out here?" he stammered, buying time.

"I finally got him to sleep." She nodded down at Bobby, relaxed in her lap. "But then he woke up again, all fussy. Sometimes fresh air and rocking helps him settle down."

"And you can relax now, knowing you're safe here," he said.

"Exactly. I never felt quite at ease bringing him outside at night. Silly, I know, but I worried that Lorna and Art would jump out and grab him."

"I don't think they'll be bothering you anymore." He believed it, too. He'd followed them when they left downtown with their tails between their legs, had watched them check out of the motel at the edge of town and made sure they drove away. He'd spoken to Dion this afternoon, and the full force of the law had been in effect. Dion was in contact with the police in the couple's hometown and was working on a restraining order here. If a trial came, Gina would have to testify, but after his conversation with Lorna and Art, Dion was certain they'd stay away.

"Thanks for what you did with the picture," she said. "In the confusion afterward, I couldn't find you. I wanted to make sure to tell you, I think that's what turned the tide."

"Only after you spoke up and told the truth." He shrugged. "And Miss Minnie did a pretty good job of telling them off."

"She did, for sure. But it wasn't until the whole town—and Dion—saw that picture that we really got rid of them."

He looked up at the stars, breathed in the smell of night blossoms. Now that he was here with Gina, he might as well talk a little. Besides, it would take a while for his brain to regain control and make him leave. "I should have stayed with you when they first came. I had something to work out, but I shouldn't have left you."

"I was upset you did," she admitted. "Pretty mad at you, in fact, but it all turned out all right." She put a hand on his arm. "You're not perfect, Buck, but you're a good man."

Just like that, he was forgiven. He shifted and knocked a boot against his duffel and it tipped out into the middle of the porch floor. She looked at it, then at him. "You're leaving?"

He looked down at the duffel, then up at her. "Yeah."

"Again, without telling me?" There was hurt in her voice.

"I wrote you a letter. Lacey has it." He looked out across the silvery, quiet street. Should he go into it with her? Would he be able to leave at all if he stayed here, talking with Gina in the moonlight?

Talking with the woman he loved?

The answer, obviously, was no.

He forced himself to stand up. To put his duffel over his shoulder. One step at a time.

Bobby stirred, then opened his eyes and saw Buck. "Buh! Buh!" he said sleepily, holding up his arms.

Buck picked the baby up, a lump in his throat. This inimitable little man had helped him to heal, and Buck hated to leave him. "Hey, it'll be okay," he said, jostling the sleepy boy.

Don't go, then, his heart mourned. *Stay!* "I could…" He started. Then stopped himself. *No. Don't reopen that door.* "See you," he croaked out, handing Bobby back down to Gina. And then he turned and walked slowly down the porch steps, feeling older than any resident of the Senior Towers.

Gina watched him go with a perfect storm of pain and confusion swirling inside her.

Why was he leaving? Because he *didn't* care for her, or because he did?

Because he was honorable or dishonorable?

"Buh," Bobby fussed, reaching toward the vacant spot where Buck had been.

Babies and dogs, they could sense who was a good person. And she could sense it, too. She hadn't trusted herself, and she hadn't made good decisions in the past, but she'd changed. Grown. Toughened up.

If Buck were a danger to her and Bobby, she'd let him go, no question. But she knew with every fiber of her being that he wasn't a danger, that he was, in fact, perfect. Not a perfect, flawless person, maybe—there weren't any of those—but perfect for her.

The sound of his truck starting pierced the darkness, and suddenly she was on her feet, clutching Bobby to her hip. She rushed down the steps to catch him. "Buck! Wait!"

But he was already pulling out in the street, his jaw square, face grim. He didn't look to the right or left, but only forward. And he drove away.

Despair gripped her heart. If he left, would he ever come back? Would he know she cared for him? That she loved him?

She walked out into the street, looking after him. She was wearing flannels and a T-shirt, fuzzy slippers on her feet, a robe billowing around her in the slight breeze. She looked like a fool.

Moonlight illuminated the shops, now dark and empty of people. The streetlamps cast a soft glow. She loved this town. But it wouldn't be home without Buck.

She started speed walking down the middle of the street, Bobby tight against her chest. She passed the

Senior Towers, where one or two windows still glowed, and thought of the parade of helpers that had come to save Bobby today.

She wanted to stay here, to raise Bobby here. But she didn't want to do it alone.

"Buck! Come back! Come back!" She started running down the middle of the main street of Rescue River, the robe flying behind her like wings, chasing those two red taillights. Waving her free arm frantically. "Hey! Come back!"

The lights were getting dimmer. She slowed to a walk, straining her eyes.

She couldn't see the taillights. He was gone. She blew out a sigh that ended in a sob and stood, holding Bobby in the middle of the downtown she loved.

"Come back," she whispered. "Please, come back."

But there was no sound except the rhythmic croaking of a couple of frogs in the creek. No sign of a truck turning around or coming back.

Bobby's fussing rose to a wail, and she felt like wailing, too. She couldn't—she had responsibilities—but she felt like it.

Despair made her shoulders hunch over as she carried her crying son back toward the guesthouse.

He had to do this. He couldn't look back.

He put on his turn signal, being careful even though there was no other traffic on the road. By the book, by rote—that was the only way he could force himself to leave Gina and Bobby behind.

He started to turn and glanced in his rearview mirror. He thought he saw something back in the middle of the downtown.

What was that? Billowy, floating, but half looking like a woman?

Memories slammed into him, of that first night he'd encountered Gina and Bobby on that lonesome road outside town. So much had happened since then. He'd relearned how to feel, how to love. He'd grown to where he could put aside his own past, his temptations, because that was best for the people he cared about. The two people he cared about most in the whole world.

The truck was coasting into the turn and he couldn't help it; he stopped and looked back, squinting through the darkness.

There was definitely someone there.

He'd better go back just to make sure it wasn't someone intent on harming Gina and Bobby. Some lowlife sent by her rich former in-laws to scare or threaten them.

He turned the truck around and headed back, slowly, trying to see.

Clouds skittered over the moon, throwing the street into darkness. He let the truck coast quietly, watching.

And then his heart gave a great thud. It was Gina, walking back, head down.

Walking slowly, as if she'd come out into the middle of the street.

As if she'd been chasing him.

If there were any chance at all…

He pulled the truck crookedly into a diagonal parking place and got out, not even bothering to close the door. "Gina! Wait!"

She turned. Her eyes widened. "Buck?"

"What are you doing out here?" He strode toward her. "I… I just had the thought…" He hesitated. And then realized he needed to put his pride aside and tell the whole truth. "Gina, if you have any interest in pursuing this thing we've got…"

Her free hand went to her mouth, her other arm around Bobby. Slowly, her eyes never leaving his, she nodded her head.

He was in front of them in two seconds, wrapping his arms around her right in the middle of Main Street. "Gina, I promise you, I've changed. I'm a new man, with a new life."

Her eyes got shiny, and as she stared up at him, a tear spilled out.

He reached down and thumbed the dampness from beneath her eye. "I know you've got baggage, and the Lord knows I do, too. But with God's help…"

That gorgeous smile spread across her face, and it was like the sun coming up. "With God's help, we just might make it work."

"You're willing to try?" He was laughing a little and yet his own throat felt tight. "Gina, I love you so much you wouldn't think there was any extra room in my heart, but there is, because I love Bobby just about as much as I love you."

She stepped into his embrace. "I love you, too," she murmured against his chest.

"Buh," Bobby said sleepily. "Buh. Buh."

They both laughed a little and cried a little. "Come on," he said, wrapping an arm around her shoulders. "Let's go home."

Headlights flashed behind them. Buck shepherded Gina and Bobby to the sidewalk.

A marked car pulled up beside them—Dion. "Everything okay here?"

"More than okay," they both said at the same time. Then laughed.

Dion gave them an assessing look. "You left your truck running, buddy, but I'll take care of it. Looks like you've got something better to do."

As they walked back to the guesthouse, Gina clutched his arm, making him stop. "But what about your reputation, the troubles you've had here?"

"I still have some reparations to make," he said, "but this community is forgiving. I figured that out yesterday, when the seniors all defended me." He smiled down at her. "When *you* defended me."

"We take care of each other here," she said.

"And you? You're okay being with someone who'll probably go to AA meetings for the rest of his life?"

"Absolutely," she said, moving closer to his side. "I trust that you've turned a corner."

He had turned a corner, Buck reflected as they climbed the stairs together. And he was sure glad he *hadn't* turned the corner out of Rescue River. Because this was the start of the new life he'd always wanted.

Chapter Fifteen

The last day of the festival was drawing to an end when Gina came downstairs, having just gotten Bobby up from his nap. She carried him toward the front room, pausing to stand in the doorway.

Buck was there, and Gina's breath caught when he smiled at her. They'd spent almost every moment together since Friday night, talking and dreaming.

It was as if the Lord had taken away all her anxiety and stress, and she was able to accept that Buck loved her, that she was lovable and that this was God sanctioned and could work. Feeling his arm around her as they'd walked through town yesterday, taking in the festival, had been bliss.

At the front of the room, Mr. Love and Miss Minnie Falcon sat telling the story of their ancestors and how the house had served as one of the most prominent stations on the Underground Railroad. They'd held visitors rapt both days, and they were thriving on the questions and interest.

Bobby started babbling, so Gina backed away, not wanting to detract from the elders' storytelling. Lacey waved her over to the front desk. "Look at this," she said, showing Gina the computer screen.

"What am I looking at?" Gina leaned closer. "Are those…bookings?"

Lacey nodded, beaming. "Starting this fall, we're booked every weekend up until Christmas." She blew out a breath. "Which means we'll have to work like crazy to get this place done, but with all these reservations, I'm feeling confident enough to cut down to part-time at work so I can help, too."

"That's wonderful!" Impulsively, Gina hugged the woman.

"I owe it to you," Lacey said. "You believed in what could happen before I did, and your work and PR abilities are what tilted the balance."

Gina leaned back on her elbows, looking around. "It does look great. And what's happening in there—" she gestured toward the front room "—that's just serendipity. Good for everyone."

"It's good for me, seeing you and Buck together," Lacey said. "He deserves happiness." She looked wistfully into the room, where her brother was kneeling to help Mr. Love hold up the large door, with its tiny peephole, that had camouflaged the fugitives' hiding place in the basement of the Falcon home.

"Your time will come."

Lacey laughed. "I wouldn't go that far. I'm just glad to see my brother happy. And you. And those two crazy rescue dogs."

"Things are going to get even crazier when my California dogs come home. My friend Haley is driving them when she comes to visit next month." But it would work out. She had faith that everything would work out, now.

As the last group of guests filed out of the front room, Gina slipped inside. Mr. Love waved to the last visitors, and then he leaned over and said something to Miss Minnie.

"Why, Mr. Love," Miss Minnie said, her cheeks pink. "I hardly think that's appropriate at our age."

"I've buried two wives, and I'm not looking for another," he said calmly. "But there's nothing wrong with companionship. And a man is never too old to appreciate a beautiful woman." He patted Miss Minnie's hand.

"Except I know you can't half see," she complained, but a smile lit up her deeply lined face.

Mr. Love turned to Buck and Gina. "Miss Minnie and I, we've been talking, and she helped me look through some of the heirlooms we had out at the old farm. I found something pretty special, as this young man knows."

Gina looked at Buck and was alarmed to notice perspiration on his upper lip and a pale cast to his face.

"I've had an offer for this particular item," Mr. Love continued, "that I'm tempted to accept, but only if the buyer can put it to good use." He pulled out an old velvet box, just a couple of inches square. "The young couple who were going to use this more than one hundred and fifty years ago never got their happy ending. This has been in a cubbyhole in the Old Rose Barn ever since, waiting for the right time to be found."

"We can't help them," Miss Minnie said, "but maybe we can help to create some happiness right here and now."

"I'm hoping." Buck took the box from Mr. Love and

walked over to Gina, drawing her toward the high-backed love seat. "Sit down a minute."

Gina's heart rate kicked up a notch, and she did as he asked.

The two elders watched, smiling, obviously in on some secret. Lacey was leaning on the doorjamb, smiling as well.

Buck knelt in front of her. "Gina," he said, "you know how I feel about you, and I want to ask you, will you marry me?"

"What?" Her voice rose to a squeal.

He opened the box, and there was a Victorian-style gold ring, its central diamond surrounded by small diamonds that formed the shape of a cross.

Gina's breath caught. "Minerva and Abraham's ring?"

Buck nodded. "You haven't answered my question." His hands shook a little, holding the ring box.

Joy rang through her like bells. "Of course! Yes, yes, yes!" She tugged him to the seat beside her.

"There's only one condition," Mr. Love said, "on my selling Buck that ring."

"What is it?" Gina asked.

"Anything," Buck said at the same time, so fervently that he drew a laugh from Lacey, still standing in the doorway.

"That the person wearing it has to stay right here in Rescue River." Mr. Love flashed a smile. "We don't want you going anywhere."

"Why would anyone want to live anywhere else?" Miss Minnie glanced over at Mr. Love, and a dimple appeared in her cheek.

Tears sprang to Gina's eyes. "I'll stay," she said,

and then she couldn't get out any more words. She just nestled closer to her future husband's side.

The sound of barking came from the next room, where Spike and Crater had been confined to their crates, safely out of the way of the festival's guests. Lacey disappeared, then returned a minute later with the dogs bounding in beside her, in hot pursuit of Mr. Whiskers. Mrs. Whiskers, who'd been weaving through Buck's and Gina's feet, jumped up on one arm of the love seat, and Mr. Whiskers leaped onto the other arm. Both glared indignantly down at the raucous canines.

Buck chuckled, then touched Gina's chin, turning her face toward him for a kiss. And, safe in his arms, Gina knew that she and Bobby had found the home and family she'd always craved.

* * * * *

Brenda Minton lives in the Ozarks with her husband, children, cats, dogs and strays. She is a pastor's wife, Sunday-school teacher, coffee addict and sleep deprived. Not in that order. Her dream to be an author for Harlequin started somewhere in the pages of a romance novel about a young American woman stranded in a Spanish castle. Her wish came true, and twenty-plus books later, she is an author hoping to inspire young girls to dream.

Books by Brenda Minton

Love Inspired

Mercy Ranch

Reunited with the Rancher
The Rancher's Christmas Match

Bluebonnet Springs

Second Chance Rancher
The Rancher's Christmas Bride
The Rancher's Secret Child

Martin's Crossing

A Rancher for Christmas
The Rancher Takes a Bride
The Rancher's Second Chance
The Rancher's First Love
Her Rancher Bodyguard
Her Guardian Rancher

Visit the Author Profile page at Harlequin.com for more titles.

HER GUARDIAN RANCHER

Brenda Minton

To the police officers and the men and women of the armed forces—because their constant sacrifice keeps our communities and our nation safe. May we show them respect and continue to uplift them in our prayers.

Now faith is the substance of things hoped for, the evidence of things not seen.

—*Hebrews* 11:1

Chapter One

The moonless sky was dark and heavy with clouds and a promise of rain that would be welcome, since most of November had been dry and December promised more of the same. Daron McKay eased his truck down the driveway of the Wilder Ranch, away from Boone Wilder's RV, where he frequently crashed on nights like this. Nights when sleep was as distant as Afghanistan, but the memories were close. Too close.

On nights like this he took a drive rather than pace restlessly. A year ago he would have woken Boone and the two of them would have talked. But Boone had recently married Kayla Stanford and the happy couple had built a house on the opposite side of the Wilder property.

Daron had his own place, a small ranch a few miles outside of Martin's Crossing. He rarely stayed there. The house was too big. The space too open. He preferred the close confines of the camper. Not that he wanted to admit it, but he liked Boone's dog. He also didn't mind Boone's large and raucous family.

His own family was a little more restrained and not

as large. And his appearance sometimes bothered his mom. He didn't shave often enough. He preferred jeans and boots to a suit. His dad, an attorney in Austin, wanted his son to join the family law firm rather than run the protection business he'd started with friends Boone Wilder and Lucy Palermo. His mom wanted him to attend functions at the club and find a nice girl to marry. His sister, Janette, was busy being exactly the person her parents wanted her to be. She was pretty, socially correct and finishing college.

Daron was still coming to terms with his tour of duty in Afghanistan, with the knowledge that he could lead friends into an ambush.

One of those friends had died. Andy Shaw had only been in Afghanistan a few months when Daron and Boone followed an Afghan kid who claimed his sister was in trouble. The sister. Daron pulled onto the highway, gripping the steering wheel, getting control of the memories. He'd thought he loved her, so when her brother came to him and said their family needed the help of the American soldiers, Daron had agreed to go.

He'd been young and stupid, and because of him, Andy had died. At thirty he didn't find it any easier to deal with than when he was twenty-six.

The truck tires hummed on the damp pavement. He headed his truck in the direction of Braswell, a small town in the heart of Texas Hill Country and just a short distance from Martin's Crossing. He cranked some country music on his stereo and rolled down the truck windows to let cool, damp air whip through the cab of the truck.

A few miles outside Braswell he turned right on a paved county road. He slowed as he neared the older farmhouse that sat just a hundred feet off the road. Only one light burned in the single-story home, the same light that was typically on when he made his midnight drives.

And he made this trip often. When he couldn't sleep. When he felt the need to just meander by and make sure everything looked okay. It always did.

But not tonight. Tonight a truck was pulled off the road on the opposite side as the farmhouse. The parking lights were on. There was no one inside. He cruised on by, resisting the urge to slam on the brakes. A few hundred feet past the house, he turned his truck, dimmed his headlights and headed back, pulling in behind the other truck and reaching in his glove compartment for his sidearm. Unfortunately it was locked in the gun cabinet at the trailer.

With quiet steps he headed toward the house, staying close to the fence, in the dark and the shadows. He kept an eye on the house, scanning the area for whoever it was who owned the abandoned truck. If it hadn't been idling, he might have thought it was just broken down and that the driver had decided to walk. But the engine running meant the driver planned to return fairly soon.

He was near the back of the house when he heard the front door slam open. He moved in close to the side of the house and rounded the corner and then he stopped. The front porch light was on and caught in its glare was a too-thin Pete Shaw with a ball bat swinging in his direction. The younger brother of Andy Shaw jumped back quick, avoiding the aim of the woman advancing on him.

"Get out. And don't come back. Next time I'll have

more for you than this baseball bat, Pete. Stay away from my house. Stay away from my family. We don't have anything."

Pete lunged at her, but she swung, hitting his arm with the bat. He let out a scream. "You broke my arm!"

"I don't think so. But next time I might." She raised the bat again. She might be barely five feet tall, but she packed quite a punch. Daron resisted the urge to laugh. Instead he took a few quiet steps forward, in case she needed him.

"I'm not going to let you hit me, Emma."

"You're not coming back inside this house." Emma Shaw swung again and Pete fell back a pace, still holding his injured left arm.

It looked as if he planned to leave. Daron remained in the shadows, watching, waiting and hoping Pete would walk away. When the other man lunged, Daron stepped out of the shadows. "Pete, I think you ought to listen to her."

Pete turned, still holding his left arm, still looking kind of wild-eyed. He was thin. His hair was scraggly. Meth. It was easy to spot an addict. The jerk of the chin. The jumpiness. The sores. A person couldn't put poison in his body and expect it to be good for him.

"This isn't your fight, Daron." Pete held up his right hand, showing he still had half a brain. "But I'll make it your fight."

Or maybe he didn't have half a brain. Andy's younger brother took a few steps in Daron's direction.

"Really, Pete?" Daron remained where he stood. "Get in your truck and get out of here. Get in a program and get some help."

"I don't need help. I just need the money. I know she's got it hid somewhere."

"I don't have money, Pete. I don't have anything but bills. You blew through the money Andy left. You bought that truck and you bought drugs."

"None of us were at the wedding," Pete countered. "I doubt you were even married to my brother."

"Go away, Pete. Before I call the police." Emma advanced on the other man, as if she were taller than her five-foot-nothing height. Daron stepped forward, coming between her and danger.

"Pete, you should go." Daron said it calmly, glancing back at the woman who didn't appear to be in the mood to appreciate his interference. He wasn't surprised. For three years she'd been telling him to go back to his life, that they weren't his responsibility.

Pete backed away, his eyes wild as he looked from one to the other of them. "Yeah, I'm leaving. But I'll be back. I want what belongs to my family."

"Go. Away," Daron repeated.

He followed the other man to the road and watched him get in his truck and speed off into the night. When he returned to the house, Emma was gone and the front porch light was off. He grinned a little at her bravado and knocked on the door anyway.

He didn't mind that she kept up walls with him on the outside. It certainly hadn't kept him from watching over them. Them meaning Emma, her aging grandfather and the little girl, Jamie. Even with their limited contact he was starting to think of her as a friend.

A friend who didn't mind closing the door in his face. He grinned as he lifted his hand to knock a second time.

* * *

Emma leaned against the door, needing the firm wood panel to hold her up. Her legs still shook with fear and adrenaline. She'd barely gotten to sleep when she heard a window opening, the creaking sound alerting the dog that slept on the foot of her bed. Fortunately her grandfather and Jamie had slept through the racket.

Racket? No, not really that drastic. She'd pounced on Pete as he climbed through the window. He'd pushed back, hitting her into the china cabinet, but she'd steadied it and herself, managing to get a good grip on the baseball bat she'd carried from her room.

Pete wasn't healthy and it had been easy to back him out of the house and take control. Or at least it had felt like she was in charge. She'd had it handled.

The last thing she needed was Daron McKay in her home and in her business. But there he'd been, standing in the shadows like some avenging superhero, ready to rescue her.

He'd been playing the role of guardian since he got home from Afghanistan. He'd been at the hospital when she had Jamie. He'd brought gifts and food in the years since her daughter's birth.

No matter what she said or did, she couldn't convince him she didn't need his help. They were making it. She, Jamie and Granddad. They'd always made it and they would continue to do so.

Yes, it would have been nice to have Andy's help. But Andy was gone. No use crying over what couldn't be changed.

The door behind her vibrated with a pounding fist knocking just about where her shoulders touched the wood. She jumped back, letting out an unfortunate squeal.

"I know you're there," Daron called out, his voice muffled through the thick wood.

She didn't move, didn't speak. Surely he would take the hint and go away.

"I want to check and make sure everything is okay. And I'm not going anywhere until we know Pete isn't coming back."

Pete might return. She should have thought of that. Of course he would return. Usually he came during the day, demanding money she didn't have. Andy had divorced her just prior to deploying and he'd made Pete his one and only beneficiary.

She'd called him after he deployed, to tell him he was going to be a dad. He'd made promises about the two of them and she'd told him they could talk when he got home, not when he was thousands of miles away and she was still hurt by his betrayal and him walking away from their marriage. Slowly, hesitantly, she touched the lock, took a deep breath and opened the door. Her gaze slid up, her eyes locking with the gray eyes of the man standing on her front porch. Drat, but the man made her feel safe. As much as he annoyed her. As much as she wanted him to go away.

"Well, you opened the door." His voice was low and rumbled, sliding over her, causing goose bumps to go up her arms. She hugged herself tight, her hand touching a spot on her opposite arm and feeling a sticky dampness.

"Ouch." She glanced down. Her hand came away stained with blood.

"You're hurt. Did he do that?"

"I backed into the china cabinet. But I'm fine."

"We need to call 911 and let them look for him." He took her by the uninjured arm and started through the house with her, guiding her as if he knew the way.

"We don't need to call the police. He won't be back tonight. He's just a stupid, messed-up kid."

"A stupid, messed-up kid who's on drugs and breaking into homes. Let me look at your arm."

"I'm fine. You can go." Bravado didn't work when her voice shook, from fear, from aftershock.

"Let me take a look anyway. Even though we both know you're fine. Is this the first time he's broken in?"

She nodded as he led her into the kitchen. Without warning, his hands went to her waist and he lifted, setting her on the counter.

"Would you stop manhandling me?"

He grinned at that, as if he thought she didn't truly mean it, and he went about, rummaging through cabinets until he found salve and bandages. He wet a rag under the sink and returned. Without looking at her he took hold of her and wiped at the gash on her arm. She flinched and he held her steady, smiling a little but still not looking at her.

That gave her time to study his downturned face, his eyelashes, the whiskers on his cheeks, the column of his throat.

She swallowed and tried to pull away. He glanced up then, his dark gray eyes studying her face so intently she felt a surge of heat in her already-flushed cheeks.

"How did you do this?" he asked as he dried the cut and then applied salve.

"I bumped into the china cabinet. Maybe I hit a rough edge."

"Maybe," he said. He opened the bandage and placed it over the wound. "It's pretty deep."

"I've had worse."

His hand slid from her arm and he moved, putting distance between them. His scent—country air, pine and something Oriental—drifted away as he backed against the opposite counter. She inhaled. Oh, and sandalwood.

No, she didn't want to notice his scent. Or his eyes. She didn't have time to notice him, to notice that she was female, still young and still willing to be attracted to a man like him.

"So this wasn't the first time he's been here?" he asked, his gaze intent, serious.

"No, it wasn't. He typically comes during the day. He likes to show up as I'm leaving Duke's." She'd started waitressing at Duke's No Bar and Grill last year, just to make ends meet. Between her tips and her grandfather's Social Security, they were making it.

Someday she'd finish her degree. She was taking classes online, and next year she would be finished and licensed to teach. Until then she did what she could. Breezy Martin, Jake Martin's wife, watched Jamie the few hours a day that she worked. She did her best to keep her daughter in an environment with few other children. It was important that Jamie stay healthy.

"You could get a restraining order," he suggested, still leaning against the counter. His arms were crossed over his chest.

"I don't want to do that. He was Andy's brother. Our marriage ended, but that doesn't mean I'm angry or that I want to cause problems."

"He's causing you problems." He brushed a hand

through his unruly hair, the light brown color streaked with blond from the sun.

"He's causing himself problems. He's an addict. My getting a restraining order won't cure him of that. His parents would use it against me. I took one son and I'd be taking the other."

"Took their son? You didn't take Andy." He glanced away. "I did."

"He volunteered for service in Afghanistan because he wanted to get away from me. If not for our divorce, he would still be here."

He opened his mouth to speak but then shook his head. "You're wrong."

She shrugged, unsure of what to say to that. She guessed she knew she was wrong. But right or wrong didn't change anything. Andy was gone. Jamie would never know her father. A family had lost their son.

"Neither of us can go back," she finally said. Because she thought they both wrestled with the past. Why else had he been driving by at this hour?

"No," he agreed. "We can't."

They stood there for several long minutes, the only sound the ticking of the clock and the hum of the refrigerator. He cleared his throat and moved away from the counter.

"I have to go. Will you be okay?"

"Of course I'll be okay."

Wasn't she always?

As she walked with him to the front door, she thought about the ten-year-old girl who had lost both parents and had been sent to live with a grandfather she barely knew. On the drive to Houston he'd repeatedly glanced at her and asked if she was okay. Each time she'd nodded to assure him. But each time he refocused on the road she would shut her eyes tight to hide the tears.

After a while she had been okay. They'd moved from Houston to this house. She'd learned to be a farm girl from Braswell, wearing whatever her grandfather thought she needed. Usually jeans, scruffy farm boots and T-shirts.

She could look back now and realize that in time she'd been able to deal and she'd been happy.

Life wasn't perfect. God hadn't promised perfection. He'd promised to be with her, to give her strength and peace. She knew there were mountains looming in her near future. She also knew they would get through the tough times. They would survive.

She had to. There was no choice.

Daron stood on the front porch, tall and powerful, a man most women would want to lean on. Just moments ago, she'd been that woman, leaning into his strong arms.

Momentary weakness, she assured herself. For that very reason she managed an easy smile and thanked him for his help. The dismissal seemed to take him by surprise, but he recovered. He touched two fingers to his brow in a relaxed salute, stepped down from the porch and headed down the road to his truck. She watched him leave, then stepped back inside and locked the door.

This time when she leaned against it, closing her eyes as a wave of exhaustion rolled over her, she knew he wouldn't be coming back.

Chapter Two

The next few days were uneventful and Emma appreciated the calm that followed Pete's midnight visit. Each morning she fed the cattle with her granddad, then headed to Martin's Crossing to Duke's No Bar and Grill to work the lunch shift as a waitress. Lately she'd managed a few extra shifts, which would come in handy with Christmas just around the corner.

She'd only known the Martin family by name before taking the job at Duke's. The last six months or so, she'd come to appreciate their family. Not only had Duke Martin given her a job, inexperienced as she was, but his sister-in-law, Breezy, had offered to watch Jamie.

Lily, Duke's daughter, swept into the restaurant on Wednesday afternoon, a big smile on her young face. Emma responded with a smile and a wave. The teenager followed Emma to the waitress station.

"Breezy has Jamie across the street at my mom's shop. She said she'll bring her over in a minute. She thinks maybe Jamie isn't feeling good."

Emma's heart sped up a little at that information.

They'd been blessed this winter. So far they'd avoided major viruses. That was the goal. And a good reason for having Jamie at Breezy's, with fewer children around to spread germs. The twin nieces that Jake had gained custody of after his own twin sister's death were now in preschool. Jake and Breezy had a one-year-old who stayed at home with Breezy.

She recovered, fighting off the moment of panic. "Is she running a fever?"

"Breezy said she isn't. Mom thought she felt warm."

"I'll check her when we get home." She maintained a smile, to make herself and Lily feel better.

Nedine, Ned for short, Duke's head waitress and right-hand woman, walked out of the kitchen carrying a tray. The older woman, tall and big-boned, had once explained she'd been named for her dad, Ned. He'd wanted a son but he'd been happy with a daughter.

The older waitress smiled at Duke's daughter and winked at Emma. "Lily, your daddy said to put you to work when you got here after school. I think you're going to be my bus girl this evening."

Lily saluted. "Will do, Ned. Hey, did the twin foals do okay over the weekend?"

Ned's face split open like sunshine. "They sure did. Prettiest little palominos I ever did see. You'll have to come out and take a look."

"I will!" Then Lily returned her full attention to Emma. "Did my mom tell you about the potluck at our church this Sunday?"

The girl reached for the big jug of ketchup and started refilling bottles alongside Emma. Before Emma could answer her, Duke entered the restaurant. He caught sight of his daughter and headed their way.

"Hair in a ponytail, please," Duke said as he gave her a hug.

Lily responded by digging in her pocket and pulling out a hair band. She pulled her dark hair back in a messy bun and kept working.

"She did tell me," Emma answered the girl's question.

"Are you going to be there? I know you go to church in Braswell, but, you know…"

Emma nodded. "Yes, I know. You have someone you want me to meet."

"Kind of," Lily admitted. "He's nice. He works for my dad."

"I'm sure he's nice, but I really don't have time for dating." Emma blinked away a flash of an image. No! She would not think of Daron McKay and dating in the same thought. She wouldn't allow his image to startle her that way, coming unbidden to her mind, all concerned and caring the way he'd been last Sunday night. At least she knew it wasn't Daron who Lily had in mind for her. He didn't work for Duke.

"Are you okay?" Lily's shoulder bumped Emma's, nearly making her drop the ketchup bottle she held. "Oops, sorry. I didn't mean to scare you."

"You didn't scare me. And I'm fine." She pulled her phone out of her pocket. "It's a phone call, that's all."

Saved by the bell. She glanced at the caller ID and grimaced. An unknown caller. She didn't need that. It most likely meant it was Pete or a bill collector or something equally unpleasant. But when the caller left a message she lifted the phone to her ear to listen.

"Oh no," she whispered as she listened.

Lily stood next to her, eyes wide, ketchup bottle

held close to her mouth. Emma took the ketchup bottle from the girl and set it on the counter before reaching into her apron for a pencil. She jotted down notes and ended the call.

"Is everything okay?" Lily, still wide-eyed, asked.

Duke came around the corner. "Lily, why don't you give Emma room to breathe? There are a couple of tables you can clear."

Lily moved away, reluctant, with slow steps and a few backward glances. Emma managed a quick smile for the girl before glancing up at her boss. He towered over her at six foot six. With his shaved head and his goatee, he used to intimidate her. Now she knew him to be a gentle soul.

"My grandfather seems to be in custody at the Braswell Police Station," she explained, still numb.

"I didn't know Braswell had a jail." Duke took the towel she was wringing the life out of and tossed it on the counter. "Is he okay?"

"Yes, I guess. He ran someone off the road. I guess I'll know more when I get there."

"Do you want me to give you a ride or find someone to drive you?" His deep voice rumbled, reassuring her.

"No, I'm good."

"If you're sure. But call us later and let us know that you're okay."

Emma nodded, still in shock, as she headed out the diner.

The city police station of Braswell, Texas, was located on Main Street, between the Clip and Curl Salon and the Texas Hill Country Flea Palace, a fancy name for a store that sold everything from secondhand can-ning jars to old books. Emma parked her old truck in front of the police station and reached over to unlatch the car seat where her daughter, Jamie, dozed, thumb in mouth and blond curls tousled. Her eyes, blue and wide, opened as Emma worked the latch. She grinned around her thumb.

"Hey, kiddo, time to get up. We have to bust Grand-dad out of this place."

Jamie giggled, as if she understood. But at three, Jamie understood things like puppies, kittens and new-born calves. She didn't understand that her favorite person, other than her mommy, was getting older and maybe a little senile. She also didn't understand bills, the leaking roof or the desperate need to buy hay for winter, which was nipping at their heels in a big way.

The farm her grandfather had bought and moved them to when she'd lost her parents wasn't a big spread, not by Texas standards. The fifty acres had provided for them, though, supplementing her grandfather's small retirement. It had been a decent living until her grandfather's pension had gotten cut, and then they'd had medical bills after Jamie's birth. Emma had been forced to sell off most of her horses, all but a dozen head of cattle and get a part-time job. The economy and the drought had dealt them a blow the past few years.

All things work together for good, she kept telling herself. All things, even the bad, the difficult, the trou-bling.

Unbuckled, Jamie reached for Emma and wrapped sweet little arms around her neck. Emma grabbed her purse and reached to open the door of the truck. It was already open, though. Daron McKay was leaning against it, December wind blowing his unruly hair. His dark gray eyes zeroed in on Jamie and he unleashed one of those trademark smiles that might charm a woman, any woman besides Emma. Any woman who had time for romance. If her favorite top wasn't in the rag pile, stained with throw-up, and if her daily beauty routine consisted of more than a ponytail holder and sunscreen, a woman might give Daron a second look.

But a woman going to bail her grandfather out of the city jail didn't have time for urban cowboys in expensive boots, driving expensive Ford trucks and wearing... Oh goodness, what was he wearing? It smelled like the cologne counter at the mall, something spicy and Oriental and outdoorsy, all at the same time. The kind of scent guaranteed to make a woman want to drop in and stay awhile.

No! She'd done this once before. She'd believed Andy, that he would help her, fix her life, make things all better. And he didn't. When things had gotten tough, he bailed. He hadn't been prepared for reality.

"Go away, Daron." Emma pushed past him with her daughter, because she was decidedly not the woman who wanted to lean into him and stay awhile. She didn't have time for anything other than reality.

Daron McKay was a nuisance and he'd been a nuisance for three years, since he got back from Afghanistan. He'd involved himself in her life because he'd come home and Andy hadn't. But Andy had left her long before then and Daron just didn't understand.

Andy had left her here alone.

Alone, broke and pregnant. Of the three she could handle alone. Other than with her granddad, Art Lewis, she'd been that way most of her life. Her parents had died in a car accident when she was ten. Art had been the only one willing to take her on.

Now, eighteen years later, the tables had turned, and she was taking care of her granddad.

"I can't go away." Daron followed her, reaching his arms to her daughter. Jamie, not knowing any better, went straight to him. He'd been hanging around for three years. Her daughter thought he was the best thing ever.

"Why can't you just go away?" she asked, knowing she shouldn't. "And how did you know?"

The wind, strong and from the north, whipped at her hair, blowing it across her face. She pushed it back with her hand and gave the man next to her, who towered over her by nearly a foot, an angry glare. Not because he was a bad person, but because he was always there. Always catching her at her worst, when she felt weak and vulnerable. He'd been in the waiting room the night Jamie was born. He'd been there when Jamie had the croup. He was always there. Like he thought they needed him.

He'd brought groceries, bought Christmas presents, provided hay for their cattle. He was kind. Or guilty. Maybe he was both. She didn't know and she really didn't have the time or energy to figure him out.

She did know he wasn't the least bit fazed by her attempt to push him away. "I heard the call on the scanner. And I can't go because I'm carrying Jamie. And she happens to think I'm amazing."

He smiled down at her and added a wink that made her roll her eyes.

"That makes two of you," Emma quipped, barely hiding a smile as she averted her gaze from the too-sure-of-himself rancher with his Texas drawl, sun-browned skin and sandy curls.

He laughed off the comment. "Yep, me and Jamie, we think I'm pretty amazing."

"It's time for you to cut the strings and realize I don't need you, Daron. I'm not your problem. You don't owe us anything. We're taking care of ourselves."

His smile faded and he glanced away, his gray eyes looking a lot like the clouds rolling over the horizon. "I'm here. Like it or not."

"I think you're upset that *you're* here instead of Andy. You are upset every time you take a breath. You have to let it go."

"He was a friend."

She looked at Jamie, then shook her head. "I'm not doing this again. We can't go back. I can't help you soothe your guilt. You have to let go."

"Your granddad ran a tractor off the road. He was fiddling with his stereo. He said they need to play more Merle and less of this stuff they call country these days. All of the good ones are dying off, he said."

Emma brushed a hand across her cheek, not wanting to think about the good ones dying off or songs about who would take their place. "I'll take care of it."

"There's damage to the tractor."

"Okay, thank you. You can go."

Daron remained next to her, matching his giant steps to her smaller ones. "Your granddad let his insurance lapse. It hasn't been paid in two months."

Emma sighed. "Could this get any better?"

It would get better, though. She knew in time they'd work through this. Jamie would be healthy and Emma would be able to work full-time. Things always got better. Sometimes they just had to get worse first.

"They mentioned having him evaluated." Daron reached to open the door for her. "They think it's time he gave up his license."

"Of course they do. But he's only eighty and he's usually careful." She held her arms out to her daughter, but Jamie ignored her, preferring instead to rest her head on Daron's shoulder. "We have to go now, sweetie."

"I'll go in with you." He glanced down at the child in his arms, her blond curls framing her face. Put a hand to her cheek as if he knew the routine. "Is she sick?"

Emma briefly closed her eyes, because for a brief moment she'd forgotten what Lily told her. "She has a virus."

And then she took her daughter and walked through the open door, leaving him alone on the sidewalk. When she got to the desk where an officer was doing paperwork, Daron was still behind her.

"Can I help you?" The officer, his name tag told her his name was Benjamin Jacobs, looked past her to Daron.

"I'm Emma Shaw. My grandfather, Art Lewis…"

The officer grinned and held up a hand. "We know Art. He's in the back entertaining the guys with stories of the trouble he got into when he was overseas during the Korean War. We'll get him processed and you can take him home."

He hit the intercom and told someone in the back that Art's granddaughter was there to get him.

"Do you have the name of the person he hit? I'm

under the impression there are damages and Art's insurance has lapsed?"

"It's taken care of." The officer went on with his paperwork.

"It can't be taken care of. He doesn't have insurance. If you'll give me the name, I'll handle it. Or will we see them in court?"

"They didn't press charges."

She spun around to face Daron. He had taken a step back, but he was still close enough to poke a finger into his chest. "I said stop."

"Stop what?"

"How many times have I told you—you don't have to rescue us. We're fine."

He held both hands up in surrender. "I know you are."

A door behind them opened and closed with a click. She glanced back and saw her grandfather with the police chief. He'd lost weight and his overalls hung a little loose. He was wearing slippers instead of his farm boots. She drew in a breath, aching because he was getting older. Why had she thought he'd be with her forever, always picking up the pieces and keeping her safe?

"Granddad, what in the world?" She hiked her daughter up on her hip and closed the distance between herself and her grandfather. "Are you okay?"

He scratched the gray whiskers on his chin. "Well, I reckon I am. What are you here for?"

"I came to get you. They said you were in a wreck."

He tickled Jamie and smiled at Emma. "Oh, I wasn't in a wreck. It was a misunderstanding. I'm sorry for worrying you, kiddo."

"I'm…" She swallowed the argument because it would do no good. And she pushed aside her fear for her aging grandfather. "I'm sure it will be okay."

Jamie's arms tightened around her neck as a violent episode of coughing racked her small body. Emma buried her face in her daughter's hair, close to her ear, and whispered for her to take a slow breath. When she looked up, Daron watched with questions in his thick-lashed eyes. He towered over her, all broad-shouldered and strong, ready to help.

There were days when she wanted to give in and let him be the hero he wanted to be.

Not today. Today she wanted to go home, help her child breathe a little easier and make sure her grandfather was okay.

"Is she okay?" Daron asked as she shifted Jamie to her other hip and pulled the hood of her jacket over her head.

"She's fine. And thank you. For being here."

"Emma, if you need anything…"

"I know."

She took her grandfather by the arm and walked him out of the police station. Daron didn't follow this time. She resisted the temptation to glance back, to see if he stood in the doorway watching.

Daron told himself to let it go. He knew that Emma was holding on to her pride by a thread that was coming unraveled fast. But he couldn't let it go. He couldn't watch her struggle to keep afloat knowing that he was partly responsible for her struggle.

Emma didn't want him in her life. He wanted to say he wasn't interested in being in her life. But he guessed if he was going to be honest, he'd admit that he was attached to her, to Art and to Jamie.

There was something about their little family. They didn't have much. He'd noticed a tarp on the roof, meaning it probably leaked. Her truck tires were worn slick. They were content with that little farmhouse, the small plot of ground they owned and the few head of cattle they ran.

Content. He sighed. It had been a long time since he knew the meaning of the word.

From the window of the police station he watched as they all climbed into her truck. She leaned to buckle Jamie into the car seat. Art said something and she shook her head, but then smiled and touched his weathered cheek.

The cop said something to him about rain. Daron nodded and headed out the door. The cop had been right. The rain was coming down in sheets. He hunkered into his jacket as he hurried to his truck. Once inside he cranked the heat and turned the wipers on high. It was cold for December in Texas Hill Country.

He headed in the direction of Martin's Crossing, and the strip mall where he and his friends Lucy Palermo and Boone Wilder had their office. Since returning from Afghanistan the three had opened a bodyguard business. It kept them busy, supplying protection and security for politicians, businessmen and anyone else who might need and be able to afford their services.

Things had changed since Boone married Kayla Stanford, half sister of the Martins of Martin's Crossing. Boone was building a house. Daron was still crashing at the RV on the Wilder ranch.

Lucy remained the same. She was still a loner. She

was still hiding things that might be buried deep, keeping her tied up in the past.

Daron was still reliving that moment when he saw his friend Andy die, caught in the blast of an IED. He remembered the face of the kid who had led them all, knowingly or unknowingly, into danger.

Just a week before that explosion, Andy had learned that Emma was pregnant. He'd shown all the guys the ultrasound picture of the baby, the tiny dot he'd claimed would be his son. Andy had divorced Emma, not realizing she was pregnant. And she'd let him go, he said, because she wouldn't force a guy to stay in her life.

Daron had made a promise to his dying friend that he'd check on Emma, make sure she and the baby were okay.

Daron had kept that promise. But after more than three years, maybe it was time to walk away.

Chapter Three

Emma came in from the barn on Thursday morning to find her granddad in the kitchen making up a cold remedy concoction that smelled a little bit like mint and a whole lot like something he'd cleaned out of the corral. He held the cup up, his grin a little lopsided beneath his shaggy mustache. His overalls, loose over an old cotton T-shirt, reminded her he'd lost weight recently. But he was still her granddad, her hero. She wanted him to live forever.

From the bedroom she could hear Jamie coughing. "I'm going to call the doctor."

Art pushed the cup into her hand. "Give her a sip of this. It'll help that cough."

She held the brew to her nose. "Art, what in the world is in this?"

"Mint to clear up her cough, some spices from the cabinet and a little cayenne."

"We can't give her this. She'll choke."

His mustache twitched. "It always worked for you."

"No, it didn't. I poured it out and then made a face so you would think it worked."

"And here I thought I'd invented a cold cure."

She set the cup down and gave him a tight hug. "You cured a lot of things, Granddad. Like loneliness and broken hearts. But you can't cure that cough. You can't cure her. And I know you want to."

His blue eyes watered. With a hand that trembled a bit more than it had a year ago, he pulled a white handkerchief from his pocket and wiped his nose. "I'd give this farm to cure her."

"I know you would. So would I." Emma brushed a hand down his arm, then turned her attention to the kitchen cabinet, intent on finding the right cough medicine and the inhaler that would clear her daughter's lungs.

But the asthma and the cold were the least of their problems.

The coughing started up again. She hurried down the hall to the room she shared with her daughter. The teenage posters of Emma's high school years had been taken off the walls and replaced with pictures of kittens and puppies. The twin beds were covered with quilts that Art's wife, a grandmother Emma had never known, had made.

Jamie was curled on her side, her blue eyes seeking Emma as she walked through the door. She'd seemed to be getting over this virus, but last night she'd taken a turn for the worse. Emma had known they would be seeing the doctor today.

"Hey, kiddo, need something for that cough?"

Jamie sniffled and rubbed her blanket against her face. Her cheeks were red and her eyes watery. Emma had given her something for the fever before she went out to the barn an hour ago. A hand to her daughter's forehead proved that this time a dose of over-the-counter fever reducer wasn't going to cut it. She leaned to kiss Jamie's cheek and managed a reassuring smile.

"We're going to get you dressed and take you to the doctor, okay?"

Jamie nodded and crawled into Emma's lap. Emma brushed a hand through the silky curls.

"Mama," Jamie cried, her voice weak.

"I know, honey. Sit up and take this medicine, and then I'll call Duke and tell him I won't be in today."

"Everything okay in here?" Art's gruff but tender voice called from the doorway.

Emma glanced back over her shoulder. "We're good. But we're going to take a drive in to town to see Dr. Ted. You want to go?"

"Nah, I'll stay here. But if you need anything, you call and I'll head to town straightaway."

"I'm sure we'll be fine. I think we just need something stronger than what I can buy at the pharmacy."

"That would be my guess." Her granddad stepped into the room, his smile tender for his great-granddaughter. "Ladybug, you need to get better so we can start learning to ride that pony of yours."

Jamie smiled a weak little smile, but her eyes lit up. "Blacky."

"Yeah, that's the one. He's a pretty little pony." Art brushed a hand through her hair. "Now, you be a good girl for your mommy and I'll make chicken noodle soup for you for dinner. They say that's a good cure for a cold. Better than my tea, I've been told."

Jamie grinned and the tension surrounding Emma's heart eased just a bit. "We'll be home soon, Art. Don't try to fix that tractor by yourself. We'll work on it together. If it has to wait until tomorrow, that's fine."

Art frowned. "Now, don't go getting sassy with me. I've been working on tractors since before you were born. I'm old, but I'm not feeble or ready for the rest home just yet."

"I agree, but there is no use getting hurt."

"No, there isn't. But you don't need to worry about me." He gave her a quick hug. "Go call the doctor."

An hour later Emma was carrying Jamie through the Braswell Hospital toward the pediatric unit, where Dr. Ted assured her they had a bed waiting. He wanted to put Jamie on intravenous antibiotics and to run some tests. In Emma's arms, Jamie felt too light, too small to be facing something so overwhelming.

Emma felt so alone. She suddenly wanted her granddad there with her. Then she started thinking about Daron McKay, and how he'd been watching over them for the past three years. Right now she wouldn't even complain about him being where he wasn't invited. Because never in her life had she felt so alone. And never had she wanted company more than she did at that moment.

As she approached the nurses' station, a somewhat familiar face stepped out from behind the desk. Samantha Martin, now Jenkins, smiled at the two of them. Duke's younger sister had a friendly openness about her. She'd married a couple of years ago, and from the tiny bump near her waistline, it appeared she might be expecting.

"Ted said you were on your way up." Samantha touched Jamie's brow and offered a reassuring smile.

"And you've got quite a fever. Let's get you in bed and see if we can get you cooled down."

Emma followed Samantha down the hall and into a room with green walls and a view of an open field that lay beyond the hospital grounds. Samantha took over, placing Jamie in the bed, covering her with a light blanket and then kissing her forehead. Emma stood back, watching as the nurse moved about the room, turning the television on to a cartoon station and opening the curtains to give a clearer view of cattle grazing in the distance.

Emma stepped into the hall to take a deep breath. She could do this. They would survive. She closed her eyes to say a heartfelt prayer for her daughter.

When Daron pulled up to the office, Boone's truck was parked in front. Daron parked next to it and got out. Hard rain was falling from a sky heavy with clouds. He hurried through the front door, pulling off his jacket and tossing it on the back of a chair to dry.

"You look bad," Boone said, surveying him critically.

"Thanks. It's pouring."

"How'd last night's job go?" Boone poured him a cup of coffee. "Here. That ought to help."

"Or rot my insides." He sat down and put his booted feet on the top of the desk. "Not bad. The senator is a hard one to stay close to. Works the crowd like a…"

"Politician?" Boone offered.

"Yes, something like that." He tossed his cowboy hat on his desk and ran a hand through hair that tended to curl in this weather. Daron took a sip of coffee and grimaced. "Let Lucy make the coffee next time."

"You say the most hurtful things," Boone shot back, his mouth curving.

"Hurtful but honest." He took another sip of coffee and decided it wasn't worth it. "I'm going to Duke's for lunch. And coffee."

"Or maybe you're just hoping Emma is there. She's going to get tired of your version of babysitting. Or is this courting, Daron McKay–style?"

"I'm not babysitting or courting. Where did you get that? I'm…" He rubbed a hand across his cheek. Man, he needed to shave. "I'm just doing what I promised."

Boone held up a hand to cut him off. "Stop. Andy volunteered to go with us."

"I trusted Afiza."

"Yeah, you did. And we trusted her brother. That doesn't make you Emma Shaw's keeper. It isn't your fault Andy divorced her, or that he didn't list her as a beneficiary."

"You'd think his family would want to help out."

"But they don't," Boone said. They'd had this conversation a hundred times before. "You can't make sense of what doesn't make sense, my friend. So either you keep hounding her, trying to help when she doesn't want it. Or you walk away and let her live her life. The problem is, if you don't mind me saying so, that you kind of like being in her life. You're attached to Jamie. You like Art."

"They're pretty easy to like." He grabbed the mail piled on his desk and started opening envelopes. A few checks they'd been waiting for.

A letter from his mom. Why would she send a letter rather than call? He slid his knife under the flap of the envelope and pulled out a card. No, it was an invitation. He glanced over it.

"Something good?" Boone asked as he got up to pour himself another cup of coffee.

"My mom, making a point."

"What's that?"

Daron glanced at the photograph on the front of the invitation, of a smiling blonde and her too-handsome fiancé. He opened the card and read over the details. "My ex-fiancée is getting married. This is my mom's way of letting me know I've missed the boat."

"It isn't like there aren't plenty of boats out there." Boone lifted his cup of coffee in salute, and the light glinted off his wedding band.

"Spoken like a man who is tragically in love."

"Nothing tragic about it, my friend. So, will you go?"

Daron glanced over the invitation and then shot it into the wastepaper basket. "I don't have time for this. I'm going to run to the bank and make a deposit that will keep us solvent and help you pay off that pretty house you've built your wife."

He was heading for the door when the phone rang. He waited as Boone answered. Then he waited because the call seemed serious.

"Well?"

"First-responder call." Boone shot him a look that unsettled him.

"Who?"

"Art Lewis. He's cut his finger pretty badly and Emma isn't there."

"I'll drive on out there and make sure he's okay,"

Daron said as he headed out the door, Boone behind him.

"Might as well," Boone agreed. "I'll follow you in my truck."

As they left town, the fire truck and rescue unit were leaving the rural fire station that served the Martin's Crossing and Braswell area. Daron flipped on the first-responder light on his dash and fell in behind the emergency units.

It took less than ten minutes and he was pulling up to the small home where Emma lived with her grandfather. Art was on the porch, a towel wrapped around his hand. Daron jumped from his truck and hurried past the other first responders.

"What happened?" he asked as he reached the porch.

Art grimaced. "That tractor. I've been trying to get that nut loosened up for ages, and of course today it came loose and my hand slipped. I cut a hunk out of my thumb."

Art started to unwrap his hand and show Daron and Boone, who had joined him on the front porch.

Daron stopped him. "No, that's okay. Keep it wrapped. And you're pale, so why don't we take a seat and let the guys check you out?"

A first responder grinned as he stepped into the group and took over. "Art, you have a way of finding trouble. Wasn't it just last year that you set—"

Art cut him off. "Let's not go over the list of past sins or we'll be here all day."

The first responder took a look at the gash and shook his head. "You're bleeding pretty good here, Art. I think we need to get you to Braswell."

"Oh, don't look so worried. I'm not going to bleed out." Art started rewrapping the wound.

"We're going to dress this a little better," the first responder told him. "Let's get you to the ambulance and we'll be in Braswell before you know it."

Art planted his feet on the porch. "I only called you young roosters because I thought you'd bandage it up. I didn't expect you to haul me in."

"Well, Art, there are just some things we can't do in the field." The first responder held his own, but the corner of his mouth flirted with a smile.

"I'm not in a field. I'm on my cotton-picking front porch."

Daron laughed and earned himself a glare from the older man. "Art, I'll call Emma. She'll be glad you went to the hospital. Is she at Duke's?"

"No, she had to take Jamie in to the doctor. I figured she'd be home by now, but you never know what the wait time is going to be."

"Is Jamie still sick?" Daron asked as the first responder continued to look Art over. They had moved him to a chair.

Art glanced down at his injured hand and then back at Daron. He grimaced a bit as the first responder cleaned the wound. "Yeah, son, she's still sick. But she's strong and her mama has faith." Art turned his attention back to the first responder, who now seemed to be trying to help him to his feet. "Son, I said I'm not going. I can drive myself if I need stitches."

Boone walked up behind Art, his beat-up cowboy hat pulled low over his brow and a look on his face that told the first responders to take a step back. "Art, how about we drive you to Braswell to the ER? They can sew you up. Plus, you can check on Emma and Jamie while you're there."

Art pushed himself out of the chair. "Now, that's an idea. Thank you all for coming. I'll just take Boone's offer and let you all go on back to your jobs, or whatever you were doing before I got you called out here."

Daron shot Boone a look. "Really?"

Boone arched a brow and grinned. "We don't have anything else on the calendar for today, do we?"

"No, nothing else. And we both love to get Emma riled up. Let's go, Art." Daron led the older man down the steps and to his truck. "You aren't going to bleed all over my new truck, are you?"

Art stumbled a bit, but his voice, when he answered, was still strong. "I reckon if I do, you can get it cleaned up."

Daron laughed. "Yeah, I reckon."

The three of them crowded into the front of Daron's truck, Art in the middle. Boone leaned back in the seat like he was in his beat-up old recliner and happy as he could be.

"Now that it's just us," Art started, "why don't you tell me what you think Pete Shaw wanted the other night?"

Daron pulled onto the main road. "You knew that Pete was out there?"

"No, not at first. I heard Emma shout and then heard Pete mumble something about her trying to kill him. I was heading for my bedroom door when I heard you say something and I just figure you're a few years younger, so you might as well handle things."

"Thanks for the vote of confidence, Art. And I'm not sure what Pete's after."

"I guess I just figured you had some idea, since you're patrolling the place like an overworked guard dog."

"What's that supposed to mean?"

Art shot him a look. "It isn't like you can hide a pearly white Ford King Ranch like this. I'm old, I get up at night and I've seen you driving by like you're keeping an eye on the place. Emma has seen you. I guess she told you to mind your own business."

Daron kept driving. "I'm not patrolling. I'm just driving by on a public street."

"Call it what you want," Art said. "I call it patrolling. Emma calls it being a nuisance. I reckon you have your reasons."

"I'd like to be able to help out, Art."

"There's nothing you can help with, Daron. I know you mean well, but we've got it handled. We've struggled a bit, but things aren't so bad we can't deal with it. This hand might slow down patching up that roof, but we got a tarp on it yesterday and that'll hold us over until I can climb up there."

"But what about Pete?" Boone asked, entering the conversation with a quiet question. "What's he after?"

"He's an addict who believes there's more money than what he got. Emma has other concerns without Pete stirring up trouble for her. I told her to call his parents but she won't. She doesn't want anything to do with Andy's family."

"Don't you think they'd like to know Jamie?" Boone asked, his tone casual.

Art guffawed at that. "They know they have a granddaughter. But they're the kind that thinks they're better than others, and that Emma wasn't quite what they wanted for their son. They encouraged the divorce. I can't say I wasn't glad when the marriage ended, as Andy wasn't particularly nice to my granddaughter, but I'm sorry his family lost him."

"Art, what's wrong with Jamie?" Daron tried to ease back into the conversation, but he saw from the corner of his eye that it didn't work.

"Now, that's something you'll have to ask Emma. And I reckon if she wanted you to know, she'd tell you."

"She's been too busy telling him to leave her alone," Boone added.

Daron didn't thank his friend for his special brand of humor. He wanted answers, and this wasn't getting him anywhere. He drove faster, telling himself he wanted to get Art to the ER a little quicker.

It wasn't the truth. What he wanted was to get to Emma's side, sooner rather than later. He could tell himself it was because he was worried about Jamie, which he was. Or he could blame it on a need to keep Andy's widow safe.

He needed to keep a promise to a dying friend. When he'd made the promise to Andy, it was about a woman he didn't know and a baby not yet born.

Now he knew them. He knew Emma as a woman of strength and faith. She loved her little girl. She loved her grandfather.

Unconditional love.

Watching her, being around them, it made him want to be a better man. The kind of man she allowed into her life.

Chapter Four

Emma stood back as her daughter was examined by the on-call physician in the Braswell Community Hospital pediatric wing. The doctor smiled as he rubbed the stethoscope to warm it; then he winked at her daughter and told her she was brave and promised she'd be getting the best dessert once they were finished with the examination.

"She's a strong girl, Mom." The doctor listened, "Another breath, Jamie."

Jamie took a deep, shaky breath. She was still pale. Her lips weren't as pink as normal. It had been so frightening, that moment when Emma realized her daughter was gasping for air. She'd hit the call button, summoning a nurse as she tried to calm Jamie, telling her it was fine, to take slow, easy breaths.

A hand touched Emma's. Samantha Jenkins moved to her side. "I'm sorry—I was with another patient down in X-ray. She's okay, Emma."

Not a question, a statement of fact. Samantha's expression was reassuring as she gave Emma a quick hug.

Emma nodded, accepting the words of encouragement, but it didn't immediately undo her fear. Her hands trembled and she couldn't seem to stop the shaking.

"Let's step into the hall," Dr. Jacobs said, patting Jamie's arm. "I'm going to have a nurse come in and give Jamie her dessert options."

"Mommy." Jamie's voice was weak.

"I'll be right back, sweetie."

Tears filled Jamie's blue eyes. Emma leaned to kiss her forehead. She wiped away the tears that rolled down her daughter's flushed cheeks and she fought the tightness in her own throat.

"Your mom will be right back, kiddo. And I bet the two of you will share a brownie." Samantha eased in next to Emma. "I'll stay with you until she gets back."

Jamie nodded, her eyes closing as Samantha trailed fingers through her hair. Emma stepped into the hall where Dr. Jacobs waited. The elevators at the end of the hall opened. Her grandfather stepped out and headed her way. Daron McKay followed. The fear that had cascaded over her gave way to relief. The tears she'd fought fell free and she sobbed.

"Let's take a walk." Dr. Jacobs inclined his head, directing her away from Jamie's room.

Her grandfather, his hand bandaged from the cut she'd been called about, and Daron, fell in next to her. She hadn't wanted to be alone. Now she wasn't. Tears continued to stream down her cheeks and she swiped at them with her hand until her grandfather handed her a clean, white handkerchief from his pocket.

Dr. Jacobs led them to a conference room with a table, bright fluorescent lights and molded plastic chairs. "It isn't comfortable, but there's more room if we're going to have several of us. Unless you'd prefer just the two of us having this conversation?"

"No, of course not." Her gaze skimmed past her granddad to Daron, standing in the doorway, his cowboy hat in his hands as he waited. "They can join us."

Dr. Jacobs motioned them all to the table. "Let's have a seat."

She sat down, the chair scraping on the tile floor. Daron sat at the end of the table, several chairs away. Her grandfather sat next to her. He put his arm around her, giving her a light squeeze. The gesture was as familiar as her own reflection in the mirror. From the very beginning, that had been his way of comforting a lost and hurting girl. She was a woman now, and sometimes felt responsible for him, but he was still her strength.

Dr. Jacobs sat across from them. He was youngish, with dark hair and dark eyes, the smooth planes of his face covered in five o'clock shadow. Yes, he was older than her twenty-eight years. But he was still too young.

"Isn't Dr. Jackson in today?" she asked.

Dr. Jacobs smiled, because of course she'd made it obvious that she was worried. "Not today, but don't worry. I'm smarter than I look."

"I'm sorry," she started to apologize, and he stopped her.

"Don't be. I know I look young. I also know that your daughter is the most important person in your life and you want only the best for her. I'm the best. I wouldn't be here if Dr. Jackson didn't think that I was qualified for the position. So let's figure out what we need to do for your daughter."

"Okay." She met his steady gaze. "What do we do?"

He glanced over the file in his hands. "We start with an echocardiogram. I'm worried about the ventricular septal defect, but I also think she has pneumonia. We'll do blood tests, start her on IV antibiotics and get her hydrated."

He listed it off, as if it were a shopping list. But it was her daughter. It was Jamie's heart. It was her life.

"She'll be okay," Emma heard herself say. Not a question. A statement of faith. God hadn't gotten them this far to let them down.

"She'll be great. I think she should stay in the hospital for a few days. And I also think we need to take a careful look at her heart because it might be time to repair the VSD."

"Open-heart surgery?" For years she'd dreaded those words.

"I hope not. We have options other than open heart. I'm an optimist." Dr. Jacobs gave her a steady look. "I'm also a man of faith. We'll do everything we can. And when we've done all we can, we stand on faith."

She nodded, closing her eyes against the fear, the hope, the onslaught of emotions that swept over her. A chair scraped. A hand settled on her shoulder. Without looking she knew that it was Daron. That he was there, standing behind her, the way he'd been doing since he got back from Afghanistan. It was guilt that kept him in her life. But today she didn't mind. Today his presence felt a lot like friendship and she wasn't going to turn that down.

Somehow she would get through this. Jamie would be okay. They would have the surgery, and she would be healthy. But it was good to have people to depend on.

"When will the surgery take place?" Daron asked, his voice deep, strong.

"I think sometime after Christmas. I want to know that she's strong enough before we send her down to Austin."

"Austin?" Emma asked, the reality of what he'd said hitting home.

Dr. Jacobs leaned a bit, making eye contact. "I'd love to tell you we could do the surgery here, but we can't. We'll contact specialists and she'll have the best of care."

"But you do believe we can wait until after Christmas?" Daron asked, his use of the pronoun *we* not lost on her.

"Yes, I think so. Unless there's a change, she isn't in any immediate danger. For now our main concern is this infection." Dr. Jacobs cleared his throat. "I know this is a lot to take in. What we want right now is for Jamie to rest, and for Mom to not worry."

"I think we can make sure that happens," Granddad said, patting Emma's hand.

"And we'll do our best, as well," Dr. Jacobs responded.

"Can I go back to her now?" Emma needed to see her daughter. She needed to hug her and to reassure herself that Jamie was okay.

"Yes. I ordered the blood test. We'll give her a little time to relax and then we'll take her down for the echocardiogram." Dr. Jacobs stood, the file in his capable hands. He handed her several printed copies. "If you have any questions, don't hesitate to ask."

"Thank you, Doctor." Emma looked down at the

files in her hands, the words swimming as she blinked away tears. Ugh, she didn't want to cry. No more tears.

The doctor left, the door closing behind him.

Her grandfather steepled his hands on the table and cleared his throat. "I reckon you ought to tell Andy's parents about their granddaughter."

"I'm not going to call them. They don't want anything to do with her."

"They might want to know about this," her granddad pushed in his quiet way. "Em, she is their granddaughter."

"No, she isn't. She's *your* granddaughter. There's more to grandparenting than a title and DNA. I'm not going to call them."

"Forgive—" her grandfather started.

"I will forgive," she conceded in a softer tone. "But I'm not through being angry."

She pushed back, the chair hitting Daron. She'd forgotten he was behind her. He grunted and rubbed his knee.

"I'm sorry," she said, her hand going to his arm. "I have to go. Jamie will wonder where I've gone to."

Boone Wilder was waiting outside Jamie's door. He tipped his hat, his smile somber. His presence made her falter, just a step. She'd gotten used to Daron's presence, his midnight drives past her house. Boone was more low-key with his interference.

"Boone," she said as she slipped past him. "You don't have to be here."

"Now, why wouldn't I be here, Emma?"

Arguing with him would have been pointless. It was their code. Whether as cowboys or soldiers, they stuck together. They took care of their own. She had become theirs when Andy died.

He followed her into the hospital room, where a nurse was setting up to draw blood. Samantha still sat next to the bed, Jamie's hand in hers. Her grandfather came in, not minding that the small room was crowded. He moved in close to his great-granddaughter and patted her hand. Jamie smiled up at him.

"Hey, Grand-girl, you sure do look pretty." He touched her nose.

Jamie managed a weak attempt at a smile and touched his bandaged hand. The gesture undid something inside Emma. She hadn't thought to ask him what happened. How exactly did he get hurt? How bad was the injury?

"You were working on the tractor, weren't you, Granddad?" she asked, watching as he moved his hand from Jamie's reach.

He winked at Jamie and then glanced up at her, his look a little more serious. "Just a little cut from that tractor."

"I told you…" She shook her head. Daron moved in behind her, his hands resting lightly on her shoulders. She breathed deep and relaxed. "I'm sorry I wasn't there."

And he was a grown man. He didn't want her telling him what he could or couldn't do.

"You don't always have to be there, kiddo. And I can get cut with or without your help. Boone and Daron came out and got me all fixed up. So right now let's worry about my ladybug."

Just like that, the room cleared. Boone and Daron slipped into the hall. Samantha smiled down at Jamie, gave her a quick kiss on the cheek and told her she would check on that brownie. Then it was just the nurse drawing the blood, Jamie, Emma and her grandfather.

"We're going to put her on oxygen." The nurse said it quietly. "She's doing fine, but a little won't hurt. Also, we've got a line in and we're starting her on antibiotics and fluids."

"Thank you." Emma sank into the chair next to her daughter. "Do you feel better?"

Jamie nodded, her eyes scrunched, her cheeks pink from the fever. "I like brownies."

"Yes, you do." Emma swiped at a tear that rolled down her cheek. "I love you."

"I love you, Mommy."

Never had any words meant so much. Except maybe when her grandfather told her everything would be okay. She always believed him, trusted him.

Movement outside the door caught her attention. And then she heard the scrape of a chair on the tile floors. She glanced that way as Daron placed a chair next to the door and took a seat, a cup of coffee in his hand and his cowboy hat pulled low. He crossed his right ankle over his left knee and leaned back. It looked like he planned on being there for a while.

She should tell him to go home. But she couldn't. Not today, when it felt better knowing he was there. He'd managed to enter her circle of trusted people. She hoped he didn't let her down.

Daron woke with a start, rubbing his neck that had grown stiff from sleeping in the waiting room chair. He'd pulled it into the hall, next to Jamie Shaw's room. It was late. The halls were quiet, the lights dimmed for the night. The quiet whisper of nurses drifted down the hallways, but he couldn't make out their words. He glanced at his watch. It was a few minutes after midnight.

Standing, he stretched, rolling his shoulders and neck, and managed to feel almost human again. His back ached, but he could live with it. He'd been living with it for a few years. He took a careful, quiet step and peeked into Jamie's room.

Emma was asleep, like him, in a chair not made for comfort. Her head rested on the hospital bed. Her hand clasped her daughter's. Jamie was awake. She glanced his way, her eyes large in her pale face. He silently eased into the room and lifted the cup of water next to her bed. She shook her head and her smile wobbled. He hadn't been around too many kids in his life, but this one had his heart. She had from the moment he first saw her through the window of the nursery at this very hospital. She'd been pink, fighting mad and none too pretty.

He guessed she knew she had him wrapped around her finger. And that was okay by him.

Not wanting to wake Emma, he brushed a hand through Jamie's hair, then raised a finger to his lips. Her stuffed animal had fallen to the floor. He picked it up and tucked it in next to her. When she seemed content, he turned his attention to Emma. She had to be cold, curled up the way she was in the vinyl hospital chair. Looking around the room, he spotted a blanket folded on a shelf and returned to cover her with it. She didn't stir.

With a wave, he headed toward the door. Jamie watched him go, snuggling into her blanket and closing her eyes. He walked down the hall, not really sure where he was heading. Of course he wouldn't leave. He was used to pulling all-nighters. Sleep wasn't typically his friend, because in sleep the nightmares returned.

A soft light shone from a room at the end of the unit. He headed that way, curious. When he got there and peeked in, his curiosity evaporated. The chapel. The light came from a lamp illuminating a cross. On a shelf beneath it lay a Bible. A plaque hung on the wall next to the display, with the words "Thy word is a lamp unto my feet and a light unto my path. Psalm 119:105" engraved on it.

Out of habit, he took off his hat. After all, this was church. It was small. There were no pews. A minister didn't preach here on Sunday. But the room had a comforting feeling, as if Jesus might walk in at any moment, clasp a hand on a man's shoulder and tell him to let go of his burdens.

It was hard to let go of the burdens he'd been carrying for several years. He'd grown too accustomed to the weight.

When he thought about letting go, he wondered who he'd be without them. Without the burdens. He guessed it was wrong to think of Emma and Jamie as burdens; they weren't. They had actually become his anchor, keeping him grounded. Because without them, he might not have wanted to survive the last few years.

He might have given in to some other ways of easing the guilt. He had plenty of friends who had found comfort in the bottom of a bottle. He also had friends who relied on faith. They seemed better off, if he was being honest.

He focused on work, and on keeping Jamie and

Emma safe. Fixing a fence from time to time when she'd let him, buying Christmas gifts that he had delivered to their house, so she wouldn't turn them away.

He eased into the seat by the window of the chapel. A picture hung on the wall with a verse about comfort. This room was meant to comfort.

He bowed his head, hat in his hands. He hadn't prayed in a long time. He guessed he'd never been much of a praying man. He hadn't been raised the way Boone had, going to church, having faith, believing it above all else. When he'd filled out the paperwork to join the army, he checked the Christian box because if anyone had asked, of course he believed in God.

He'd prayed for Andy to live. Now he would pray for Jamie. And God had better be listening. Because she was a little girl. She was three years old with her whole life ahead of her. She had a mom who would do anything for her. And she had a granddad who loved her "more than the stars in the sky."

That was what Art had told her when he said goodbye to Jamie, before Boone gave the older man a ride home.

Daron hadn't been raised going to Sunday school. He'd been to church a few times with the Wilders. That was the sum total of his experience with prayer. But he felt as if he had the basics down. Petition God. Ask the Almighty to spare a little girl.

When he heard a noise, he looked up, heat flooding his face. He stood, nearly knocking the chair over in the process. He jammed his hat back on his head and faced the person standing just inside the doorway.

Emma, head tilted, dark hair framing her face, studied him as if she'd never seen him before. "I didn't expect to see you here." She brushed a hand over her face and shook her head. "Not that you wouldn't pray. That isn't what I meant."

He waited, a grin sneaking up on him, as she found words for what she meant. She was cute. He'd avoided that thought for a few years because Andy had been married to her and there were lines a man didn't cross. But tonight, in a softly lit chapel, sleep still in her eyes and her dark hair a bit of a mess, he couldn't deny it. He guessed his brain was a little sleep addled, too.

"I meant, I thought you'd come to your senses and left," Emma finished.

"Should I be insulted that you were surprised to find me in the chapel?" Daron teased. "Or because you thought I'd leave you here alone."

"Stop." She held up a hand. "Please, not right now."

She looked vulnerable and alone. Instead of arguing, he closed the distance between them and wrapped his arms around her, pulling her close. She didn't fight. That took him by surprise. He was more surprised when she rested her cheek against his chest.

"I'm glad you're still here," she whispered. "I'm so tired of being alone. I have Jamie. I have Art. And of course I have friends. But sometimes I feel so stinking alone."

"I'm not going anywhere, Emma."

She left his arms and walked through the room to the cross. Her head bowed. He watched from the doorway as she prayed. He marveled at how she kept going, even seemed to be happy most of the time. By the world's standards she didn't have much, but he figured she had more than most.

Eventually she turned around, her expression telling him she hadn't expected him to still be there, waiting for her.

"What happened between you and Andy's parents?" he asked as they walked back down the hall, past the nurses' station, past rooms where children slept, some alone and some with parents close by.

"Other than the money, you mean?"

Andy had mentioned the money to him, that he'd divorced her and made his brother, Pete, his beneficiary. Once Andy learned about the baby, he'd meant to switch it back. He hadn't. But there had to be more.

"Other than the money," he said. "Because Pete got the life insurance, correct?"

"Pete believes Andy had another policy. And I think he did, before we got married. But he dropped it because he thought what he got through the military was enough. Pete doesn't believe me." She shrugged slim shoulders and paused a few feet from Jamie's door. "They didn't believe Jamie was Andy's daughter. We divorced so quickly. He left for the Middle East soon after. It didn't add up to them. But I'm not going to beg them to see her, or invite them here to hurt her."

"But Jamie is their granddaughter."

"They told me if she's really Andy's, they'll take her away from me. It's an empty threat. They can't take her. But the fact that they'd threaten it is enough."

He took her by the arm and guided her in the direction of the waiting room, where he fixed them each a cup of coffee. She took a seat, propping her feet up on a coffee table. He handed her a cup and sat down next to her.

"Andy and I were friends but I don't know his parents very well," he said. "But if there is some way I can help…? Is that why Pete shows up every few weeks?"

"You really have to stop camping out on the road. We don't need for you to protect us," she told him as she lifted the cup to take a sip.

"I don't sleep a lot. Keeping an eye on things is the least I can do."

She set the cup down on the table next to her. "I don't know what to do about Pete. You losing sleep isn't going to change that. And it isn't helping you, is it?"

He ignored the last statement, because he wasn't going to get bogged down in the subject of nightmares and shrapnel injuries.

"Pete's on meth. He used to be a decent kid, but his brain is melting." The subject of Pete was easier to tackle.

"I agree. Andy knew it, too. I just don't understand why he…" She stopped and shook her head. "No use asking why. It won't change anything. I don't want you to feel as if we're your responsibility. We aren't. And we really are doing okay. Things are tight, but we've got this."

"I know you do."

But he couldn't walk away. If someone had asked him if it was the guilt that kept him tied to her, or something else, he would have avoided the question. He wouldn't even allow himself to think about all the reasons he stayed in her life.

He'd always prided himself on being loyal. A loyal man didn't let himself get involved with a friend's wife.

Even if that friend was gone and the woman in question was hard to walk away from.

Chapter Five

Jamie was released from the hospital on Saturday morning. Emma helped her put on the fuzzy slippers, the only shoes they had with them, and handed her the teddy bear Daron had brought her the previous day. Throughout Jamie's stay he'd remained close at hand. Emma had tried to tell him to go home, or to work, whatever he needed to do. But he'd refused. Instead he'd slept in a chair in the hall or the waiting room. He'd brought her coffee, insisted she eat, and he'd entertained Jamie with sock puppets he bought in the hospital gift shop.

A light knock on the door frame interrupted her musings. She turned, not surprised to see Daron standing there. Her heart did something crazy and unexpected. No, not unexpected. She was a living, breathing woman, so of course she noticed that he was tall with shoulders broad enough to lean on, arms that held a woman tight and a dimpled Texas cowboy smile that knew its own charm.

He'd been kind to them. He'd been there for her during some of her toughest days. She appreciated him.

Even though he was a bit of a pain. Like a stray dog that just couldn't be convinced he needed to keep moving on down the road.

"Your chariot awaits," he said in a low voice as he removed his hat. "Art said to let you know he's got stew for dinner."

"You've seen Granddad?"

Jamie was tugging at her hand and whispering. Emma glanced down at her daughter and smiled.

"What do you want, sweetie?"

"Did Daron really bring a chariot?" Jamie whispered, her eyes round.

"No, honey, he didn't. That's just a saying. He brought his truck."

Daron stepped into the room, as if he'd been invited. Emma didn't know when, but in the past few days she had sort of invited him into her life. She certainly had leaned on him for the last few days.

But she didn't want to get used to it. She had Jamie. And Granddad. They were a family. Daron was only temporary. She'd been telling herself that for a few years now. Sooner or later he'd work through whatever it was that kept him up at night and he'd move on. Maybe he'd go back to Austin. Maybe he'd get married and have kids of his own.

Jamie was holding her arms up. To Daron. He gave Emma a quick look, asking permission. Her hesitation was brief; then she nodded. Daron lifted Jamie gently, her arms wrapping around his neck. Her grin split open and the dimple in her cheek deepened. It hit Emma that they could be father and daughter. Both had hair more blond than brown, unruly curls and that dimple. Hers in the left cheek and his in the right. It made them a matched set. Like bookends.

But they weren't father and daughter. She cleared her throat and took a deep breath, getting past the thick emotions that settled in her chest. Wordlessly she packed up the few things still scattered around the room.

"Ready to go home?" Samantha asked as she breezed into the room.

"All ready," Emma said. She held their overnight bag and the bouquet of flowers Duke Martin had sent from all the folks at Duke's No Bar and Grill.

"Here's the prescription." Samantha handed her a paper. "We called it in to the Braswell Pharmacy. It should be ready. And Dr. Jacobs would like to see her in a week. He'll arrange for you to meet with the surgeon in Austin. Probably in the next couple of weeks."

Emma nodded, hoping her fear didn't show. Daron reached for the bag she carried. He hefted it over his shoulder and motioned her forward.

"Sam, thank you for everything." Emma hugged the other woman. "I'm glad you were here."

"Me, too. And if you need anything, just call."

Moments later they walked into bright sunlight and fresh December air, crisp and clear. The sky was the color of robin's eggs, the haze of heat gone. Emma drew in a deep breath, for brief seconds closing her eyes as she exhaled. When she opened her eyes, Daron still stood next to her, Jamie's head against his shoulder.

"You okay?" he asked.

"I'm good. It just feels good to be outside and to breathe fresh air." She motioned him forward and he continued across the parking lot in the direction of his truck, the pearl-white paint gleaming in the winter sunshine.

He'd installed a car seat in the back of the truck cab. It didn't surprise her. Jamie gladly climbed in, tucking her stuffed animal under her chin and cuddling into the blanket Emma had brought for her.

"Time to go home," Emma said, kissing her daughter on the cheek.

When they pulled up to the house, Jamie perked up. Her dog was on the front porch, tail wagging. Granddad opened the front door as Daron pulled right up to the porch.

"We can walk, you know," she muttered.

"Of course you can," he said as he eased to a stop and pulled the truck's emergency brake. "But why do that when I can give you front-door service?"

She unfastened her seat belt but didn't move to get out. "Thank you, Daron. For everything."

He winked, a gesture telling her it didn't really matter. But it did. They both knew it. He'd seen how much it mattered. "Anytime."

What should she say to that? No, he shouldn't do this "anytime." Anytime required something more than his hovering on the periphery of their lives, rescuing them, protecting them. Out of some sense of obligation, she thought. And how long could he go on, feeling so guilty?

"Daron, it's too much," she said quietly, stopping him from reaching in the backseat to unbuckle Jamie.

"Too much?"

She bit down on the corner of her lip, trying to explain, to find a way to release him from whatever it was that kept him tied to their lives.

"You don't have to do all this. I don't know what happened, but I know you feel some sense of obligation to us. You don't have to. I don't blame you for Andy's death." She studied his face, the shift of his eyes away from her, the way his throat moved when he swallowed. "Let go. It happened and you don't have to continue this, whatever it is."

"Friendship?" He smiled only faintly as he looked at her.

"Is that what it is? Or is it that you're still worried that you owe us something?"

"It isn't guilt, Emma."

She arched a brow.

"Okay, maybe some guilt," he admitted with an amused expression that didn't quite touch his eyes.

"You don't have to feel guilty. You didn't take anything from me. It was already taken. Andy left me. Our marriage had ended, because…" She shook her head. "No, I'm not going to discuss this right now. But we were over and I'm sorry if he said something that made you feel responsible for us. So stop. You don't have to watch over us this way."

"It's been a long three years, Emma. I consider you a friend. And I'm not one to walk out on a friendship."

"Friendship is a cup of coffee and a phone call, not midnight drives, patrolling my road."

He chuckled. "You make me sound a little creepy. But if it takes coffee and phone calls for you to consider me a friend, then I could use coffee. And we could all use more friends."

They sat there for several minutes as she tried to gather up the courage to truly let him in.

"I could use a friend," she admitted. "I've been so busy, I've lost track of the ones I used to have."

He held out a hand. "Then we start today as friends."

"And you stop the crazy stalker/protector thing you've been doing." She took his hand, his fingers strong around hers.

"Nah, I don't think I can do that." With that settled, he reached in the backseat for Jamie. Somehow he'd twisted things around and she'd accepted his interference in her life. All because he'd used the word *friend*.

She wanted to argue but couldn't. He had Jamie in the front seat with them, and he was buttoning up her jacket, as if he'd been doing it all her life.

Jamie's arms were around his neck. The perfect sunny day had disappeared as they'd driven, and the blue sky was now heavy with clouds. A few drops of rain splattered against the windshield.

Jamie leaned in, touching her nose against Daron's. Emma's heart stuttered over that moment, the gesture her daughter usually reserved only for mother-and-daughter moments.

Daron caught her eye and winked, but he couldn't know what it meant, to share that moment with her daughter. To him it was simply a cute gesture.

"We should go inside before this turns into a downpour," he suggested just as a deafening clap of thunder vibrated through the truck.

"We might be too late." Suddenly rain pounded against the dry earth and beat against the windshield of the truck. "Maybe it will let up soon."

"Yeah, I'm sure that's what Noah said after the first thirty days. Let's make a run for it. I've got Jamie. You get the bag."

They flew from the truck, heads down against the drenching, but it did no good. They were soaked to the skin as they hurried up the steps and rushed through the front door. The house was warm, but a bucket sitting in the middle of the living room floor reminded Emma that the roof still leaked. Drat.

Granddad handed them towels. "I've got coffee brewing and lunch on the stove."

"Looks like we'd best take care of that leak first." Daron rubbed his hair and face with the towel and handed it back to him. "This rain isn't supposed to let up for a few days."

"Too wet to get up there and put down shingles," Granddad told him, leading the way through the living room to the kitchen. "The bucket will keep us from getting flooded out, and as soon as this clears up, I'll get up on the roof."

"Do you have another tarp?" Daron asked, taking the cup of coffee her grandfather poured for him.

Emma took Jamie from Daron's arms and pretended this conversation about her roof wasn't humiliating. She'd already patched it. And added the tarp the previous week in hopes that they could sell some cattle to pay for the new roof the old house so desperately needed.

"Yeah, I think there's one in the shed," Granddad answered.

Emma held her daughter close, draping a blanket around her. The two men went on discussing the roof.

She had to stop this. "We can fix the roof ourselves, Daron. You've really done enough. Our roof isn't your problem."

He stopped midsip, the cup poised in front of his

mouth. His brows arched. "I hate to remind you, but I believe friendship was your idea."

Wide-eyed, Jamie was watching the adults from Emma's arms, her gaze shooting from Daron to Emma and then to her granddad.

"Why don't you put that little mite down?" her granddad suggested. "I bought her a new cartoon the other day."

"Thanks, Gramps, I will. Daron, please. You don't have to do this."

She walked away, leaving the two men staring after her. Their voices carried. She could hear their soft murmurs as she tucked Jamie in her bed, giving her the stuffed animal that was her favorite. It had been a birthday present from Daron.

In three years he hadn't missed a birthday or Christmas. There had been mysterious deposits in her bank account that he wouldn't take credit for. Groceries had been delivered.

Jamie snuggled up with the stuffed horse, holding it close to her face, brushing her cheek against the soft fur. She loved that horse. As Emma brushed a hand over her daughter's soft blond curls, Jamie's eyes grew heavy with sleep. Her little-girl lips turned in a slight smile that said her world was just as she wanted it.

After a few more minutes, Jamie slipped into sleep, her eyelids fluttering only once, her arms tightening around the pink horse. Emma tiptoed from the room. When she got to the living room, Granddad was tending one of his famous pots of stew, cooked on the top of the woodstove.

"Where is he?"

He turned, looking sheepish and guilty as he tugged

on his whiskered chin and stirred the concoction in the cast-iron pot. "He left."

She peered into the pot of meat and vegetables, the broth thick and savory. She'd make rolls later to go with the stew. It was perfect for a blustery day in December.

"Gramps, why do you look so guilty?"

"I reckon *you're* going to tell *me* why." He reached for salt and added a dash. "We've been making this stew together for nearly twenty years, haven't we, kiddo?"

The memory took her back, the two of them finding ways to be a family. "Yes, we have. And you're avoiding the question."

He stopped stirring, and when he started to lick the spoon, she stopped him. He put the wood spoon on a plate and tugged at his beard again.

"I'm not getting any younger," he started. "I don't like to admit there are things I can't do. And things I wish you didn't have to do. There are days I'm more than a little angry with Andy for not getting the paperwork done to make you his beneficiary. I'm more than a little angry with his family for taking the money and not thinking about their granddaughter. But there isn't much I can do about that. We get by fine on my Social Security and what you make at the diner. And it won't be long before you have your degree. I guess if we had stayed in town years ago instead of buying this place, we'd be doing even better. It is what it is. But the one thing I can do for you is teach you to accept help."

"He's helped us enough."

"I don't think this is about what he thinks he owes you. It's about a man trying to be a friend. Or maybe a little more."

She'd been about to walk away, but the last statement stopped her. She looked up at her grandfather and shook her head. "You have clearly lost it. I'm the furthest thing from the type of woman Daron McKay would be interested in. He's here because he feels obligated. He thinks he owes us something because of what happened." And it still hurt. Andy had been her husband, her friend. He'd been everything she thought she wanted, and then he'd abused her trust.

He'd cheated on her.

He'd left her alone. As much as he had hurt her, she still missed him. She cried at night because he'd died too young.

Granddad put an arm around her shoulders and kissed the top of her head. "I might be talking like a grandfather who is proud of his girl, but I think you are everything any man worth his salt would be interested in. You're a strong woman of faith, a good mom and pretty as a speckled pup."

She nodded. "And you are still a little prejudiced when it comes to your only granddaughter. But this conversation is pointless." She stood on tiptoe and pulled him down to kiss his scraggly, unshaved cheek. "What are you and Daron up to?"

Then she heard the truck pull up out front, saving her the trouble of interrogating her grandfather. She walked out the front door, leaving him to tend to his stew. She would tend to sending Daron on his way.

It was still raining when Daron left his place and headed back to Emma's. It had taken him less than fifteen minutes to find a tarp in the storage room of his barn. It would probably take longer to convince Emma to let him put it on her roof.

He pulled up to the old farmhouse. It was a decent place, just in need of some work. He jumped out of his truck and there she was, standing in the rain, the hood of her jacket covering her head and hanging down over her brow. She looked up at him with dark eyes and a mighty big frown.

"Go home, Daron. When it stops raining I'll fix the roof."

He took her by the arm and moved her toward the covered front porch with the lawn chairs and a small grill. She jerked her arm free and stomped up the stairs, as much as a hundred-pound woman could stomp. When she turned around to face him, he managed to keep a straight face.

She was the most kissable female he had ever met, with those rosy lips and that big frown, raindrops trickling down her cheek. He took a closer look to make sure they weren't tears. Nope. Just rain.

He'd been in Emma's life for a few years now. When had he started noticing her lips? Or the darkness of her eyes, like coffee on a cold winter day?

He grinned, just a little. Enough to earn himself another narrow-eyed glare. Back to business.

"I'm not going home. You have a sick little girl in there. The last thing she needs is a leaking roof. The last thing you need is for Andy's parents to use that roof and her stay in the hospital against you."

She paled at the mention of Andy's parents.

"Emma, I'm sorry. I shouldn't have said that."

She glanced away but not before he saw the moisture in her eyes. "I'll get to the roof."

"You're wearing yourself out. Let me do this." As they stood there, the rain slacked off a bit. "I checked the forecast. It's going to rain all week and this looks like the best time. I'm not going to stand here and argue with you."

"Of course you aren't. But if you're going up, so am I. You can't do this alone."

She walked off in the direction of the shed. He guessed she was going to get a ladder. He hurried to the truck and pulled out the supplies he'd brought from his place.

He was gathering everything up when Emma returned. Without the ladder.

"It's gone," she explained. "I know it was in the barn. I used it for the last tarp."

"Let's have a look. Maybe Art put it somewhere?"

She shook her head, but she walked past him into the house. When she returned, she didn't look too happy. "Art hasn't seen it."

"So someone stole the ladder?"

She shivered and pushed her hands deep into the pockets of her jacket. "Yes. It isn't the first thing that's been taken. Things have been disappearing for a year or so. Not much. Tools. An old saddle. Now the ladder."

"Pete?"

She shrugged. "Maybe."

"I'll head back to my place for a ladder. Emma, he has to be stopped. I'm worried that he isn't in his right mind."

"Because he isn't. I knew Pete before. He was a good guy. Always a little wild, but decent."

Daron opened the door. "Go inside, where it's warm. I'll be back in fifteen minutes."

This time she didn't argue. Instead she headed back inside and he went back to his place. It gave him time to think. Gave him time to clear his head.

When he got back she met him on the front porch, tiny in her big jacket with brown work gloves covering her hands. He wanted to talk her out of going onto the roof with him. He knew she wouldn't listen.

He moved his ladder into position and headed up to the roof with the tarp, tools and nails in the pockets of the tool belt buckled around his waist. She joined him up there. The rain had let up. It was easy to find the leak.

They stretched the tarp and pounded tacks to keep it in place.

He gave a quick look at Emma on the opposite end of the tarp, holding it as he tacked it to the aging, broken shingles.

"I'm going to need a pot of coffee after we're done," he called out against the wind.

She nodded but didn't answer. Her shoulders shuddered and she had to be freezing. He worked a little faster, getting the tarp down in record time.

"Let's go," he said. He motioned her toward the ladder. "You go first."

She went down as he held the ladder. The wind caught her jacket and she swayed a bit, but held tight. He waited until she was firmly on the ground and holding the ladder from there before he started down. Close to the bottom, the wind gusted. The ladder wobbled. He felt it going and jumped.

"Emma, get back," he yelled as he fell sideways, the ladder going in the other direction.

His body hit hers and he twisted to keep her from

falling. Pain shot through his spine, making him see stars. The ladder clattered to the ground, and Emma's arms were around him.

"Are you okay?" she asked, her arms still surrounding him, her body close.

Daron took a deep breath and let his arms ease around her. Just for support, he told himself. But she felt good in his arms. She smelled good, like spring flowers and rain. He wanted to hold her a little closer, a little longer, but he knew better. "Yeah, I'm good. Every now and then I get hit with a spasm. Jumping off a ladder probably didn't help."

Still in the circle of his arms, he thought she leaned in close and sniffed. Soon after, she seemed to realize where she was and what she'd done. She pulled back abruptly. "Let's get you that coffee."

He started to reach for the ladder, but her hand on his arm stopped him.

"We're both soaked," she said. "Forget the ladder. Coffee and a bowl of stew are more important."

He followed her inside, where they both shed their coats and shoes. She moved immediately to the woodstove. He followed, holding his hands out to the warmth. The aroma of the stew filled the room. His mouth watered.

"Is that your stomach growling?" she asked, humor lacing her tone.

"Might have been yours," he answered.

Art called out from the kitchen that the coffee was ready. And he asked if they noticed that the roof wasn't leaking anymore. Emma laughed a little and the sound made him want to pull her back into his arms.

"Coffee sounds good," he said too quickly. But he needed to move away from her, away from temptation.

If he'd had any sense at all, he would have gone on home. Instead he stayed. For coffee. For a bowl of stew. For time spent with this family. Because they had entered his life as an obligation but in the past few years they'd become a little bit more.

He never really allowed himself to think about what that meant. To him, they were just more.

Chapter Six

Sunday dawned cold and blustery but without rain. Emma bundled Jamie up for church while Granddad went out to warm up the truck. They were going to the Martin's Crossing Community Church for the potluck. After all, she'd promised Lily. It would be good to go to the small community church. Their own church in Braswell had grown over the past few years. Growth was good, but Emma had missed the smaller congregation that had once felt a lot like family.

Now she felt a bit lost in the crowd. She might have spent her first years in Houston, but she was a small-town girl at heart.

"Ready to go?" Granddad, dressed today in starched jeans and a button-up shirt, stepped into the living room. He carried the pie she'd baked.

"All ready," she responded. She reached for Jamie's gloved hand and the three of them walked out the door.

By the time they reached the church at the end of Martin's Crossing's Main Street, the sun had come out and was warming the air. Somehow it still smelled of winter, of snow, of Christmas. It helped that the nativity was up on the church lawn and the town was decorated.

Three weeks till Christmas. She sighed at the thought. She was nowhere near ready for the holidays. Worry assaulted her as she walked next to her grandfather, carrying her daughter in her arms.

Darker thoughts were dispelled as they entered the church and were greeted by Duke and Oregon, their daughter Lily at their side with one of the little ones they'd recently adopted. A little girl named Sally.

"Good to see you all this morning." Duke shook Granddad's hand and handed him a program. "You all can join the Martins. We're midway up on the left. There's plenty of room."

It was a good plan. To sit with Jake and Breezy Martin, Samantha and Remington, Brody and Grace. With the Martins they would feel as if they belonged in this congregation.

As they walked up the carpeted aisle, Jamie spotted Daron. He was sitting with Boone Wilder and his large family, all of them taking up two pews. Jamie pulled away from Emma and headed for the man sitting at the end of a pew, his cowboy hat in his lap and a hand brushing nervously through his hair.

"Daron," Jamie said, immediately crawling into his lap.

"Hey, there's my favorite girl." Daron shifted her, then glanced back over his shoulder. "And her very serious mommy."

Jamie giggled.

Boone Wilder stood, holding out a hand to Emma and then to Art. "Good to have you all. Join us?"

Emma glanced longingly in the direction of the

Martins. It would be easier, less complicated, to sit with the Martins. She could sit behind Samantha. She could sing and not be distracted.

But Art was already accepting the offer. There was a shifting of bodies to make room for a few more. It was no problem, Boone Wilder's younger brother, Jase, assured them. So somehow Emma landed in the pew next to Daron, her daughter sitting on both of their laps.

"You don't get to look more nervous than me," Daron whispered.

"What do you mean?" she responded.

"I don't go to church often. So I have the market cornered on nervousness. I can't believe sitting next to me is more nerve-racking than coming to church for the first time in, well, months."

"I think it might be."

He chuckled and leaned in, his head touching Jamie's. Emma's daughter laughed and snuggled against him. It was too much. It hurt deep down, where she'd placed her hopes and dreams for a future with a man who hadn't shared those dreams.

But she didn't want to think about Andy. Not today. She didn't want to think about how she'd lost him twice. Once when he cheated on her and then divorced her. Next when an IED detonated in Afghanistan.

She closed her eyes against the onslaught of pain.

Daron seemed to notice, because his attention refocused on her face and he shifted Jamie. His hand touched Emma's arm.

"I can't do this. It's too much." She held her arms out to Jamie to go.

"Don't leave on my account. I'll go."

"No. It isn't you. Stay and give Art a ride home, if you don't mind. I just can't breathe in here."

She took Jamie and left, knowing people were staring, whispering and wondering about her unusual departure. When she got to the truck she put Jamie in the seat, and then she climbed behind the wheel and waited until the world righted itself.

It didn't. Not for a long time. Her chest ached and it hurt to breathe. Jamie started to cry.

"So that's what a panic attack looks like," someone said from the open passenger-side door.

She jumped a little. "Oregon. I'm sorry. I shouldn't have run out like that."

"We do what we have to. But I didn't want to leave you out here alone. You're okay now?"

"I think so. Embarrassed but okay."

Duke Martin's wife, Oregon, climbed in with her. Jamie was happy, nibbling on a cookie and playing with a book. Oregon must have given those things to her without Emma even realizing.

"Don't be embarrassed. We all have stuff we work through, deal with. Sometimes it helps to talk to a friend."

Emma nodded, accepting the offer. They had become friends in the past year. "It was just leftover emotion. I have days when I think I'm over it, that I've moved past Andy's death, the divorce, the pain. And then it sneaks up on me."

"When you see your daughter sitting on the lap of a man who is decent and kind."

"He's in our lives because he feels guilty. He isn't her daddy, Oregon. Lately he feels like a friend. But we aren't his problem and I don't want to count on anyone else the way I counted on Andy."

"Oh, how well I understand. But will you do me a favor, Christian woman to Christian woman?" Her smile was amused and knowing.

"Okay, you know I can't say no to that."

"I do. Give God a chance. Let Him heal your heart and trust that there are good men out there, men who cherish and who are faithful. Men who won't let you down."

"I'll try to do that." She glanced at the clock on her phone. "You should go back inside. No need for us both to miss church."

"Why don't we both go back inside? The message was going to be short today and I'd say they're already moving on to the potluck. Or getting close to it."

Go back inside. She glanced over her shoulder at the pretty little church, the scene of her crisis. It wasn't as if she could avoid these people indefinitely, Daron included. "Okay."

They entered the church together, taking a seat on a back pew and listening as the sermon came to a close. From where she sat, Emma could see Daron. She watched the expressions on his face change, saw his pain, his guilt.

She could help him, she realized. He didn't have to feel guilty for what had happened. He should have healing. Maybe even find faith.

Years ago she'd learned that friendships happened for reasons a person didn't always understand. Some relationships were just for a season, to teach, and to help.

Maybe this friendship of theirs was meant to help

him work through what had happened to him over-seas. Maybe he needed her as much as she needed him.

There. She'd finally admitted it, at least to herself, that she did need him as a friend.

Ladies were washing dishes and men were wiping down tables and putting up chairs. Daron knew how to make himself useful. He took a load of chairs and headed for the storage closet, allowing a quick glance in the direction of the kitchen, where Emma helped do the dishes. The church fellowship hall had been overflowing until about thirty minutes ago, when the potluck meal wrapped up and people started gathering up their covered dishes, saying their goodbyes and heading home.

Daron could have left. Instead he'd remained behind, keeping an eye on the woman who had escaped him at the beginning of church.

"Are you going to keep walking or just stand there gawking?" Boone said, coming up behind him, pushing another load of chairs.

"I'm walking."

"You're just worried about her, right?" Boone winked as he said it.

"You know, some people think you're charming. I don't get it," Daron shot back.

"It's the dimples and the pretty eyes. I'm taken, though."

"I feel sorry for her," Daron shot back.

Boone laughed, loud and long enough to draw some attention to the two of them. Happiness could be so annoying. Daron pushed the chairs into the storage closet, and when he walked out, he flipped off the light and shut the door behind him, leaving Boone inside and in the dark.

Boone came out chasing after him, but Daron escaped to the kitchen, the women and Boone's wife, Kayla. The two of them slid into the room, the women turning to stare. Kayla gave Boone a sharp look and he managed a grin that had her eyes softening almost instantly. Daron tried that same look on Emma, but she just shook her head and turned back to drying dishes. Jamie sat on the floor nearby playing with plastic bowls and measuring cups.

"Art went on home," Daron told Emma as he edged a little closer to her.

"I know. He said you'd give me a ride. You really don't have to. I can get someone." She glanced around at the dwindling crowd.

"I don't mind. Actually I thought you might like to come out to the Rocking M. I haven't been there much lately, but I think I might…" He cut himself off. There were things he didn't tell anyone. Not even the woman pretending to be a friend.

Boone knew. Boone, Lucy and Boone's mother. Maria Wilder had a way of listening. It encouraged a guy to talk about his secrets and his fears.

"You might try what?" Emma asked.

"Putting up a Christmas tree. Making the ranch a little more homey."

"I see."

"You could help. You and Jamie." He backtracked when she looked perplexed.

"I don't think that's a good idea."

People were moving around them. Older women in comfortable shoes, a mom with a toddler on her hip, one of the older men who seemed to enjoy being the only man in the kitchen. Emma started to pull away from him. And for whatever reason, he couldn't let her go.

"What isn't a good idea? Helping me put up a Christmas tree? Taking an afternoon to rest and have fun?" He saw the corners of her mouth tilt, just barely.

"Daron, stop trying to tempt me with that sweet smile." Her cheeks turned pink as the words slipped out.

"I have a sweet smile."

"You know you do. And you know that we can't do this. We agreed on being friends, but I can't do this, Daron."

"I'm confused. What is it you think I'm looking for?" He followed her across the kitchen, where she tossed the towel she'd been carrying into the pile of used towels and dishrags. "Oh, you think I want *more* than friendship."

She spun around to face him. "Stop. Just stop."

He put his hands up and took a step back. Behind him he heard Jamie. She toddled up, her blue eyes wide, watching the two of them. "I'm trying to be your friend."

"I know." Her features softened. "I guess I don't want to get lost in something that isn't real. I'm a mom. I'm divorced. In my heart I guess I'm a widow. My life is complicated right now."

"I'm sorry," he said, leaning in close to keep the conversation between them. "I pushed. And I probably teased. I just…want to spend the afternoon with you and Jamie. Something that doesn't include me driving past your place, pulling in and pretending I didn't mean to be there, or showing up at the diner just to check and see that you're okay."

"Are we friends or am I just your latest mission?" she asked, her eyes darting to see who might be close enough to hear.

"Friends."

"Then stop driving past the house. Stop checking on me."

"Help me put up my tree," he continued, watching as she weakened a bit and waiting as something that felt like hope flared up inside him.

"All right, we'll go. I have to let Granddad know we won't be home till later."

He gave her a sheepish grin that he hoped would cover a multitude of his mistakes. "I already told him."

She stomped off, but he knew that it was more in protest than in irritation. He felt pretty pleased with himself. Then he melted a little because Jamie had stayed next to him. Her hand was on his knee and she looked up expectantly. He picked her up and her sticky hands touched his face.

"Well, kiddo, looks like we're going to put up a Christmas tree."

"Christmas presents." Jamie giggled and patted his cheeks again. She leaned close to his ear and whispered, "I want a puppy."

"I bet you do." He carried her to where her mom was gathering up her purse and jacket and Jamie's soft blanket.

"Come back anytime," Oregon Martin was telling her. "We know you have a church in Braswell, but you can consider us your second church family. And, Emma, we'll all be praying for Jamie."

Emma hugged the other woman tight. "Thank you."

Then she turned those dark eyes on him and he realized he was in over his head and he wasn't sure if he knew how to swim in these murky waters.

"Ready to go?"

She nodded. Oregon gave her a questioning glance, so he jumped in and said, "I told Art I'd give them a ride home."

Jamie chimed in. "And Christmas trees."

Oregon looked confused but she didn't ask.

They managed to escape with no further incidents. He draped the blanket over Jamie and placed a hand on Emma's back to guide her out the side door of the church and across the parking lot to his truck.

On the way to his place, she broke the silence, reaching to turn down the radio. "People are going to talk."

"Yeah, I guess." He didn't dare grin. "They probably already do. Mostly about how I've lost it and how I need to admit I like you. Mostly they say I need to cowboy up if I'm going to ask you out."

"They say those things?" she asked.

"And a few more."

"You aren't going to ask me out," she stated flatly, giving no room for argument.

He'd argue anyway. "If you say so."

"You're making this pretty complicated, aren't you?"

He laughed at that. "Yeah, I do like complications. But I'll be out of your hair for a few days. I have a security job in Austin and then one in Houston."

"Good," she said, but it didn't sound like she meant it. And he was glad.

"Don't worry—I'm not going to stay gone." Now for

the serious stuff. "I'd really like to go with you when you go to Austin to the heart specialist."

She nodded but didn't say anything.

He guessed there ought to be a program for guys who couldn't stay out of dangerous relationships.

Step One, admit you like to be a hero...

Chapter Seven

Emma had driven past the Rocking M. By most standards it was a smaller ranch, only a few hundred acres. It was still quite a bit larger than her grandfather's small farm. The front of the property was surrounded by white vinyl fencing. The driveway was blacktop, not gravel. The house at the end of the blacktop was a fantastic stucco, wood and stone lodge home with a covered front porch, stone-lined flower gardens and a few willow trees. In the distance she spotted the stable and other outbuildings.

"I shouldn't let it sit empty," Daron said as he pulled into the garage.

"Then why do you? Your parents used to stay here quite a bit."

"They got tired of the drive and they aren't really ranchers. My grandfather, my mom's dad, had a ranch. She thought she wanted that life back, then realized she wasn't much of a country girl anymore."

"So they handed it over to you?"

"Yeah, they did. Boone would tell you I'm not much of a rancher, either. But I'm not ready to give it up."

They entered the house through a utility room and then walked down the hall to the kitchen and great room with vaulted ceilings and large windows overlooking the countryside. Emma put Jamie down, but her daughter was unsure of this big new space, the hardwood floors and shiny kitchen. Jamie held tight to her hand, eyes wide, studying the surroundings.

"I don't have any toys," Daron said, his expression troubled.

"No one would expect you to."

"I do have coffee, however," he offered. "And a tree."

He pointed to the giant tree devoid of decorations. It was situated in front of the large windows in the living area.

"You planned this?"

"Not really. I wanted a tree. Today, when you showed up at church, I thought you'd probably enjoy decorating it. Or Jamie would."

"Then we should have that coffee. Where are the decorations?"

"The decorations are in the garage," he said. "I'll get them and you start the coffee. There might be instant hot chocolate in the pantry, if Jamie would like that. And cookies." He'd obviously thought of everything.

"I'll take care of it. You get the decorations." She watched him walk away; then she circled the kitchen with its dark cabinets, granite countertops and appliances that made her want to cook. And she didn't really like to cook.

She found the coffee and started a pot brewing. Jamie sat on the floor nibbling a cookie that Emma gave her. She leaned against the counter and watched her daughter jabber to herself. Jamie looked up at her, all wide-eyed and sweet. She looked so much like Andy. Sometimes it was so hard, seeing his face, his expressions, on their little girl.

Even though she didn't want to get lost in the past, there were days she wondered if he would have come home to them, been faithful, been a husband and father. After all, they had Jamie together. Would they have gone through with the divorce had they known Emma was pregnant?

They were all questions that would never be answered because she and Andy had never gotten the chance to talk, except for that one phone call when she'd told him she was pregnant. He'd deserved to know.

"Everything okay?"

The question startled her. She regrouped and nodded. "Yes, just thinking."

"I see it, too. How much Jamie looks like him."

"Yes, and someday she'll want to know." She left the sentence unfinished. But they both knew. Someday Jamie would want to know about her dad.

"I'm sure she will. I'm sorry." He set the tubs on the floor and stood there, tall, strong, a little bit lost. She liked that about him, that little bit of vulnerability in a man who always seemed strong.

She picked up the coffee cups she'd found and poured them each a cup. She held one out to him. "Here's to friendship and forgetting the past. To letting go."

"A nice lecture hidden in a phrase of good cheer." He took the cup and lifted it in a salute.

"It wasn't," she started. "Okay, a little. Honestly we all have things we have to learn to let go of."

"If it was as easy to do as it is to say."

His expression shuttered and he walked away, taking the cup of coffee with him and stopping by the tree. Emma picked up Jamie and followed.

She didn't ask questions, not at the moment. Instead she sat in a rocking chair near one of the floor-to-ceiling windows and watched as he opened boxes, occasionally stopping to take a drink of his coffee.

Jamie climbed down off her lap and walked toward the box of glittery red ornaments. Daron handed her one and helped her hang it on a low branch of the tree. Emma moved from the rocking chair and lifted a laminated card with a ribbon attached. The angel and manger scene on the front didn't set it apart from any other Christmas card. She turned it and read the inscription on the back.

"Dear Soldier. Thank you for serving our country and keeping us safe. Jesse. Third Grade."

The words undid something inside her, something tightly wound that she usually kept a hold on, to keep her emotions safe, unattached from this man who had been watching over her for three years. That something unraveled a bit and she swallowed quick to keep it from turning into tears that were burning at the backs of her eyes, tightening her throat. She reached for another ornament, an angel colored in childish scribbles. Also laminated and a ribbon attached.

"Don't cry," he warned in a low voice.

"I'm not going to cry."

He pushed a tissue into her hand. "Yeah, you're going to cry. You're starting to get emotional, thinking I'm sentimental. I'm not. It just seemed a waste to throw away an art project some kid put all that work into."

"Of course," she said, shoving the tissue into her pocket. Unused.

"There are letters, too. Don't start reading them or we'll be here all night."

She shook her head. And as he helped Jamie hang another bright red decoration, she hung a card with a picture of the baby Jesus and on the back, a note from a little girl named Annie whose daddy was serving in Iraq and so she prayed for all the soldiers.

There were more. Letters. Cards. Homemade ornaments. From elementary school children across the country who had signed with first names, the words misspelled and sometimes smudged. But they told a story of a soldier who had cherished each and every missive.

No, he wasn't sentimental. And as she read through the cards he found crayons and plain paper for Jamie to add her own work of art to his tree. Her heart tugged a little because she really did want this man for a friend. If friendship was easy and didn't include strings.

"I asked him to go," he said while bending over Jamie, without looking at Emma. "That day, when the boy came to get us, to help his sister. I asked Andy to go with us. I didn't think it would be a big deal."

"Of course you didn't," she answered, looking up to meet his gray eyes. He quickly looked away.

He gave Jamie a few more crayons and told her he liked the tree she was coloring. She told him with a smile that it was Baby Jesus. He agreed that it was a very good Baby Jesus.

"I knew about you, and about the pregnancy. I wouldn't have put him in danger."

"I know you wouldn't. He made the decision to go with you. It wasn't your fault. It wasn't his fault. We can't live our lives second-guessing ourselves."

"Of course." He straightened, stretched and pasted on a look that was probably meant to appease her, to stop her from pushing the conversation further.

A friend would ask if he was okay. A real friend. She wasn't sure if she qualified yet. But here she was, helping him decorate his Christmas tree. She'd made coffee in his kitchen. She should push, get him to talk.

She let her attention drift to her sleepy little girl. Emma reached and Jamie went straight to her, arms out. She carried her to the sofa and snuggled her under an afghan before returning to the tree and to Daron. He had gone back to decorating.

"It wasn't your fault, Daron," she repeated as she stood next to him to hang a decoration. "Life isn't fair. It wasn't fair that my parents died in a freak car accident on wet roads. It wasn't fair that Andy died. Or that his parents refuse to believe Jamie is their granddaughter. It isn't fair that Pete is addicted to meth. Life isn't fair. But it's beautiful and complex. Every day I watch my daughter learn a new word, smile at something she's only just discovered. It's beautiful."

"It is beautiful." He looked down at her, and his gaze softened. "You…"

Emma held her breath. Because there weren't supposed to be moments like this. She was a single mom. He felt attached to them because of an event that had been out of his control. But the thread between them became a tangible thing. The air in the room buzzed as the moment stretched out. His fingers barely connected with her cheek but somehow pulled her up on her tiptoes, as if that invisible string was lifting her to meet him.

His lips touched hers. He tasted of coffee and cookies. It was warm and inviting and it made her feel truly alive to be in his arms. She hadn't felt alive, not like this, in a very long time. She'd simply been existing, being a single mom, a college student, a waitress.

For those few minutes in his arms, she was more. As his lips grazed her cheek and hovered near her temple, she wanted to be more than the solitary person she'd become. She wanted to trust her heart. Because this man was good and kind. He cared deeply.

He kept cards from schoolchildren he'd never met.

But trust was such a fragile thing and hers had been broken, shattered by Andy's infidelity, his willingness to walk away when he realized she didn't fit in his world or his plans for the future.

The heart was a funny thing. Once broken, it tried to avoid being broken again.

She slipped from his arms, the invisible string untethering so that she could back away. She touched her lips, still feeling the aftereffects of the kiss.

"I'm sorry," he said calmly. Hadn't he felt what she felt? Maybe that was the part of her heart she shouldn't trust, the part that felt so much when others seemed to feel nothing in return.

"Don't." Her hand slid from his shoulder. "It was a kiss, nothing more."

"Sure, nothing more," he said, the words sounding unsure. Maybe he wasn't as strong as she gave him credit for.

It was time to change the subject, to let the moment go.

"The tree looks beautiful. And I do love the homemade ornaments. Do you use them every year?"

He glanced at the tree, as if he'd forgotten its existence. She hid her amusement, then chastised herself for being so pleased that he seemed a little off-kilter.

"We're going to discuss the tree right now?" he asked, brushing a hand across his mouth.

"It seemed safe."

"Okay. Yes, I do. I put the tree up and water it and then I go to the Wilders'."

"Why?"

He let out a sigh. "This is the problem with women. Kiss them and they want to know all your secrets."

She heard the humor in his tone and a little bit of frustration. She decided to go with humor. "Kiss and tell, McKay."

"I don't sleep at night. Thus my stalkerish behavior, driving past your house, making sure you're all safe and sound. I pace a lot."

"Nightmares?"

He put the lid back on one of the tubs that had held decorations. "Yeah. Nightmares."

"You were injured, too."

He nodded at the observation. "Yes. I was hit with shrapnel."

"We've never discussed this." She picked up a card that had been left on the coffee table.

"We weren't friends," he said with a grin.

"No. And now we are. So tell me about the injuries."

"Oh, you're one of *those* friends. The type that believes she has a right to know everything."

"Something like that. After all, you know everything about my life."

He picked up their coffee cups and headed to the kitchen. Her phone rang as he was pouring more coffee.

Daron listened to Emma's phone conversation. Even hearing only one side, he knew there was a problem. And it sounded serious, meaning she'd have to head home. He poured out the coffee and hit the power button on the coffeemaker. She ended the call.

"The tiller is gone. I don't know why Granddad was out in the shed, but he said it's practically empty. We don't go out there much in the winter." She slipped the phone into her pocket. "I can't afford this. I know it's Pete, although I don't know why he targets my family. I don't want to press charges. But I can't support his drug habit."

"He's going to have to get help. And if that means you pressing charges, then you have to do that. Let's head on back to your place. Did Art call the police?"

"Yeah, the nonemergency number for the county. They'll be out tomorrow to take a statement and a list of missing items."

He watched as she woke Jamie, holding her daughter close and trying to maneuver her arms into her jacket.

"Take the blanket. Then you won't have to stuff her into the jacket."

She nodded and wrapped the blanket tightly around Jamie. "Thank you. I'll get it back to you tomorrow."

"I'll be gone on a job."

Her eyes darted his direction. "Oh, that's right. I forgot."

The strangest thing happened; he realized he'd miss

her. He guessed it wasn't the first time he'd had that thought. How did you miss a person when she wasn't a real part of your life? He guessed that after today, he'd miss her more.

He could call that kiss a mistake. Or just a moment. But what it did was change things. It changed a lot when a man kissed a woman, and when she stepped away, his first thought was how to get her back. And keep her.

The job would give him time to get away and put things in perspective.

"We should go. Before your granddad starts a search on his own." He laughed it off, but he wasn't sure it was really a joke.

"He did mention tire tracks at the side of the road. He said it looks like they went north."

"Maybe I should hire him?" He took Jamie from her. The little girl wrapped her arms around his neck.

"Only if you switch your business from security to private investigator."

He shifted Jamie to his left hip and pulled the keys out of his pocket. He winced as a spasm tightened in his lower back. Emma caught the look.

"I'm fine," he said.

"Of course you are. I didn't say anything."

When they got back to her place, he parked next to Art's old truck. Jamie was still sleeping. He got her out of the backseat. As they headed for the house, Art stepped out on the front porch.

"I wasn't expecting the two of you to head back here. I can hold down the fort." Art showed them his .22.

"Art, you have to put that away." Emma stepped up

on the porch and took the weapon from her granddad.
"That isn't going to solve anything."

"If it's Pete, he's hopped up on meth. You don't
know what he might try next."

"He won't hurt us," she insisted.

Daron wanted to argue Art's side. Pete might hurt
them. Instead he handed Jamie over to Emma and took
the gun from her. "We'll put this away. And, Art, let's
have a quick look in the shed. But we aren't going to
touch anything. Let's make a list of everything you
thought was in the shed and things you think might
be missing. If you have paperwork on the tiller, that
would be helpful."

"I have it filed," Emma said as she walked through
the door Art had opened for her.

Daron followed Art to the shed at the back of the
yard. "Art, I'm going to be out of town a few days."

"I'll keep them safe for you."

Daron opened the door to the shed. Did he argue that
it wasn't for him? That they weren't his to keep safe?
They were Art's family. But he didn't argue. Emma
needed to focus on Jamie, on the upcoming surgery.
She didn't need to worry about Pete and what he might
do next.

Sometimes a man made a decision that would
change everything. He guessed he'd been making decisions like that since he got back. Including the one
he was about to make.

"If something happens, call me. And I'll make sure
that either Boone or Lucy drives by here, just to check
on things."

Art peered into the inside of the shed. "That's a lot
more than a guilty conscience talking."

"I'd kind of like to think it's a thing friends would do for friends."

Art stepped out of the shed and he looked Daron head-on. He might be getting older, but Art Lewis was still a tough old man and the look on his face wiped away any humor Daron felt.

"Sure, okay. But let me give you some advice, Daron. Back in my day, if a man liked a woman, he just came out and said something. Usually he started out with 'I sure like that perfume.' And then he might ask if she'd like to catch a movie or get some ice cream."

"Ice cream, Art?" Daron couldn't help laughing.

Art gave him a sheepish look, his blue eyes twinkling.

"Well, I guess young people these days don't get ice cream."

"Maybe if they're fifteen."

"You're wearing my granddaughter's lipstick on your cheek. I guess ice cream would be a mite silly at this point."

Daron wiped at his face while pretending serious interest in the contents of the shed. "What was hanging on the hooks?"

"Some halters and a couple of bridles. Emma won't be happy about that. One was her show bridle. Not that she's had much chance to show. She had to sell her good mare. Shame, really. She's quite the trainer."

"When did she sell the mare?" Daron didn't know why it mattered. He didn't want to think about why he was asking.

"Six months ago. She decided college and a way to support Jamie were more important than raising horses." Art said it over his shoulder as he looked around the shed.

"Who bought her?"

"Duke Martin. Probably hoping she'd be able to buy the horse back someday."

"We'll find her stuff, Art."

"Don't break her heart in the process. Andy did a number on her. She's not gone out with anyone since he left her. She says Jamie is her life and she doesn't have the time or energy for a relationship. But she's young. Too young to give up."

"I don't think she's giving up," Daron said. He closed the door of the shed. "The tiller, bridles and halters. You'll have to tell Emma because the police will need descriptions."

"Yeah, I know. I just hate it. It's like Andy took a big chunk out of her heart and his family has been chipping away at the rest ever since."

"We won't let them," Daron assured the older man. "We'll keep her safe."

"I'm guessing you are part of the 'we'?"

Daron didn't know how to respond to that. He didn't feel like the person Emma should count on. Not when he was the person who had put her in this situation in the first place. One moment. One decision. Lives changed forever.

Because of his decision to ask Andy to help them out, Daron was now in Emma's life. In Jamie's life. In Art's life. When he'd started on this journey he thought it would be a short one. He'd get home, make sure they were okay and taken care of. But here he was, three years later, and he was still in their lives.

No escape route. He guessed he'd planned the mission without a clear way out.

Chapter Eight

The weather had warmed by Friday. Emma left the grocery store and headed for her truck, a bag under each arm. She'd worked the breakfast shift at Duke's, and as soon as she picked up Jamie from Breezy Martin's house, she was heading home to fix soup for Art. He'd caught a cold and wasn't doing well.

It didn't help that the house was drafty and damp. She'd build a big fire tonight and they'd have something warm to eat. She stored her worry for a later day. She didn't have time for it right now.

She definitely didn't have time to get sick. She could feel the virus tickling her throat and lurking in her head. She refused to give in to it. She didn't have time for that, either.

As she got in her truck, she waved at Boone Wilder. He was getting out of his truck and heading into Duke's. If she had more time she'd talk to him, tell him he didn't have to take over where his friend left off. She didn't need their bodyguard services. If Boone wanted to help, he should convince his friend Daron to move on with his life.

Three years was too long for one man to be stuck in the past. Stuck worrying about her. Stuck in his own nightmares. And because she knew that about him, she now worried about him.

She liked him.

Purely as a friend, of course.

It was easy to let him be a friend. No strings attached. No complications. No worries that she wouldn't meet his parents' standards. No fear that she wouldn't fit into his world. No heartache when he realized he'd married a woman who would never feel comfortable in his world.

He would never hurt her because she wouldn't give him the chance.

She started her truck and backed out of the parking space, waving to Oregon Martin when she appeared at the front door of her shop. Oregon's All Things was just that, a shop with a bit of everything. All handmade by Oregon.

The truck shuddered a bit as she shifted gears. Like everything else on the farm, the truck needed repairs. Actually, if she was completely honest with herself, it needed to be replaced. She started it every day with a prayer that it would keep running. One more day. Her prayer for so many things.

She cranked the radio up. If she listened to music, if she sang along, it distracted her. It also meant she couldn't hear the death knock in the engine, telling her it wouldn't last much longer. Her worrying wasn't going to change things, so she might as well be happy where she was in life.

Where she was wasn't so bad. She rolled down the windows because it was damp and chilly but it felt good. The air smelled clean, like farmland and winter. The song playing on the radio was a favorite of hers.

She was going home to fix soup and the yeast rolls she'd put in the fridge the previous evening. She had a half dozen steers she planned to take to the auction. The money would get them through the next few months. It would help while she was in Austin for Jamie's surgery.

The surgery. Thinking of it caused a tight knot to develop in her stomach. Sing, she reminded herself. About peace. "It Is Well" came on the radio. One of her favorite versions of the song. A song about a man who continued to think it was well with his soul, even after the loss of family and fortune.

"Whatever my lot, thou has taught me to sing. It is well…"

Suddenly the engine popped and sizzled, and the truck rolled to a stop.

She leaned her forehead against the steering wheel and laughed. Crying would have taken too much energy and she doubted it would get her home. Besides, it was just another stupid thing to get her down, to steal her joy, to rob her of peace.

No, she wasn't going to let it get to her. She leaned back and thought about her tired feet and the two-mile walk back to town because her phone was dead. She gathered up her purse, her tips for the day stashed safely inside, buttoned her jacket and stepped out of the truck. Back to town was definitely closer than Jake Martin's house, where Breezy had Jamie.

The wind whipped at her hair. She pulled up the hood of her jacket and started walking. She didn't make it fifty feet when a truck eased in behind her.

She turned as the gray Dodge moved to the shoulder. And then she started back toward her truck, picking up the pace when she heard the door of the other truck creaking open and slamming shut.

"Emma. Wait."

She didn't wait. Instead she ran to her truck and climbed in, locking the doors. She watched in her rear-view mirror as Pete hurried to her truck. He was thinner than the last time she'd seen him. His light-colored hair was thin and greasy. There were sores on his face.

"Emma, I just want to talk."

"I don't want to talk. Pete, just go. I don't have anything. If I had money would I be driving this truck?"

He braced his hands on the top and peered in at her. His eyes were watery and rimmed with dark shadows. She felt for him. He hadn't always been this person. But he'd made the wrong choices.

"I need help. I need money." He closed his eyes but continued to rest against her truck. "I'm tired, Emma. I can't keep doing this."

"Then get help. Go to your parents and tell them you need help."

"I haven't seen them in months. I can't see them because I don't want them to know. You have to help me." He looked up at the overcast sky. "I need five thousand dollars."

"Oh, come on, Pete, even I know that meth isn't that expensive."

"I owe some people. Some really bad people."

"I'm sure you do."

"No, you have no idea." He shook his head. "I'm warning you. I'm in with some bad people. I've been dealing and I owe them."

"Did you take their money, Pete? Or use up the merchandise?"

"I don't have time for this, Emma. I just need money. If you could loan me some money. You were Andy's wife. I'm your brother."

"Andy divorced me."

"I know. I'm sorry." He looked about to cry.

She rolled down the window, unafraid. "Pete. You're strung out and you need to sleep. Get some help. Go to your parents. It isn't as if they don't know."

"I can't." He breathed in, his lungs raspy, his hands on the truck shaking. "I can't. But you have to understand. These people are bad."

"What are you saying, Pete?"

"These aren't the type of people who forgive."

"Okay, fine. They don't forgive. You should go. You're starting to scare me and I need to get home to my family."

"How's Jamie?"

"None of your business."

He brushed a hand over his face. "Let me help you with your truck. I should help you. Andy would want me to do that."

"Pete, you don't have to help me."

This guy, who had been stealing from her a week ago, now wanted to help?

"Yeah, I can help. Let me look at the engine. Or I can call for a wrecker."

"You could do that for me. But then you have to leave. And, Pete, you have to get help."

"I wish that was possible." He pulled his phone out of his pocket, then shoved it back in. "Never mind. Your watchdog is here. I'll leave."

He took off at a run back to his truck. She watched in the rearview mirror and then she got out of her truck as Boone Wilder approached, looking menacing with his hat pulled low and a glower directed at the other man, now in his own vehicle.

"What did he want? Did he stop you here?" Boone was reaching for his phone.

She put a hand on his to stop him. "My truck engine blew. He actually stopped to help. And I don't know, maybe to warn me. Or ask for money. I'm not sure."

"What did he say?"

"He's in with some bad people and he owes them money. I'm not sure why that would worry me, but he acted as if it should."

Boone continued to watch as Pete turned on his vehicle and left. "Yeah, it should worry you. If he's in with the wrong people, it should worry us all. I don't get how someone gets into that stuff. But they do. Good families, dysfunctional families, it can happen to anyone."

"Yes, it can. I told him he needed to get help."

"He isn't interested?"

"Not at this point." She pushed the truck door open. "My phone is dead. I'm supposed to pick up Jamie from Breezy's. And now this."

He wrapped her in a friendly hug. "I'll call a wrecker and we'll go get Jamie."

"Thank you," she said. "It's been a long day."

"A long year. Or three?"

"Yeah."

Boone pulled out his phone, made a couple of calls as he paced the shoulder. "The wrecker will drag the truck out to your place. Unless you have somewhere else you want it taken?"

"No, have him take it to my place. It isn't going to get fixed for a while."

She wasn't going to say how worried she was. She needed this truck. It was her only transportation to work. But she still had the steers. She could use that money to get this truck fixed or get a decent older truck. They would get by.

"I can loan you one of our farm trucks," Boone offered as he opened the passenger door of his truck for her.

"We'll be fine."

"I know you will, but I'm offering."

She nodded and blinked back the moisture that welled in her eyes. She wouldn't cry.

And she wasn't going to allow herself to wish that Daron McKay was in town. She'd never felt this before, this need for someone, to lean on them. She had her granddad. She had Jamie.

So why did she feel so lonely? Why did she want to call Daron and tell him about her rotten day?

The screen door of the camper banged shut. Daron rolled on the couch and covered his face with the blanket. Or tried to. The blanket wouldn't budge. He yanked on it and tried to move, but a heavy weight held him pinned.

"Get, you smelly mutt." He didn't remember letting the dog in, but he'd been so tired when he got home that morning he hadn't really paid much attention.

The dog groaned, and then something hit his foot. Hard. Daron sat up, pushing the dog to the floor in the process. He reached fast for his sidearm and then he flopped back on the miniature couch.

"Go. Away," he snarled at Boone as he dragged the blanket back over his face. "I drove straight home from Houston after the event was over last night."

"Why didn't you stay in Houston and rest up?" Boone took his customary place in the recliner and kicked back, hat low and arms crossed over his chest. It looked like a casual pose. Daron knew him well enough to know it was anything but.

"I wanted to get home." He didn't want to go into reasons. He didn't want to talk about missing Emma Shaw. Just thinking about it made him feel like the worst kind of man.

"Okay, well, did your rush to get home have anything to do with Emma?" Boone asked.

"What? Emma? No." Daron paused for a moment. Then he went on. "Is she okay? Is Jamie okay?"

"Yeah, she's fine. I just gave them a ride home."

"A ride home?" Daron reached for his boots and pulled them on. He pushed the dog away. The collie had a thing for lying on his shoes.

"From what I could tell, her truck engine blew out. She's fine. No transportation now, but she's okay. She's about the toughest woman I know. When I left her, she was heading to the field to hay their cattle. Art's down with a cold."

"You didn't offer to help?" He was already pulling on his jacket. Out of the corner of his eye, he saw Boone grin. He got a little suspicious. "What?"

"Nothing." Boone raised his hands. "I offered her a truck. She said no. I offered to help her feed her livestock. She said she does it every day."

"I have a farm truck at the ranch. I'll take her to get it." Daron had a hand on the door, but he remembered his manners. "Thanks for letting me know, Boone."

"Anytime. One more thing." Boone pushed himself up from the recliner and followed him out the door. "Pete was there when I found her on the side of the road."

"Maybe you should have started this story with that, rather than finishing it?"

"I'm telling you now, so relax. She said he kept mentioning he's in trouble with some bad people."

"Great. Leave it to Pete to get in with some drug cartel. He needs to go to rehab."

"He needs money. Sounds like he owes someone a lot of money, and it's probably the type of person who doesn't like waiting for it."

Daron sighed out loud. "I'm going."

"Figured you might. Call me if you need anything."

"Will do."

Daron climbed into his truck and headed down the drive. On the way to Emma's, he told himself it was nothing personal. He was doing the same thing he'd been doing for the last few years, keeping his promise to Andy.

But he wasn't good at lying, not even to himself. Something major had shifted. For the last three years he'd kept her solidly in the category of "client." He'd managed to keep his professional distance.

He'd blown it the day he kissed her.

Big-time.

Fifteen minutes later he was pounding on Emma's door. She didn't answer. Art opened the door looking a little worse for wear and none too happy. The older man stood on the inside of the screen door and glared out at Daron.

"Is there a reason you're pounding on my door, Daron McKay?"

"Sorry, Art. Boone told me about Emma's truck breaking down. I wanted to make sure she's okay."

"That's a lot of pounding for a blown engine. She's out in the field. One of her mama cows didn't come up at feeding time. I offered to go with her, but Jamie is sleeping and Emma seems to think I need my beauty rest. I told her I'm not getting any purtier to look at."

"I'll go check on her."

"Go on with you, then. But you might not want to ruffle her feathers."

"I reckon no matter what, her feathers are gonna be ruffled," Daron said, managing to keep a straight face.

Art chuckled. "You do manage to bring out the best in her."

Art started to cough and Jamie peeked around his legs, her thumb shoved in her mouth. Daron felt a change of plans coming on as the older man doubled over with the force of the cough, and Jamie seemed worried, unsure, her blue eyes filling with tears.

"I have an idea. How about if I stay here with you and Jamie? If Emma doesn't show up soon, then I'll go looking for her."

Art finally managed to catch his breath, but his face was red. "I guess that'll suit, since you don't seem to think we can manage without your help."

"I'm not meaning to interfere, Art."

"I know you're not. Jamie here is supposed to be napping."

Daron picked up the little girl. "Then I'll read to her and maybe she'll go to sleep."

He carried Jamie to the living room and covered her with a quilt. She curled on her side and grinned as she shoved her thumb in her mouth. "Read the princess book?"

"You got it, kiddo." Daron looked around and spotted a horsemanship magazine on the table. "This has pictures and I don't see a princess book."

"I like horses." She closed her eyes. "And princesses."

Art walked through the room, shaking his head.

Daron sat on the edge of the sofa and started to read about a mare that had a good showing at a national event. The horse had been an underdog, not favored to win. The breeding wasn't the best. The training was local and the rider was the owner. But they showed everyone. The page was dog-eared more than once.

He showed Jamie the picture of the horse. She told him it was a bay. He agreed. She knew her colors. He turned the page and showed her another horse. "Chestnut," she said when she saw the pretty red filly. They played "name the color" for a while.

Every few pages he glanced at his watch and then out the window.

Jamie was dozing when the front door opened. He winked at Emma. It was a flirty gesture and probably wasted on a worn-out cowgirl whose braids were coming undone and whose daughter needed heart surgery.

"Boone told you, didn't he?" Emma asked as she stopped in front of the woodstove to get warm.

"He did. Jamie and I have been reading a magazine

about horses, waiting for you. Unless you need help. I didn't want to get in the way."

"I found the heifer I was looking for and put her in the corral. She'll probably calve tomorrow. Or maybe tonight. She seems prone to orneriness."

"I have an extra truck for you to use," he said, glancing down at Jamie. She was sound asleep. "If you want, I'll drive you out to get it."

Emma sat down in a nearby rocking chair. Her forehead was furrowed, and after a long moment, she finally nodded. "I want to say I don't need your truck. But that would be my pride talking. I need to be able to work and take care of my daughter."

"Then we'll leave Jamie in Art's capable hands and run over to get the truck." He stood, letting Jamie nestle into the couch as he pulled the blanket up around her. "Will the two of them be okay together for fifteen minutes or so?"

Emma had moved from the rocking chair and she leaned over her sleeping daughter. Lightly she brushed a curl from Jamie's brow. It was easy to see her concern for her child. She didn't have to tell him. He doubted if she talked about it much with anyone. In the next couple of months, though, her daughter would possibly undergo open-heart surgery. It wasn't an easy thing to think about.

"They'll be fine," she said as she moved away from the sofa and the sleeping child. "Let me tell Art where I'm going and I'll grab my purse. If you don't mind, I need to stop by the feed store in Martin's Crossing."

A few minutes later Art was in the recliner in the living room, Jamie was still sleeping and Daron was following Emma to his truck.

"What are you going to do about Pete?" he asked as he pulled onto the road. "He's no longer just a stupid addict looking for money. He's probably involved in things he wishes he could get out of. If he's coming to you for money, he's desperate."

"I don't think he'll hurt us."

"No, maybe he won't. But you don't know who he's involved with. Emma, these people don't care who they hurt. They just want their money."

She covered her face with her hands. "I'm so tired. I'm tired of Pete dragging us into his problems. I'm tired of trying to make everything work for everyone else. I'm just tired."

"I know," he said quietly, giving her a minute to pull herself together.

"I'm fine. I really am. And I'm not sure what to do about Pete. I would really like for life to be simple again."

He pulled into the parking lot of Martin's Crossing feed store and backed his truck up to the loading dock. "I do know."

She turned that dazzling smile on him, the one he hadn't seen too often. She'd spent more time frowning at him than smiling. He'd gotten on her nerves, always hanging around. Now it seemed as if the two of them had become a habit. She was used to him always being around. He was used to her telling him to go away. But all of a sudden, she wasn't too eager to run him off. And he wasn't too eager to leave.

As they got out of the truck and headed to the entrance of the store, he caught sight of a familiar truck. Pete.

Nothing about this felt right. And leaving Art, Jamie

and Emma alone and defenseless, that didn't set well with him. She wasn't going to like it, but her life was about to get a lot more complicated.

Chapter Nine

The truck Daron loaned her was about ten years newer than her old farm truck. It shifted easily, started without pumping the gas and didn't die going up hills. On Saturday morning she drove through the field looking for the cow she'd expected to calve. She parked and got out. There were several head gathered under a tree. She walked the area, checking behind brush.

She found a section of fence that the cattle had ridden down, pushing their heads through to get grass on the other side. After all, it was always greener over there. She headed back to the truck for tools and work gloves. She pounded the posts back into the ground, made sure they were sturdy, then tightened the few strands of barbed wire.

The sound of a cow in distress caught her attention. She stood still, listening. *No. No. No.* Not the heifer. She hurried back to the truck and drove in the general vicinity she thought the sound came from. As she pulled up to a stand of trees, she caught sight of the black cow stretched out on her side. She was heaving, raising her head to cry out and then heaving again.

"This is not how I wanted this to go, Mama." Emma knelt beside the heifer. "I'd prefer you do this on your own."

She got up and hurried back to the truck, but then remembered, it wasn't her truck. She didn't have her calving jack, gloves or anything else she might need to pull a calf. She did find some rope. She could make do if things didn't happen on their own.

When she got back to the cow, she was heaving, pushing. The calf's hooves were out. The cow looked as if she'd been at it a long time. She was worn slick, too tired to really try.

"Listen, Mama, I understand. Really I do. Twelve hours of labor, all alone. Believe me, I get it. But you've got to get this baby out or I'm going to lose you both. And I don't want that."

Obviously the cow didn't really care what she had to say.

"Okay, you push, I'll get these ropes around those hooves and we'll do this together."

On the next push she got a loop around each hoof of the calf. It wasn't going to be easy without the calving jack to wench the baby out, but she'd done it this way before. It took muscle, and probably more strength than she had. But somehow her adrenaline kicked in. Fifteen minutes later the calf was curled up on the ground and the mama cow found a little energy to clean her up.

Emma sat down on the cold ground a short distance away. She was too exhausted to care that it was damp. She didn't really mind the cold. It was a good morning, watching that new baby get up on her legs, wobble a bit, then find her first breakfast, safe at her mother's side.

A truck idled up. She turned, not surprised to see

Daron McKay. He got out of his truck and a few minutes later he was sitting next to her.

"Art was worried." He leaned back to watch the heifer and her baby. "Can't see something like this in the city."

"No, probably not. But it's an amazing thing to see. I'll text Art." She sat a few minutes longer. "What are you doing here?"

"Good to see you, too, Emma." He sat with his knees up, his arms resting on them, his gaze focused on the cow. "I have a crew at your house, putting new shingles on that section of roof."

She started to tell him he shouldn't have. But the new Emma was trying to be grateful. She'd been praying about it, about allowing people to help her. She couldn't do it all on her own. And Granddad was getting too old. It was time to admit that maybe it was okay to accept help.

Pride was a difficult thing to let go of.

"You're not going to tell me to stop interfering?"

She bumped her shoulder against his and then rested it there. And it felt good. "No."

"That's good. Because there's something else I have to tell you."

"I don't like the way that sounds," she admitted. The calf finished nursing and took a few awkward steps.

"No, you probably won't. But I want you to hear me out. I'm worried about Pete and what he's involved in."

"Me, too," she said.

"I've asked Lucy to stay with you all for a while. Just to keep an eye on things. She's between jobs and she doesn't mind."

A stranger in her home, watching over them? She

bristled at the idea. "I can watch out for my family just fine, Daron."

"I know you can. But I'd feel better if she was here."

"We are *not* your problem. I know you believe you are responsible for Andy's death. You're not. An IED killed him. It injured you and Boone. You don't have to do this."

"I know I don't." He sat there, arms crossed over his knees, and then he slowly looked at her. "I'm doing it for you."

Her heart thawed just a bit. There were dozens of reasons to pull away from him, and only one reason to lean toward him, to kiss him on his cheek. Because he was kind.

So she kissed him and then she stood, because she needed to go to the house, to let her granddad know she was okay. She needed space from this man because he was burrowing into her heart, and she thought that when he left there would be a Daron-size piece of it missing.

"I have to go check on Jamie. We have a doctor's appointment Tuesday. In Austin."

He stood next to her. "I know. When I left she was sitting with Boone telling him all about the Christmas tree and what she wants for Christmas."

"She wants ponies and kittens and puppies." Emma knew the list by heart. "Oh, and an elephant."

"I'd like to see you put that in your barn."

"If I could give her an elephant, I would." She smiled.

"You would give her anything." He laughed. "I would give her anything. I think right now Boone is wondering if he could find an actual elephant."

He opened her truck door for her. She would have hugged him at that moment, but she needed a shower. It was a point in his favor that he would even stand next to her. She wondered what type of women he dated. It was a dangerous thought, because she knew the world he came from. Married to Andy, for a short time, she'd been a part of that world. "Don't worry," he said.

"I'm not. Okay, maybe a little."

"About Jamie?" he asked as he leaned against the open truck door.

"Yes, Jamie. And Pete. Sometimes I even worry about you."

He showed her that dimple in his cheek, the one that could make a girl develop a serious crush. "Now, why would you worry about me?"

Why would she? He was standing there, all tall and confident in blue jeans and a cowboy hat.

"Because you're still hanging around here instead of moving on with your life."

The dimple deepened, throwing her off-kilter. "Sweetheart, that is where you're wrong. I'm exactly where I want to be. And I am moving forward with my life."

Her heart slammed against her ribs. "Don't say things like that."

"Why not? Unless I mean them?" he asked. His grin disappeared, but the look on his face was just as dangerous. "I mean it."

Then he closed the truck door and walked away.

Daron parked next to Emma. As she got out of the truck, she looked a little worse for wear. It was barely eight in the morning and she'd probably been up for several hours already. Her grandfather had been up since six and he said she'd already been long gone. Jamie had still been asleep when Daron got there, but she'd woken up and was busy entertaining Boone when Daron left the house to go find Emma.

The roofing crew was hard at it. There were four men and he guessed they'd get a big portion of the roof done by evening.

"This is too much," Emma said. "I'm working at being more accepting of help. But a new roof isn't just help."

He walked with her toward the house. "Accept it, Emma. I'm also going to put plastic on the windows. That might help keep the wind out."

"Thank you," she said softly, and he didn't look down. He didn't want to see tears and he doubted she wanted him to see. "I'm going to take a shower and then you can introduce me to Lucy. But really, she doesn't have to stay here."

"She does. And she agrees."

He didn't tell her the rest. He had the police doing some checking on Pete and who he might be in trouble with. Emma left him in the living room. Jamie was showing Lucy a book about elephants and explaining why one would be a good pet. Lucy had never been much of a kid person, but she was softening up, her hand even stroking Jamie's blond curls.

Daron didn't know all of Andy and Emma's story, but he could guess that his friend had done a number on Emma's self-confidence. Andy would have expected a lot. And then there was the fact that he hadn't been faithful. Idiot. He'd been given a gift and he hadn't cherished it.

Daron went to the kitchen and put on a fresh pot of coffee. Art was cooking up some eggs and bacon on the stove. He looked a little run-down but better than he had the previous day.

"Art, I can do that."

Art faced him, spatula in hand. "It's the least I can do, make you all breakfast. We appreciate this. I'd appreciate it more if I knew why you thought we needed a bodyguard."

Daron sat down at the kitchen table and explained. Because Art deserved to know. He had a right to protect his family. Art turned off the stove and removed the pan of eggs from the burner. "That boy needs to be locked up for his own safety."

"Yeah, he does. Unfortunately something has to happen in order to do that."

"I reckon. But I hate that something always has to happen before a person can get help."

"Me, too."

Emma entered the room, her hair damp from her shower. She'd changed into jeans and a pale blue T-shirt, her feet bare. She glanced at him, shy, then went to the coffeepot. She hugged Art before pouring herself a cup.

"We have a new heifer calf," she told her grandfather.

"That's good news. You had to pull her?" Art asked as he scooped out eggs and bacon and handed her the plate. "Jamie had cereal for breakfast."

"Thanks, Granddad." She rose on tiptoe to kiss his cheek. "Yes, I had to pull her. It wasn't too bad. The cow was just worn out and needed a little help. I need to transfer stuff from the old truck to Daron's. I didn't have the jack or gloves."

She sat down across from Daron and raised her gaze to meet his. "Do you want breakfast?"

"In a minute."

Lucy joined them, pouring herself a cup of coffee. "Jamie is drawing pictures of elephants. In case we wondered what she wants for Christmas."

Daron pushed a chair out with his foot. "Join us."

Lucy nodded, but she filled her a plate first.

"Lucy, I don't think you've met Emma Shaw. Emma, this is our partner Lucy Palermo."

Lucy gave Emma a somewhat pleasant look. That was as pleasant as Lucy got. She'd had a rough childhood, even rougher teenage years. She kept to herself, a habit learned from her mother. Don't trust. Don't talk.

"Nice to meet you, Emma. I've heard a lot about you." She shot Daron one of her rare smiles. It looked more like a smirk.

"Nice to meet you, too." Emma set her coffee cup on the table. "You really don't have to do this. I know Daron is worried and..."

Lucy raised a hand to stop Emma. "I'm here because I'm worried, too. This is something we all talked about."

"Maybe I should have been included in this conversation *we* all had?" Emma said with a bit of bite in her tone.

"We're discussing it now," Lucy shot back.

"Good, this is promising." Boone entered the room. "Lucy, we need to get you declawed. Daron, haven't you called the vet?"

Daron laughed and so did Art. At least two of them

were on the same side. "I tried, but the VA is back-logged and can't declaw for several months."

"You all are so funny," Lucy snarled, and then she dug into the breakfast. "Remember, I'm armed."

Daron glanced at Emma. "Lucy does love her weapons."

"I'm a good bodyguard and don't you forget it, Daron McKay. I'm more than a pretty smile and flashy gray eyes."

He put a hand to his heart. "Ouch. You got me there. My weapon is my dimple."

Boone sat down at the table with them. "The two of you are like siblings in the back of a van on a long vacation."

"Something Boone knows all about." Daron got up to take his cup to the sink.

"Yeah, if it has to do with siblings, I know a thing or two. But we need to discuss this. I have to put together a crew for a big oil CEO coming to Houston for meetings. Daron, you're staying here to man the office for a week or so?"

"Yes, and to plan for that big conference in January."

"That leaves me here," Lucy said. "I'll be able to help you in Houston if you need me. And if Daron needs me at the office, I can manage."

"I don't need twenty-four-seven protection," Emma tried to protest. Daron wanted to tell her he understood. She didn't want them all invading her life. But for now, this was best. They were all in agreement. They'd served with Andy. They cared about her.

Jamie entered the room, killing any further conversation. She crawled onto her mom's lap and began to draw more elephant pictures. Emma leaned close, kissing the little girl's head.

"This is an elephant with big ears, Mommy." Jamie pointed at the picture. "And it likes kittens."

"So the elephant wants a pet kitten?" Emma asked.

Jamie nodded, her head tucked beneath Emma's chin. Daron leaned against the counter and watched the two of them.

There was definitely no way he was getting out of this situation without losing a big chunk of his heart.

Chapter Ten

Emma hefted a tray of Monday meat loaf specials and headed for table ten. She said a quick hello to an older friend of Art's, sidestepped Ned and managed to get to the table without losing a single plate. She counted that as an accomplishment.

After she'd served the customers, refilled their drinks and chatted briefly, she headed back to the kitchen. Duke was stirring up something chocolate. She wanted chocolate. Badly.

"Have a bite," Duke offered. He grabbed a spoon and scooped her out some. "Chocolate pie filling."

She took it, relished it and tossed the spoon in the sink. "That's amazing."

"Better than cake?" he teased.

"Definitely better than cake."

"About your mare," he said as she headed out of the kitchen.

She paused and then did an about-face. "What?"

She never asked about Bell. She didn't visit. She pretended the horse had never existed because it was easier than giving up on a dream. If she pretended the dream hadn't existed, it hurt less.

"I'm only telling you this because I think you have a right to know. Daron is trying to buy the mare. We told him she's not for sale, because that's the deal we made with you. But if you're okay with the urban cowboy buying her, we'll go ahead."

"I'm not okay with him buying her." She closed her eyes and counted to ten. Twice. When she opened her eyes she was still on the edge of angry. "I don't want him to buy that horse. Not because of his city roots but because of his stupid guilty conscience. I don't want pity gifts. I don't want this. Any of it."

She pulled her apron up to her face and growled into it. Behind her the door opened and Ned chuckled. Emma dropped the apron back into place.

"He's infuriating."

Ned full-blown laughed. "Got to be talking about the urban cowboy. Honey, let me tell you something. Yes, he's infuriating. But he's also a wonderful-looking man. I'm old, but I look at him and thank my Good Lord above for allowing me to at least look. You've got him running in circles after you and you're about to send him on down the road?"

"I don't want his pity or his guilt. I thought we were friends. I can use a friend."

Duke poured filling into a prepared pie shell. "He offered to buy her horse back. I thought I should check with Emma before I made any deals."

"Troublemaker," Ned quipped as she turned in an order. "You knew it would rile her and you love to cause that boy problems. The whole lot of you have been picking on him for about twenty years now. But he's stuck with it. He hasn't left that ranch. He hasn't walked away from his friends. I guess we probably should stop calling him city boy. He's as country as the rest of us."

Duke laughed. "Just with shinier boots."

Emma found her sense of humor. "He does have pretty boots."

Ned snorted. "If that's what you're noticing when you look at him, then I think the two of us need to have a long, long talk."

"Ned, seems like *you* ought to ask him out." Duke handed Emma a pie. "Ready for the fridge."

"Now, what kind of woman would I be if I tried to take Emma's man?" Ned asked as she headed back out of the kitchen. "Besides, I'm too old to take that road again."

"I'm with Ned. I've already been down that route. I'm fine being single."

Duke gave them both a look and shook his head as he went back to his pies. "You all are trying to out plan God. I remember when I tried that. And one day I turned around and found I had a daughter and that the woman I didn't remember was the love of my life. You never know what will happen tomorrow."

"I hope only good things," Emma said. She could use some good days.

"Surely you don't think the Lord is worried about marrying me off, Duke Martin?" Ned cackled a bit. "That ship done sailed. Not that sweet little Emma here can't believe in second chances."

"I think I'm happily single, too." Emma shot her boss a look. "The horse stays at your place. Yours or Jake's. You are *not* to sell it to Daron."

She walked back into the dining room of the restaurant, and there sat Daron McKay, in the flesh. In the last few days she'd gotten used to his continuous presence. No matter where she went, either he or Lucy followed. One of them always seemed to be at the house, too.

It did make her feel better, safer, to have someone watching over Granddad and Jamie while she worked. Today Lucy had even kept Jamie so she wouldn't have to go out in the cold to Breezy's. Emma knew that was a big deal for the other woman, who had freely admitted she wasn't a kid person.

Not that the two of them had shared their deepest secrets. They talked about the weather, about horses and about what to fix for dinner. Occasionally they touched on the surface of their real lives.

She didn't hold on to any real hope that she and Lucy would be best friends.

Her heart skipped to Daron. Because even annoyed, she was glad to see him. And that frightened her. Relying on him, on anyone, scared her.

Except Granddad. He was her one safety net. He had always been there for her. It wasn't that she didn't believe another person could do the same, it was just more comfortable to rely on her grandfather.

She carried water to the table where Daron sat, alone.

"You asked Duke if you could buy the mare," she said as she set the glass in front of him.

"Duke has a big mouth," Daron said as he picked up the menu. "I'm here to follow you home."

"Good. Wonderful. But the horse isn't included in this bodyguard business. I'm letting you all invade my home, my life, and I'm doing that to keep my daughter and grandfather safe. That doesn't give you the right to interfere in the rest of my life."

He pointed to the seat across from her. She sat down, waiting for his explanation. She didn't look at him. Looking might mean falling. For his excuses. Not for him.

"Art told me how much the mare means to you."

She closed her eyes, wishing it were true. She loved the mare. She was a beautiful animal. She was a hope and a promise. And not at all what people thought. Because she wanted that horse. She wanted the dream.

But not the way it had happened.

"No. Daron, just no. Don't go there. Don't bring this up. Just let it go. I don't want the mare back. She's beautiful and wonderful and I don't want her."

"But Art said…"

Emma stopped him. "There are things Granddad doesn't know. And there are things I'm not going to tell you. Just let it go. I don't want the mare. I want the Martins to have her. Someday I'll have a foal out of her. That will be enough."

She could see the wheels turning in Daron's head, and she wondered how long it would take him to connect the dots. But maybe he wouldn't think about it past today. Maybe he would understand the story was too difficult to tell. Only Oregon knew. That was enough.

"Okay, no mare." He leaned back in his chair. "You know, I'll listen if you ever want to talk."

"I know you will. But for now I have to get back to work. Did you want to order?"

"Nope, I'm just here to follow you home when your shift is over."

She got up from the table, hoping he meant it, that he wouldn't push.

He reached for her hand, stopping her escape. "I'll be at your place early tomorrow morning."

"Why?"

"I'm driving you to Austin tomorrow. For Jamie's appointment."

"You really don't have to."

"I think I do. We'll do chores before we head out, so Art doesn't have to. And while we're gone, Lucy is going to try and convince him to go to the doctor for that cough."

"I hope she can convince him," she admitted. "I haven't been able to get him to go."

"Lucy can be very persuasive."

Lucy wasn't the only one. But she didn't have a chance to tell him that. She found herself busy for the next hour. Folks working on the Christmas bazaar had finished up for the day and were taking a late lunch.

When she finally clocked out, Daron was still there. Duke had joined him for a glass of tea and a slice of pie. The two were talking horses and the price of cattle.

"I'm heading home now. Duke, I'll see you in a couple of days."

Duke stood. "You make sure you let us know how the appointment goes. And if you need anything at all, just call. We're praying for you both, Emma."

"Thank you, Duke. We appreciate it so much."

Daron got up to follow her out. "I'll be at my place tonight."

That took her by surprise. "Okay?"

"It's closer. In case you need anything."

"We have Lucy with us," she reminded him.

"I know." He shrugged, like it didn't matter. "It will be good to stay at my place. Boone's brother, Jase, has been crashing at the camper. It's hard to pace with him constantly wanting to analyze what might be wrong with me."

"All right, then. See you in the morning."

She almost invited him for dinner. But she didn't. Instead she said goodbye to him at her truck, knowing he would follow her home, then go on to his place.

It was better that way.

Daron fixed himself a bologna sandwich that night and he sat on the front porch to eat it. In the field cattle grazed. His cattle. There were horses, just a few. When he wasn't there to take care of them, the ranch hand, Mack, did whatever was necessary.

He loved the ranch. He'd been raised in the city, but small-town life was what fit him. At least at this point in his life. He didn't mind coming up behind a tractor and poking along at twenty miles per hour. He loved the smell of fresh-cut hay in the field.

In the past few months he'd thought about moving back to the city, but he knew it no longer suited him. He'd changed since his tour in Afghanistan. He didn't want a job at his dad's law firm. He didn't want the committee dinners and society functions that his parents enjoyed.

He didn't mind that they enjoyed their life. He just wanted them to see that it wasn't for him.

He went back inside, where he'd built a fire earlier. After sitting outside, where it was cold, he felt good to sit down in front of it.

He dozed. But in the dark he was running. Jamie

and Emma were ahead of him. They were running, too. Emma held Jamie in her arms. He was yelling at them to stop. He ran faster, but he couldn't catch up. The blast came out of nowhere. He couldn't reach them.

He sat up with a start, perspiration beading across his forehead. It had been a dream. Of course it had. He rubbed his face to clear the sleep from his eyes, from his mind. Then he got up.

In the kitchen he drank a glass of water while staring out the window at the darkened countryside. He refilled the glass and downed it again. His heart returned to a normal pace. He pulled his keys out of his pocket, pushed his feet into his boots, grabbed a jacket off the hook by the door and headed out the back door.

Minutes later he was driving past Emma's house. He slowed as he drove past. There was a light on in the living room. Someone else couldn't sleep, either. Probably Lucy. Like the rest of them, she sometimes had nightmares.

A shadow moved near the barn. He slowed, turned and idled back. At first he thought it might be his imagination. But he saw it again, crossing the yard. He turned into the drive and pointed his headlights in the direction of the shadow.

He jumped out and headed toward the woman in the bright beam of his headlights.

"What are you doing out here?"

"I could ask the same of you," Emma quipped. "I thought you were going to stay at your place tonight. In order to do that, you actually have to stay."

He walked with her toward the house. "I couldn't sleep."

She accepted the hand he offered, surprising him.

"Me, either," she admitted. "When I woke up I thought I might come out and check on the new calf. I brought her and the mama up yesterday."

"And they're doing okay?" He wanted to ask if she understood how dangerous it was for her to be out there alone. But he remained silent.

"They're good. Do you want a cup of tea?"

"Might as well, since I'm here. But do you mind telling me where Lucy is?"

"I had her take my bed tonight. She's been sleeping on the couch."

"Gotcha."

He followed her to the house. It was starting to rain. Just a light mist, but already the air felt cooler, more like winter.

The house was quiet, lit only with a lamp in the living room and a light above the kitchen sink. Night sounds settled around them. The creak of the old house, the wind picking up, the patter of rain against the windows. She put the cups of water in the microwave and then stood there until it buzzed. Daron sat at the old table, with a yellow Formica top.

All in all, it felt pretty good to be there in her kitchen. It felt restful, something he didn't often feel. He told her that, and she smiled as she stirred sugar into the cups. When she joined him they were silent for a minute. The tea smelled of cinnamon and other spices.

"Why don't you sleep?" she finally asked, taking a cautious sip of her hot tea.

"Nightmares. Tonight you were there. Right before the explosion I called your name."

Her hand slid across the table and met his halfway. Their fingers intertwined, the peaceful feeling grew.

He couldn't remember ever feeling so good about his life, even before the military. But if he ever told her it felt right, sitting in that kitchen with her, holding hands, she'd probably run him off and say something about his guilt.

This wasn't guilt. But it also wasn't the time to tell her what he thought it might be. Which was about the best thing that had ever happened to him.

"It was just a dream, Daron. Here we are, all fine."

"Yes, all fine. With Pete and his friends somewhere getting high and with Jamie needing surgery. It's all fine?" It made him angry and he didn't know why. She was entitled to be fine with her life.

Her fingers tightened around his. "What would my faith be if I didn't trust that God could handle this? Yes, I worry. I am sometimes afraid. But in the end, I have to trust. I can either trust or fall apart. I choose faith."

"I wish I had your faith."

She grinned at him. "You'll have to get your own. Mine is being used."

He laughed, then looked down into the cup of amber liquid. "Yeah, I'll have to find my own. I've been working on that."

"And maybe you can find some peace."

"I'm working on that, too. One step at a time, Shaw. Don't push a guy too hard."

"You have to understand something, Daron. My marriage was over. Andy was not good to me." She bit down on her bottom lip, and her eyes looked damp. "I don't like to talk about him, about what happened. It seems wrong. He's gone and he can't defend himself."

"I know," he answered. His own voice was a little tight. If he could undo her past, he would.

She cleared her throat and quickly swiped at the corner of her eye where a tear had escaped. "It's over. It's in the past. I don't want to go back and relive it again and again."

"Why did you sell the mare?"

She sipped her tea and in the silence he could hear a clock ticking the seconds away. Outside, a coyote howled.

"The mare was an apology gift from Andy." She shrugged and then took another sip of tea before continuing. "We tried to work things out and obviously it didn't work. But I have Jamie and I'm not sorry. She's the best thing he ever gave me. The horse is beautiful. But my daughter is everything to me."

"Yes, you have Jamie. And if I say anything else, it'll just be wrong. I'm sorry."

Daron sat back in his chair, absently rubbing the back of his neck. It was hard to find words when everything he wanted to say would have revealed his feelings for the woman sitting across from him. And she wasn't ready to hear it.

As they sat there in silence, he thought about all the ways he would show her a man could be trusted. He wouldn't let her down. He made that silent promise. Somehow he would be the man she could finally count on.

It didn't slip past his attention that this night mattered. A lot. Maybe God wasn't as distant as he'd always thought. Maybe his faith was more than a box checked off on a military form. And maybe this woman would someday accept what he really wanted to tell her.

Chapter Eleven

They left for Austin at six the next morning. Lucy had fixed them a thermos of coffee. The gesture had been unexpected. She'd also given Emma a quick hug and told her not to worry. Art and the farm would be fine. She'd make sure of it. And Emma should just focus on making sure that little girl was okay.

It was a few minutes before eight when they pulled up to the Children's Hospital. Daron had been silent for some time. Emma had been okay with the silence. She'd needed time to think and to pray. Now she was fed up with the silence. She needed for him to say something.

If she were truly honest with herself, she really needed a hug, but she wasn't going to ask for one.

"Here we are," he finally said.

"Yes, we're here." She bit down on her bottom lip and stared up at the big building, all metal and glass. She wondered if it had paintings on the walls and a doctor who sometimes wore googly eyeglasses to make the children laugh.

"We should go in," Daron said.

"I wish we didn't have to," she said, reaching for her purse and for the backpack with snacks, blankets and stuffed animals. "But the sooner we get it over with, the better."

"Yes, come on, Emma, you're not a quitter. You're David going after Goliath with a tiny pebble and a lot of faith. You're Daniel staring down lions."

"And who else?" She smiled as she quizzed him.

He chuckled. "That's all I've got. You've used up my entire repertoire of famous Bible guys who had faith."

They entered the building, Jamie holding tight to Emma and Daron carrying the backpack. Emma allowed herself a few seconds to think that this was how it felt to be part of a couple. *Relish it, then get it out of your system*, she told herself. It almost worked.

She wanted to relish a little longer. But she didn't have the luxury to feel this way. She had Jamie in her arms and a specialist waiting to tell them what would be their next mountain to climb. Their next battle to win.

But she knew they'd conquer all. She knew it the way she knew if she took a breath there would be oxygen.

The specialist was a woman named Dr. Lee. She had dark hair and warm, almond-shaped eyes. Jamie took to her right away, climbing on her lap, taking turns with the stethoscope. Emma watched, taking in every expression on the doctor's face as she examined the little girl on her lap. She turned to her computer and browsed over the notes, Jamie still on her lap.

After a careful examination, Dr. Lee invited them to walk with her. She showed them the examination rooms, explained the parent policy of staying with their children, eating meals with the children, even helping with their recovery if they needed baths, physical therapy, etc.

She led them to an office and invited them to sit. She then poured them coffee and gave Jamie a juice box and apple snacks.

"I would like to do more tests," the doctor told them, her expression serious. Her gaze settled on Jamie, who was busy eating the apple slices. "We want to do the best thing for Jamie and I would rather not rush to judgment and make the wrong choice for her. So we will let you go home today and I will have my office call you later with a schedule for tomorrow."

"Tomorrow? But we live in Braswell. It's a two-hour drive." Daron rested his hand on her arm and gave his head a quick shake. "Okay. Tomorrow."

Dr. Lee's expression remained neutral. "We do have housing if you need a place to stay."

"No, I have family in town." Daron's hand was still on her arm, keeping her from protesting the assumption that she would stay with his parents. With his parents? The idea of it sent a tremor up her spine.

"Good, because I don't want this to be a hardship." Dr. Lee handed a packet of material to Emma. "This is some information for you to look over. There are two very good options if we decide Jamie needs surgery. Of course there's the more standard open-heart surgery. But there's also a cath lab procedure in which we would go through her neck or her groin. Not so invasive. But of course neither procedure is without risk. I don't want you to worry, because the risks are not what we focus on. We focus on the best way to make Jamie a healthy little girl and to give her a very bright future."

"Thank you, Doctor," Emma said. She stood, shook the doctor's hand and gathered her daughter in her arms.

They left a few minutes later, riding down the elevator in silence. They walked across the parking lot in that same silence. Jamie was now in Daron's arms, her head on his shoulder.

"I can't stay in Austin," she said as they got in his truck.

"You have to." Daron started his truck and backed up. "We can stay with my parents. They have plenty of room. They're constantly calling, wanting me to visit. So they'll get their visit and the bonus of meeting Jamie. They've heard a lot about her. About you both."

That didn't help settle her nerves. His parents knew about her. It was hard to say what they knew or what they thought. She decided to keep her doubts to herself.

"Are you sure they won't mind?" she asked instead of bringing up all the reasons the McKays might not want extra company.

"I'm sure they won't mind."

Two days, staying with his parents. She had a feeling they would mind. Very much.

His parents lived in a gated community on the edge of Austin. The lawns were large, sprawling, fenced. The driveways were long and protected. At the end of one of those driveways, Daron came to a stop. The house in front of them was French provincial with pale, gray brick siding. It was two story with multipaned windows, a double door of heavy wood, expansive flower gardens and a three-car garage.

She hadn't brought extra clothes. Or food for Jamie. She hadn't brought anything they might need for an overnight stay. During the drive, Daron had been on the phone with his parents, so she hadn't been able to tell him that this wouldn't work. She couldn't barge into their home with nothing but the clothes on her back.

"Stop worrying," he said with that dimple, the one that should have distracted her.

"What do you mean, stop worrying? I'm walking into your parents' home, unannounced, with my daughter. We didn't bring anything for an overnight stay. We're almost two hours from home. So you're right—I shouldn't worry."

"Trust me," he said. "There's a mall nearby. We can get what you need for one night."

"Of course." Because she had tons of disposable income.

"Let's go inside. Jamie looks like a girl who needs a nap. Maybe her mom needs a nap, too."

"I don't nap," she said.

"I don't nap," Jamie repeated with a giggle.

Daron shot her a look as he got out of the truck. When he opened the door for her, he took Jamie and leaned to kiss Emma on the top of her head.

"Like mother, like daughter," he whispered. "Both stubborn."

"I'm not," she said, but humor caught up with her, and she grinned.

"Yeah, you are. Lucky for you, I like my women stubborn."

"I'm not," she started again. She wasn't his woman. He shouldn't say things like that. She tried to object, but she didn't get to because he was leading her up the front walk to the house and the door was being opened by a woman who had to be his mother. Her hair was the same shade of not-quite-blond, not-quite-brown. She had his gray eyes. She had his height. She didn't have his smile.

"Mom." He hugged her. "Good to see you."

"Really? Because your avoidance would say otherwise." Her gaze shot past him.

"This is Emma Shaw and her daughter, Jamie. Emma was married to Andy."

"Yes, I know." She held out a beautifully manicured hand. "Emma, I'm Nora McKay. It's a pleasure to meet you. We have heard quite a bit about you."

"It's nice to meet you, Mrs. McKay." They walked through the house, and it was even more overwhelming inside than out. The rooms were large with high ceilings. The furnishings and décor were expensive.

And yet Daron always seemed at home when he sat at their chrome-and-Formica table. He didn't seem to mind the green upholstered sofa that Granddad had bought new when they moved in twenty years ago.

She reminded herself that he had a beautiful home of his own but he stayed in a camper on the Wilder Ranch.

"Are you hungry?" Mrs. McKay asked.

Jamie chimed in. "Cookies?"

"No cookies," Emma told her.

Mrs. McKay thawed momentarily and smiled at Jamie. "I do have cookies, but I think you should probably have lunch first. Daron, I'm going to let you take care of things. I have a meeting in the city."

He kissed her cheek. "We'll be fine."

Nora McKay gave a quick nod in Emma's direction. "If there's anything you need, let one of us know."

She left. Emma slumped against the counter of the kitchen and let out the breath she'd been holding.

"She's not a fire-breathing dragon," Daron teased. "And even if she is, I'm a dragon slayer."

Emma stood up straight. Jamie was sitting on the floor playing with the baby doll she'd pulled out of her backpack.

What Emma wouldn't give to be three years old and totally unaware of the world and its problems. What she wouldn't give to go back even a few weeks to the days when Daron McKay was just a nuisance and not her dragon-slaying hero.

Then again, maybe not.

That evening, after a day they could all agree had been long, Daron walked Emma to the room she and Jamie would share for the night. They'd found what she needed at a local department store, then had dinner at a chain restaurant. She and Jamie were both exhausted.

"Do you need anything?" He had Jamie on his hip and an arm around Emma. He pulled her a little closer than usual, and she leaned into him, taking him by surprise.

He held her for just a minute. When she pulled away, there was a glimmer of amusement in her eyes. "That was nice."

"Yeah, it was," he agreed. Wholeheartedly. "Mind if we try that again? Because I'm not sure if it was real, or my imagination."

"It was just a hug," she teased.

"Yeah, but I think it might have been more."

She moved into his arms and then it was the three of them because Jamie raised an arm and pulled her mommy closer. Yeah, definitely fantastic.

"I'm not sure what we're doing," she whispered

against his shirt. "I'm afraid, Daron. Of so many things. I'm not ready for this. I'm not ready to feel. Or to be hurt. I have to focus on Jamie and…"

He stopped her by settling a kiss on her brow. "Stop. You don't have to worry."

Jamie reached for her mom. Emma took her and stepped back from him, moving out of his arms and out of his reach.

"I'm patient, Emma."

She rested a hand on his shoulder. "I know. Good night, Daron."

The door closed behind her. He thought he heard her lean against it and sigh. He smiled and leaned close. "Go to bed."

"I will," she answered. And then he heard footsteps leading her away from the door.

Daron turned to go downstairs and saw his mom waiting for him. She wasn't smiling. That didn't bode well.

"Mom," he said, meeting her at the top of the stairs, and they walked down together. "I was going to talk to Dad."

"He's in his office. She seems like a nice girl."

"Yes, she is. She's been through a lot."

His mom gave him a careful look. "So have you. And as your mother, I don't want you to go through any more."

He followed her into the den, where his dad was sitting, an open computer on his lap. He glanced up at them and went back to work. James McKay loved his job. He loved his family, too. But he knew how to focus better than anyone Daron had ever met.

"Dad." Daron took a seat and watched as his dad closed out a file and shut down the computer.

Daron guessed this was going to be another "you're wasting a good education" lecture. From his mom it was going to be a "don't get involved" lecture.

He might as well start things off on the right foot. "You all know that I'm thirty, right?"

His dad pulled off his reading glasses and set them on the table next to his chair. And just like that, Daron felt sixteen again. But he wasn't. He cleared his throat and looked from one parent to the other, because at thirty, he knew himself a little better than he had a dozen years ago.

"I know you're a man with a law degree and I have a practice that I'd like to keep in the family. It was my father's law firm, Daron." His dad sounded tired. Daron relaxed a bit because maybe this was a conversation they needed to have.

He wasn't a lawyer. He had the degree. He'd passed the bar. But he wasn't going to step foot in a courtroom. Ever. "I do know that. And I appreciate that it means a lot to you to see it stay in the family. I'm happy that I have a sister who is interested in the law. I have a business of my own. Someday I might have a son," he said. "And when I do, I'm sure I'll want him to follow in my footsteps. But I would also accept that he might want to find his own path."

Nora McKay smiled. "What you're telling your father is no, thank you?"

"I'm telling him that I'm not a lawyer. That doesn't mean I can't help you out from time to time. I can help manage the business. I can provide security, should anyone need it. But I'm not a lawyer."

"Are you a rancher now?" his dad asked. No sarcasm, which was a good thing.

"I think I might be. And that's the last question I want to answer. For now."

His mom watched him closely. She'd made it a habit, watching him. As if she thought he might lose it one day, no warning, just go crazy.

"I'm fine," he said to her without her having to ask. "I'm happy where I'm at. I have good friends in Braswell. It might not be what you wanted for me, but it's where I am and I'm good."

"And Emma?" his mom asked simply.

"That subject is off-limits."

"We only want the best for you," his mom said as she stood to leave the room.

"I know you do, Mom." He stood, also. "And she's the best thing for me."

She gave a curt nod and left them alone. His dad motioned for him to push the table between them.

"Chess?" his dad said.

"I'll beat you."

His dad smiled. "Yes, you usually do. So how's the business?"

"Good. New clients, repeat clients, exactly what you'd expect it to be. It's keeping the three of us busy and we have a good team that we call when we need extra people on a job."

"I guess you're going to make a career of it, then?"

"I guess I am."

His dad moved his first piece. "Still sleeping in Wilder's camper?"

Daron moved and then he sat back in his chair. "I'm starting to move back to the ranch."

"Really? What changed?"

What had changed? It was simple. A little faith. And a woman who made him fight through the nightmares.

"A lot," he answered. And left it at that. His dad was a brilliant lawyer. He could read people. He knew if someone was guilty and he knew if someone was lying to him.

So any question he asked, he probably already knew the answer. The real question was, did Daron know?

Everything good that had happened to him in the last few years was connected to a woman and a child, their faith, their smiles.

It was unsettling that they meant so much to him, had probably meant that much for some time, and he was just now figuring it out.

Chapter Twelve

It felt good to get home. Even though home meant sharing space with the ever-serious Lucy. Emma sat at the table across from Granddad. Lucy walked into the kitchen but paused. Emma motioned for her to join them.

"You're not bothering us," Emma said. "We're just talking about the visit to the hospital."

"How'd it go?" Lucy asked as she sat down with them.

"They've put her on vitamins and another dose of antibiotics. They're going to let us get through Christmas and then they want to do the procedure. They did several tests and realized they can do a catheterization rather than open-heart surgery. They'll go up through her groin and close the hole with a special mesh device."

"And that will work? I don't know how they can get anything through the veins of a girl that little." Granddad wore his super-skeptical look.

"They can do it." She placed a hand over his. "We're

going to worry, but we're also going to have faith. We've gotten through everything together."

Lucy stood abruptly and excused herself.

Granddad waited until he heard the door close. "That young woman has a lot on her mind."

"Yes, she does. I'll go check on her. If Jamie wakes up, you can yell for me."

"I think if that little girl wakes up, she and her old granddad will be just fine. You go tend to Lucy."

Emma walked out the front door, pulling on a jacket as she went. She didn't have to go far, though. Lucy was sitting on the edge of the front porch, the dog, Rascal, next to her. Emma sat down next to her. The dog moved and sprawled on Lucy's lap so that his front paws could rest on Emma's legs.

"This dog is an attention hog," Lucy said in her normal brusque manner.

Emma would have been put off by the tone if she hadn't gotten to know the woman. Lucy hid kindness beneath her tough exterior. "Yeah, he is. You okay?"

"Hmm, oh yeah, of course." She ran a hand down the black-and-white coat of the border collie. "I'm good."

"Right. Because you didn't act at all upset in there."

"No, not at all." Lucy shot her a look. "You get under a person's skin, Emma. You have to remember. I'm not here to talk feelings with you. I'm here to keep you safe."

"Of course. But you can't spend this much time with someone and not think of them as a friend."

Lucy laughed. "Oh yes, you can. I've spent a lot of time with a lot of different people, and I can't say that I ever wanted to be friends with them."

"Okay, I was wrong."

Lucy sighed. "No, you might be right. But I'm not someone who shares my life. Not with anyone."

"I see. But if you ever want to talk…"

Lucy moved the dog over and got up. "If I was going to talk to anyone, I would talk to you. But don't let that go to your head."

"Never."

"And there's my backup for this evening. I have to drive up to Stephenville to check on my mom." Lucy indicated the Ford truck pulling into the drive. Daron's truck.

"I think we'd be fine on our own for an evening," Emma protested as she watched him getting out of his truck. He stretched, rubbed his lower back, then climbed up in the bed of the truck and grabbed a couple of boxes.

"I don't think he's taking no for an answer," Lucy said as she walked back into the house.

Emma picked her way across the yard, avoiding puddles left from that afternoon's rain. "I didn't expect to see you so soon."

He hopped down from the bed of the truck and grabbed the boxes he'd set on the tailgate. "Lucy needs some time off. I brought a few things."

"It looks that way. What did you bring?" She picked up a third box that he'd left on the tailgate. "What's this?"

"That's the nativity. These are decorations and lights. I thought we'd do something to get in the spirit of Christmas."

"What, you think I have no Christmas spirit?" she asked as she led the way to the house. "I happen to have plenty of Christmas spirit. And decorations. I just haven't put them up yet."

"Thus my spare tree and decorations. I can't sit in a house with no lights and no tree. I kind of guessed your stuff is in an attic and I don't want to climb up a ladder. So here I am, with everything needed to make this house look like an elf threw up on it."

"Since you put it that way," she joked, opened the door and motioned him inside. "Try to be quiet. Jamie is sleeping."

She was wrong about that. Jamie was definitely up. The minute she saw Daron, she ran across the room and attached herself to him. He put the boxes down and picked up the little girl.

"We're going to decorate a tree this evening. And I brought fried chicken from Duke's, so no one has to cook."

He was thoughtful. Emma knew that, but each time he did something like this, it became more obvious. He was touching their lives in sweet little ways.

Granddad grabbed up the bag from the grocery store and headed off to the kitchen with it. Jamie started looking through an open box that contained store-bought decorations and small plaster figurines to paint. She picked up a tiny star and followed Art from the room.

"This was really nice of you," Emma said as he pulled out a small tree that just had to be shaped and fitted together.

"Nice?" He arched a brow. "I thought it was sweet. The kind of thing that makes a woman swoon."

"Is that what you're going for, swooning?"

"Maybe a little." He said it with a tone that might have been hopeful or teasing.

"Well, I'm not one to swoon. The last time I did, there was no one to catch me."

"I'll catch you," he whispered. He leaned in close, grazing her cheek with a feathery kiss.

"No." Suddenly she was afraid. Because what if he didn't catch her? What if he thought she was the woman he wanted in his life but then realized she didn't fit?

"Stop thinking," he warned. "I can see the wheels turning in your head, and I think you're wrong."

"What if I'm right? What if this is temporary? What if one day we're at a family dinner or a social gathering, and you look across the room and you realize that you made a mistake?"

"That won't happen."

She shook her head. "You don't know that."

"No, maybe I don't. But I want to try this, Emma. I want you to try."

Jamie returned from showing Art her tiny treasure. Emma knelt next to her daughter and admired the star.

"Do you want to paint it? With pretty yellow paint and sparkles?" Emma asked.

Jamie nodded and dug around in the box for the yellow paint. "I can paint it."

"Yes, you can. And we'll write your name on the back so you'll always know that you painted this yourself."

Jamie smiled up at her, big eyes and soft curls. "I like to paint it. Daron paints it, too."

"Do you want me to help you paint?" Daron asked, finding another paintbrush in the box.

They were gathering supplies for painting when a shot vibrated the air and glass shattered. Daron grabbed Emma and Jamie and pushed them to the ground, covering them with his body as another shot rang out. From the kitchen, Art said a few choice words.

"Granddad, are you okay?" Emma called out. She pushed herself out from beneath Daron, but he held tight.

"Don't move." His arms keeping them close.

"Daron, you have to let us up. We have to check on Granddad." She turned in his arms, brushing her hand across his face. "We're safe."

"I know. Just give me a minute."

"This isn't a nightmare, Daron," she said.

"I know. Believe me, I know." He was still holding her, holding Jamie. He moved, taking them with him, half dragging them to the kitchen.

Art was sitting on the floor, holding a towel to his thigh.

"Granddad, you're hurt. They shot you."

Art shook his head. "I think it's just glass from the kitchen window. They ruined my pants."

She laughed until she stopped wanting to cry. Pete had done this. She wouldn't have believed he would do something like this to her, to his niece.

She heard Daron on his phone, calling 911. He kept them in a corner, protected. Safe.

Daron stood to the side, watching the road, the field, as paramedics loaded a very upset Art into the ambulance. Boone stood nearby, also watching. Just in case whoever had done this came back. Daron didn't think they would. This was a warning. He didn't know what the warning meant, but he knew that he wasn't walking away from Emma and Jamie.

Emma stepped close to his side. He kept his attention on the surrounding area. Without speaking she pushed a piece of gauze to his cheek. He flinched at her touch and she lightened the pressure.

"You're bleeding," she finally said.

"Just from glass. I'm fine."

"We're all okay." She pushed the gauze into her pocket and unwrapped a bandage. "Stop thinking this is your fault."

He let her tend his wound, which was nothing more than a scratch, really. "Is Jamie sleeping?"

"Yes. She's with Kayla. Boone brought her, in case we needed her."

"That was good of him." Daron moved his eyes away from the horizon, just briefly, to look at the woman standing next to him.

She was small, but strong. Her dark hair was pulled back in a ponytail and she wore fuzzy slippers with her jeans and flannel shirt. He wanted to pull her close, inhale the scent of her hair and just hold her. Man, he really wanted to hold her.

But wasn't that what had gotten them in this position? He'd lost focus. He'd been living some strange dream, decorating Christmas trees and baking cookies. Now there were shattered windows and glass everywhere. The Wilder brothers were boarding up the windows. Getting new windows put in would have to wait until tomorrow.

"Pack a bag for each of you. Art will need a few things, too. I think they might keep him overnight, but he'll need clothes when he leaves the hospital tomorrow." He gave the order as she stood there, brows drawn together, probably trying to figure him out.

"Why would we need a bag?"

He glanced down again, this time getting lost for a moment in her dark eyes. The anger flashing in those dark eyes helped him get back on track.

"Because you're staying at the Wilders' for a while."

"We can't stay at the Wilders'. They don't know us. And I'm sure they don't have room for three more. That's ridiculous."

"It isn't ridiculous. Tonight someone shot at your house. If we'd been standing two feet to the right of where we were, if Art had been standing in front of the sink…" His voice shook as he drew the picture for her. "Someone could have been killed tonight."

The color drained from her face and she wobbled a little. He put a hand on her elbow to steady her.

"But Pete wouldn't do that. He wouldn't try to hurt us. He wants money, but he isn't mean."

"Meth changes people. And it isn't just Pete. It's whoever Pete is in debt to. My guess is Pete owed money, so they bargained with him. If he would deal for them, they'd forgive his debt. Or give him a discount. And then he probably spent the money he made rather than turning it over to the boss."

"How did he get messed up with this business?"

Daron shrugged. "Good people get involved in bad stuff, Emma. That's how life is."

"Yes, I guess. I just wish there was a way to help him."

"He could have gotten you killed. There are people willing to hurt you to teach him a lesson."

"I know," she said, her voice soft and tremulous.

He didn't want her afraid. He wanted her fighting mad, willing to stand her ground. But he wanted her safe, too. "It isn't forever. We'll figure out who Pete is connected to and we'll get rid of them."

"I wish we could get Pete some help."

He still had hold of her arm. "Yeah, me, too. But first things first. Let's pack those bags. And tell Art you'll see him at the hospital."

She peeked into the back of the ambulance, where Art was arguing that it was only a flesh wound and he didn't need to go to the hospital.

"Art, you have to go." Emma patted his foot and he howled. "Just a flesh wound?"

Art grimaced, eyes narrowed. "I didn't say it doesn't hurt. I just said I don't need to go to the hospital. And I don't want you there, either. Stay home with Jamie."

Daron stepped in behind her. "She's not staying here, Art. You don't have to worry."

"That's good. Don't let her come to the hospital. Boone already said he's going to follow the ambulance. I reckon once I get there, they'll give me something to make me sleep. No reason for Emma to drag Jamie there." Art leaned back on the stretcher. "Now go, so they can get me outta here."

Before he could stop her, Emma was in the ambulance next to her granddad. She leaned over him, kissed his forehead and told him she loved him.

Art patted her arm and told her she could save all of that nonsense for his eulogy, and he doubted he'd need one of those for another twenty years or so.

Daron helped her down and they watched as the ambulance pulled away. "Let's get you packed."

"Why do we have to do this?" she asked as they went inside to throw a few things in suitcases.

Daron zipped up the bag she'd packed for Jamie. "We have to do this because we don't want anyone else to get hurt."

"Right," she agreed. "It just makes me mad. This is my home. I don't like to be run off by thugs."

"I don't like it, either, but there's not much we can do. You can't have Jamie here. It isn't safe."

"I know. It just makes me angry. I'm going to pack our bags."

"I'm going to check the livestock and put a leash on your dog. I'll take him to my place and keep him in the kennel."

"Are you sure?"

"Yeah, I'm sure."

An hour later they were pulling up to the camper he'd called home for the last few years. Boone's big old collie was on the front porch. There was a light on inside.

"You're sure they're expecting us?" she whispered. Jamie was sleeping in the seat next to her.

"Yeah, and let me tell you, the Wilders know how to show hospitality. If you haven't met Maria Wilder, Boone's mom, you'll love her."

"I'll owe her."

"She won't see it that way." He carried Jamie. Emma followed.

The door of the RV opened as they stepped onto the porch. Lucy motioned them inside.

"You were going to see your mom," Emma said.

"Yeah, you know how to create excitement." Lucy

teased, an unusual thing for her. "There's food in here. Mrs. Wilder stocked the fridge. There are clean sheets on the bed and one of the sisters—I can't remember her name because Boone has too many siblings—came down and cleaned the place up a bit."

She stepped aside so Daron could carry Jamie down the short hallway to the bedroom, such as it was. It was a small room, big enough for a bed and a built-in dresser and closet. Jamie didn't stir.

Emma watched from the doorway; then she moved back down the hall to the living area. She sat on the sofa and just stared.

He knelt in front of her and took her hands in his. The door opened. Lucy left.

"It's going to be okay."

"I know. I really do. I don't have a clue what God is doing, but I know He's doing something." She squeezed his hands and then lifted them, kissing the knuckles of one and then the other. "The storms make us appreciate the calm."

"Yeah, this is a crazy storm we're mixed up in."

"It seems like that's what I do best, getting you mixed up in my storms. I'm sorry."

"Don't be. I've found some peace in this storm. Maybe a little faith."

Her eyes watered and he groaned.

"Don't cry. Please." He leaned forward, caught her mouth and kissed her sweetly.

"I should cry more often," she whispered. Her lips brushed his again.

"Yeah, and I should leave because staying here with you is dangerous."

"Thank you. For being there tonight. For protecting us."

He stood, his back tightening in response to the treatment he'd given it the last few hours. She noticed and stood up, too. Her arms went around him and she moved her hands to his spine working out the knots. He leaned in.

"I have to go," he repeated. She rose on tiptoe and touched her lips to his.

"Yes, you do."

The door opened. They broke away from each other. Lucy laughed, unapologetic. "Should I sing about two little lovebirds, caught kissing in a tree? K.I.S.S.I.N.G. First comes love, then comes—"

"Stop," Daron growled at his partner.

She snickered and headed for the fridge.

"I'll see you tomorrow." He kissed the top of Emma's head, then shot Lucy a warning look.

He left, but he didn't go far. He backed his truck out of the drive and went a hundred feet down the drive. He parked and pulled a blanket out of the backseat.

He trusted Lucy, but he didn't trust Pete. He didn't trust drug dealers who were desperate. He had let Emma down once. On a dusty street in Afghanistan he hadn't been able to save Andy. Tonight he would make sure he didn't let anyone down.

Chapter Thirteen

Emma got up early the next morning. She sat on the front porch of the camper. The only chair was an old lawn chair. It wasn't comfortable, but it served its purpose. As she was sipping her morning coffee, she spotted the truck just down the driveway from the camper. The white King Ranch was parked off in the grass.

She wrapped the blanket around her shoulders, picked up her coffee cup and walked down the driveway. Daron was asleep in the backseat, head against the side window, a small pillow under his cheek. She rapped on the window and he jumped, wiped his mouth and then came fully awake.

"You are an idiot," she said through the glass.

"I thought you knew that," he mumbled.

"I did, but this confirms it. I'm perfectly safe with Lucy, and if she thought you didn't trust her, she'd probably shoot you."

One side of his mouth quirked up. "Yeah, probably. I'll be over in a second for coffee."

"There's a fresh pot. I was going to make biscuits and gravy, but Lucy is making breakfast burritos."

"Gotcha."

"I'm calling Andy's parents today. I think they need to know about Jamie *and* about Pete. I've prayed about it. I have to forgive them. Even if they continue to reject us, I have to forgive."

He pushed open the back door of the truck and climbed out. His curly hair was all over the place and he brushed a hand through it to settle it into place. She wanted to help but resisted the urge.

"I think that's a good idea." His voice was still husky from sleep. His eyes were soft.

"I'm going. If you want breakfast and coffee, come on." She started walking back toward the camper.

"I'm coming with you." He caught up with her, his arm sliding around her waist.

It felt perfect, the two of them on that gravel driveway, his arm around her. But perfect, she knew from experience, could fade into something altogether different. She forced her mind elsewhere. She didn't want to think bad thoughts about him. She didn't want to relive the past.

"So this is where you stay. Even though you have a perfectly good house to live in," she said.

He glanced down at her, questions dancing in his eyes. But he went with it. "Yeah, this is where I stay. When you meet the rest of the Wilders, you'll understand."

"I've met Boone's dad. And his brother, Jase. I think a sister. I'm not sure which one."

"There are a few of them. They're all good people."

"So are you."

She slid from his grasp and walked up the steps of the camper. He followed,

Lucy was fixing Jamie a plate, and Jamie was telling her a story about the kitten she wanted for Christmas. Apparently, if she couldn't have an elephant this year, it would be okay. She could get one next year.

"Daron." Jamie's eyes lit up. "Lucy made burritos."

"I didn't know Lucy could cook." Daron helped himself to an already-made burrito and then poured himself a cup of coffee.

"If you all are okay, I'm going to go ahead and make this call." Emma poured herself another much-needed cup of coffee. "When I'm done, I'm going to head to Braswell to see Art."

"I'll drive you," Daron offered.

"That would be good." And then she walked outside, unsure and more than a little nervous. With unsteady hands she dialed the number for Andy's parents.

After several rings Mrs. Shaw answered. Loretta. Emma had never called her mother-in-law by her first name. Loretta Shaw had never invited that familiarity. In the beginning it had been all right. She'd had Andy's support. Or believed she had it.

"Mrs. Shaw, it's Emma."

There was a long pause. "Emma. What do you need?"

Hesitant, Emma continued. "I wanted to let you know that Jamie is having surgery. The first week in January."

"I'm sorry to hear that."

"She's your granddaughter. I know this is difficult, but I…" She resented Andy for what he'd done to her. Emma resented the Shaws for their lack of support. But she would never resent her daughter. "I thought you might reconsider. But if you don't, I want you to know the door is always open for you to contact me and see her."

"Andy was very clear, Emma. He told us that Jamie isn't his."

The pain of that betrayal hurt worse than everything else Andy had done.

"He lied, Mrs. Shaw." She'd never been so blunt with any of the Shaws, but she was tired of being accused. "I'm not sure why Andy lied. But he did. Jamie is your granddaughter, and on the eighth of January, just a few short weeks away, she's having surgery. A very serious operation."

"Thank you for letting me know."

"Mrs. Shaw, there is one other thing."

A long sigh could be heard from the other end of the line. "What is it?"

"You might not be aware of this, but Pete needs help. He needs a good rehab program. He's dangerous, Mrs. Shaw. Last night someone shot through our house. Pete threatened me. He's been stealing from us."

"I don't want to hear any more of this." Mrs. Shaw sobbed and hung up.

Emma became aware of Daron standing on the porch with her. "She hung up."

"You have to understand, she doesn't want to hear that she's already lost one son and the other is probably on his way to prison." Daron leaned against the porch rail while she sat on the lawn chair.

"Of course she doesn't. I don't blame her. But if she'd listen, maybe they could get him some help."

He nodded, took a sip of his coffee and stared out over the fields. "It's beautiful here. When I first got back to the States, I couldn't imagine being anywhere else. I wanted to spend my life on the porch of this camper."

"I can see why," she said. "Standing here, it's hard to believe there is anything other than good in the world."

"I think standing here taught me that there still is good in the world." He pulled truck keys out of his pocket. "I have an appointment this morning."

"We're fine. I'm going to see Granddad. We'll probably head home after he's released."

"No, you'll head back here. I want you here, where I can keep you safe. I'd prefer that you don't tell anyone where you're staying. And stick close to Lucy."

"Daron, I don't want this to be my life. And I don't want my relationship with you to be one where you feel obligated to keep us safe."

"I don't feel obligated. See you later." He took the few steps and looked back up at her when he reached the bottom. "The Christmas bazaar is this weekend. If you and Jamie would like to go, I'd love to take you. Not because I'm obligated, but because I want to spend time with you."

He didn't give her a chance to answer. She watched as he walked down the driveway to his truck, and her mouth pulled up at the corners.

Boone rode with him to Jake Martin's. "Tell me again why you're going to look at Jake's livestock? Because I'm confused why a man who never stays at his own place is suddenly interested in putting a few head of horses on said acreage."

"None. Of. Your. Business," Daron answered again. "Sometimes I wonder why I keep you around."

"I'm worth more alive?" Boone shot back. "Or you would be lonely without me."

"I'm not sure either of those fit."

"Back to horses."

"I told you I plan on staying here. I do plan on living on that ranch."

"Gotcha. Mystery solved. This has something to do with a woman."

Daron hit the brakes and pulled to the side of the road. "Get out."

Boone pointed to himself.

Daron repeated it. "Get out. Your happy-in-the-morning self is about to get on my last nerve. Out."

Boone laughed, and then soon they were both laughing. "Touchy, aren't we?"

"Yeah, I guess I am."

"O love, how hath thou changed the man."

"Don't, Boone."

"Buying a woman a horse is almost as serious as buying her a ring. You realize that, don't you?"

"I didn't say I'm buying her a horse. When did you get so nosy, like someone's cat lady neighbor with binoculars?"

"But I'm right, aren't I? And you have to understand, this is commitment. For a guy with self-diagnosed commitment phobia, this is big. It's almost like we're going to pick out a diamond for her."

"Yeah, I realize it."

Boone openly laughed at him. "This is great."

"I'm glad you're so amused." Daron kept driving, keeping his lips firmly in a straight line. He wouldn't show his amusement. Not to Boone. It would be the same as exposing weakness to a predator.

"Let's discuss this situation with Pete. Do you think he was messed up on drugs and took the shot? Or do you think it's his friends? Business partners. Whatever you'd like to call them."

"I think it's the business partners. Pete's messed up, but I don't really believe he'd hurt Emma and Jamie."

"Meth changes people, Daron. You know that."

"Yeah, I do."

They'd lost classmates to the drug. Good, smart people who made the wrong choices, tried something they couldn't untry.

"The police have a lead or two. It would be good if they could get Pete to testify." Daron turned onto the drive that led to Jake Martin's place.

When they pulled up to the stable, Jake was waiting. He had a little girl hanging on his leg, holding tight as he walked. She was giggling and having the time of her life.

"Pardon me, gentlemen, but this little nugget insists on coming to the barn with me. She says to help, but usually we manage to get a lot less work done when we're together. Mainly because instead of working horses, we chase kittens."

"You wouldn't happen to have any kittens you want to get rid of, would you?" Daron asked as they headed into the barn. "Or an elephant."

Jake gave him a sideways look. "I'm not even sure how to respond to that. I thought you were here for a horse, and I'm all out of elephants. Only a kid could get a man to ask a question like that. Or get him to consider kittens."

"Do you have any kittens or not?" Daron asked again. This was getting complicated. He no longer felt like himself. It was his face in the mirror, but someone else taking up residence on the inside. Someone who cared that a little girl wanted kittens and elephants. Someone who cared that a woman had given her heart and had it rejected by the man who should have cherished her. He'd given her a horse as a last apology and parting gift.

"Slow down, partner," Boone said in a low, easy tone. "You're here to buy a horse, maybe get a kitten, so why do you suddenly look like you could hurt someone?"

"Sorry. I'm good. So, where is the horse Emma Shaw sold you?" Daron asked Jake. He'd picked up his little girl. She was now on his shoulders, his hat on her head.

Daron wanted that. He wanted a little boy that looked like Emma, with her dark hair and dark eyes. Or a curious little girl who would be Jamie's best friend.

"She's out here. She foaled a few weeks ago. Best-looking little dun we've ever had on the place. Nice colt."

"Would you sell him?" Daron asked as they walked back into sunshine, the pasture stretching out in front of them. A couple dozen head of horses grazed in the early-morning sunshine.

"I might be tempted to. Next fall, maybe. What is it you're looking for exactly, McKay? Do you want horses for yourself or for Emma? I know she doesn't want that mare back. When we bought the horse she told us she loved the animal but she just couldn't look at her."

"Yeah, she has reasons."

"I'm sure she does," Jake said. "I have a nice bay mare. She's four. I have a two-year-old gelding that shows a lot of promise. I guess it depends on who and what you want the livestock for."

"How much for both?" It was a start.

Jake set his daughter back on the ground and took his hat off her head to place it back on his own. He named a figure. Boone whistled. Daron pulled the checkbook out of his back pocket. "Sold, if you'll throw in one of those kid ponies I know you raise."

"My POAs don't go cheap, McKay."

Daron didn't doubt that. But a Pony of America seemed the perfect horse for a little girl. Not too small, good disposition. A horse she could grow into.

"Looks to me like nothing around here goes cheap, Martin. You just robbed a man without a weapon. The least you can do is throw in a spotted pony."

"I've got one. He's about ten. Good as gold with kids. I bought him last year, but he doesn't show well and the girls all have horses."

"Package deal?" Daron continued. "Oh, and a kitten."

"The kittens will be ready to go in the next couple of weeks. Pick one today and I'll make sure it's delivered."

"For Christmas?" Daron smiled down at Jake's little girl. Melody, he thought her name was.

"Yeah, for Christmas. You drive a hard bargain, McKay."

They left and Boone managed to stay silent until they were driving down the road.

"That's a mighty big diamond ring you just bought, partner," Boone drawled with a chuckle as punctuation.

Daron didn't respond, and kept on driving. But it got him thinking. About rings. He guessed if this was a marathon, he was miles ahead of Emma in his thinking. He'd just bought her horses. She was still trying to push him away.

He knew he needed to slow down. But he'd never been good at waiting. But he had a feeling if he didn't pull back on the reins, she'd show him the exit real quick.

Chapter Fourteen

Emma came home from work Saturday exhausted and ready for a nap. Lucy looked up as she entered the camper, their "safe house" as Boone liked to call it. Emma paused just inside the door and watched as Lucy helped Jamie hang a pretty star on a tiny Christmas tree.

"Another tree?" Emma said.

"Boone said we'd be here until after Christmas." Lucy swept back her long, dark hair. It was an impatient gesture, but she managed a smile for Jamie. "His mom, Maria, brought down the tree. She said it's not quite two weeks until Christmas, but Jamie definitely needs a tree."

"I'm sure you'd rather be somewhere else? With family?" Emma asked as she kicked off her shoes and headed for the kitchen and a glass of water.

"No, not really. I only have my mom. She's remarried and they usually visit my stepfather's family in California."

"You're not close, you and your mom?" Emma knew

better than to dig into Lucy's life. But occasionally she tried.

"We were in the foxhole together for too many years to be close."

"Foxhole?"

Lucy handed Jamie another ornament. "We survived too much together. Blame is a horrible thing. Maybe someday we'll work through it."

"I see. Can I get you something? Coffee, water?"

"No, thanks. I'm going to take a quick walk and get some fresh air. I'll let you help with the tree. Oh, there are gifts to be wrapped."

"Gifts?" She sat down on the edge of the couch. "I haven't been shopping yet."

"I told him no, but he never listens." Lucy stretched. "Oh, and he said he'd take you all later for the daily visit to Art. He said Art is enjoying himself with the Jenkins family."

"It was good of Samantha and Remington to take him in. I bet he is having a good time with Remington's grandfather."

"They're kind of cut from the same cloth. I heard they've been terrorizing the neighbors, shooting bottle rockets at crows or some such. Nothing to hurt anyone, just acting like teenagers."

"I worry about Granddad, but he isn't slowing down much."

"He's a good grandfather," Lucy agreed. "I'll catch you in a few. Boone said to let you know he plans to take you all to the Christmas bazaar tonight."

"I wonder if it has ever occurred to him to ask, not tell?"

Lucy was tugging on her running shoes. "No, I don't think so. Some advice?"

"Sure."

"Stand your ground with him. I know from experience that when he starts getting this way, I play opposites with him. He says go, I stay. He says smile, I frown. It keeps him on his toes. He's a pretty boy who is used to getting his way in all things."

"Thanks. I'll remember that."

Lucy bent to kiss the top of Jamie's head, saluted to Emma and out the door she went. For a run, not a walk. Emma lowered herself to the floor next to Jamie.

"It's almost Christmas. What do you want? Other than elephants and kittens. Elephants are hard to come by this year."

Jamie giggled. "A giraffe."

"Did someone tell you to ask for a giraffe?" Emma asked.

"Boone," Jamie said. And she reached to hang a pretty globe on the tree. "Boone said tell Daron I want a giraffe."

"Boone is very bad."

"He should be in time-out?" Jamie asked, sitting back with her little legs stretched out in front of her. Her smile was everything good in Emma's world.

Emma pulled her close and kissed her cheeks until she giggled and said, "Stop, Mommy."

Then Jamie kissed Emma's cheeks.

"I love you, Jamie."

Jamie put a hand on each side of her face and leaned close. "I love you, Mommy. And so does Daron."

Emma closed her eyes and leaned in close to her daughter, smelling her sweet little-girl scent and promising herself she wouldn't be broken again. She wouldn't feel less than. She wouldn't apologize for who she was. She wouldn't let a man hurt her. Ever again.

And she would teach her daughter to be strong and to believe in herself. Because little girls should feel cherished and grow up to be young women who valued themselves.

Jamie leaned in and whispered, "Mama crying?"

"No, I'm not." She wasn't. She had weathered the storms of her life and she'd come out stronger. "So, what about Christmas? Other than a giraffe?"

"A baby that pees."

"Not a real one, I hope?" She heard the front door open. Emma looked over the top of Jamie's head at Daron. He was watching them, a guarded expression on his face.

Jamie laughed at his question. "Yes."

"No," Emma said. "But I think we can do a doll. And what, might I ask, is in the bags in the bedroom?"

Daron shrugged. "Stuff."

"We need to talk."

He sat down and waited. "About what?"

"About little girls and how they feel when they really like someone but that person is only in their lives for a while."

"Who isn't going to be around?" he asked.

"Stop, Daron."

"I'm not going anywhere, Emma," he said. He glanced at his watch. "Actually I am going somewhere. I'm going to see Art and then I'm going to the Christmas bazaar. Teddy Dawson has his pony ride set up and I heard there's some pretty amazing boiled shrimp."

"Ponies?" Jamie dropped an ornament in the box,

the tree forgotten. She hurried to Daron, crawled up on his lap and gave him a hug.

"You don't play fair," Emma accused.

"Nope. I play for keeps," he quipped. "How long will it take you all to get ready?"

"Fifteen minutes." She gave in too easily. Lucy would have given her a look for that. She hadn't stood her ground. She hadn't said no. She didn't want to say no to Daron in their lives.

When she thought long and hard about it, the only thing she wanted to say no to was him leaving them.

The town green surrounded the Martin's Crossing Community Church. This was where they held the bazaar that brought locals and tourists alike to Martin's Crossing. They came to listen to music, buy homemade crafts, toys and clothes, and eat the many different types of food that a festival such as this one always offered.

"Shrimp?" Daron asked as they wandered through the crowds.

"I have shellfish allergies," Emma told him. "I want a corn dog."

"Corn dog?" He looked appalled. "When you could have anything else, you want a corn dog?"

"Corn dogs are important festival food," she informed him. "They aren't amazing when they're the frozen variety heated up in the oven. But at a festival when they're hand-battered and deep-fried? Amazing."

"Better than a steak sandwich from the VFW guys over there?"

She nodded and kept walking. "You've never tried one, have you?"

"I've had corn dogs."

She arched a brow and waited for him to come clean.

"Okay," he admitted, "I've never had one at a fair. When we were kids, my mom wouldn't allow us to eat carnival food."

"Seriously?" She had to laugh. "Why?"

"They aren't sanitary."

"The hot grease would kill any germs."

He moved next to her in line. "I'm taking your word for that."

"Good. Because I also want a fried Snickers."

He blanched. "Can a human body handle that much grease?"

"Of course it can. And you'll love it."

"If you say so."

She leaned against his shoulder. "You've lived a very sad, sheltered life."

They ate at a picnic table close to a blazing fire pit. The heat felt good. Although it wasn't freezing cold, there was a definite chill in the air. Jamie managed to eat part of her corn dog, then had other things on her mind.

"Can I ride the pony?" she asked Daron, tugging at his sleeve.

"You bet. Why don't I take you, since your mom is still eating? Emma, catch up with us in a minute?"

She nodded and took another bite of fried candy bar.

When she finished she tossed her trash and headed across the lawn to the pony ride. Jamie was on a pretty spotted pony with Daron walking next to her.

Emma stood at the edge of the small fenced enclosure watching her daughter live out her dreams of being a cowgirl. Daron said something and Jamie smiled big. She hoped he wasn't making promises.

A hand clamped down on Emma's arm. She pulled away but the grip tightened. She turned to face the man at her side. Pete. He looked worse. His face was sunken. His hair greasy.

"Emma, you have to help me."

Those weren't the words she expected. Her fear eased a little.

"I can't help you, Pete. You know that. I would like for you to get help, though." She stepped back from him and he released her arm. His gaze shot past her, to someone she couldn't see.

"You can help me. I need money. Andy said he left you a life insurance policy."

"He didn't."

The words were barely out of her mouth when he fled, running through the crowd, pushing people as he went. She turned, knowing Daron must be close. He made it to her side and scanned the crowds. But Pete was gone.

"You okay?" Daron asked.

"I'm fine. He believes I have a life insurance policy from Andy. That's why he keeps coming back. He's delusional."

"Meth does that. It makes people paranoid. It alters the brain's cell structure." He glanced back into the crowd and that was when she realized he didn't have Jamie.

"Where's Jamie?" She panicked.

"I saw Pete with you and I left Jamie with Oregon and Lily."

She released her breath and closed her eyes. "Don't do that to me."

"I wanted her safe."

"I know." She continued to breathe slow and steady, calming her racing heart. "I'm sorry."

His hand rested on her back and he guided her through the crowd. "Should we head back to the Wilders'?"

She nodded. "I think so. We came, we ate, we rode ponies. That's about all the excitement I can take for one night."

But she stopped in a clear area where, for one moment, it was peaceful. There were Christmas lights, a choir in the background singing "O Little Town of Bethlehem" and the nativity near the church. "I love it here. I can't imagine living anywhere else. And even with Pete trying to steal my joy, there is peace." She touched Daron's arm. "Do you feel it?"

He looked stunned, as if he doubted her sanity, but then he nodded. "Yes, I do."

He brushed his thumb against her lips. The gesture was sweet and it caused her to think of how it felt when he held her. When he kissed her.

But she wasn't going there. This thing between them had become tricky. It had opened doors that she'd closed, barred, locked and bolted shut.

"We should go now," she said. Because being with him like this now, this felt dangerous.

Daron sprawled on the sofa in the living room of the camper. Lucy was in the recliner. With Pete's appearance in town last night, he'd decided they should both be on duty. And she'd gotten to the recliner first.

That left him tossing and turning all night, and thankful when the sky finally lightened enough to call it morning.

He pushed himself up from the lumpy piece of furniture and made his way to the kitchen and the coffeepot. Footsteps in the hall warned that he wasn't the only one up. He brushed a hand through his hair and went back to making coffee. Emma appeared, looking sweet and sleepy. Her hair was loose, framing her face, making her eyes look large and luminous.

"Do you mind going to church in Martin's Crossing today?" he asked as he poured her a cup of coffee. Then he stuck a couple of slices of bread in the toaster.

"I guess not. Why?" She took the coffee and sat down at the booth-style table.

"I feel more comfortable there. I know the layout and the people."

"Because of Pete?"

"Yeah, because of Pete."

"I don't understand why he can't be arrested."

"No evidence he's committed a crime. He comes to your house asking for money. We could try for a restraining order."

"And what would that do?"

"If he comes within several hundred feet of you, your daughter or your property, he can be arrested. But the problem is, if he's determined, he's going to ignore the order."

"Exactly. Do you think he would just go away? If I had money, which I don't. Would he leave?"

He joined her, sitting across from her at the tiny table. "I don't think so. I think he's like most junkies.

He'll go through the money and come back begging for more."

"Yes, you're right," she said softly, then lifted her cup to take a drink. "I really want to go home. Not that this camper isn't lovely, but I miss my kitchen and my space. I miss my cattle."

"We can spend the day there. Maybe take some lunch out there. I had the windows fixed yesterday."

"You shouldn't have done that. I can take care of these things, Daron. It's my house, my family."

He raised his hands, stopping the argument. "I know it is. I know I have a tendency to go full throttle. I just want to make this easier for you."

"But you have to understand, we're not your problem. And I can't repay everything you're doing for us."

He got up from the booth and walked over to the sink, rinsing his cup before facing her again. "I didn't ask you to pay me back. I do know that you're not my problem." He paused, shaking his head. Lucy was in the recliner, probably feigning sleep. "You don't owe me anything. I'm not doing this out of some sense of guilt."

"No?"

"No," he repeated. He looked at the clock on the microwave. "We should get ready for church."

"I'm not going to church," Lucy snarled from the living room. "You know I draw the line at church."

"Yeah, Luce, I know."

Emma had slipped away. He heard the door down the hall close. He heard her talking in soft whispers to her daughter. Jamie giggled, the sound undeniably happy. He guessed the faith of a child was this: heart surgery in the future, not a lot of money, someone waiting to bring harm, and a three-year-old able to giggle.

When they got to church the building was crowded. The pastor told them it was the pre-Christmas rush. Everyone wanted to get in good with the Lord before the big birthday party. Occasional Christians, the pastor called them. They showed up for the special occasions. Christmas. Easter. Daron guessed he kinda fit into that group. His family had been occasional Christians, too. They were good people, his parents. They had a strong marriage. They loved their kids. They just didn't spend much time inside a church.

Maybe they'd had faith, but he didn't remember it getting passed on to him or his sister, Janette.

He watched Emma as she hurried over to hug her grandfather. Daron followed the two of them to a pew they were sharing with Boone and Kayla. He slid in next to Boone. That left Kayla, Boone and Jamie between Emma and him.

He didn't much care for that.

"Do you want to take Jamie to children's church?" Kayla asked. "I think they're having a puppet play today."

Emma looked down at her daughter. "Do you want to go?"

Jamie nodded, so Emma lifted her and left, squeezing past him to get out. "Want me to go with you?" he asked.

She shook her head. "No, of course not. I'll be right back."

Boone told her where she would find the children's church. She hurried away, talking to Jamie as she went.

Daron glanced at his watch. He would give her four minutes to get there and back.

"She's safe here," Boone assured him.

"I know she is."

He glanced at his watch again. Three minutes. He'd give her one more minute and then he was putting the building on lockdown.

Chapter Fifteen

"**Y**ou are going to have to give her to me, Emma." The voice came from a doorway on the quiet hallway that obviously wasn't the way to the children's church.

Emma had gotten confused, taken the wrong door. She'd known it and had started back. And then she'd heard the voice. Pete's voice.

He stepped out of the shadows. "I've been waiting, hoping to catch you alone today."

"Pete, don't do this." Emma backed away. She held her daughter against her and tried to calm her as Jamie started to sob. "She's frightened. You're her uncle. Why don't you say hello to her, Pete? She has Andy's eyes. Blue, just like his."

Pete glanced but then looked away. She saw remorse. She knew she could get to him if she kept talking, connecting him with his niece.

"She's going to be in the hospital in a couple of weeks. You should come visit her. I called your parents. They might come see her."

"I don't think they will," he mumbled. "You're nice, Emma. You just weren't good enough. They wanted

Andy to marry someone who fit into his world, not the poor farmer's daughter from Braswell."

"That's mean, Pete." She kissed Jamie's brow and rubbed her back as she held her close. "Jamie is three now. Did you know that? She wants kittens and an elephant for Christmas."

He almost smiled. "Emma, stop. Please stop. You don't understand how much trouble I'm in. I won't hurt her. I'll just spend time with her until that boyfriend of yours can get money from his family. They have plenty. I get that Andy left you high and dry, but it looks like you've bounced back just fine."

"I don't have a boyfriend, Pete. He's just a friend. You know that. He and Andy were friends, so he's checked on us and helped us out."

"I'm not stupid, Emma." He tilted his head, chin up. He was tweaking. Great.

"I know you're not. I'm just telling you that you're wrong."

She had to keep him talking. She knew Daron would notice how long she was gone. He'd come looking for her. Pete noticed her shift to look at the door at the end of the hall.

Before she could stop him, he grabbed Jamie from her arms. From out of nowhere he produced a knife. "Stay here, Emma. Please stay here. Understand that I am sorry, but I have to get money or they're going to hurt all of us."

"Pete, don't do this. You could help the police get these guys. You could do the right thing."

He shook his head and ran down the hall. Jamie was screaming. "Mommy!"

"Jamie, Mommy is here. Don't worry." She let him get a short distance ahead of her and then she ran after him.

He got through the glass door to the outside. Before she could reach it, he jammed something under it so she couldn't open it. She screamed and pounded. He kept going, Jamie yelling for her mommy, the knife hanging loosely in his hand. Halfway to his old truck he dropped the knife and kept going.

Emma watched him drive away. She wanted to know the direction. She pulled out her phone and called 911. As she did the door behind her opened. Footsteps sounded on the tile floor. Daron was yelling at her, telling her to give him details.

Boone was there. Kayla. Granddad. Her world was fuzzy and cold. Numb.

Nothing made sense. Pete had taken Jamie. She tried to explain, to describe. Sobs were choking her, making it hard to talk. But Daron got the details, and after a quick hug, promising it would be okay, he left. Kayla held her tight, promising that if anyone could get Jamie back, it would be Boone and Daron.

"I want to go home," she whispered into Art's shirt a few minutes later. "Granddad, I want to go home. I want to be in my house when they find her and bring her back. I want her to know that we're there waiting for her."

"You got it, kiddo." Art wrapped a protective arm around her and led her through the church. People tried to talk. They touched her arm. They told her they would pray.

As they walked out the front door, Lucy arrived. She pushed through the crowd, positioned herself on

Emma's other side, opposite Granddad, and told her to hang tight, that they'd be home in a minute.

A few people followed them to the farm. Boone Wilder's mom, Maria. Duke and Oregon. Remington and Samantha. They sat together in the living room as the police questioned her. They asked the same questions over and over again. She kept answering, trying to remember if she'd left out any details.

"I just want my baby. She's sick," she sobbed. "She has medicine."

Art stood, looking taller and more menacing than a man in bib overalls should look. "I think she's had enough, boys."

The two police officers focused their attention on him for the moment. "Mr. Lewis, we have to question her. That's how we're going to find your granddaughter."

"I understand that, but she's answered all of your questions. She's answered them several times. I don't know what you're hoping to learn from her, but she told you everything. Now I'm asking you gentlemen to back off and let her breathe."

One of them started to rebuke her grandfather. Lucy stepped in. "I think we're all a little stressed. I think you can give the family time to breathe."

The officers stood up. "Mrs. Shaw, we want to find your daughter. We're sorry that we've had to question you this way, but we want every detail so we can find her and bring her home."

She nodded. "I can't think anymore. I just can't. I need to go outside. Lucy, can we go out to the barn? Please."

"Is there something in the barn?" the younger officer asked.

Lucy scrunched her nose at him. "Yes—animals. Fresh air. Space."

"We'll be in the yard, not too far away." The older officer opened the door for Emma and he followed them out.

"Where are we going?" Lucy asked as they crossed to the barn.

"I don't know. I just need to think. I need to breathe. I can't remember everything Pete said. But maybe he gave me a clue. I just have to remember."

"I called his parents. They're on their way. They said they would keep trying his phone."

"That's good of them."

She sat on a square bale of straw next to the barn. It was cool but clear, the sky brilliant blue. Jamie was out there somewhere. With Pete. Or maybe with Pete's dealers. She fought back the panic. "Lucy, will you pray with me?"

Lucy sat down next to her. "I'm not a praying person, Emma. You know that."

"Why?"

"Because my experience with religion wasn't congregations full of friends and family. It wasn't kind."

"I'm sorry. Do you mind if I pray?"

Lucy stared at her for a moment, then took hold of her hand. "I'll pray with you."

They bowed their heads and Lucy prayed. It was heartfelt, sweet, simple. When she said the final amen, Emma kept her head bowed. She let tears trickle down her cheeks.

Suddenly a hand touched her back. Daron moved in front of her, knelt and took her in his arms.

"You didn't find her?"

"We know where she is. Pete has her in Braswell in an old house. He doesn't know that we know. But I want you to come with us. I want you to talk to him and see if we can reason with him. We don't want her hurt. We don't want to have to hurt him."

"She's in Braswell. Alone with Pete."

"There are people watching the house. They won't let anything happen to her."

"Okay, let's go."

They took Lucy with them to Braswell. Emma sat between Daron and his partner. She closed her eyes, praying that God would somehow loosen up Pete's heart and give him a clear mind. A conscience. Just for a few minutes if he would do the right thing.

The house in Braswell was exactly what Daron described. It was a drug house. Empty with broken windows. Brown weeds covered the lawn. It might have been a pretty house at one time. Two stories with a small front porch. But time and poverty had gotten the best of it. The window boxes were empty. The shrubs were nearly to the roof.

She didn't wait for instructions. When Daron stopped to talk to Lucy, Emma moved to the broken window on the porch.

"Pete, it's me. It's Emma. I'm here to get Jamie. Tell her that I'm here, so she won't be afraid." She peeked inside and saw Pete in a corner, her daughter on his lap asleep. Pete held a finger to his mouth, but it was too late. Jamie stirred, then woke up screaming for her mommy.

"Now see what you've done."

"I'm sorry. But, Pete, you have to take responsibility. You've kidnapped your own niece. You can rationalize all you want, but this is on you. You know that you can make this better or worse. You can hand her over and get help. It's up to you. I want you to someday apologize and do your best to be the uncle she deserves. Be the person you deserve to be."

"They'll kill me if I don't pay them."

"That's something the police can help you with. Maybe you can help the police?"

He kept hold of Jamie, but Emma could see that he was trembling. She climbed through the window and stepped carefully over broken glass. Pete scooted farther into the corner.

"Pete, give me my daughter."

He stood, holding Jamie away from him, toward her, and then he lunged. The bullet hit him in the shoulder, taking him down. Emma grabbed her daughter and jumped back. Jamie was crying. Maybe they were both crying. It was hard to hear. Pete was screaming that he'd been shot. Police were ramming down the door.

Daron was there, gathering them close, telling them they were safe. His arms remained close around them as he led them from the house littered with needles and old clothes. The stench of the place remained in her nostrils as she walked back to his truck.

Lucy wrapped a blanket around her.

"That was stupid, you know." Lucy gave her a serious look and shook her head. "Of all the stunts you could have pulled, that was the worst."

"I had to."

Lucy clucked a few times like an old mother hen, totally out of character. "Yeah, I know."

The police questioned her again. This time she was sitting in Daron's truck and he was next to her. Jamie was in her arms, telling her that Uncle Pete gave her a lollipop and said he was sorry.

As they loaded Pete in the ambulance, his parents arrived. They talked to the police and to their son, and then they waited. For her, she realized. They wanted to see their granddaughter. Emma was both thrilled and frightened.

Daron opened the door of the truck. "Do you want me to send them on their way?"

She shook her head. "No, I'll talk to them for a minute. But then Jamie and I want to go home."

He led the Shaws to his truck. Emma and Jamie remained inside. She watched as he spoke to Andy's parents, people he had known most of his life. She tried to read their very guarded expressions. She wondered if they had ever looked at the cards and pictures she'd sent. Or would today be the first time they really saw their granddaughter?

Mrs. Shaw approached the open door, her husband behind her. Lucy was nearby, her most menacing look directed at the couple. Emma felt her chest loosen, the fear ebbing away.

"Emma. Jamie." Mrs. Shaw wiped at the tears trickling down her cheeks. "My goodness, Jamie, you do look like your daddy."

Jamie didn't speak. She cuddled against Emma and looked at the woman she should have known.

"Jamie, this is your grandmother and grandfather Shaw."

"Uncle Pete needs a time-out," Jamie sobbed, and buried her face again.

Mrs. Shaw cried, "Yes, he does. Emma, I am so sorry. Please forgive us."

"Of course." Emma kissed Jamie's cheek. "We forgive you. We're just very tired right now and we want to go home."

"Of course you do." Mrs. Shaw touched Jamie, the gesture timid. Her hand rested on Jamie's back for a brief moment. "I hope that we can visit. When you're up to it."

"Yes, we'd like that."

Mrs. Shaw hugged both Jamie and Emma before walking away with her husband.

Daron watched the Shaws leave; then he got back in his truck. He sat behind the wheel for a minute before he turned the key in the ignition.

"This has been a long day," he finally said.

"You can say that again," Lucy said from the backseat. "Emma, you are about the toughest case we've ever had."

Emma laughed a little. He was glad to hear that laugh. It meant she was already bouncing back.

"I'm so tired," she said after a minute.

Jamie, buckled in the seat between them, was already dozing, her thumb in her mouth. Emma leaned close to her daughter. He saw her breathe deep and then touch Jamie's hair.

"The police want us to go by the ER. She should be checked out—just as a precaution." Daron waited until he was actually on the road to the hospital to make this announcement. He guessed that made him a chicken.

Emma gave her daughter a careful look and nodded. "Yes, of course."

The ER staff was expecting them. They had an exam room and Dr. Jacobs was waiting. Daron was thankful it was someone Jamie knew. It made it easier that she knew his smile, his voice. He allowed her to sit on her mom's lap and he talked about ponies and kittens. Daron stood in the doorway, watching over them.

He guessed he'd have to figure things out now. He had been watching over them for the last few years. He'd known for a couple of years that Pete was being a nuisance, so his presence had seemed necessary. Or so he'd told himself.

Dr. Jacobs finished the exam and handed Jamie a big stuffed horse. "I heard you were coming and that you'd had a pretty eventful day, so I went down to the gift shop to see if they had any ponies. This was the only one, but they assured me he doesn't eat much, doesn't make messes and he can sleep in the house."

Jamie accepted the gift, and whispered, "Thank you."

Daron watched as the good doctor said goodbye to the patient and her mother. A new emotion washed over him. Jealousy.

He shrugged and let it roll off. Water off a duck's back, he told himself.

Chapter Sixteen

Christmas morning dawned overcast and cool with flurries falling. Jamie ran out the front door and yelled, "Snow."

It wasn't really snow, but living in Texas Hill Country, they would take what they could get. Emma followed her daughter out, holding a jacket out to slip her arms in. Jamie wiggled into the jacket, then tromped down the steps of the porch and into the yard. She stood for a full minute with her face up and her tongue out. The flurries turned into large white feathery flakes. They were the type that fell hard and fast but then ended as quickly as they began.

Granddad wandered to the door. "You girls are silly. Aren't we going to head over to the McKay Ranch?"

"Yes, soon." Emma tilted her head and caught a few flakes with her own tongue. Jamie saw and laughed.

Emma wasn't in a hurry to go to Daron's. She was afraid. Of a lot of things. Of what she felt. Of the future. Of spending this day with his family. Old emotions were rearing their ugly head. She wasn't good enough. He didn't really want her, just the idea of her.

He'd realize that soon and then she'd be left with a broken heart.

No, she caught herself. Not a broken heart. A heart could only be broken if a person loved someone who hurt them. She didn't love Daron. They were friends. She cared about him. They had shared some sweet moments.

That didn't make it love.

But he'd invited them to spend Christmas with him and his family, and she'd accepted. Partly because she wanted time with him. She found herself missing him now that Pete was in jail and he'd helped the police get the cartel that he'd been working for. She also thought that she would tell him soon they needed time and space because she was afraid they'd been thrown together and that it was possible she was confused about what she felt. Or maybe he was confused.

She knew that someday she would marry again. She didn't want a second failed marriage.

This was her putting the horse before the cart, thinking that there was more to her relationship with Daron than maybe there was. And that was why she had to take a step back and discover the truth. What she felt. What he felt.

Granddad had fixed breakfast that morning. It was a Christmas tradition. Every year he made the same thing for Christmas breakfast. Biscuits and gravy, cinnamon rolls, eggs and bacon. Afterward they would usually tell the Christmas story and then open gifts.

This year Granddad read the Christmas story from the Bible and then they jumped in the truck, Daron's truck, and headed south in the direction of the McKay spread, as her granddad called it.

With each passing minute, Emma's apprehension grew. Her granddad shot her a careful look. "Em, if you don't breathe, you're going to pass out. Calm down. It isn't like you haven't met these people before. It's Christmas, so smile and stop looking like you're heading to the hangman's noose."

She nodded and managed a grimace that was meant to be a smile. She took a few deep breaths and wiped her palms down the sides of her jeans. She looked at the jeans she'd picked, with boots and a long tunic-style sweater. Maybe she should have worn a dress?

Art shook his head. He was pulling up to the house. There were several cars already parked out front. She guessed them to belong to his parents and maybe his sister, Janette.

"We're here!" Jamie said gleefully.

Emma smiled down at her daughter, got out of the truck and they walked hand in hand to the front door of a home that looked more like a lodge and less like a home. A woman about her age answered the door.

"You must be Emma! And Jamie and Art. Please, come in. We're all in the kitchen. Mom doesn't really cook, but she has a great caterer. We brought everything down in coolers. It's amazing."

Emma allowed Janette to lead her through the house to the kitchen. Art was muttering about electric bills and wasted space. She sent him a warning look and he just chuckled and kept on talking.

Standing in the kitchen, Daron smiled when he saw them. Emma froze, trying to fit this man into the image of the one she'd known for several years. This man was dressed in slacks, a soft gray button-down shirt and black boots. His face was freshly shaved. He smelled wonderful, all spices and mountain air kind of wonderful.

He lifted Jamie and then wrapped an arm around Emma. Art was already picking over the food and talking to Daron's dad.

"I want an elephant," Jamie whispered to Daron.

He hugged her tight. "I know you do. I'm afraid the store was all out of elephants this year. I did get something pretty cute, though." To Emma he said, "You look beautiful."

She wanted him to mean it. She wanted him to mean that she fit. That she didn't have to be someone else.

"Have you seen Daron's new horses?" Janette asked as they walked to the living room, where the tree sparkled and presents wrapped in bright-colored paper were piled high.

"New horses?" She shook her head. "I guess I haven't."

"Big mouth," Daron said as he scooted past his sister. "I was going to show you today. One of them needs some work. I bought them from Jake."

"Not..." She bit down on her lip.

He shook his head. "Not the mare. I wouldn't do that. But the mare has a foal. Pretty nice colt."

She shook her head and he gave a brief nod. "You can show me your horses later."

A noise from under the tree offered a welcome distraction. Jamie was scurrying, trying to find it. She grabbed at a blanket and laughed, a real belly laugh, the kind that made a mom so happy. Even if the thing her daughter was laughing at was a living, breathing creature. A kitten.

"My kitty." Jamie dropped to her knees and tried to open the cage. Janette got down on the floor to help her. The kitten was long-haired, gray and had blue eyes. It mewed and, as soon as the door was open, crawled into Jamie's lap.

"A kitten," Emma said. She managed to frown at Daron. She wanted to be upset with him. But the kitten and her daughter made a beautiful picture, and she couldn't be mad. She shifted her gaze from his because she didn't want to be lost in what she felt for him.

"We should open gifts," Nora McKay suggested, watching the two of them and then shifting her eyes away. She started passing around the many presents from under the tree, enlisting Jamie as her helper.

Jamie took the responsibility very seriously, holding her kitten under one arm as she delivered gifts. There was a pile for her, and when all the gifts were passed out, Jamie leaned to kiss a wrapped present and then she kissed her kitten. Emma sat down on the floor next to her daughter.

"Let Jamie open hers first, and us old people will watch." Daron's dad had leaned back in a chair, his feet propped up on an ottoman. "This is my favorite part of Christmas and it's been a long time since we've celebrated one here at the ranch with a child around."

Jamie didn't have to be told twice. She happily started opening gifts, occasionally pulling her kitten back to her lap when it tried to get away. There were games and books, dolls and a preschool art kit.

Emma watched as Jamie played. She watched and wished that everything could be as perfect as this moment.

Soon, with all the presents opened and the wrapping paper shoved into garbage bags, they all settled down and she knew that it was almost time to talk to Daron.

Art was talking to Daron's dad. His mom and sister were with Emma, clearing the table. Jamie was curled up on a pallet of blankets with a sleeping, purring kitten.

She'd named the kitten Buster.

Yes, it all seemed perfect. But she knew from experience that perfect had a way of falling apart.

Daron walked up behind Emma. She half turned, smiled and went back to drying dishes.

"Walk with me?"

She paused and he thought she might say no. "Okay."

She hung the dish towel on the bar and followed him. He wanted to take her hand, but he had a feeling she wouldn't let him. Not in front of everyone. They walked side by side, not speaking. When they got to the stable, she waited for him to push the door open and she went in ahead of him.

The horses were in stalls. He flipped on lights and she went immediately to them, stopping first at the POA, Pony of America. The small gelding was showy with his Appaloosa markings. He had a nice head and good eyes. For Daron it was always about the eyes.

"This one is too small for you," she said in a soft tone without looking at him. Her hand was on the neck of the pony.

"Yeah, I guess. I just thought someday..." He paused because he didn't know what he'd been thinking, not really. Cart before the horse—that was what had happened that day. Without knowing their future, he had assumed she and Jamie would always be in his life.

Man, he really wanted them in his life.

But he had a bad feeling about this. "Say something."

She put her face to the face of the pony. "He's beautiful."

"Not what I was looking for."

"I know." She moved on to the mare in the next stall. A pretty girl, all showy and expressive.

Daron stepped next to Emma. "Is it because of the kitten?"

She shook her head. He saw a tiny lift of her mouth. "No."

"Are you going to tell me that we're through?"

"What are we, Daron? Friends? Your charity case? We make you feel better about what happened in Afghanistan?" She shook her head. "Forgive me. That was wrong. So wrong."

He shrugged it off. "Maybe those were my intentions at first, to soothe my guilt. I think we both know that. I felt guilty for what happened. And after years of driving past your house, checking on you, it became a habit."

"Right. So how do we know what we really feel? What part of this is habit, what part is real?"

"All I can tell you is what I feel. It's not a secret." He wanted to pull her close, kiss her, tell her she didn't have to be afraid. But he knew that now wasn't the time. She was going to have to figure this out on her own.

He was going to have to let her. He couldn't remember ever having a broken heart. Maybe once, in fifth grade when he had a crush on the art teacher. He'd brought her flowers, written her a poem and she sat him down one day and said someday some girl would come into his life and it would be wonderful. But Miss Craig had a boyfriend and she planned to get married that summer.

He'd been waiting twenty years for that someday girl.

She was standing next to him crying silent tears as she told him, and he shook his head as he listened.

"I think we shouldn't see each other for a while. Because I need to know what I feel. And I need for you to know. I don't want to get six months down the road and realize, or have you realize, that this is wrong. I don't want you to look at me with disgust because I wore the wrong shoes, or fixed my hair the wrong way. I just can't be that person again."

"You aren't that person. You are incredible, strong and independent. I don't care if you go barefoot."

She laughed a little, the sound ending on a sob. "Oh, I think you would. And I would care. If I looked across the table and saw regret in your eyes, I don't know if I could handle that."

"I'm not Andy."

"No, you're not. And I'm trying so hard to not compare. Because it isn't you. It's me. I'm broken. I need to be whole. When I give my heart, I want it to be my whole heart. For the person I love. For my daughter. I want her to know that she has two parents who will love each other, respect each other and stay together for each other and for her."

He kissed the top of her head. "I want that, too. I'm not going to argue with you, but I think we are a good fit. And I think our time together clarifies everything we feel."

"No, because we've been through too much. Not just in the last few weeks but in the last few years."

"Okay, I'm going to give you time. But I want to be very clear about one thing. I know what I feel for you. It isn't pity. It isn't charity. This isn't coming from a guilty conscience."

"But some time apart will help you know for certain."

He drew her to him, touching his mouth to hers, tasting her tears as he kissed her. She clung to him for a moment and then she let go.

"That isn't friendship, Emma."

"I think I should go now."

"If that's what you think you need to do. I…" He shook his head. "No, I don't understand."

"Neither do I," she admitted quietly. "I just feel like this came out of nowhere and I need to know for sure, you need to know, what it is we're feeling."

"And you think we can do that apart?" He shook his head. "Emma, I don't want to be away from you, not even for a day. So I guess I know how I feel."

"Then I'm the one who has to know for sure what you feel, and what I feel. I should go."

"If that's what you want."

He walked her back to the house. She gathered up the stuffed elephant Daron had bought for Jamie, and the games from his parents, the books from his sister. Her granddad had been given a hand-carved checker set. Daron watched as she smiled and talked to his parents, his sister. She stopped to tell Jamie something about her kitten.

He'd forgotten his gift for her. Other than the horses.

But he couldn't tell her now that the horses were for her. He handed her a small box. "You can unwrap it later."

She held it for a moment, then tried to give it back.

He shook his head. "It's for you, Emma. It wouldn't suit anyone else and I refuse to take it back."

She put the box in her purse and thanked him. And then she pulled a box from her bag and handed it to him. He opened his gift. A Bible. It was engraved. He opened it and she'd written in the inside that she hoped this Bible would guide him on his journey, wherever it might take him. And she hoped he knew that he had a friend who would always be praying for him.

It sounded like a pretty serious goodbye to him.

Chapter Seventeen

The first day of the New Year dawned cold and rainy. Emma drove out through the field, still in Daron's truck. She had called to tell him she'd sold her steers and was getting her old farm truck fixed. He told her to keep his truck as long as she needed it. He wasn't using it.

He'd asked how she was and she'd told him she was fine. Of course she was fine. And he'd said the same. But she wondered if either of them was truly fine. Fine didn't feel like this, like her world was broken apart and needed to be fitted back together again. Fine didn't feel like waking up every morning wondering if she should call him and tell him she'd made a mistake. Or wondering if he would call and ask to talk.

Or maybe fine was all of those things. And she wanted more than that. She wanted her world to be beautiful again.

She'd told him she needed time apart. And he was giving her that. Relationships shouldn't be rushed into. She'd made that mistake once before.

She didn't tell him she'd opened his gift, but

she should have. She should have thanked him for the bracelet. It was beautiful. And even though she shouldn't, she wore it every day. Because it felt like a piece of him was with her. But then, there was also the kitten. That crazy little feline that followed them around, playing with shoes as they walked, climbing on furniture and terrorizing the dog. It was such an innocent-looking little ball of fur. She smiled at the thought of Buster and how much it was loved by Jamie. And when Jamie talked to her kitten, she talked about Daron.

The cattle came running from the other side of the field. She stopped the truck to drop the round bale, lowering it to the ground with the spike and then pulling away. As the cattle converged on the bale of hay, she got out and grabbed the bag of feed off the back of the truck and carried it to the trough. As she stepped away, the cattle were moving in, nudging and pushing. She climbed back into the truck and headed back to the house.

Granddad normally took care of morning feeding, but he'd been in the kitchen fixing breakfast and she'd needed the fresh air. She needed time alone to think.

Lucy was getting out of her truck as Emma got out to close the gate and latch it. She waved and Lucy headed her way.

"I thought I'd stop by and see how things are going," Lucy said as they walked into the barn, where the lighting was dim and dust danced on the few beams of sunlight.

"I'm good. We'll be going to Austin next week for Jamie's procedure. Did you see your mom?"

Lucy shrugged off the question. "No, but I've seen

my partner. Remember him—Daron? He's on a job in Dallas. He looks like someone ran him over with a semi."

Emma headed out the back door of the barn. She fed the chickens, gathered the few eggs and walked back inside. Lucy waited, patiently.

"I'm trying to not hurt him, Lucy. I don't want him confused about what he feels."

Lucy shook her head. "It's really none of my business. I'm the last person who should be giving advice about relationships."

"I don't mind your advice. I just really felt as if everything had moved so quickly and it was wrapped up with Jamie's illness and Pete's addiction. It just needs to be unraveled so we know what we are feeling in each situation."

"That makes sense to me," Lucy agreed. "Can I be there, at the hospital with you?"

"I would love that." She reached for Lucy and pulled her into a stiff hug. "You're not a hugger."

Lucy pulled back. "No, I'm not. I'll forgive you this time."

"Since we're still friends, let's have a cup of coffee and see if Granddad made cinnamon rolls."

"I love that idea."

They were heading to the house when a familiar white truck pulled up. Lucy said something like "uh-oh" and went on inside, leaving Emma in the yard to face Daron.

He got out of his truck, patted her dog, and then he looked at her. She looked at him, too. She wasn't ready to admit how much she missed him.

"Hi."

He pushed back his hat and grinned. "Hey."

"I didn't expect to see you. Lucy said you're in Dallas."

He shrugged off her comment. "I wanted to stop by. I'm home for the day and then back to the job. My mom called. She wanted me to tell you that you and Art are welcome to stay with them when you're in Austin for Jamie's surgery. She insisted, so I told her I'd pass it on."

"That's really nice of her, but she doesn't have to."

"Emma, where are you planning to stay?"

"A hotel. I made reservations."

"Stay with my parents. Please. They'll be upset if you don't. Go the day before the surgery so Jamie can rest up. Stay with them as long as needed. They'll enjoy having you there. My dad says he's going to teach Art to play chess."

She nodded, heat climbing into her cheeks. "Tell them thank you, we appreciate it."

"She's going to be fine." He brushed a hand down her arm, and his fingers touched hers. And then he noticed the bracelet. She saw a hint of a smile. "You opened it. I thought you might not."

"I did, and thank you. It's too much, but I love it."

"Tell Jamie I'll bring her something special to help her recover."

"Not an elephant," Emma warned.

He had started to walk away and he turned, winking as he smiled that slow, easy smile of his. "Not an elephant."

Daron got in his truck, shifted into Reverse, then sat there watching as Emma walked up the steps. She paused on the front porch, but she didn't turn. Pathetic fool that he was, he waited.

After a few minutes he backed out of her drive and headed toward Dallas. Driving away from her was the hardest thing he'd had to do. He had wanted to pull into her house, convince her that what they felt was love and that she should give him a chance. Give *them* a chance.

Instead he'd respected her wishes and hadn't pushed. He could only hope, and pray, that she was heading in the same direction he was. Because the last few days had made things pretty clear for him. She and Jamie meant everything to him.

Boone was waiting for him at their hotel, and also the site of the convention they were providing security for. Daron walked into the room and found his partner sitting on the bed watching a John Wayne movie.

"Pretty stereotypical," Daron said as he pulled a bottle of water out of the fridge.

"What?" Boone reached for his hat and shoved it down on his head. "I think I'm a lot like John Wayne."

"Whatever."

"Did you see her?"

"Yep. I passed on the message from my parents and left. Lucy was there." Daron sat down on the edge of his bed and swigged down half the bottle of water.

"That's an odd pair, Lucy and Emma."

Daron shrugged. "Not really. Makes sense to me that they'd be friends."

"Yeah, I guess. But have you ever known Lucy to have a friend, other than us two?"

Daron clicked off the TV.

"What are you going to do now?"

"My job. I've been distracted for the past month, and distraction can get a guy killed."

"Yeah, it can."

They both went to a dark place. Daron guessed it was the same dark place. A place where he'd been fooled by feelings for a woman and because of it he'd led a few guys into danger. And one of them had died.

Chapter Eighteen

Emma tried to pretend it was any other morning. For Jamie's sake. For her own. But it wasn't. They weren't at home; they were in Austin staying with Daron's parents. And even though Jamie was too young to understand what was happening, she had an idea that it was a big day. She'd been fussy for a few days. She'd cried last night that she wanted Daron.

That had taken Emma by surprise. Jamie always wanted her mommy. Sometimes she wanted Art. But last night she'd wanted the person who had been their rock during a difficult time.

Emma had to admit, she missed him, too.

His parents were wonderful. They were kind and caring. They loved their son. They might interfere in his life and want something different from him, something other than the career he'd chosen. But they were good people.

Emma turned on the lamp. It was still dark outside, but she could hear people stirring. Daron's parents insisted on going with her to the hospital. Granddad, of course, would be with her. He was always with her.

He was her rock. She wouldn't forget that. He'd been wiping her tears and cleaning up her messes for a long time.

Her granddad had taught her what a real man was and how he should treat a woman. He'd been everything to her: a mom, a dad and a grandfather.

Jamie huddled on the bed in her robe. "I want cereal."

"No cereal this morning, sweetie. Later you can eat."

"I'm hungry."

Emma gathered her daughter up. "I know, honey. I promise you'll get to eat. Just not right now."

Jamie sobbed against her shoulder. "Mommy. Please."

"Soon. And you're going to feel so much better. You're going to run. And you're going to chase the kitten."

"I can run fast."

"Yes, you'll run even faster." And not be tired after playing. She wouldn't need to catch her breath after chasing her kitten.

Two hours later the nurse escorted Emma, Art and the McKays to a surgical waiting room where they would be given updates. The pediatric cardiologist had explained the process of threading the catheter through the vein in Jamie's neck to fix the hole in the ventricular septum. He explained the possible problems and what they would do if any of those problems occurred.

Emma sat by the window and prayed. She prayed for her daughter, for the surgeons, the nurses, the anesthesiologist. The door to the waiting room opened.

The Shaws, Andy's parents, stepped in. Mrs. Shaw

looked unsure. "We wanted to be here, for you and for her. Is that okay? We understand if you don't want us."

"No, please stay." Emma wiped at her eyes. Silly, useless tears. "The procedure just started. It could be several hours."

"Can we get you anything?" Mr. Shaw asked.

"I'm fine," Emma answered. Then she let the rest of them talk in soft whispers, about Jamie, about the weather and about politics. She watched the clock. The minutes ticked by so slowly. Her heartbeat caught the rhythm of the clock. Each tick, each heartbeat, one step closer.

The door opened again. Her heart did a funny catch. She turned, hoping, expecting. Wanting Daron. It was a nurse, smiling at all of them.

"I wanted to update you. We're halfway there. She's doing great. The doctor said he doesn't foresee any problems at this point."

Emma blinked back more tears. She nodded and thanked the nurse, who slipped quietly out of the room.

She wanted to call Daron. She wanted him to know that Jamie was doing well. Of course they'd known she would. She thought about how different it would have felt had he been here. She was surrounded by people, but she felt alone. If Daron had been here, she wouldn't have felt alone.

He was her partner. He'd become her partner the day he stepped into her hospital room after Jamie was born. He'd brought flowers and told her he would always be there if she needed anything.

She'd sent him away. Now she was in the wilderness alone. She closed her eyes and took a deep breath. No, not alone. It was almost as if God was speaking to her heart. She wasn't alone. He had this. He had a plan. He had the path before her and He would be her light.

The nurse returned a little over an hour later. "We're all finished. She did great and she'll soon be moved to a room."

Emma stood. She couldn't sit. She had to hug some- one, so she hugged the nurse. "Thank you."

The nurse returned the hug. "You're so welcome. She did the hard work. Jamie and Dr. Lee."

The nurse left. Emma stood in the center of the room surrounded by people she hadn't expected to have in her life. Granddad, of course. Andy's parents, though, they were a surprise. She accepted their hugs and well-wishes.

"We're going to go now," Mr. Shaw told her. "Can we visit tomorrow?"

"Of course you can." She hugged her ex-mother-in- law again. "Jamie will like that."

After they left she hugged Daron's parents. "Thank you for being here with us. And for letting us stay with you. It has meant so much."

Nora McKay held her in a tight hug. "Of course we wanted you with us. And I know Daron wanted to be here. He's been working in Dallas."

"I know." She walked away, back to her window.

"Should someone call Daron?" she said, without looking back at his parents. It was easier to sit facing the window. That way, she didn't see their concern. She didn't have to make conversation.

"What if I just show up?" The voice, low, so sweetly familiar that it almost undid her.

She flew out of the chair. He was standing in the

doorway, his hair a mess, a suit with the tie loose around his neck and the jacket unbuttoned.

"You're here."

"Yes, I'm here. I had to be here."

She wanted to touch him, but they had an audience, a very interested audience. She focused on the tie, hanging loose around his neck. She straightened it a bit and smoothed down his collar. "I'm glad you're here."

She caught his gaze and held it. "I've missed you."

"I've missed you, too." He exhaled, then pulled her close. "I hope you understand what this has been like for me. I hope, and I mean this with love, that you've been just as miserable."

"I have. I really have."

The door opened again. The nurse smiled at them all. "Mom, do you want to come down and see your little girl?"

"Yes, please." More than anything. "Can Daron come with me? She'll want to see him."

"Is he family?" the nurse asked, still standing in the doorway.

"He's my best friend."

The nurse smiled. "I think we can allow a best friend today. Especially if it will make our patient happy. Before the anesthesia hit she was telling me about a kitten and a guy named Daron that her mommy loves."

Emma felt heat crawl into her cheeks.

"You love me?" Daron whispered as they walked down the hall.

She didn't answer.

At the door to the cardiac intensive-care unit, the nurse stopped them. "We have her in here for now, just to monitor her and make sure all her vitals are strong.

We'll probably move her to a regular room in the morning. I'd like for you both to scrub hands and arms and put on a gown, and let's limit the visit to five or ten minutes right now. We'll need to do some work with her and she's going to be tired. But I promise in about thirty minutes or so we'll come back and get you for a longer visit."

"Thank you." Emma moved to the sink the nurse had indicated. She scrubbed her hands and arms.

Daron waited until she finished and was gowning up before he stepped forward to wash. She held a gown out and he slipped into it. Hand in hand, they walked through the doors into that brightly lit and sterile world.

When Emma spotted her daughter, she wanted to cry. She wanted to pick her up and hold her. But she couldn't. There were tubes, monitors, IVs. She looked so small and fragile in the hospital bed, surrounded by equipment, monitored, watched by a nurse.

"She's going to be fine," Daron said. "She's strong and she has a mommy who's tough."

She leaned into him. "Yes, she's going to be fine."

Jamie opened her eyes, then opened them wider when she saw Daron. She smiled, just a tiny smile but it was her smile. She whispered, "Mommy?"

Emma kissed her cheek. "Mommy is here. And Daron came to see you, too. We love you."

We. She didn't know that they were a "we," but it felt right for the moment. They could be a "we" when it came to Jamie. The two of them were both there for her.

She sat in the chair next to her daughter's bed and held her hand until she fell asleep. Daron had slipped away, telling her he would meet her in the chapel.

When the nurse told her she'd have to leave for a bit,

Emma kissed Jamie again and slipped from the room as her daughter slept.

Where was the chapel? She vaguely remembered seeing a small prayer room near the surgical waiting room. She headed that way. When she got there she peeked in and she saw Daron at the window. His head was bowed. She waited and finally he turned.

He had flowers and balloons.

"I don't know if they'll let her have flowers," she said.

"They're for you." He looked up at the balloons with the words Get Well Soon printed on them, and he grinned. "It's all they had in the hospital gift shop."

Daron looked awkward with the bouquet. He handed them to her and she took them, looking up at the balloon with the get-well message.

"I know you need time," he started, pushing a hand through his hair. "But I don't," he said next. "I don't need time to know that I love you. I love Jamie. Every moment since Christmas, I've missed you. You are my life, Emma. You are my next breath. Good grief, you have me spouting poetry. I know this is not the best time. I know you're worried about Jamie. But I can't do this life thing without you."

"Get well soon?" She looked up at the balloon and laughed.

"You'll never forget this moment," he assured her with that dimple showing in his cheek. He settled a hand on her waist and pulled her close.

"No, I guess I won't." She leaned close, breathing him in, wishing he would kiss her.

"I don't want time to think. I want time with you.

Let's just pretend that balloon says something totally different."

She felt lighter than she'd felt in days. A giggle erupted and she touched his cheek. "What does the balloon say?"

He dropped to one knee and she couldn't breathe. The room spun in a crazy way and he smiled up at her. "The balloon says I love you and I plan to love you more each and every day. I want to have a family with you. I want to grow old with you. Will you marry me?"

Tears began to fall and she laughed through the haze of moisture. "We'll need a bigger balloon."

"This is not a moment when you want to tease a man." He was still on one knee. "I just poured my heart out to you. Don't leave me hanging. Or kneeling, as the case may be."

She put the flowers on the table next to them and leaned to cup his cheeks and kiss him.

Daron stood up, holding her hands in his. She'd kissed him. That meant he probably ought to kiss her back.

"Will." He kissed her. "You." He kissed her again. "Marry." And again. "Me?"

And then he settled his lips on hers, kissing her the way he'd wanted to since she walked into this room. He kissed her until he hoped her knees were weak, and so was her resolve to resist him.

When he pulled back she was clinging to his arms. "Please answer me."

"I can't. You keep kissing me," she said.

For that he kissed her again. Her lips were sweet beneath his, and her hands held tight to his shoulders.

This time when he pulled away from her, she nodded. "Yes, I think I will marry you."

He picked her up and swung her around the small room. Her foot hit the flowers and he caught them before they could hit the floor.

"I love you."

"I love you, too." She wrapped her arms around his neck and held on as he scooped her up. He grabbed the flowers and put them in her hands, then carried her back to the waiting room.

As they stepped through the door, everyone inside stood and applauded. His parents. Art. They all looked pretty pleased.

"I guess I don't need to announce that I'm the happiest man in the world?" Daron asked as he set Emma on her feet next to him.

"I think we were all just waiting for the two of you to figure things out," Art said. "Good thing, because I was tired of waiting. I'd just like to tell you, I hope you've got an in-law room in that big house of yours."

"Art, we have plenty of room for you."

The door opened again and the nurse peeked in. "I'm glad you all are celebrating. Our little patient would like some company."

Daron walked down the hall at Emma's side. Always at her side. That was where he planned to stay. Forever.

Epilogue

April was the perfect month for a wedding in Texas. The reason was simple: the bluebonnets were blooming. Nothing was more beautiful than Texas Hill Country in spring.

She also chose to get married in the country church where Remington Jenkins was pastor. The church was situated in a valley with fields of wildflowers spreading out from it like deep purple carpet. It was as if God was the florist for her wedding.

"Are you almost ready?" Lucy stepped into the room wearing a black evening dress.

She wasn't a bridesmaid. The bridesmaids wore dresses the color of spring. No, she was one of the groomsmen. She and Boone. Oregon and Lily were the matron of honor and bridesmaid. Oregon wore a pale lavender dress. Lily's dress was pale yellow. The bouquets were filled with wildflowers in shades of yellow, purple and white.

Jamie was her flower girl. Her blond hair in ringlets and a wreath of baby's breath atop her little head. She carried a basket of flower petals that she would sprinkle along the aisle of the church. If the petals survived. At the moment she had several of them lined up on the windowsill and she was arranging them like little flowers.

"I'm almost ready." Emma looked into the mirror. She hadn't known until recently that her grandmother's wedding dress, the same wedding dress the Lewis women had worn for three generations, was in a box in Art's closet. He'd had it sealed, in case she should ever want it.

He hadn't told her before. She didn't ask why.

Oregon stepped forward to adjust her veil.

"You look beautiful," Oregon said softly, a shimmer of tears in her eyes. "I'm going to cry."

Lily groaned. "I don't get that. It's a wedding. It's a happy time. I think when I get married, I'll elope."

"Don't you dare," all three of the women said in unison.

"I should go check on the groom," Lucy said as she opened the door. "He's a little bit nervous. He actually sent me in here to make sure you didn't duck out the back. I think Boone made him watch the movie *Runaway Bride*."

"Tell him I'm not going anywhere."

"Except down the aisle," Oregon added. "And tell him she loves him."

"Yes, I love him." She loved him so much it hurt.

The next person to pound on the door was Granddad. Oregon let him in. "My goodness, you are beautiful, Em."

"Granddad, have I told you how much I love you?"

"I love you back." He took her hand and slipped a pretty ring on the finger of her right hand. "I want you to have this. It was your mom's. Now, don't cry. Something borrowed, something blue, something old and something new. I guess I said that wrong, but I'm close. That ring is old. I believe it was my grandmother's. And now it's yours. But I'm also giving you something new."

"And what's that?"

"New hope and a new beginning." He grinned. "Now, that's something not everyone can give their girl. But you deserve it and I'm glad you stopped being afraid to accept it."

"Me, too, Art. Me, too." She hugged him tight. "I think it's time."

"Yes, I believe it is. Do you like my new bibs?"

She laughed and dabbed at her eyes with the tissue Oregon pushed into her hand. Art preened a bit in his dark blue bib overalls beneath a sport coat.

"I wouldn't have you any other way. You look very handsome."

"I thought so. I even let Allie at the Clip and Curl trim my hair and give me a shave. I kind of liked that." He rubbed his hand across his very smooth cheek.

He crossed the room to Jamie, kissed her cheek and told her she was as pretty as a field of wildflowers.

Oregon peeked into the hall. "It's time."

She opened the door wide. She went first down the hallway and Lily followed. Jamie walked in front of Emma and her grandfather. Emma put her hand on Art's arm and they took their time walking down the dimly lit hall to the outside door. They walked out into fresh air and she breathed deep as Art guided her up the front steps of the church. Jamie waited for them at the top of the steps. She had a flower petal on top of her head and she was grinning as if she might be up to something.

Music was playing. Someone was singing. Emma had picked the song and now she couldn't remember which one. She could only think of one thing—Daron. After today they would be married. She, Daron and Jamie would be a family. And Granddad. She smiled up at her grandfather.

"Here we go, kiddo." He smiled down at her. "I sure love you and I'm sorry that life has been hard, but you've been a blessing to an old man. And I hope this young man is a blessing to you."

"Granddad, I'm going to look terrible if you make me cry. My nose will be red and mascara will run down my cheeks. But I love you, too."

They both laughed a little. Jamie glanced back at them and Emma nodded, indicating her daughter should take her walk down the aisle.

Emma looked toward the front of the church. Lily and Oregon were on the left, smiling, holding their bouquets. Boone and Lucy stood on the opposite side. And next to them, Daron. He wore a Western-cut tuxedo. His hair had been trimmed. Her heart filled to over-flowing because he caught her eye and then he smiled at Jamie, encouraging her. She sprinkled flowers as Art and Emma started down the aisle.

As they got to the front of the church, Jamie turned and with that mischievous grin she picked up the basket and tossed flowers in the air. Wildflower petals fluttered around Emma as Art released her and she stepped to Daron's side.

Remington smiled at them, at the wedding party,

and then he began. "You may be seated. Who gives this bride in marriage?"

Her granddad stood nearby, chest puffed out in pride. "Me and the Good Lord."

The guests laughed a little. Granddad winked and took his seat.

Emma wanted to remember every word, every moment of the ceremony. But later what she remembered most was her hand in Daron's and Jamie at her side. And it felt right. It felt like they were a family.

She looked up at the man who would be her husband and he gave her a slow wink and that steady, easy smile of his. He placed the ring on her finger and she placed one on his. And then he kissed her with Jamie standing between them, hugging both their legs.

With the crowd cheering, he lifted Jamie and took Emma by the hand, and they walked back down the aisle with wildflower petals floating through the air and a song being played. She thought it might have been "Can I Have This Dance?"

She only remembered that it felt so right to stand next to Daron and know that now and forever he would be hers and she would be his. And maybe in a year or two Jamie would have a little brother or sister.

Yes, her heart was full to overflowing. And God had indeed blessed her with this second chance.

* * * * *